ENEMY TERRITORY

ENEMY TERRITORY

Douglas Terman

BANTAM BOOKS
NEW YORK · TORONTO · LONDON · SYDNEY · AUCKLAND

ENEMY TERRITORY

A Bantam Book / November 1989

Library of Congress Cataloging-in-Publication Data

Terman, Douglas, 1933–
    Enemy territory / Douglas Terman.
        p.   cm.
    ISBN 0–553–05377–9
    I. Title.
PS3570.E676E5   1989
813'.54—dc20
                                                                89–6837
                                                                CIP

Published simultaneously in the United States and Canada

DEDICATED TO

Tom Clark (The *WALRUS*)

The schooner JACINTA (*PAMPERO*)

Harry-Ott

AND TO ALL THOSE WHO PASSAGE
WHERE DEEP WATERS FLOW

ACKNOWLEDGMENTS

For all their helpful research assistance, comments, and insights: Tom Alibrandi, Tom Clancy, Clive Cussler, Jake Eddy, Dr. Sandy Foot, Milan Fryscak, Captain David Howe, George Lowe, Colonel Don Masuret, Lt. Colonel George Ojalehto, Preston Peters, Dr. Porter Smith, Chip Taylor, Greg Tobin, and Dr. Chuck Wagner.

And especially, for the love, encouragement, and the endless hours of her time that she gives to me—my wife, Seddon Johnson.

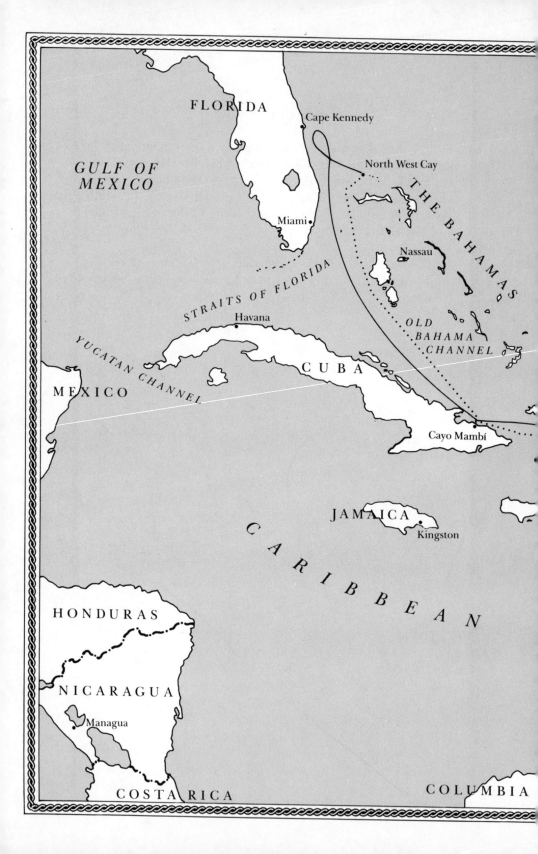

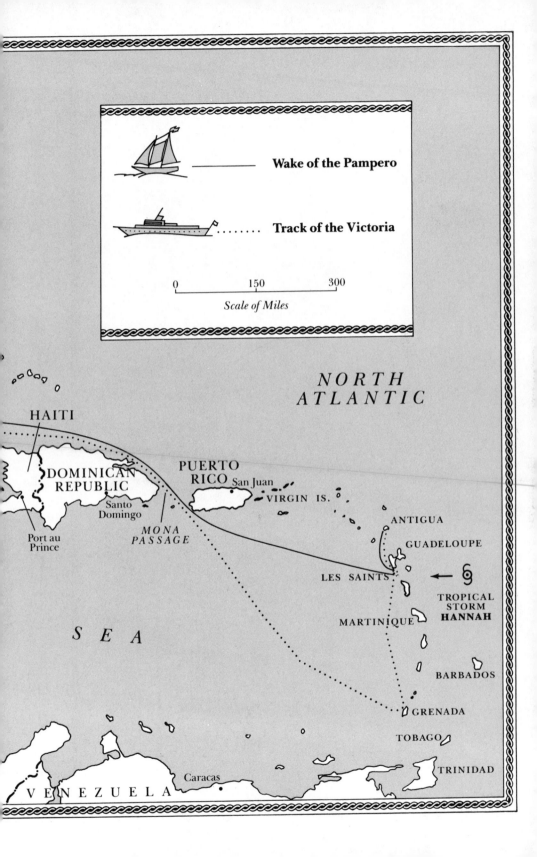

Wake of the Pampero

Track of the Victoria

0   150   300

Scale of Miles

NORTH
ATLANTIC

HAITI

DOMINICAN
REPUBLIC

PUERTO
RICO   San Juan

VIRGIN IS.

ANTIGUA

Santo
Domingo

GUADELOUPE

Port au
Prince

*MONA
PASSAGE*

LES SAINTS

TROPICAL
STORM
HANNAH

MARTINIQUE

SEA

BARBADOS

GRENADA

TOBAGO

Caracas

TRINIDAD

VENEZUELA

PART ONE

THE VIETNAM ERA

1.

July 10, 1969

Bracken was at flight level 180 over the Gulf of Tonkin, an F-4-D Phantom fighter strapped to his back. The gulf below him was a bright glare of dazzling sun reflected back from shattered glass. He scanned the horizon carefully in small increments.

Up to the northeast of the gulf he saw the *V* of a wake, spearheaded by the black splinter of a ship. He glanced down at the clipboard strapped to his thigh. "USN Cutter *Roxbury* on Foxtrot Station" was his own barely decipherable scrawl. He knew that on her fantail was a rescue chopper; a clapped-out fighter jock's insurance policy if it came to that.

Unconsciously, he breathed a little more deeply. The oxygen hiss was picked up by his mike, then echoed back in his headphones.

"What's the status?" he said into the mike.

"Bad case of the whips, jingles, and brown flapping woohoos, if you're inquiring into the status of my own personal vital signs."

The problem with Willie was that if it took two words to give an answer, he always dragged it out to twenty. He would have made one hell of a politician.

Seated eight feet behind him, framed in the convex rearview mirror, he could see the distorted reflection of his Electronic Weapon Systems officer, Captain Eugene Williams. Willie had done three years during peacetime and transferred to the reserves, then been recalled to duty in 'Nam. Unbelievably, he took the recall in good grace and talked about staying in, allowing as how the service, as opposed to stinking up a chem lab in a no-name Ohio high school, provided a decent monthly paycheck and enough bennies to raise his rug rat. But Willie had begun to belly up to the Officer's Club bar a little too frequently in the last month. Bad vibrations for a short-timer with only two weeks left in his tour.

"Going away party for Major Dum Dum," Willie said into the intercom. "Killed half a bottle of sake, the other half like near

1

killed me. It was Pearl Harbor all over again and the good guys lost again." Dum Dum, as he was universally referred to, was Major Daniel D. Dunn, the squadron intelligence officer, a misnomer if one ever existed.

Bracken smiled into the oxygen mask. Why in hell anyone would drink Japanese rice wine was beyond him, unless Willie was trying to anesthetize himself against the gut fear at the tail end of his second tour. But that was his business, because Willie, despite his perpetual hangovers, was first class on the scopes.

"The state of your liver aside, what gives with the black boxes?" Bracken prompted.

Willie gave him a big zero with his thumb and forefinger, reflected in the mirror. "Radar crappy, ECM crappy. In brief, O great leader, system status is absolutely normal."

Bracken nodded, confident that the electronics were serviceable, then checked his watch. Another eight minutes to the coast, then another seven to target.

Off to his right wing tip and slightly behind were two other Phantoms stacked up in a loose echelon. He rocked his wings slightly and flipped them the bird. Radio silence, but they rocked their wings in acknowledgment. Good karma. Casey flying his wing and the new kid, Springmaker, on Casey's. Once more into the breach, he thought.

He relaxed for a minute, wanting to feel the machine with his senses rather than through the interpretations of needles, numbers, and video displays. Bracken pulled off one of his flying gloves and lightly drew his fingers along the aluminum sill of the canopy, trying to sense the health of the beast that rumbled beneath him.

In the better aircraft he had found that there was a kind of high-tension electricity that flowed between him and the ship: the sensation of a minute but pulsing voltage as if the airframe's nervous system were alive. *Triple Nickel,* otherwise identified as AF048–555, had a pulse of her own, and on this afternoon in September, the pulse was sure and strong.

Satisfied, Bracken pulled the glove back on and relaxed marginally. Ahead of him the coast was emerging from haze, the crumpled mountains, the wet stinking jungles, the highlands beyond beginning to take form and definition. As always, when he closed the coast, he felt his heart rate pick up, his sphincter contract. Very high pucker factor, particularly this mission.

Housekeeping to do. He checked the gauges, fuel remaining,

weapons-arming status, exhaust gas temperature, panel, power settings, and IFF.

"All quiet?" Bracken asked.

Willie hesitated, his head stuffed into the scope. "Quiet as Ashtabula on a Sunday night. Little fuzz from search radar up the coast, but it's not steady—more like they were just trying to keep their hand in. No electronic countermeasures, no surface to air missile radar—" He paused. "At least not yet."

There would be, Bracken knew. His flight had drawn the dam on the Quin Ho Reservoir for today's mission. This was the third strike against that stinking mound of mud. Rece photographs showed minimal damage from the initial strike on Monday. Wing Headquarters had sent in a second mission on Tuesday. Awesome damage, said the rece guys. Then three days of bad weather; more than enough time for the NVA to triple their surface-to-air missiles and radar-controlled antiaircraft. Today's strike—"the *coup de guerre*" Major Dum Dum had triumphantly told them because *he* sure as hell didn't have to put *his* ass on the line up here—was going to be a bitch.

Bracken reached up and poked the belly button of the plastic Porky Pig that swung from a string looped over the gyro reset knob. "Bring me home safe for three more weeks, buddy, and I'll buy you a lifetime pass to Disneyland."

"You say something?" Willie asked.

"Talking to myself. Symptoms of premature senility."

"You should live so long," Willie replied without inflection.

Some had dolls, one guy in Charlie flight was reputed to wear the same unwashed underwear whenever he flew hard missions. Other guys had their own talismans. Carved tikis from Fuji were the current vogue.

"You want my latest duck joke?" Willie said.

Williams had at least two per mission, particularly when they were getting close to the target. "Shoot."

"Duck walks into a pharmacy and says, 'Gimme a tube of Chap Stick and put it on my bill.' "

"Ugh . . ."

"Got another . . ."

Bracken checked his watch, then the mission outline. "Save it for the trip home. Time for descent to approach altitude. You set?"

"Do I have a choice?"

He thumbed the radio transmit button. "Foxtrot flight, this is

One. Ordnance arm switches on, ECM on, and power back to eighty-three percent. Trail astern and keep your separation staggered. Start descent *now*."

The three Phantoms ponderously peeled off, one following the other, power back but gaining speed as they descended. Beneath each of their wings were slung sixteen 500-pound iron bombs: maximum "wall-to-wall" ordnance load.

They know we're coming, Bracken thought, sunlight and shadows sweeping across the cockpit as he corrected his heading. Eating their midday rations of rice and mangos and tea, then tensely sitting around in their gunpits smoking cigarettes, telling stale jokes, just as tired and bored and scared shitless as we are.

The approach to the dam was up a narrow valley with a dogleg to the left. He had watched six reruns of the rece films the night before. Two known quad ZSU-23 millimeter emplacements, one on either side of the dam but probably three times that many by now. Two more ZSU-57-2 flak emplacements up on the ridges of the hills overlooking the valley. And by now they would have SAM-2s and SAM-7s in place. He knew that in his bones.

Seventh Air Force had let it be known that they wanted maximum effort, maximum results on this mission. The guy who was head of targeting was a former Strategic Air Command bomber pilot, aka SAC, aka "squares and checks," who prided himself on "mission accomplishment." Which meant filling in the squares with checks, regardless that those squares and checks represented missing men and aircraft. A classic was "Mission 187B, January 17, 1968. Six armed patrol vessels in the river port of Dong Hoi neutralized and/or sunk. Heavy damage to port refueling facilities" . . . which translated into a bunch of old men in fishing boats being blasted into dog meat, their sampans reduced to match wood and an outhouse-size community water tank riddled into Swiss cheese.

But the dam—missions 393, 397, and 404—was now his favorite target and he would keep spending lives and aircraft until the dam was breached. The mission objective was to "destroy reenforced structural dam and neutralize surrounding enemy troop concentrations with the result of denying the lower Ho valley to enemy food production." From what Bracken had been told by Bravo flight's leader, the dam was an earthworks affair, the sill at least 300 yards wide and the base likely three times that much. It sucked up 500-pound bombs like a dry sponge sucking up raindrops. And damage to the dam today, if any, would be repaired before dawn, and another mission would bust their collective chops trying to gut the thing out. To Bracken, the dam represented the pointlessness and futility of the whole war.

He leveled *Triple Nickel* off at three hundred feet above the deck.

"Fourteen seconds to the mouth of the valley. Come right about six degrees," Willie instructed, his voice bone-dry. "Search and surface-to-air radar up ahead."

Bracken checked Willie in the rearview mirror but could see just the top of his brain bucket, his face buried in the scopes. Better, Bracken thought, than having to look outside.

Strung out in a switching tail were the other two Phantoms, both of them laying down plumes of kerosene exhaust as they followed in his wake.

Tracers now floating up from the approaches to the valley. Hadn't been there before, so the NVA had moved more stuff in. Bracken unconsciously hunched down in his ejection seat, edged the power up another five percent, and braced himself.

He blasted the Phantom into the valley, held it level for five seconds, and then racked *Triple Nickel* into the dogleg turn, leveled again, and looked ahead for the earthworks and sheen of the lake beyond the dam.

Black puffballs of flak dotted the valley and tracers arched over from the ridges. He double-checked the arming switches and squinted at the range ring.

"They've got a missile lock-on," Willie said, his voice up half an octave.

Bracken could hear it himself, the high-pitched whine of the radar tracker that would guide the missile.

He wasn't worried about that one. Some smartass NVA was just trying to spook them because the SA-2 wasn't effective against low-flying aircraft. He pressed on up the valley, now weaving, the flak getting heavier.

The airframe of *Triple Nickel* was taking minor hits now, the *karump* of fragmentation shells splattering her with shrapnel.

The floor of the valley was thick with smoke; probably from burning truck tires set aflame by the NVA gunners to obscure the target. And the walls of the windless valley obligingly contained the smoke in a stratified haze, cutting ground reference to zero.

Triple Nickel bucked, then shuddered. Major hit. Bracken didn't dare look at the panel. Ahead, he could see cannon tracers converging on the center of the valley from two gun emplacements that he guessed were at the ends of the dam—which would at least give him a rough idea of where the dam was. He rammed in full military power and bit his lip, guessing that he could toggle off the bombs in less than three seconds.

More thuds into the fuselage, and the Phantom was vibrating heavily, as if it were out of rig. The instrument panel was blurred by the vibration, Willie screaming something, the plane now getting kicked around by the heavy bursts. Bracken stabbed the bomb release, then racked the plane over hard to the right, the g forces dragging down on his flesh, sagging his eyelids, his cheeks, his lips. He kept her down on the deck, hugged the trees for a few more seconds so the bastards couldn't hold an infrared lock-on. Then, almost without thinking, he flicked the throttle around the horn into afterburner and heard the simultaneous explosions and the boot in the rear kicking *Triple Nickel* into overdrive.

He was out of it now, still on the deck, flying up the slope of the valley, the trees only a couple of wingspans below him. Fireflies flickered through the leaves—mainly small arms stuff.

Now!

He pulled back on the stick and stood the Phantom on her tail, the altimeter whirling madly in its glass cage, gaining precious altitude, then looked back. He saw both Phantoms, Casey having split left after hitting the target as they had agreed and Springmaker still over the target, pressing in like the Great White Hope of the West. Springmaker never pulled up. There was a great gout of flame which carried on into the earthworks, throwing out pieces of junk and bodies and mother's dreams in an expanding black and red balloon of fire.

Willie was shouting into the intercom. "Main buss power gone, radar's out. Everything's dead back here 'cept me."

"You take any damage?" He was starting to collect himself now, getting his scan going. The state of *Triple Nickel*'s health was reflected in the screaming swarm of amber warning lights on the panel. Up through nine thousand now and accelerating, because like a good horse she was going to run her heart out before she died. But die, Bracken knew, she would.

"Right leg's numb and my pants are wet. I hoped it was piss, but this stuff is red. And there's a couple of major drafts back here as well."

"How bad?"

"Nothing that a McDonnell Douglas factory refab job couldn't handle in three or four months. Until then, consider this bird as a loose gaggle of aluminum panels flying in formation."

"Give me a heading to the coast."

"Computed that during preflight. Try oh nine seven magnetic, about sixty miles."

Bracken eased the vertical ascent over into a climbing arc, slowly coming right until the noonday sun was just off his right wing. The directional gyro seemed frozen, so he checked the backup compass and made a final correction based on pure good faith. To keep her in afterburner or not? Prime question, because if he was leaking fuel, he wanted to convert as much of the fuel remaining into altitude. He decided to keep the torch lit and glanced down at the panel again. Up through 18,000.

He stared ahead for the glint of the sea but knew it was too far, then checked the horizon. Heading seemed good. He could see the foothills that lapped the city of Ha Tinh and the mountains beyond off to the southwest. Time to check in.

"Fox Two, this is One. You copy?"

Casey's voice came back instantly, smooth and polished; like he spit-shined it every morning. "Roger One. I'm at your five o'clock, about two hundred yards and closing. One of your gear doors is blown off, there's some damage to the aft section of the fuselage, and you're trailing fuel."

Cheerful bastard, Bracken thought.

He glanced at Porky, and the pig stared back cross-eyed, his idiot smile noncommittal. "Get me home, you turkey," Bracken swore under his breath. The pig, probably resenting being mistaken for a turkey, promised nothing, just twisted slowly in the noose, his face now in shadows.

Passing through 22,000 feet, *Triple Nickel* flamed out. For a second Bracken froze as he listened to the engines spool down, not believing that she would die this soon. Beneath them was rolling flatland, whereas down toward the coast there would be a combination of swamps and jungle. And if Willie was leaking blood, he would need medical attention and fast. Bracken nosed her over to keep her above a stall, gaining time and mileage from the dam.

"Fox Two, we can't make the coast and we don't want to go down in the jungle. We're punching out."

"Roger, One. We'll see you down."

Casey—always the professional. Nothing maudlin like "good luck" or any of that crap.

Triple Nickel was descending now like a greased brick. Down through nineteen, then fifteen thousand. He dropped the gear and flaps, then eased back on the stick, slowing what remained of *Triple Nickel* to a sedate crawl of 155 knots. "You ready, Willie?"

"You first, John."

In his last act as aircraft commander of *Triple Nickel,* Bracken yanked the pig from his noose and stuffed him into the pocket of his flight suit, then zipped it shut. He bottomed the ejection seat and pulled down his visor, clamped his legs together, jettisoned the canopy, then squeezed the ejection grip.

All the while listening to the pig in his pocket stutter in a muffled cartoon voice, "Tha-tha-tha-that's all, folks."

2.

September 13, 1969

The man who called himself Lu Duc Lee sat in his chair, hands folded together, his fingers interlaced, the thumbs, pad to pad, slowly rubbing against each other. For three or four minutes, as he always did at the beginning of an interrogation, he silently studied Bracken.

Lu wore no uniform, no badges of rank—only a faded black Mao jacket and pants. He was smooth-shaven and probably in his mid-thirties, perhaps just a shade older if you noted his thinning hair.

He wore frameless amber-tinted glasses in the manner of the French, and had taken them off only once in Bracken's presence. In those few seconds, Bracken discovered that though Lu had Oriental features—an almost hairless face, prominent cheekbones, and almond-shaped eyes—he was not pure Oriental. Eastern and Western genes had mingled somewhere in his ancestry; probably Colonial French and Vietnamese, like many that Bracken had seen in Saigon. The facial muscles had a quick energy, and his controlled smile revealed fine teeth that were slightly yellowed from a two-pack-a-day cigarette habit. The only thing Bracken had discovered in those few short seconds was that Lu's eyes were gray-blue—the color of glacial ice under Arctic sunlight.

"What information are you going to give me today, Bracken?"

"Captain John R. Bracken, U.S. Air Force, Serial Number 29574A."

Drawing one finger slowly down the side of his nose, Lu smiled. "You are a non-person, Bracken. You have no officer status. Your country has never declared war against the Vietnamese people. Therefore, you are a mercenary killer. As such, you have no rights or privileges under any convention and you continue to exist only at my rapidly diminishing pleasure." Lu said this evenly, without inflection, just part of the ritual.

These were the first moves in a game they played in each

9

interrogation. The opening by Lu, the standard response by Bracken, the bored threat by Lu, complaints about the conditions by Bracken (always ignored) followed by Lu's carefully edited news release, supposedly verifying his claims that America was losing an aimless war with no will to fight it.

Lu flicked a package of cigarettes across the table, another part of the continuing ritual. Marlboros this time; never the same brand for long. Sometimes Luckies, sometimes Pall Malls. Bracken supposed that they were taken from dead or captured Americans —a subtle but unspoken verification of Lu's news reports, part of the psywar gambit that he played so well.

"Gave 'em up for Lent," Bracken replied, not wanting to look at the pack yet unable not to. God, he wanted one—but to accept even one was to give away what little he had left of his independence.

Lu nodded politely, retrieving the pack. He lit a cigarette and inhaled deeply with pleasure, held the smoke in his lungs, then exhaled, blowing a blue haze through the light of his shaded desk lamp.

Leaning back, Lu studied Bracken more carefully, as if Bracken were a rare tropical fish in a small glass bowl, there for the minor pleasures of distracted observation. The feeling was magnified by Lu's sometimes habit of tapping a precise point of air in front of him, as if he were trying to gain the attention of the specimen contained within.

"I am pleased to report that the war is not going well for your country, Bracken." Lu's perfect, accentless English was a product, he said, of six years as a student, the school and its location unspecified. He shuffled through a sheaf of papers. "More than 44,000 American deaths to date, 133,000 total casualties. Yesterday, six American B-52 crew members whose plane was shot down were pitchforked to death by North Vietnamese peasants. You see, your valiant comrades bombed a children's hospital"—he paused and looked up—"just as you incinerated peaceful field workers planting rice in the area beneath the Ho dam."

"And it was water buffalo chips that they slung at me, right?"

Lu smiled. He reached down to the floor and retrieved a manila folder, looked up at Bracken for a moment, then back to the contents of the folder.

"I want some medical attention for Captain Williams," Bracken demanded.

Lu shook his head. "You know the house rules, Bracken. I

ask, you answer. What you *want* is of no interest to me. The penalty for not following the rules is a reduction of half your food ration for today." He arched his thin eyebrows. "Is there anything else you *want*? Don't you want to gamble for double or nothing?"

"Half of nothing is nothing," Bracken shot back. "Williams's leg has never healed, never set properly. Without proper attention, he's going to lose it."

"Yes—so I'm told. But we have very limited medical facilities here. Until he signs a war crimes confession, he must remain in our correctional facility. Once he does, we will transfer him to a hospital, where he will receive professional attention. And once recovered, he will join other prisoners in what you Americans call the Hanoi Hilton. And if you choose to cooperate, you could also join him." He scratched his chin lightly with his fingernail. "Kissinger, I am told, is begging for a cease-fire. For those Americans who are rehabilitated, that could mean going home . . . soon, perhaps."

It was something new and unexpected. Bracken didn't want to even think that it might be possible. He considered himself in suspended animation—no present time, no future, no past, just living second-to-second as long as his heart beat. He could handle it without hope, but hope would alter his perspective, and that was the danger.

Lighting another cigarette from the butt of the previous one, Lu then said, "I see your lips forming another question. Do you wish to play for tomorrow's food allowance as well?"

Bracken knew that he couldn't afford to. A day's ration was weak tea, a scoop of partially cooked rice, and orange sludge which Lu referred to as pumpkin soup. Sporadically, there was a ration of a rotten banana to commemorate some NVA national holiday. Overall, Bracken estimated that half the calories he took in were lost to diarrhea. He finally shook his head.

"That's very wise of you." Lu glanced at his watch and then down to the papers he had extracted from the folder. He read for several minutes in silence, occasionally stretching his lips in a smile, then placed the papers on the table and leaned forward, fingers splayed into a steeple. "Until now, I had the impression that you were just a pilot, but your service record would seem to indicate otherwise."

"Who says?"

"U.S. Air Force Form—" He bent over and squinted, examining the bottom of the page. "Two-twelve."

"Where did you get that?"

Lu arched his eyebrows, always a dangerous sign. "That could mean an even further reduction of rations, but I'll accept your momentary indiscretion. There are people in the South who are patriots. They work for our government by working for yours. At great danger to themselves, they feed us information." He tapped the papers with his finger. "This is your military background, Bracken, laid out in every detail. Tell me first about the Black Hangar training."

There was suddenly a raw, throbbing emptiness in the pit of Bracken's stomach, as if something had been wrenched away by a surgical claw without benefit of anaesthesia. The Black Hangar was a special-weapons course given at Lowry Air Force Base, Colorado, for career officers. Special weapons was a euphemism for nuclear weapons. And the course covered not just basics but what the weapons did: blast, heat, radiation, fallout, and electromagnetic pulse.

"It was just an indoctrination course. There was a training quota to meet, and somebody in the squadron had to go. My number came up. I slept through most of it."

"Oh, Bracken—what am I going to do with you?" Lu asked softly, wagging his head. "You lie so quickly and convincingly. This meticulously detailed record indicates that you studied there for seven months and received the third highest marks in a class of sixteen. This document sheds a whole new light on our relationship. I think, tomorrow, we will increase the duration of our conversations. In the meanwhile, I've made some rearrangement in your living quarters." He rapped on the table, and from the darkness the two guards stepped forward, banging the heels of their boots together.

Lu rose, his face now in the shadows. "Be prepared, Captain John R. Bracken, U.S. Air Force, serial number 29574A, to discuss in detail specific characteristics of the American Mark 17 nuclear weapon."

The twin set of North Vietnamese guards—whom Bracken had tagged as Huff and Puff, based on the first guard's repeated threatening gestures and the second's chipmunk cheeks—arm-wrestled Bracken into a new cell. They slammed the door shut and Bracken listened as the multiple bolts thudded into their recesses.

Like the cell he had been existing in for the past four months, the dimensions of the concrete floor were roughly eight by six, the walls approximately ten feet high, no window, a steel entrance door with a peephole at eye level and a slop door at the bottom. The furnishings consisted of a straw-filled mattress, a shit bucket, and a water tap. But this one had subtle differences. Set into the walls on either side were wire mesh grills, probably there for cross-ventilation.

Bracken flopped down on the mattress, physically exhausted but his mind zeroing in on the new reality of the background information that Lu now had. Lu was getting serious, and that sent a chill through his body.

He knew that it was a dangerous attitude, but he actually respected Lu, found him to be reasonably civilized, even humorous at times. Without any other human contact—he had discounted Huff and Puff as human—he generally looked forward to the distraction that Lu's daily interrogation offered.

Sure as hell, he had given Lu information, but only information that Lu would have already extracted from the hundreds of pilots that had gone down over 'Nam, and even that information Bracken had distorted. But he had drawn a line on signing any confession. The chances had been that Lu would eventually tire of him and release him to ordinary prisoner status.

But now a new element of uncertainty had been added with his 212 file in Lu's hands. With the exception of some rough handling by NVA troops when he and Willie were captured, and Lu's methodology of cracking a prisoner's will through slow starvation, no one had actually physically abused him. But now that might change, and he wondered, like any other prisoner facing torture, just how much he could take.

And he worried about Willie because they might use his deteriorating condition as a lever. He'd seen Willie, briefly, about two weeks before on the way back from interrogation. The right leg of Willie's flight suit was cut off, and he had been using two sticks of bamboo to support himself. Although he had lost thirty or forty pounds, Willie's right leg was swollen to twice its normal girth and was wrapped with strips of brown-stained muslin. Willie had glanced at Bracken and marginally shaken his head, warning him not to talk. They passed in the corridor, both of them with guards prodding them from behind. Bracken, even now, could not shake the rotting pork smell that Willie trailed behind him.

The sound had been in the background for a few minutes, but until now he hadn't really noticed it—just a faint persistent clicking. Bracken pulled himself to his feet and wandered around the cell, trying to pinpoint its location. Not at the steel door, not the grill, not the wall, not exactly. The water tap? He bent down and placed his ear against it, the vibrations distinct now. Bracken rapped on the spigot with his knuckles three times.

The tapping stopped for a few seconds, then resumed. Two groups of one to five clicks, a pause, and then another group. It came back to him now—the prisoner code that had been worked out by POWs in Korea, now taught to all U.S. pilots during survival training.

He ignored the taps and feverishly started to scratch rows and columns of letters into the whitewashed wall with the handle of a metal spoon. It took him thirty seconds to scratch out

$$
\begin{array}{ccccc}
A & B & C & D & E \\
F & G & H & I & J \\
L & M & N & O & P \\
Q & R & S & T & U \\
V & W & X & Y & Z
\end{array}
$$

The K was missing but C was used as a substitute.

Hunkering down next to the spigot, Bracken tapped eight times in a row, trying to signify that he was ready to transmit. The tapping stopped. Then, laboriously, he began his own message, forming each letter, using the first clicks to designate the row number and the second to designate the column number. It took him more than a minute, but he got off his first message— WHO U.

A pause, then the response: LT RON LEVIN USN—WHO U.

Lu had warned Bracken in the first meeting that any attempt to communicate with another prisoner would be punished by the flailing of his bare soles with a split-bamboo cane. Lu had called it "institutional policy."

Bracken was leery. Something that Lu had cooked up? He hesitated, then tapped WAIT, sat back, and thought. He had to ask a question that would establish the bona fides of the other tapper.

He couldn't use military jargon. Lu would be up on that. But presuming that the tapper was about his age and American, they probably shared a common slang. Maybe something about girls or what they ate as kids on Saturday nights at the drive-in. It came to him. Laboriously, he tapped out: *WHAT IS GRINDER*.

Short pause, then the long reply. *EITHER STRIPPER OR HOAGIE—DEPENDS WHAT PART OF UR ANATOMY U WANT SATISFIED*.

Relief, hope, and joy flooded through Bracken. He rapidly tapped out *CAPT JOHN BRACKEN USAF*.

For the next three hours Bracken caught up with the world.

Levin, a carrier pilot, had been shot down during a mission against torpedo boat bases at Hon Gay only two weeks earlier. From Levin he learned about the escalating war and the massive B-52 raids that were pulverizing Hanoi. Learned about the peace activists and LBJ's resignation. Learned that Kissinger was actually negotiating with North Vietnamese in Paris. Levin also told him about the ventilation slots at the top of the cells—that at night, after the guards stopped pacing the cell corridor and retired to the guard room, it was possible to stand on the shit bucket and whisper back and forth without too much difficulty.

Bracken finally asked about Willie. Levin signaled that he had communicated with another prisoner who had talked with Williams in the latrine. *LEG BAD*.

Bracken tapped back: *WHERES WILLIAMS*.

The answer came back. *CELL OTHER SIDE OF U AS OF LAST WEDNESDAY*.

Later, after the lights were switched off, Bracken tried raising Willie by whispering through the grill, but there was no response, only the sound of hoarse breathing.

"Start off with how you were selected for special-weapons training, Bracken." Lu skipped all the preliminary sparring.

"I have a kind face."

"If you don't give me straight answers, Bracken, you will have no face left before this day is over. Again—why were you selected?"

He knew the correct answer wouldn't compromise anything, but it was a start down a path that would lead to other questions, then to answers that would betray secrets and, more important, the trust that he had sworn to guard.

"I've got no idea why, old buddy."

Lu took a deep breath and slowly expelled it. "Let's get down to specifics. What is the yield of a Mark 17 warhead?"

"I've never been close enough to the crater to measure it."

Resting his elbow on the table, Lu cupped his chin in his palm. He looked at Bracken with distaste. "The house rules have changed, Bracken. I have a preliminary list of questions which you will study. I will want you to write down the answers in the fullest detail that you can remember. That will be just the start. Our sessions in this room will be eight hours a day, every day of the week. Others will join me in the interrogation. Some of those are more impatient than I am and their methods are more direct."

"I won't answer any questions." Bracken realized how thin his voice now sounded. His armpits were soaking wet and sweat trickled down his back.

"But you will, Bracken. All of those questions and more and then even more until you are sucked dry. In the end, Bracken, you will be nothing more than a husk that will be blown away in the wind." He shoved the list of questions, a pad of paper, and a ball-point pen across the table. "I'll give you thirty minutes to consider your future. I strongly advise that you give us your unconditional and free cooperation." Lu stood and left the room.

The list of questions was laid out in Lu's neat handwriting. Give the man an A-plus for neatness. The questions reflected an intimate knowledge of nuclear weapons and their plumbing.

Question 3. What type of seal is used on the electronics bay support cover of the Mark 17? Transfer valve—how reliable? Leakage? How often is the seal replaced? Any known in-flight failures of this valve?

Question 13. Describe backup fusing of the warhead. Attachment of the crystal shock transmitter. Screw-in or welded? Type of sealing compound and its manufacture.

Question 21. Describe sequence of APCHE checkout equipment in reliability test mode.

Question 28. Describe metallurgy and identification of warhead casing. Thickness? Rockwell hardness? Tensile strength?

Christ, Bracken thought. This wasn't something that the NVA would have any knowledge of. Not in this depth. The Chinese? More likely the Soviets. Then Bracken realized the significance of Lu's blue eyes. Might it be that Lu wasn't part French but, rather, part Russian? It would explain the absence of badges of rank on his uniform, his veneer of sophistication, and his near-perfect command of English. The whole thing, although a little shaky, fitted together. The Soviets were supplying the NVA with arms. Wouldn't it be logical as a quid pro quo for them to get first crack at interrogating captured American officers?

Bracken's Russian was limited. He'd done three months in the air force language school at Monterey and some independent self-study, so he had a very rough working knowledge of the language. For the next quarter of an hour, he thought about his response, practicing.

Lu came back. With him, besides the guards, was another man, who stood back in the shadows, leaning against the concrete wall of the basement cell. Lu stepped forward, placing a tape recorder on the desk, then setting a microphone on a stand in front of Bracken. He turned the machine on, then tapped the microphone with his fingernail, setting the levels.

He glanced at the blank pad of paper. "You haven't started your homework."

"I think I can supply some of the answers. I'm not strong on technical stuff, but I remember a little of it."

Lu gave him a thin smile. "I think you will do better as time passes and your memory is exercised."

Motioning to the package of cigarettes, Bracken casually asked, "Could I have one of those?"

Obviously pleased, Lu shook one from the pack and tossed it across the table. It rolled to a stop just short of Bracken's fingertips. He picked it up, tapped it carefully, and placed it between his lips.

"And a light, please?" The humble-pie routine.

"Of course." Lu moved to Bracken's side of the table and flared his lighter, holding it to the tip of Bracken's cigarette.

"*Spaseba,*" Bracken said casually, thanking him in Russian. He sucked in on the cigarette.

Automatically, Lu answered, *"Nye za . . . shto . . ."*

Uttering the last word, Lu's voice had hesitated and trailed off into a whisper.

"Vyi ez kakoy chyahstye Sovyetskova Soyuza?" Bracken said softly. "Let me guess. Maybe Khabarovsk? No, I doubt that. You're probably a warm-weather boy—more southern. Like Buryat, or perhaps lower Mongolia?"

Lu reached over and snatched the cigarette from Bracken's mouth, dropped it on the concrete, and stamped it out with his boot. He turned toward the door and said something in rapid-fire

Vietnamese. The other man grunted, muttered something under his breath, and left the room, slamming the door behind him.

Turning back, Lu said, "For the rest of your life, Bracken, you'll be sorry for that indiscretion." He motioned the two guards forward, instructed them in Vietnamese, and then stood back from the light cast by the desk lamp, his upper body in darkness.

They shackled Bracken's wrists together, then bound his arms behind the chair with two canvas straps, one around his elbows and another set just under his shoulders, then secured his legs and arms to the chair with belts. Huff remained behind him while Puff left the room, returning in a few minutes with two wooden bars. Bracken felt the bars being pushed into the webbing of the straps behind him.

"The problem with this corrective measure, Bracken, is that one never passes out from the pain. The straps are tightened with the bars, the elbows first, then the shoulders. Eventually, the joints pop out of their sockets. It just goes on and on and you scream your lungs out, but there's no release. For today, I'm not even interested in getting answers from you. That will start tomorrow." He nodded toward the guards.

"*Da skorava,*" he said, and left the room.

As Lu had promised, Bracken was fully conscious through the next four hours, mad with pain, screaming until his throat was raw and he couldn't scream any longer. A little after seven he choked on his own vomit. The guards then unstrapped him, pushed him over on the concrete floor, and kicked him in the stomach until his windpipe was cleared.

Bracken, semiconscious, was wheeled to his cell on a gurney with squeaking wheels just after nightfall.

3.

September 14, 1969

The guards, AK machine pistols slung across their backs, came for Bracken just before dawn. As he silently screamed, they lifted him onto the gurney, strapped him down with canvas webbing, and then trundled him along corridors, past wire-mesh gates, across a rain-flooded courtyard, and finally through the doors of a dispensary whose walls were covered with peeling green paint. They locked the gurney's wheels and left.

He lay there, immobile, panting, his heart jackhammering against the wall of his chest, his mind fading in and out. Bizarre images moved across his mind like figures dancing on the ground-glass viewfinder of an unfocused camera—until the screen finally went blank.

He awoke sometime later. Gusts of wind still rattled the windows, but it was the end of the storm and a pale sun was breaking through the clouds. Bracken couldn't see outside because a patterned wax paper had been ironed against the glass, but there were the shadows. He identified them in sequence as a tree branch, a man, a giant bird, and death, then faded out again.

An hour later, he thought. The sun higher, the shadows shorter. The pain was still intense and he tried not to move at all. He desperately wanted to urinate, didn't have the will to hold it, and soiled his pants.

The place smelled of his own warm urine, lye soap, and the overlying scent of carbolic acid. Two portraits, one of Ho Chi Minh and the other of Vo Nguyen Giap, stared down on him in silent admonition.

The rest of the room was a crude collection of rough shelving stocked sparsely with American and French medical supplies, many of their labels scorched, and a makeshift operating table built from packing cases. An oil lamp, hanging near a naked light bulb, still smoldered, choking its glass chimney with soot. In the corner near the door stood a full-length mirror, an eye chart, and a rusty scale.

19

He was fully awake now, but he couldn't tell how much time had passed.

Sounds of scuffing footsteps in the corridor, a pause, a muffled conversation.

Two sturdy women and an old man stood over him, all of them clothed in the same black jackets and pants. The younger of the two women looked down at his damp flight suit in apparent disgust.

The old man wore the wisp of a white goatee trailing down his chin, his brown face runneled with wrinkles like an earthen field that had been furrowed by the erosion of a heavy rain. After releasing the webbing, he unzipped Bracken's flight suit from neck to crotch and began to probe. His fingers were gentle and practiced, but his eyes were neutral and distanced from feeling, as if Bracken were no more or less than a machine that had unexpectedly malfunctioned.

The old man grunted twice and turned away, impatiently yanking open and slamming closed drawers in a cabinet until he found what he was looking for. He returned with a wooden tray and, holding several needles up to the light, squinting to insure that they were the proper instruments, pricked each one in turn into the right eyelid, both earlobes, along the hairline, the folds of the neck, below the heart, the hip, and then the left side of the abdomen. Curiously, the needles produced no pain. To the contrary, Bracken felt a warm, easy glow, almost euphoric.

The two women positioned themselves on either side of him, each one bracing one of their feet in his armpit, then drawing his arms out in a crucifix. The old man stood behind Bracken's head, mumbling directions in impatient staccato monosyllables. The women then interlaced wrists, overlapping their grips, and, with their other hands, pressed in on his biceps. Almost simultaneously, Bracken heard two distinct, wet *pop*s.

"I fix you," the old man said in a phlegmy voice. He plucked out the needles and laid them on the tray. The two women left the room at the old man's hand gesture. He then turned back to Bracken. "I think I fix you again, many times." He coughed, turned, and shuffled out of the dispensary doors, the echo of his wooden clogs reverberating down the empty corridor.

"This process is totally unnecessary," Lu said, standing over him. "You are intelligent. No one will fault you for giving out information which we already know and only want confirmation on. Why not spare your body further pain?"

Bracken was naked, on his knees, hands bound, a doubled leather thong banded around his forehead and stretched behind him to his ankles. Lu nodded and Huff tightened the thong with the wooden stick.

"Don't . . . know . . . anything," Bracken tried to gasp. Nothing really came out of his mouth, just silent words formed on his lips, blowing saliva bubbles. It was the third day. On the second day, Huff and Puff had shoved bamboo splinters under his toenails; Lu, his hands clean, had waited beyond the door.

"Question fourteen again, Bracken. What electromagnetic pulse levels are produced by a one-megaton warhead?"

"Don't . . . know," Bracken croaked.

Standing over him, Lu shook his head and made a circular motion with his hand. Huff immediately released the pressure, then cut the thong.

"I give you high marks, Bracken," Lu said. "You tolerate pain fairly well for a Westerner. But time has been wasted. I think we will now move on to another approach." He signaled someone in the darkness at the back of the room, and cold air washed over Bracken as the door opened and then closed.

They brought Willie in on a stretcher twenty minutes later. The stench of his gangrene clawed at Bracken's nostrils.

"I have already discussed the house rules with Williams," Lu said. "He knows the type of information that I'm seeking. You'll have half an hour together. Then we'll resume." He tossed a package of Pall Malls and a book of matches on the table. "Enjoy your visit." He left the room, followed by the others.

Bracken lit one for Willie and put it between his lips. "How's it going, sport?"

He nodded down at his festering leg. "I'm still kicking," he said without irony.

Bracken took the cigarette from Willie's lips and drew on it. He wanted to get Willie's mind off the immediate, something to reestablish the old link between them. "What was that joke you were going to tell me before we punched out of *Triple Nickel*? The one about the duck."

Willie shut his eyes, no animation in his face, the words mechanical. "Man with a duck squatting on his head walks into a shrink's office. The shrink says, 'Are you the patient who called about a paranoia problem?' and the duck says, 'Yeah, Doc, I want to get this guy off my ass.' "

Bracken tried to laugh, but it came out as a racking wheeze. He took another drag on the cigarette. "Bad corner I painted us into, Willie," he finally said.

"Whither thou goest, etcetera."

"What did the dink tell you?"

Willie lay his head back on the stretcher, staring at the ceiling. "Said you were being quote uncooperative unquote. That he needed only your confirmation of information that he already had. And if he didn't get it, he'd tell the goon squad to massage us with the big bamboo until you did." He moved his head, locking his eyes on Bracken's. "So Lu wants details on the Mark 17. Shit, the thing's obsolete. And what are the Vietnamese going to build one out of anyway—cow pies and coconuts? So what's the big deal in telling him?"

"He's a Soviet," Bracken said. "Not Vietnamese." He filled Willie in about the response in Russian and the blue-eyed theory.

"*Now* it's absolutely, fucking obvious," Willie said cynically. "He's some kind of stir-fried Paul Newman who likes to read Tolstoy in the original." Willie turned his head and looked up at Bracken. "I'm going to lose it."

"Lose what?"

"My leg, you asshole. One of those things you use for walking on, running on, dancing on. I've got red streaks up to my crotch. If someone touched my leg with a feather, let alone a bamboo cane, I'd go berserk. Just the pressure on it, lying here, is driving me nuts."

"You spell it out, Willie. What do you want me to do?"

Williams lay back on the stretcher, his eyes locked on Bracken's. "Two things on my list. You know that Marlene walked out on me. No idea where she is and, frankly, Scarlett, I don't give a damn. But I've got a fifteen-year-old daughter, Jill. She's living with Marlene's sister. If I don't come out of this, I want you to make sure that she gets my insurance. She may need some additional help as well. Like her old man, she's a little flaky around the edges."

Bracken silently nodded, no point in arguing.

"Item two. I'm with you on this thing. I'll try to hold out. You do what you think is right without regard for me. It's five to one that I won't make it through another week anyway."

"We're both going to make it—" Bracken started.

"Which we both know is horse hockey. I want your word."

"You have it."

Willie took a long breath and settled back. "Then let the games begin."

They held out for two hours and forty minutes.

During that eternity, Lu would ask a question and Bracken would reply, giving explicit instructions to Lu as to how to cram his elbow up his asshole. Lu would compress his lips, then nod to Huff, who handled the split bamboo cane. Willie fainted three times, and each time, Puff revived him with spirits of ammonia. The fourth time, Willie passed the threshold of tolerable pain, shrieking *"Oh my God Bracken, tell him, tell him!"*

And for the next six hours, Bracken did; helpless, defeated, and guilt-ridden.

They let him alone in his cell for five blessed days. No contact with Levin, whose cell was now empty. Bracken was sure that Willie was in the next cell but Willie wouldn't or couldn't talk to him. Still, in the early morning hours, Bracken could hear what he thought was mumbling, sometimes sobbing, sometimes just raw gasping for breath.

On the third day, the food ration improved dramatically. Two scoops of rice, twice the quantity of orange sludge, some stringy meat, and two bananas. After nightfall, when the guards had pulled out of the corridor and back into their pen, Bracken tried to get some kind of response out of Willie, standing on the shit bucket, almost yelling. But Willie didn't answer. Bracken molded two thirds of his rice ration into a ball and lobbed it through the connecting air vent, then followed it with most of the meat. But there was no response.

On each succeeding day, they brought an improved ration of food, gradually adding more calories. Some of it was straight out of GI field rations, including candy bars and cookies. Bracken still shared his ration with Willie, throwing stuff up through the ventilating duct but never getting a response.

In the early morning of the fifth day, Huff and Puff opened the steel door. Lu stepped past them, into the cell.

"On my recommendation, you're going to be transferred to other quarters, Bracken. But first we're going to clean you up."

They led him down the corridors, through a door into the guards' quarters. Beyond that through a second door was a squat hole and a concrete shower stall.

"Shower and wash your hair," Lu said. He looked bored.

The water wasn't hot, not even warm; the soap had the strong scent of lye and was gritty. It was the greatest shower Bracken had ever had.

They gave him a threadbare towel and he rubbed down. Then Lu handed him a box wrapped in oiled paper. It was his flight suit, neatly mended, washed, pressed, and stinking of strong disinfectant. At the bottom of the box were his dog tags and the plastic pig.

Lu led him to the dispensary. He was given a shave and a crew cut by a tiny old woman who sang to herself in a toneless singsong as she clipped him with dull shears. When she was finished, she handed him a mirror. The eyes were baggy, the face thin to the point of being hollow. It was the first time he had seen himself in six months. Somehow, he thought, he looked a great deal older but not necessarily wiser.

"We will now have one final discussion, Bracken. Some papers to sign, but the unpleasantness is over. I have cut orders to transfer you to Hanoi. The food will be adequate. You will be able to exercise and talk with other prisoners. If things go as scheduled, you will leave Vietnam in a year or so."

To Bracken, it was like being reborn—the light at the end of the tunnel from which he had believed he would never emerge. "And Williams?"

Lu stood up. "How things change. You have already forgotten the house rules, but yes, we will also discuss Williams."

Bracken floated down the corridor on callused bare feet, the spark of hope alive within him, knowing that somehow he had survived. A dangerous concept to accept, he knew, but nevertheless, he had a feeling of rebirth that he could not suppress.

Following Lu, Bracken climbed concrete steps, out through a steel grated doorway and into the spring sunshine of the cobblestone courtyard. Willows overhung the crumbling brick walls. He looked up and saw clouds building in the morning sky.

Across the grass of the courtyard, up creaking stairs and onto the porch of an old French colonial house. Bougainvillea climbed trellises and spider plants overflowed earthen pots that hung from the rafters. Lu entered through open French doors into a spacious, sunlit study. There were deep cushioned chairs, a couch, and a tooled leather-topped coffee table. Opposite the couch against the back wall was a sideboard with dented and tarnished candelabras at either end, backed by a mirror held in an ornate golden frame made out of intertwined cupids. One wall was

devoted to library shelves, and the third framed an ornate mahogany desk. Lu motioned Bracken to the couch and sat down
behind the desk.

They remained in silence for a few moments, the galvanized
roof sheeting above them creaking as it expanded in the heat of
the morning sun.

For a long while, Lu studied Bracken as if he were trying to
decide something, finally nodded to himself, then pushed a button on his desk. A woman brought in a serving tray with two cups
of fine bone china, a thermos of coffee, a dented silver pitcher of
condensed milk, and two packs of American GI sugar.

"The coffee's a very excellent blend from Jakarta," Lu remarked, filling Bracken's cup. He offered a pack of Luckies and a
brass Zippo. And why not, Bracken thought. The bargaining was
at an end. He lit one with the Zippo, then, as an afterthought,
examined its case. *To Andy with love—Gwen.* He dropped the
Zippo on Lu's desk as if it had burned his hand.

"Shot down over Haiphong. He was given a proper burial.
Keep the lighter, Bracken. It's yours. And take it back to the
country it came from."

Resting his elbows on the arms of his chair, Lu held his
coffee cup balanced in the bowl of his hands.

"I give you credit, Bracken," he said. "You played the game
better than I expected from one of your background and race.
But when you leave this country, you will take with you the sure
knowledge that massive firepower and slogans do not win wars.
Your country is arrogant. Your leaders sit in safe bunkers and
plan victory by expending people like you without a second
thought. But as time progresses and when your country encounters other Vietnams, as it surely will, they may well remember
their lessons learned in this country: That the true strength of
revolution and its ultimate victory reside in the will of the oppressed masses. And have you finally learned, Bracken?"

The graduation speech, pure Lu rhetoric. Bracken hedged
his response. "Sure I've learned something, but right now I want
to discuss Williams."

"Yes ... Williams," Lu answered. "He has signed a war
crimes confession. That normally carries the penalty of summary
execution, but due to his physical condition, the penalty, depend-
ing on your cooperation, may be waived." He lowered his cup to
the table, played with it for a few moments, and then looked up,
making eye contact with Bracken. "It is within your power to free
him."

"So free him."

Lu shook his head. "Not that easy, Bracken. He will be freed after you answer a few more questions about the criminal activities of your air force."

"What questions? Christ, we've been through all of that. Gimme a break."

Lu compressed his lips, momentarily losing control, his face tight with anger. "Have we spent so many months together that you don't understand? Your country did not declare war against the People's Republic of Vietnam. As such, you are a criminal, not a soldier. You have no rights except those that I confer upon you."

There was silence between them for several minutes, then Lu gradually relaxed in his chair, regaining control of himself. The spring sunlight glancing off his slick black hair, the shadow of his head falling elongated across the mahogany desk. He finally spoke, his voice softened. "I have a few final questions to ask you. If you cooperate, you will be transferred to Hanoi. And by doing so, you will have the power to free Williams. Otherwise, it is just a short walk back to your cell. There, I will continue the painful process of your reeducation."

The velvet hammer, Bracken thought. "Let's see the questions."

Opening the desk drawer, Lu withdrew and then passed him three pages of foolscap, double-spaced, neatly typed.

He stood up and walked over to the couch, sitting down next to Bracken. "Before you read this, I want to explain some realities." His voice was conversational, almost apologetic. "I know what your opinion of me must be, but you have to understand that each of us was ordered to fight with the weapons provided; you with a deadly aircraft that carried tons of violent death, and I with the instruments necessary to persuade men to give me the information that my superiors demand. Oddly, we share much because we are victims of the same war and of the policies that dictate our actions." He paused, leaned over, and refilled both their cups.

Bracken started to interrupt but Lu shook his head. "No, John, not yet. I want to set things straight. Let me have my say."

Lu's use of his first name astonished Bracken.

Lu slowly extended his hand. "You fought your battle well, but it's over. Forgetting the past, knowing that we will never meet again, just for this brief moment can we be friends, or at least not enemies?"

It was bloody in-fucking-credible, after what Lu had put him through, but it would be stupid to antagonize him now, Bracken realized. Give him the gesture, regardless of what lies beneath the surface. Mechanically, Bracken took Lu's hand and slowly shook it.

Lu smiled, pumping Bracken's hand several more times, not letting go. "Good. Then we are friends, Captain John Bracken. And like you, do the American people also want peace and friendship with the Vietnamese people?"

It was an odd way to phrase a question, Bracken thought, out of context. "Yeah," he answered automatically. "I guess the American people want an end to the war. I sure as hell do."

Awkwardly, Lu withdrew his hand. He turned and glanced over his shoulder, and Bracken followed his gaze. On the wall behind them was a large electric clock, the second hand frozen. Ten thirty-three. Bracken wondered how long this dog and pony show would last.

Picking up the typed pages, Lu riffled them. "This is a standard confession we ask your pilots to sign. Some of these things are factual, others are assumptions, much of it is just crude propaganda." Lu frowned briefly and turned toward Bracken. "I just remembered something. You're a career officer?"

"Yes."

"And to sign this, even though I would imagine that you will tell your superiors that it was done under duress, will hurt your career. Correct?"

"It wouldn't help. And I wouldn't sign it except to spring Williams. And Williams will substantiate why I had to sign it. The review board will take that into consideration."

Pursing his lips, Lu nodded thoughtfully. He was silent for a few seconds, then sighed. "Still, we have to go through this for my records. You know what paperwork means. And if I didn't, I'd be censured by my superiors." He thumbed through the papers, slowly shaking his head. "How crude and unbelievable some of these allegations are. Poison gas, bombing of hospitals. I doubt that such things are any longer believed by the American press." He stroked his temple with his finger, thoughtful. "All right. I'll make this final interview as brief as possible, John. Suppose we do this—I'll read the allegation, then you repeat it in your own words and tell me what you know about the subject. I'll make a brief notation of your response and you'll sign it. Fair enough?"

Bracken was astonished that it was going to be this easy. "Fine with me."

Squinting, Lu read, "The U.S. Air Force equipped our aircraft with rockets which had poison gas warheads. We were told to fire them into civilian population centers, particularly at schools and hospitals." He looked up at Bracken. "The person who wrote this has an overripe imagination."

Nodding, Bracken agreed. "You and I know that's a crock of shit."

Picking up a pen, Lu unscrewed its cap and jotted something down on a pad of paper. He then turned toward Bracken. "Repeat the allegation that I've just read and then give me, in your own words, whether you believe that it's true."

"Something like 'headquarters slung rockets on our aircraft with warheads filled with poison gas. We were directed to fire these into civilian population centers, particularly schools and hospitals.' That's the allegation. The truth is that there never was any poison gas used and that we were specifically instructed to avoid damaging population centers at all costs. Period."

"I have no quarrel with that," Lu answered, and made a note. "Tell me, John, just for my own information, could you see schools and hospitals from the air? Traveling at hundreds of miles an hour at low levels, how could you be sure that you were hitting a factory and not a hospital?"

"It was never a problem. Schools don't have smokestacks, and the hospitals were plastered with red crosses on their roofs. Most of the time they were easy to spot. Also, our reconnaissance guys would pinpoint them and every pilot going in any given area was responsible to memorize their locations."

"You mean the locations of the hospitals and the schools."

Agitated, Bracken said, "Of course—that's what I just said— the hospitals and the schools."

Skipping down the page with his pen, Lu hesitated at midpage.

"Allegation number three. 'It was common practice with pilots in my squadron, provided that they still had ammunition remaining after their primary target was hit, to fire at civilian hamlets, buses, and field-workers.' What's your appraisal of that allegation?"

Bracken couldn't remember the allegation exactly, so he paraphrased it in his own words. "Coming back from a mission, if we had any ordinance left, we'd fire into villages, at buses, and at civilians working in the fields. The truth is that it might have happened, but it was never sanctioned by official policy. I heard of South Vietnamese pilots doing that but not our guys."

Laying down the sheaf of papers, Lu tiredly massaged his forehead. "I'm tired of this, Bracken, but we have to go through the entire list." He unbuttoned the top of his jacket, scratching at his neck. "I'm thirsty. Some more coffee, perhaps a cold beer? I think that my kitchen woman has some San Miguel."

Bracken's throat was dry, and he closed his eyes for just a moment, imagining that somewhere on this planet there was still cold beer. "A brew for me," he answered, trying to keep his voice neutral.

They worked together for another couple of hours. The woman came in with more beers, sardines on crackers, and a tray of GI canned cheese.

Allegations of indiscriminate bombing, "fragging" of officers by disgruntled enlisted men, rampant use of hard drugs. Bracken went through each allegation and told Lu what he thought about it. Most of it Bracken denied knowledge of. The important thing, Bracken felt, was to convince Lu that the charges, for the most part, were vastly overstated and therefore weren't believable. Lu seemed grudgingly convinced and Bracken's hope was that, in the future, other downed airmen wouldn't be tortured to extract a confession which, in any case, bordered on the ridiculous.

Stretching, then standing up, Lu smiled. "I think that should do it. What you've said makes sense. The war is near its end and, as you say, forced confessions are usually crude, transparent propaganda."

Lu extended his hand once more. Bracken stood up, feeling the beer. He took Lu's hand and shook it briefly. Home free, he thought.

Casually, Lu turned and looked at the clock, and so did Bracken. Only twelve-fifteen, although he was sure that more than three hours had passed. The second hand was stopped but not in the same place.

"You would probably like to see Williams now, I imagine. I've signed his release papers. He's free to leave with you."

Williams was strapped down on the operating table in the dispensary, tubes from an oxygen cylinder leading to his nose, a tube from an IV needled into his left arm, and drain hoses from his bandaged leg snaked into a basin on the floor beneath the table. The room stank of death.

"What took you so long?" Williams said in a muffled voice, his puffy eyes barely open.

"You look like a plumber's nightmare, Willie. But we're going to Hanoi, together."

"That's not the way I read it." Williams cranked his head around to look up into Bracken's eyes. "You think I'd make it over thirty klicks lying in the bed of a truck? Think again. I wouldn't last to the parking lot outside. Goat-beard says the leg comes off this afternoon, but the blood poisoning has already spread too far. He doesn't have any antibiotics. Even if I pull through the operation, he says I've got less than three days before I croak. The other good news is that he doesn't have any anaesthetic to spare beyond what he keeps for his own people."

"He uses acupuncture. It works."

"Like it worked on me, Bracken. He lanced my leg this morning and I nearly blew the windows out screaming."

Bracken placed his hand on Willie's face. It was like touching a glowing wood stove. "I'm staying. I've got a compatible blood type."

"Pack it in, John," Williams said wearily. "Don't blame yourself. Just get out of here while you can."

"I'm staying, Willie."

Williams reached up with his right hand and gripped Bracken's arm. "Listen to me, buddy, and listen good. Goat-beard went to get tea. He'll be back soon and that's all the time we've got together. I want you to do what I tell you and no arguments. You copy that?"

The sun must have been covered by cloud because the room darkened, the shadows blurring.

"Whatever, Willie."

Dropping his head back against the soiled pillow, Williams's eyes went unfocused, his voice tired. "My old man taught me to make lists if I wanted to get anything done. 'Lose your list and you're lost,' he always said. So I got a list, but there's only three things on it, John. Number one on my wish list: plant a headstone for me in some nice, quiet place that looks out over a valley. I don't care where, as long as it's real nice."

There was no room for argument. Dumbly, Bracken nodded.

Sweat speckled Williams's forehead. "Second thing. Lu had me sign something. I don't know what the hell it was, and if you get out of 'Nam, I want you to tell Jill that I never signed anything of my own will. I don't give a rat's ass what the government thinks. But I want my girl to know."

Bracken started to say something, but Williams cut him off.

"Last thing on my list." He turned his eyes toward the shelving. "My degree in chemistry finally paid off. Second plank up. Dark brown bottle with the green label. Bring it here."

The writing was in French, the liquid contents almost gone. There was a stylized red flame on the label, warning that it was highly flammable. Bracken touched the glass bottle, wanting confirmation, not sure.

"This . . . ?" He turned back to Williams. Williams had jerked the oxygen tube from his nostrils.

"Hey!" Bracken moved to the bed, picking up the tube, but Williams pushed his hand away.

His eyes were closed, his breath now coming in short gasps. "Let me do it my way . . . just this once . . . bring the fucking bottle. Gauze pads on the metal tray. Two of them."

The cloud had passed and diffused sunlight lit the room.

Willie drew him down so that Bracken was just inches from his face. Willie's breath was sweet yet sour. "I've had one helluva run, John. And you were a friend—the best. But now it's time to call it a day." He clasped his hands together over his chest. His lips moved soundlessly for a few moments. He finally opened his eyes. "Just a few drops at first so I don't gag. Then the rest of the bottle."

Bracken's eyes were flooded, his whole body shaking. From the hallway he heard footsteps approaching.

"Sleep well, Willie," Bracken said almost to himself, and put the gauze over his friend's mouth, then started to drip tears of chloroform and his own onto the fabric.

Lu, watching from behind the one-way mirror, found that he had a constriction in his throat. He lit a cigarette, noticing that his hand, which held the lighter, shook slightly.

They are a stupid, arrogant race, he thought. But brave.

4.

March 2, 1972

Fog, scud, and rain tramped in alternating ranks of gray across the Bay, driven before a raw Pacific wind. The horn on Alcatraz Island lowed softly, its muffled moan reverberating against the window of the restaurant, producing its own sympathetic vibration. Alone, with a drink in his hand and a crumpled cigarette smoldering in the ashtray on his table, Bracken watched as gulls wheeled in tight circles over the trawlers that surged against the pier of Fisherman's Wharf, their bright eyes cocked for the scraps of trash fish that were thrown overboard.

Not sure of the time that it would take to reach the restaurant, Bracken had left the hotel far too early and taken the cable car, then walked the rest of the distance from the terminal on Hyde Street to where the restaurant was perched above a complex of trendy tourist traps bordering the waterfront.

He was not looking forward to meeting Gillian Williams, but it was something that he could no longer avoid.

It was early March and Bracken was practically the only tourist on the wharf. He'd been an hour early and had spent most of that wandering through the shops, smelling sandalwood incense, citrus-scented soaps, and herbal teas. The scents would be exotic to those who had never walked the streets of Saigon, but now the cloying-sweet stench turned his stomach. He temporarily sought refuge in a pottery shop that seemed to be big on saving the whales. Until he turned over a mug with a laughing whale who implored the purchaser to "Save Me" and discovered that the mug had been made in Japan, where they killed whales like they made cars—very efficiently, in great numbers, and with collective corporate pride. The slack-faced, pimpled brunette behind the cash register never looked up from reading a romance novel as he collided with dangling ceramic wind chimes that guarded the door.

With only half an hour to kill, he had finally retreated to the restaurant, its only customer, and settled into a booth overlooking the Bay. By four-fifty he had finished his third Bloody Mary.

Now he vainly tried to signal a waitress who was rubbing herself against the mellow mahogany rim of the bar, chatting with a bartender who looked as if he would be more comfortable with someone of his own sex. Bracken finally caught her eye. She scowled, nodded distractedly to him, then turned back to the bartender and resumed her monologue.

Gillian arrived before his drink did.

Not what he had expected. Willie had called her a "kid." Bracken had added the numbers and calculated that she was now fifteen, maybe sixteen. But there was a subtle maturity in her face and a braless swelling beneath her shirt. Her hair was uncombed and hung down in tangled blond ropes, her face free of cosmetics and yet too pale, too plump. Her glasses were little squares in an antique silver frame. She strode to his table in a pumping gait and dropped into the chair opposite him, the smell of dampness, sweat, and the sea wind upon her.

There was no smile, no nervousness, none of the things that teens normally do in the presence of an adult stranger. She pulled out a cigarette and lit it with a complicated brass thing. Aware of but ignoring the phony standards of an adult with a cigarette still smoldering in an ashtray, he tried to form a parental frown of disapproval, but she ignored it.

"You were my father's pilot," she said.

He extended his hand. "Yes," he answered, giving a weak facsimile of a smile.

She ignored his hand, tapped her ashless cigarette agitatedly against the ledge of the window, and turned in profile to watch the Bay.

She could be pretty, he thought, except for the harshness that already lined her eyes. High cheekbones, clear skin, the mouth a bit lopsided but humorless. She raised the cigarette and puffed on it dramatically, then turned back to him.

"Why are you here, Captain Bracken?" She strung the words out, as if they were alien things on her tongue.

He mustered the second attempt at a smile. "Because of your father. He wanted me to meet you. Willie thought a lot of you," Bracken added, lying, because he had never talked to Willie about life beyond the horizons of Southeast Asia. That subject was closed to the men who flew combat and knew the attrition rates.

"And did you score a big pile of medals?"

It wasn't going well. "A couple," he offered, not knowing what the response was supposed to be.

His drink arrived, flagged by a heavy stick of limp celery, the surface of the drink sprinkled with a dusty substance which looked like fly droppings. The blond waitress flipped two stained menus in front of them and returned to rub her body against the bar, her laughter irritating in the otherwise silent chamber of the mahogany-paneled room.

Jill ignored the menu. "And what are your medals for, Captain Bracken?"

"The same thing that your dad got them for—staying alive one week to the next, collecting what the squadron commander handed out on Saturday morning roll call. Medals in Vietnam were GI issue—like quinine pills and aspirin."

"Then you must have a lot more than he did. You've obviously lived longer."

"I never counted them." He looked down at the menu, irritated, wanting to make the best of it, knowing that it was already a disaster.

He hesitantly reached across the table and took her cold hand in his, gently squeezing it. "I liked your father, Jill. I loved him even. I'm here because he was a fine man and a friend and he would have wanted me to talk to you."

Her hand was unresponsive in his, her eyes averted, watching raindrops splattering in volleys against the windowpane, distorting the Bay into a blurred landscape of mottled gray. There were no tears yet. "I loved him, too, but I cried my last months ago. I could have forgiven him for the first tour because they made him do it, but then he volunteered for a second—something he didn't have to do."

"That wasn't the way Willie did things," Bracken said. She had given him a chance to rebuild the bridge. He put the first plank in place. "Your father was damned brave. He'd been through one combat tour, and those who survived as many missions as he did learned the trade and made others safer by their knowledge." It sounded like a quote from a Command and Staff school manual, except that it was true. "He was the best."

Suddenly, she yanked her hand away. "That's how you see it, isn't it? You and all the bastards like you." Her voice was loud, ringing hard against the walls of the empty room. The waitress and bartender turned and stared.

"How many little kids did you and my father incinerate?" she spat at him, her face contorted in fury. "How many women will bear monsters because of the gas you spread? Is that what you got your medals for?"

She slashed her face around toward the Bay, her hair flying in a cape of damp blond strands, tears streaming down her cheeks.

A gull, perhaps in dumb sympathy, hovered in an updraft of the complex, only feet beyond the glass, eyes cocked, watching her, then wheeled and flew away toward the sea.

She slowly lowered her face into the crook of her arm, savagely but slowly twisting it, her chest heaving.

Bracken knew that nothing he could say would help.

She went to the women's room while he paid the bill, cursing himself for automatically overtipping. The waitress reciprocated by mechanically reciting in a bored voice that he should have a fabulous day. What utter bullshit. He hadn't had a nice day in the past three years and didn't expect any in the near future.

Silence between them, they walked through the complex toward the street, little dazzles of falling rain catching amber glitters from the plaza arc lights. He took her arm, guiding her under the overhanging awnings of a shop filled with stuffed toys. He handed her the manila envelope.

"I don't want you to look at this now, Jill. Not for a week, not even for a month."

"What is it?" she asked weakly, wearily.

"Some photos that I took of your dad in 'Nam. A diary that he kept. A couple of cartoons that he drew." He paused, trying to put it together. "Jill, he died bravely. It was just bad luck."

"You got that wrong, asshole," she snapped back, her eyes fierce. "It was JFK and LBJ and Nixon and all the turds like you that worked for them—all you cocksuckers were just dying to play with your G.I. Joe war toys."

She twisted away from his hold and headed west toward Leavenworth Street.

Bracken started to follow her, rain already soaking his cheap trench coat. As he passed a VW van, the door swung open and a woman stepped out, blocking his path.

She was thick, in her forties, obviously braless, shrouded in a flowered muumuu that immediately started to darken under the splattering rain. Bracken abstractly thought that the women's undergarment industry must be going through a rough time.

Her glasses were a huge plastic-framed infinity symbol, almost covering her sagging cheeks. She planted herself squarely in front of Bracken, her mouth set in a tight line.

. "You've done your thing, Bracken. Fuck off."

He started to brush past her, and she swung at him with her fist, grazing his cheek. "I told you to leave her alone," the woman shouted, flailing her fists. For emphasis, she heaved the avalanche of her body into his, catching him off stride.

He did a Bojangles backstep under the impact, then stood there, embarrassed, unnerved, unsure how to respond.

A look of smug triumph spread over her face, her glasses skewed over her nose by the violence of her attack. "All you war hero, jockstrap types are the same. No balls."

Jill was half a block away. She looked back once, her face a flash of white in the dusk, then kept walking, legs and lack of understanding stretching out the distance between them.

It would be impossible to catch her. He turned back to the woman. "Who the hell are you?" he demanded, already knowing.

"Willie's sister-in-law. We've had enough grief from your dirty little war. Get the hell out of here before I flatten you." She rocked forward on her feet, balling her fists, cheeks bulging out in anger.

The rain was coming down in hard pellets, part sleet. The cable car terminal was three blocks away and he was already soaked and felt very old.

"I won't bother her," he said. "I came to meet her because Willie would have wanted me to. That's all."

She pushed her glasses back onto the bridge of her nose, wrinkled her nose as if she had smelled something bad, and then slid her bulk back into the VW.

He stood in the gloom of late afternoon, watching the VW lurch down the street, stop to pick up Jill, and merge into the growing traffic.

So much for coming to the aid of a damsel in distress. Bracken admitted to himself that white knights in flimsy armor sometimes lost to the dragon.

"You understand that was a preliminary hearing and will not necessarily result in a trial by court-martial," the colonel said. His thick eyeglasses reflected multiple bars of light from the overhead fluorescents. He was in his late fifties, a little thick around the waist, and wore no combat ribbons. His uniform was artfully tailored to conceal the spare tire overlying his gut.

"I understand, sir," Bracken answered, worming deeper into the chair, overly conscious of his ill-fitting uniform that had been bought off the rack in the Kam Ran Bay BX just hours before he was flown home.

The room was a classroom of sorts: the walls a standard puke green, the floors tiled in linoleum, buffed and waxed by generations of fatigue-duty airmen until the cracks between the tiles had ceased to exist, now forever bound together with a tacky paste of aging floor wax and dirt. There were two blackboards, a couple of fire extinguishers, a bulletin board, and five worktables, one of them now placed at the head of the room.

Facing Bracken and behind the table were six officers. Bracken read their histories by the ribbons that they wore, by the look in their eyes, by the way they whispered and passed notes to one another, and he was not encouraged.

The other colonel flanking the senior officer had four stacks of ribbons from World War II but none from Korea or 'Nam. Enclosing the two bird colonels like parentheses were two lieutenant colonels, both overweight administrative types. Neither was rated nor had been in combat theaters. Bracketing the lieutenant colonels on either end like flimsy bookends tilting away from the mass between them was a major with Korean ribbons—one of them an Air Medal which Bracken had first taken as a good omen—and the other, a first lieutenant who seemed to be present for the sole purpose of supplying coffee to the other five senior officers. After four days of testimony, Bracken no longer had any illusions about the outcome.

Beyond the partially closed venetian blinds, a hard California sun threw thin blades of yellow across the floor. Bracken wished there were a clock ticking to stifle the silence.

The senior colonel finally spoke in a reedy voice, inhaling in little gusts between phrases. "Captain Bracken, do you have any further questions or formal statement to make to this board of inquiry?"

"No sir."

"Any further comments?"

Bracken got to his feet. He felt damp stains on his uniform, and he could smell his own sweat. Not good sweat, as in hard work, but fear sweat, anger sweat.

"I was tricked by Lu. I never knew there was a film being shot through a one-way mirror. They edited that film to cut the parts that would give it away as a propaganda stunt."

One of the lieutenant colonels lifted his hand and the senior officer nodded to him. The lieutenant colonel glared down at Bracken. "The clock on the wall pretty well shows that the filming was continuous, yet you claim that there was editing between some of the scenes. How do you explain that, Captain Bracken?" He leaned forward, pushing out his head on the thick stalk of his neck like a reptile tasting the air for a prey's scent.

Bracken shifted his feet. "They had to run the clock backward between the scenes to pick up continuity. I call your attention to the sunlight on Lu's desk. From one scene to the next, the sunlight patterns suddenly shift. Any idiot can spot it."

The lieutenant colonel flushed, his voice coming up an octave. "Several million people worldwide who saw that film didn't notice, Captain Bracken. And I must ask you again for the record, it *is* you talking, it *is* you in the film, correct?"

The film that Lu had shot had been released by a French crew who claimed that they had filmed it with Bracken's full consent. It had first been shown on EuroVision TV but copies had been picked up by the major American networks. For a week Bracken's name had been a household word—but not the kind spoken in front of minors. There had been the predictable spate of death threats, hate mail, and condemnations from the Veterans of Foreign Wars. But the thing that had frosted Bracken were two cables of congratulations: one from a rock star who was making megabucks by singing antiwar songs while on a permanent draft deferment, and the other from a southern born-again congressman, praising him as a "witness for peace."

Bracken finally nodded.

"I didn't hear you," the lieutenant colonel prompted, his face still flushed.

"Yes, sir, that was me in the film."

The combat major raised his hand. The senior bird colonel sighed a little and nodded to him.

"I have to agree with Captain Bracken. The whole film is jerky. As he says, the sunlight shifts a great deal between cuts."

"You're obviously a technical expert in film editing," the colonel said.

The major stiffened slightly. "Well . . . no, sir, of course not. It's just obvious that—"

"*Nothing*, Major, is obvious. Millions in Europe and this country saw that film. If it was so damn obvious, why didn't they notice it? Have you read anything in the papers, seen some commentator on the tube, anything that would indicate otherwise?"

"Sir—" He must have hesitated because, as a career officer, he surely could predict the ratings on his next officer's effectiveness report if he continued to press the point. He looked down at Bracken, an impersonal apology in his eyes, as if he had just witnessed a mugging but didn't want to get involved, then answered, "No, *sir*. I haven't seen any comment on the editing. I have no further questions."

Bracken was getting ready to deliver a barrage on how these fat sons of bitches had never been in combat, let alone been starved and tortured. That the will to resist was a perishable commodity, that the Code of Conduct for captured Americans was as outdated as a scrap of paper called the Geneva Convention.

"And I don't think any of us have any further questions either," the senior colonel said. He looked around, challenging the other board members. "Do we?"

"Sir!" Bracken snapped. "I have—"

The colonel rose, ignoring him. "This inquiry is closed. All of you gentlemen are dismissed. Bracken—you'll remain here with me."

Bracken watched them file out, hoping at least the combat major would look at him, but the major seemed to be overly preoccupied with studying the neck of the man in front of him. The door closed behind them.

"You have two choices, you whining little prick," the colonel spat at him, his face only inches away. "You're entitled to a court-martial, or you can resign. I would personally welcome a court-martial because then we'd have a chance to really nail you to the cross. Nice phrases like, 'aiding and abetting,' 'collaboration,' and 'traitorous behavior.' But division headquarters thinks it would better if you just disappeared. Resign, Bracken. The last thing this country needs is a traitor's trial. The left-wingers would try to make a saint out of you and the right-wingers would try to crucify you. Given my druthers, Bracken, I'd just as soon see you strung up by the balls and then shot."

The low-frequency roar of a jet in afterburner on the takeoff roll rumbled, the reverberation of its sound rattling the windows.

For Bracken, it was hard to believe that it was all finished. "Sir, permission to speak."

The colonel gritted his jaws, the muscles jumping in his neck, a vein dangerously pulsing on his temple. "Speaking's over with, Bracken. I've heard your version. Four days of wasted time spent on this board of inquiry. I've got a war to fight, and so do the other loyal officers on this board. You've had your chance. Many of the fine men that were prisoners never gave in. What made you so special that you had to squeal a pack of lies about your country to the NVA?"

"Sir—Captain Williams . . ."

"That's so much horse shit, Bracken," the colonel shot back. "Williams was made of a lot tougher stuff than you. Volunteered for his second tour. Like all of us, he took his chances."

"Up yours, Colonel," Bracken shouted, "and up all the other rear-echelon motherfuckers like you. You bastards have never been closer to combat than the latest intelligence summary. You aren't fit to write the rules if you haven't played the game."

The colonel stepped back, his eyes deadly, his face flushed to the color of raw meat. Seconds ticked away, the colonel breathing hard. Slowly regaining composure, he finally spoke in a hoarse whisper, his face inches from Bracken's.

"Oh, how I'd like to get my hooks into you, Bracken. I'd give you my personal guarantee of twenty years at hard labor, but I'm going to ignore what you've said for the good of the service. Your resignation is on my secretary's desk. I want it signed in two minutes, *mister*."

He wheeled away, slamming the door violently behind him.

Bracken's resignation was approved and processed within forty-eight hours, a standard of bureaucratic efficiency he had never before experienced in the service. Whether he was in the process of clearing personnel, records, or finance, he was summarily moved to the head of the line with no grumbles from the others who waited. He realized that the word had gotten around. Faster than the speed of light.

Rubber stamps slammed on ink pads, check lists ticked off, entries made, all by people who were silent and would not look at him. Bracken gave up trying to make chitchat and endured the agony.

In the evenings that he spent at the Officer's Club, the

process was the opposite. A drink ordered from a table never came until he moved to the bar, and even then, reluctantly serviced, usually the wrong order. Tips were pushed back across the bar at him. Other officers made too much space for him, overly casual as they turned their backs. Bracken had never known rejection, and he felt it more keenly than had they confronted him in anger.

After finishing the second day of processing, Bracken had only to pick up his papers and mustering-out pay on the following morning. He hung out in the bachelor officer's quarters until eight P.M., wanting to avoid the pre-dinner drinkers, then wandered over in civilian clothes, taking a seat in the dining room on the far side from the bar.

It was Friday-night happy hour. A few heavy drinkers clustered around the bar, but even they were beginning to drift off. For those who remained, glasses clinked and men laughed in earnest, self-confident ways, their hands steady, their smiles open, the best of a warrior race. A small dance band was unpacking their instruments, setting levels on the sound system, blowing riffs and arpeggios, just goofing around before they started the set.

He had been in O-clubs like this thousands of times. Corny, but it was a family, a band of brothers who didn't sell soap or hawk their souls to market swampland building lots. As dumb as it sounded—and one never, never talked to civilians about this—flying was a dangerous occupation. Out of Bracken's preliminary flight class of 42, only 29 were still kicking. Average life expectancy of a fighter jock in peacetime: about 53 and damn well less in wartime. Shared mutual danger and self-assurance was the glue that stuck them together, and Bracken was slowly beginning to realize that he had become unstuck.

He ordered a second double Gibson, a steak rare, salad, and baked potato, then leaned back, trying to shut out thoughts, yet knowing that he would wake three or four times through the night as he had on past nights, listening to the creak of his mattress, the ticking of his alarm clock, and the distant sound of aircraft, halfway to the moon, screaming through the night.

McCarthy, the Korean-combat major from the board of inquiry, was standing over him before he realized it. He started to stand but McCarthy shook his head.

"Don't get up, Bracken. You mind some company for a few minutes?" Without waiting for a reply, the major scraped back a chair and eased himself into it. He flagged the waitress with his fingers held up, wiggling them like rabbit ears, and without any verbal order being passed, an amber drink was set before him within a minute.

He lifted it, saluting Bracken. "Here's to my namesake and his legacy."

Puzzled, Bracken slowly lowered his glass. "What's that supposed to mean?"

McCarthy swallowed heavily, set his glass down, and wiped his lips with the back of a hairy hand. "Senator Joe McCarthy—you remember the witch hunts of the fifties? That's what you went through, Bracken, whether you realize it or not. You're one of the tainted lambs that are sacrificed on the military's altar of self-purification." He took another sip from his moisture-beaded glass. "Nothing personal, understand? Just that you were at the wrong place at the wrong time, mouthing the wrong words."

"Is that what you think? That I turned on my country?"

McCarthy shrugged. "Does it *really* matter, Bracken? Because whatever you and I think isn't worth dog shit. You got screwed by the fickle finger of fate. If I'd been in your shoes, I'd have probably been suckered into the same trap and then you'd be sitting in my chair right now, embarrassed to be at the same table but knowing that there, but for the grace of God, go I."

"You made that damn plain at the inquiry, didn't you? Really said what you believed," Bracken shot back. He lit a cigarette, took two quick puffs, then snubbed it out.

"Nope, I didn't," McCarthy answered softly. "But God knows I wanted to. I tried to support you, but they weren't buying it. We both know that every time I opened my fat mouth, Colonel Ding Dong shoved his shoe in it. I've got a wife, two kids, plus one in the oven. And I've got a career that I want to hang on to. I'm not one of the fair-haired boys destined for the stars, but I'll make it through twenty years of service and then have a paycheck for the rest of my life. It's a matter of priorities, friend."

The waitress brought another drink for McCarthy, along with Bracken's steak. Ordered rare, Bracken could see that the steak had been overdone, the surface charred to a gritty crisp. The baked potato was shriveled, and the lettuce was wilted with no dressing on it. He shoved the dinner aside.

Tentatively moving his moisture-hazed glass along his cheek, McCarthy carefully asked, "Something that I've been wondering. What about Williams?"

"What about him?"

"You told the board that Williams never gave the NVA anything."

"That's the way it happened: you know from the records that the NVA never released any confession signed by Williams." Bracken had never been able to understand why they hadn't, but since Willie's confession hadn't been released, Willie's reputation was spotless as a nun's knickers and Bracken wanted to keep it that way.

"And that's why I think you told the NVA more than you admitted. I saw your file. Crypto clearance, training in the Black Hangar, other stuff that they'd love to get their hands on. But Williams was vulnerable—wounded, needed medical attention. He'd have told them anything to save his ass, but maybe he didn't have anything significant to give them. So it fits that they'd turn to you for classified information for the tradeoff that you could get Williams a better deal."

"I didn't tell them anything else," Bracken said adamantly. Shit—McCarthy had seen through him like a pane of window glass.

McCarthy shook his head. His eyes were a little dull and his movements now betrayed how much he had had to drink. "If I had been you, I would have given them the combination to the White House safe to save my buddy's life. You did, didn't you?"

Bracken tensed, reflexes taking over, bunching his fist, but McCarthy saw what was coming and lifted his fingers in the V of a peace symbol.

"Back off, buddy. Just an off-the-record opinion, so forget it. Anyway, I understand why. He was going to die and you knew deep down in your bones that you were going to live. The guilt and all that psychological crap. Any one of us, me included, would have done the same." He drained off the rest of his drink and set the glass down overcarefully on the tablecloth. "You know, Bracken, when it came to the vote, I cast my ballot to toss you out of the service."

"You self-righteous prick!" Bracken had said it loudly, and people turned to watch them, the room hushed.

"For one simple reason. If you had stayed on in the service, you'd be waiting every day for that letter in the mail with a tape of your voice, spouting off classified stuff to some NVA interrogator. They'd have you by the short and curlies—and they always will. To me, that spells security risk."

Bracken hadn't thought of that before. Not that the stuff on nuclear weapons was unknown to the Soviets, because they paralleled American research and development . . . but they could use it against him as blackmail if he stayed in. Of such stuff traitors are made. Reluctantly, Bracken realized that he would have voted the same way as McCarthy. There was an expression for such cases: Dismissed for the good of the service.

He leaned back in the chair, the fight gone out of him.

"So what do you do now, Bracken?"

"Outside of fishing on the coast of Maine with my old man, I don't know much except flying. The airlines probably. They're hiring."

Leaning over the table, McCarthy moved his now empty glass in small circles, spreading the condensed moisture over the cloth. He shook his head. "Don't even bother trying."

"Why?"

"It's an old-boy network. The word goes out. Yours was the fourth board of inquiry for ex-POWs that I've sat in on in the last fifteen months. I finally understand the ground rules as to how they handle a case like yours. They're not interested in logic, truth, or sweet reason. This country's losing a war, and they want either scapegoats or silence. So, in a case like yours, they sweep it under the rug by allowing you to resign. You signed a release stating that you wouldn't spill the beans to the press, Roger that?"

Bracken nodded.

"So nothing surfaces. No grumbling in the ranks, all proud soldiers we. But they put the word out and it filters down through the aviation grapevine. You'll just break your ass and get nowhere trying."

"Nice to know."

"Not nice to know, but that's the way it's set up. And forget about a government job at any level. Forget about anything that requires a security clearance. Forget about defense contractors or vendors. Save yourself some grief and go fishing. It's supposed to be a great life."

McCarthy pushed his chair away from the table and slowly stood up, a little wobbly. He extended a hand. "I'm truly sorry, Bracken. But I did what I had to."

The two of them clasped hands briefly. Couples at other tables were still looking, as were some of the officers draped over the bar. The room was silent except for the hush of air-conditioning and a lonely scale on the clarinet.

McCarthy dipped into the pocket of his Class A uniform and extracted a crumpled business card. "I have a brother in Kansas. He sells shoes. On my say-so, he'd hire you."

Bracken took the card, not looking at the printing. "I doubt that I'd be any good at hustling your brother's leather, but thanks for the offer." It didn't come out right, not the way he had meant it.

McCarthy flashed a hostile grimace. "I read you loud and clear, Bracken. Cutting bait will probably offer more possibilities of advancement for a man possessing your level of intelligence." He turned and trundled across the floor on rubbery legs through the maze of tables, colliding with some of them.

Bracken celebrated the start of his new life as a civilian with two more Gibsons, wrapped the steak in a napkin, and ate it on the way back to his quarters under a clear, starry California night.

The following morning, Bracken picked up his discharge papers, settled his bills, and called a cab. He checked out of the BOQ in civilian clothes, carrying two B-4 bags. A crate with a few possessions would follow, once he had a forwarding address. Bracken wondered abstractedly how long that would be.

Leaving Vandenberg Air Force Base, the cabbie asked him for the third time, "Where to, bud?" Good question.

"Downtown. I'll tell you where to stop." He got a shrug and a flick of the meter flag for a reply.

The barren hills of southern California flowed past his window. It was slightly overcast with pockets of fog lying in the valleys. Occasionally, he could catch a glimpse of the sea beyond. He tried to organize his thinking, but nothing concrete came up, just undefined ideas. What he needed most, he realized, was a place to hole up and time to think.

At least he wouldn't starve for a while. Never married, he had salted away a lot of his salary from 'Nam. Big plus: he had a small inheritance from an aunt he had never met. All told, he figured that he had a bit over $33,000.

He settled back against the vinyl seat of the cab, watching the meter tick off the dollars. It wasn't the end of the world, he kept telling himself, except that it was. Flying was an opiate, and he was hooked, already felt withdrawal symptoms. He knew that he would have to buy some wheels and had thought of something practical, maybe a van. In Lompoc he saw a Ford dealership and told the cabbie to pull over.

Two hours later and thirteen hundred and fifty dollars poorer, he headed east into the Mojave Desert in a candy-apple-red 1968 Ford pickup with painted yellow flames licking its sides. Airbrushed on the driver's door in gold and green lettering was its name: The Thing. Not exactly the low profile that he had wanted, but when he had seen the care that had gone into rebuilding the engine, then checked the compression and listened to the transmission, he knew that The Thing would last a lot longer than Detroit had ever intended.

He drove through the day and night across the Great Salt Desert, stopping just before dawn west of Provo, Utah. He slept restlessly for four hours in the bed of the truck under a canvas tarp, then pushed on. He arrived in Blackhawk, Colorado, just as the sun was going down.

Blackhawk had been a silver mining boom town less than a hundred years earlier, then had busted flat when the ore ran out. It had never recovered, except for an expanding crop of summertime day-trippers who wanted to see what the Wild West Was Really Like. What they found were bartenders in bowler hats, waitresses in can-can skirts, storefronts full of sandalwood soap shaped like six-shooters, and fudge candies molded into sheriff's badges.

He had been up to the town a couple of times when he had been stationed at Lowry Air Force Base in Denver, mainly in the winter. It was off the après-ski circuit, had no lifts, no condos, no dogsled rides, no boutiques, and only two bars. Perhaps best of all, at least in the winter, it had an advertised population of sixteen.

He slung his bags onto the porch of the Mine Shaft Hotel and checked in.

The couple who ran the place didn't ask much more than how long he wanted to stay and what he liked for breakfast. Bracken had learned that people who lived in remote places rarely pried, and this couple was blessedly no different. His room was tiny, sparsely furnished, and immaculate. In the evening, the owner lit a fire in the potbellied stove which glowed a dull cherry-red and roared a song of its own. The bed had a down comforter, the sheets were real cotton, and the bathroom was twenty-three ice-cold steps down the hallway.

He spent the first week hiking over mine tailings, poking

around abandoned shafts, tracing streams up through the melting snows to the higher isolated valleys. For three days he panned for gold with a bent pie tin and came up with a couple of traces.

In bare patches where the snow had melted, there were spring flowers probing up between blades of grass, yet in the aspen glades, deep drifts still lay in purple shadows, fragmented sunlight glancing off crystalline corn snow. He saw the tracks of otter and beaver, deer and lynx.

And all the time he thought. Had he remembered his imprisonment as it really was or as he now wanted to believe it had been? Had he betrayed himself, Williams, and his country? Why had Lu gone to the elaborate trouble of taping the "confession," yet never revealing that Bracken had previously blabbed highly classified data on a nuclear weapon? There were no easy answers, and in the end he gave up the process of self-flagellation because although he felt no guilt, there was still remorse for Willie's death, and he had to purge himself of it.

On the tenth day he borrowed an old Underwood typewriter from the owners of the hotel and wrote for two days, exactly as he had remembered it. There was no reason that he could think of for doing it except as a mental emetic. In the evenings he went to the Glory Hole Bar and nursed two Gibsons through three hours, chatting with the owner, swapping stories from the Maine coast for stories of the high Rockies. He met an old geezer whom the locals called Billy-the-Goat, a recluse who lived in the hills, running a little placer mine whose location he was defiantly determined to keep secret but couldn't possibly after the second drink.

Bracken felt life slowly returning to him. He was beginning to get itchy, wanting to move. On the last night he took the pile of over thirty pages of his typed work and burned them in the potbelly, listening to the fire roar, the rafters creak, and the wind moan, all in harmony. He no longer saw Willie's face in his dreams and slept solidly for the first time in months.

On the following morning, in brilliant sunshine and melting snows with the creeks flooding, he headed The Thing east, 289 cubic inches howling a V-8 symphony under the hood.

Bracken detoured south to St. Louis, to the Air Force Records Center. His own record's jacket hadn't caught up with him yet, and a plump woman sergeant gave him what passed for courteous treatment. Yes, Captain Eugene Williams had designated his daughter Gillian as beneficiary and, yes, they had her address in San Francisco, confirmed on a smudged copy on AF Form 2889.

He cleared out of St. Louis by noon, across the border into Illinois, heading east on Route 70. In a town called Pocahontas, where he detoured for what the billboard advertised as the "Most rib-stickin' meal you'll ever eat," he found a bank whose name he had confidence in—the Grain Farmer's First Trust. His father had always been big on banking with people who were close to the soil or the sea. The bank looked like something Butch Cassidy and the Sundance Kid would have turned up their noses at. There was a single teller's booth and a plain pine interior which smelled of O-Cedar. The teller was a sweet old lady who looked as if she would have been more comfortable working under gas lights than fluorescent.

He set up a trust account in the name of Major Eugene Williams and funded it with $2,000 of his own, then did the paperwork that would allow the air force death benefits to be deposited directly. He had to pay another $150 to a local lawyer who smelled of talc and wore creaking shoes to draft a document that made provision for an automatic payout to Gillian Williams in the sum of $180 per month. That rate of disbursement would keep the account solvent for nearly a year, and by that time Bracken recklessly believed that the Veterans Administration would get around to sending regular checks.

Heading east out of Pocahontas with a pigeon feather he had picked up off the street stuck in his hair, he whooped a war cry and felt like a thirteen-year-old kid just out on summer vacation with a whole glorious summer ahead of him. Buried in the back of his mind, he realized that his attitude was unrealistic. He had limited funds and limited talents, but then again, unlimited freedom.

He howled across the Midwest with the speedometer quivering in the high eighties, collecting a speeding ticket and ingeniously talking himself out of another two. But once he got to the Alleghenies, he started to slow down and meander. Bracken spent four days in Latrobe, Pennsylvania, with an old flying buddy and got soggy from drinking too much beer. Then north to Lake Erie and along the shore into New York State, eating out of Burger Kings and sleeping in the back of the pickup. He crossed Lake Champlain by ferry into Vermont and drove through the Green Mountains, taking the back roads, admiring cows, and eating meals of Twinkies and Cokes from roadside country stores.

At Wells River he crossed the bridge into New Hampshire and stopped in a Gulf station to figure out the easiest route to Maine.

The gas pump attendant allowed as how he didn't know how you got "theah from heah." The boss shrugged and said that everything east of the town was hostile Indian territory.

About to leave, Bracken noticed a Porsche 911 up on one of the racks, black oil dribbling from the transmission. Beneath the Porsche, a woman in a white ski parka, oblivious to the dirty ice melting onto her jacket, looked up at the bowels of the machine with disgust.

She turned to him. "This thing was made in the Black Forest on a Monday morning by hungover elves. It spends more time in the shop than your average mechanic. You know anything about Porsche transmissions?"

She had long auburn hair and gray-green eyes. A little on the skinny side but with nice bone structure.

Bracken shrugged. "It's all black magic to me."

"You were asking about getting to Maine. What part?"

"Boothbay Harbor."

She raised her sunglasses so that they rested on her hair. "North on three-oh-two, then east on two. When you hit the Maine border, get on twenty-eight until you hit the Interstate and then just follow the signs."

"You from Maine?" She was a little on the hard side, he thought—aggressive, open, and yet he liked her for it. Refreshing, after all the compliant air force wives he had known.

"Mum and Pops have a summer place up in Northeast Harbor."

"You headed there?"

She looked him over, appraising him for a second before answering. "Not that far. I live about fifty miles from here. If you've got room, I'd like to hitch a ride. It's on your way."

He put out his hand. "John Bracken."

She took his hand and shook it firmly. "Penny Antee. My pop's idea of a joke."

In the truck, bumping over spring frost heaves, they started to trade backgrounds. She had been an art major at Radcliffe, no marriages, age twenty-three, and "did pottery." She worked part-time for a friend of a friend who was trying to get a flight school going but she talked about going back to Radcliffe for her master's in the fall.

Other than telling her that he had resigned his commission and planned on trawling the banks off Maine, Bracken gave away nothing more.

The turnoff to Stone Mountain showed up on a highway marker. He offered to take her there, telling her that he couldn't resist small airfields, and that as a kid he had gotten hooked on grass fields and first flew a Piper J-3 at age thirteen. His real reason for the detour was Penny Antee.

The field wasn't much more than 2,600 feet of cracked asphalt, a sagging hangar, and a combination home/office. A sign on the lane read SCENIC FLIGHTS AND PILOT INSTRUCTION, D. HOOPER, CHIEF PILOT.

He carried her luggage to the door. A stiff northwester was blowing. The ground was still brown but the trees were tipped with buds. Across the valley he could see the crests of the mountains still frosted white. He had a good feeling about this place. Like it was home.

"Come on in and have some herbal tea," she offered. "Warm up your bones."

There was only one bone that he really wanted to warm up. He gave her a guileless and sunny smile of grateful acceptance.

The office was actually the kitchen with a counter tacked on. There was the obligatory bulletin board with a couple of fly-speckled FAA notices two years out of date, a small case that held charts for sale, and a printed notice: ONLY GOD GETS CREDIT. MORTALS PAY CASH, with the added notation, written with a felt-tip pen, OR VALID MASTERCARD.

A note on the table said that Don Hooper, chief pilot, was out on a business trip down to Boston and wouldn't be back until Friday.

She shrugged off her ski jacket. Underneath she was wearing a white polo shirt. Underneath that, obviously nothing. Bracken enjoyed. Things had definitely changed stateside, and not all to the worse.

"Looks like Don's down in Boston again, trying to talk the bank into another loan extension. I guess you won't have a chance to meet him." She put on a teakettle and fussed around with a spoon, doling out spoonfuls of ginseng tea. "How do you like it? Honey or cream?"

Bracken nodded abstractly. "Both. How does the flight school do?"

"It could be better."

"And the charter business?"

"The same. Don's problem is that he's shy. It comes off as if he doesn't like people. With someone else the business would probably take off." She smiled. "Sorry, bad pun."

He spent the next hour looking over the property. The hangar first. Inside was an aged Aztec twin, the blue and white paint faded and chalked, but the cabin was clean, the carpets brushed, and the windshield polished. Squeezed back in the corner of the hangar was a Cessna 150 single-engine trainer disguised by the same shabby appearance but, again, the engine and electrics well maintained. Bracken, without thinking about it, was adding up assets. Outside, he jogged up the runway and down the property lines, smelling the wind and snorting like a young colt with a world of green grass just beyond the fence.

Back in the house, Penny had tea made and some slices of wheat-germ bread toasted on a grill over one of the burners. She dished out no-sugar-added-all-natural-ingredients-so-help-me-God raspberry jam.

"I'm not prying, but what keeps you here?" Bracken already suspected.

"Don." She smiled without embarrassment. "He's a sweet guy. We met a year ago. Things seemed to go together. There isn't much office work to do other than answering the phone, and with all the spare time I've got, I can mess around in the garden or go hiking. I'm also studying ceramics and boning up for grad school. The profit potential for an arts and crafts center in this area is truly awesome."

Bracken drank his tea, which tasted as if it had been brewed from dried blades of Astroturf, all the time thinking hard. Finally blurted it out. "What does he want for the whole operation?"

She invited him to dinner and he went through the books while she washed up. It wasn't *that* bad. Tomorrow he would test-hop both aircraft and check through the spares inventory. *Bracken Airways.* It had a substantial ring to it.

He slept on the living room couch for the first two nights, then, after they had shared two bottles of California rot-gut red on the third evening, in her bed.

When Don Hooper came back, they settled the deal in one day. In return for twenty-two thousand and an assumption of the mortgage, Bracken started his own airline. Hooper even threw in his station wagon.

Penny left with Hooper, and Bracken suddenly realized how

much he missed her. But four days later, unannounced, she returned, offered him a check for seven thousand from the proceeds of the sale of her Porsche as her investment in the business, and asked for a job in the office. It was a deal he couldn't refuse.

They married under budding apple trees a month later to the strains of a string quartet. Bracken had opted for banjos but Penny had gently vetoed the idea. What the hell, he thought, content at last.

PART TWO
THE
PRESENT

5.

May 4

Lu awoke to a light tap on his hotel door. For a minute he simply lay in the lumpy bed, the duvet pulled up to his nose, tracing the cracks in the ceiling plaster, trying to match them with some vaguely remembered roadmap. France? The GDR? Iowa? Maybe Italy, for there was a hole in the center of the ceiling that had been poorly patched with cracks radiating outward from it and Lu had immediately thought of it as Rome. Didn't all roads lead there?

Edging his body out of bed, he padded to the door, listened, and opened it. On the corridor floor was a tray with a dented pot of tea and two lumps of sugar in a glass. He carried it back into his room.

For twenty minutes he sat in a chair, his feet propped up on the windowsill, sipping the lukewarm liquid and watching the rain pelt down on Red Square, the line in front of Lenin's tomb an endlessly renewing chain of plastic raincoats and umbrellas. In the corridor a maid impatiently rattled his doorknob.

Irritated, he shouted, *"K chortu."* It was doubtful that she would go straight to the devil, more likely to the tea samovar located in the linen closet next to the elevator shaft. He heard her give an exasperated grunt and shuffle down the corridor, dragging along her creaking cleanup trolley. It was typical; nothing, but nothing in the Soviet Union was ever lubricated, except with vodka, bribes, or lip service.

The other side of the bed was rumpled, the woman gone with the first tints of dawn, only the faint scent of her Swedish hand lotion still hanging in the air like the smell of decaying lilacs. Lu breathed a tired sigh. Out of sheer boredom and loneliness he had picked her up in the hard-currency bar of the National Hotel. She was a minor Latvian party functionary in Moscow for a trade meeting. Therefore politically safe. They had chatted about the failure of *perestroika*, the Islamic uprisings in the southern republics, and the recent Eastern bloc labor unrest, until a group of Finnish tourists sat down in the booth behind them within easy hearing distance. With that, the conversation had stalled and he had finally invited her to his room because both of them had accepted from the very beginning that this was the way the evening would end.

He set the teacup down on the rug and removed the framed photograph from his briefcase. His son stared back at him, stiff, unblinking, expressionless, almost unknown. The photographer had tinted the portrait. The cheeks were unnaturally rosy, the almond eyes westernized, the Oriental genes neatly airbrushed out.

Looking at the photograph, he felt a tightness in his chest. I'll call him again before noon, he promised himself, but he knew that his father's housekeeper would have a ready excuse. It was generally, "Sasha's out playing," or "He's on an errand for your father." Lu had called three times yesterday, the boy's fourteenth birthday, and the excuse was always that his son was not home. He had gotten the same story for the last ten years.

Lu had seen his son only three times. Once, just after birth, Lu had gently touched the squalling red bundle of wrinkled flesh who suckled Yekaterina's breast.

Two days later, the uterine infection had set in, but Lu didn't have the three hundred rubles for "enhanced treatment" to pay the butcher who called himself a doctor. Lu desperately wired Yekaterina's brother for money, the only person he could turn to. The transfer was delayed for five days by downed telegraph lines, and by then the infection was too far advanced. The doctor took the money anyway and went through the motions. Lu buried Yekaterina in a hole blasted out of the frozen sod of Us't Kut nine days after their son was born.

Yekaterina's death left Lu few choices. He was father to an infant child with no mother to care for him. Lu's travels kept him out of the Soviet Union for months at a time, sometimes years. He could give Sasha over to a state orphanage, but he knew what they were like. There was only one other alternative.

With a great deal of grumbling, Lu's father had taken in Sasha as his ward on the condition that Lu would pay for the boy's expenses and the salary of a full-time housekeeper. That commitment took over half of Lu's income for the next decade.

Lu saw Sasha again just after the boy turned five. Lu's father was a retired pensioner in Mamontovka, a suburb of Moscow.

The old man was drinking even more now, usually in a stupor by noontime. He refused to talk to Lu, who had called from the metro station, new lieutenant-captain's stars on his shoulderboards. Lu called an hour later, this time getting the housekeeper. She said in a hushed voice that it might be possible for Lu to see his son if it was done discreetly, away from the apartment. He met her in the park and had two minutes with his son, who frowned at the strange man in the mustard-colored uniform, then ran away with his rubber ball to hide in the shrubbery.

The only other time Lu had seen Sasha was two years earlier, when the boy was twelve. Rather than trying to contact the apartment, Lu telephoned all the schools in Mamontovka, using his father's name, asking for the extension number of Sasha's mathematics teacher. Something about a book that Sasha had lost and was going to be punished for.

The administrator at district school number seven acknowledged that Sasha was enrolled, but her records indicated that there was no punishment pending against Sasha, who, by her records, was a model student. Lu asked for Sasha's schedule; how he could get the book back into Sasha's hands. She not only told him but commended Lu for being a responsible citizen and protecting State property.

Lu found Sasha with three other chess players on an enclosed porch. Sasha was in the last stages of the end game, backing his opponent against the king's row with a rook and a brace of pawns. It wasn't an elegant checkmate, but it was effective and played out with calm deliberation.

The boy looked up, frowned at the man who mirrored his genes, then looked down again, finishing the game. The opponent asked for a rematch, but Sasha stood up and walked away.

Lu followed him, unsure of himself, what he could say, how he would say it. The boy wandered into the school yard and sat down on a concrete bench under a dripping linden tree, ignoring Lu. Lu stood there awkwardly, long seconds ticking away, the boy's face averted. Till finally the boy withdrew a money purse from his jacket, opened it, and removed a cracked photograph. He held it up to Lu, his face set, his voice controlled. It was a photograph of Lu and a very pregnant Yekaterina, taken on the edge of a frozen lake thirteen years before.

"Why didn't you come before?" Then, realizing that he had just overstepped the boundaries of acceptable behavior, the boy lowered his eyes.

"Because," Lu answered, "I couldn't. I'd tried to call. I've been gone." It sounded stupid—worse than that, criminally inadequate.

But the boy nodded as if he understood. "It's all right. I know that they won't let you see me. I overhear telephone conversations by hiding under the stairwell. Grandpa has told me to forget about you, that you are a bad father who doesn't care about me. But I know the real reason is that he doesn't want to lose the money you send him for me." He hesitated for a second. "Truly, I don't think you're a bad father. I broke into Mother's old trunk and found the photograph, read the letters you'd written to her."

The boy was thin, his clothes threadbare, knees and knuckles raw from the cold. He was small for his age, a remote but proud face. Lu said, "I loved your mother more than anything, and we both wanted a son, a fine son we would name Sasha."

The boy absorbed this information without emotion, his eyes now straight ahead, focused on infinity. He finally stood up, then, placing one shoe in front of the other as if he were walking a tightrope, followed a seam of mortar between the bricks toward a bench on the other side of the courtyard. A flight of geese flew over, honking. For a few seconds they both looked up, watching the formation until it disappeared behind the housetops.

Then he sat down on the bench and absently picked at the peeling paint, his gaze still averted. "I remember, or I think I remember," he said. "You came once before. A long time ago. You wore a uniform. What do you do?"

"*Komitet Gosudarstvennoy Bezopasnosti.* I'm a major now."

"Then you guard our borders. I saw a film about the KGB in school. They were all good men and they had dogs to help them."

"Yes. We keep our enemies out." And our people in.

The boy suddenly stood up. "I have to go back now. I am in a school chess tournament. The next match starts in a few minutes."

Lu hung on a thread. "Do you want to see me again—or for me to write to you? I checked with the school's administrator. I could post it to the school chess club, and I'll enclose an address for you to answer."

Seriously, the boy pondered the idea for a few minutes. "Yes, I'd like that," he said. The boy formally offered his hand. "Yes. I'd like that very much, I think," he repeated, shook Lu's hand formally, as an adult would, and walked away, moving in zigzags along the seams of mortar between the bricks toward the schoolhouse.

* * *

Lu took a lukewarm shower, shaved, inserted his contacts, and dressed, then packed and locked his suitcase, leaving it under the bed, taking only his briefcase with him. In the lobby he checked that his KGB tail hadn't spotted him, and slid out the porter's entrance.

The ludicrous part of it was that Lu was a deep cover KGB agent, "off the books," who reported only to his immediate superior, the Colonel. His cover for being in Moscow was that of a Malaysian importer attending a trade conference, thus automatically targeted by lower echelon KGB apparatchiks to be tailed. Sometimes, he thought, it was like living in a hall of mirrors, where each re-reflected image grew dimmer and more distorted until there was nothing left except the blurred suggestion of a man, a stranger even unto himself.

It had been a late spring and the trees on Prospekt Marksa were not yet fully in bud. For three days now it had rained intermittently, clogging the gutters with broken twigs and grass clippings.

He rolled up the collar of his plastic raincoat and headed north, instantly blending into the sullen crowds.

Moving up Prospekt Marksa, Lu varied his pace, sometimes pausing in front of stores and, alternatively, pushing past clotted groups of shoppers as if he had suddenly remembered an important appointment. The mass of pedestrians was the usual mixture of student and worker groups in from the countryside on obligatory political tours, housewives endlessly searching for goods that were never available, a mixture of military uniforms topped by faces with frozen expressions, and the few, like himself, who had the subtle stamp of indeterminate middle-bureaucratic authority in both dress and manner.

At the intersection of Petrovka and Marksa, he illegally crossed the street, then stopped, looking into the Metropol restaurant, using the plate-glass window as a mirror, trying to identify any tail. A woman crossed over behind him, but she then entered a shop that featured women's plastic shoes from Romania.

He backtracked down Prospekt Marksa for a few minutes, checking faces, watching for any reversal in direction that might flag a tail.

Not fully convinced that no one was following him, he again reversed direction back to the north, once more crossing the street, turning up Neglinnaja, then right onto Solanka. He bought a packet of dried prunes and a copy of *Izvestia* at one of the kiosks, then sat on a bench in the misty drizzle, casually scanning the pages but flicking brief glances over the top of the paper at the pedestrian tide that ebbed and flowed along the street.

Finally satisfied, he wadded up the paper, tossed it into a trash barrel, and crossed the street, where he entered an unmarked door. The hallway was dimly lit with bare bulbs, the tile floor stained and cracked, a musty scent of mold and damp plaster prevailing the place. Halfway down the corridor was a wooden barricade with a sign warning of "work in progress." In the Soviet Union, that will be the day, he thought.

Ignoring the warning, he stepped past it. At the end of the hallway he dropped a plastic card in an unmarked mail slot and waited. Overhead, a miniature TV camera swiveled toward him. Thirty seconds or more ticked by, then the door latch buzzed and he pushed inside.

The anteroom was sterile but well lighted. Lu presented his credentials to an armed KGB lieutenant who stood behind a thick, armored glass plate. The lieutenant made no comment but thoroughly checked them. Satisfied, he returned both identity card and passport, then motioned the man identified as Louis Aleksandrovich Rogov toward the elevator.

On the seventh floor he passed through a second security check, was issued a red-bordered visitor's pass and escorted to an office at the far end of the corridor.

The man behind the desk had blue collar tabs and the badges of rank of a KGB colonel-general. He heaved his bulk out of the chair, his face flushing with the effort.

They met, Lu's hand extended. Colonel-general Mikhail Pavlovich Mishukov ignored the hand, embraced him, dry-kissed him lightly on both cheeks, then stepped back.

"Time treats you well, Louis Aleksandrovich," the colonel said, looking over the rims of his glasses. "Sit down, sit down. Smoke if you wish. You will have tea?"

"Tea, yes. I rarely smoke now. Perhaps I'll resume when our medical researchers perfect the neck-down transplant."

The colonel laughed dutifully at the old joke and pressed a bar on his intercom, ordering tea and pastries. Lu thought that time had not been equally kind to the colonel. He had gained a good deal of weight, and his face had a pudgy pallor to it that looked unhealthy. There were rumors of heart disease.

"And your father—how is he?" the colonel asked with bored politeness.

"Retired in Mamontovka. I don't see him much." An understatement.

The colonel nodded absently, his glasses sliding down his nose a few millimeters. Unconsciously, he pushed them back up. There was a grease spot on his tunic, and he seemed to be no more dangerous than a favorite old uncle. Which was deceptive, because the colonel was second deputy director of the KGB's department Victor, first chief directorate.

"And your son?"

"I don't see much of him either, but now that you're posting me back to Moscow, perhaps I'll be able to spend more time with him." Also an understatement.

"Yes—your posting. That's why I called you in." The colonel absently tugged at a fold of skin on his neck. "Remembering things as I get older seems to be more of a task, like straining curdled milk through a sieve. Only the solids remain and the rest leaks through—part of the inevitable aging process."

Which Lu knew was the deception that the colonel used to cover both his survival and success.

The intercom buzzed, and moments later a sergeant wheeled in a tea trolley that supported a silver samovar. To the side was a plate of doughy buns and some jars of English jam. The colonel poured the tea and added heated milk, then slid back into his chair.

Behind the colonel, meshed-metal curtains blurred the outline of Dzerzhinsky Square below and the building beyond, the old All-Russian Insurance Company, which some of the western press still called the "Lubyanka." With the noon hour approaching, the sidewalks were crowded, but standing serene and remote in the middle of the square surrounded by flowers that had been freshly planted was a statue of Felix Dzerzhinsky, proud founder of the KGB, quizzically half smiling, facing toward the Kremlin as if still soliciting his long-dead master's approval.

The colonel slowly leafed through a report, alternately turning a page, then sipping his tea. "You did exceptionally well in California, Louis Aleksandrovich. But there are some blanks to fill in. In the summary, you report that there were no apparent repercussions? You're sure?"

Lu shifted in his chair, trying to appear relaxed but still tense. The colonel had specified that the mission report be personally typed and limited to a single copy, for the colonel's eyes only. Lu was uneasy about the implications.

"Nothing that surfaced. On this particular *Titan* failure, the investigation seemed to focus on a possible design defect in the solid booster. As you can obviously appreciate, the *Challenger* has had a Pavlovian effect on American thinking. Now when a rocket blows up, they always suspect the solid boosters first because they *expect* them to fail."

"The man who actually destroyed the *Titan* was one of the graduates of the Gelding operation?"

"Yes. Fairly typical. A former U.S. Army helicopter pilot whom I processed in 1970. Under interrogation he gave up highly classified information on field communications codes used in the Mekong Delta. We filmed the standard confession of war crimes, which we released to a French TV crew through the usual back channels."

"Any problems in either recruiting or controlling him?"

"Not really."

The colonel obviously wasn't satisfied, and he pressed for details. "Tell me about his post-Vietnam background and how you approached him. This is important because I plan to use one of the other Geldings in a future operation."

"After being repatriated, he was threatened with a court-martial for the war crimes confession, with the alternative of resigning. He obviously chose to resign, then held a steady job for a year in his brother's real estate business and seemed to be making a normal recovery until his wife suddenly died. After that he started to drink heavily, got fired, then held a series of short-term jobs. There were several minor arrests for drug abuse and drunk driving. When I tracked him down, he was working as a night watchman in Long Beach. I left a tape of his interrogation in his mailbox along with the address of a bar he frequented. We met two days later. It wasn't difficult to recruit him."

"And after the *Titan* failure, all the loose ends were cleaned up?"

Lu nodded. "Zazyadko, one of our men from the consulate in San Francisco, took care of it. Driving back to Los Angeles in a dense fog that night, the Gelding drove his pickup off a cliff on the Pacific Coast Highway. It seems that the brake system was defective. The vehicle burned. So did the man."

The colonel momentarily twitched a smile. "And the equipment?"

"The Gelding dropped the equipment off at a prearranged spot. Zazyadko picked it up and reported two days later that he had broken up the unit and buried what remained in a garbage landfill."

"No loss," the colonel said. "We've developed a much improved model. More tea?"

Lu shook his head. So the colonel was planning a similar operation.

Minutes passed in silence as the colonel tapped a tattoo on his desk with a pencil, studying Lu. He flicked through the folder, then looked up. "I'd intended to post you back to Moscow Center for at least three years, perhaps to the U.S.-Canadian Institute as an instructor, but that has changed. The *Titan* project was a trial run: Marshal Khokhlov's brainchild. Frankly, when he first suggested it, I gave it one chance in three of succeeding. Obviously, I was wrong. Marshal Khokhlov now foresees a second, more ambitious project." The colonel leaned back in his chair and folded his hands across his paunch like an all-knowing Buddha, waiting for Lu's response.

"Do I have a choice? Because if I do, I'd vastly prefer the Moscow posting."

The colonel shook his head. "You have no choice. But once you've successfully completed this project, I promise you there will be no more overseas assignments."

Lu didn't like the ring of that, more the colonel's inflection than the words. He sighed. "What's the project?"

The colonel gave him a thin smile. "The American Space Defense Command is playing games with us. We don't have all the intelligence in place as yet, but our source, an aide to a senator on the Intelligence Subcommittee, has relayed to his controller that the Americans are preparing a secret orbital test of a Star Wars weapon—project code-named Excalibur."

"How in hell could the Americans get away with it without the word leaking out? Under the revised ABM treaty, I thought that no Star Wars testing could take place outside the laboratory."

"I'm told that access to the actual mechanics of the project is very tightly controlled. Our source doubts that even the American President knows the full details of the project. It's a carryover from the previous administration. Such projects have a life of their own, as you know. Our reasoning as to why they're risking exposure is that the Space Defense Command must believe that they have a major breakthrough and are thus willing to take the gamble. To minimize exposure and to disguise what they're doing, they've casually leaked that this test is a laser communications experiment involving two separate satellites, one Japanese and the other American." He tapped his finger against the folder. "It's all in here."

"Is our response actually approved in principle or is this just a contingency study?"

"In between," the colonel replied. "If our planning indicates better than a ninety percent probability of success, there will be a full presentation to the Politburo before the plan is implemented. In the end it will come down to a fight between the pacifists and the patriots—so what else is new? By my estimate, I would say that they'll be evenly divided and the deciding vote will be vested in our revisionist son-of-a-bitching general secretary. I expect that he'll straddle the fence, which just might break his balls this time."

He pushed the file across his desk. "I'll give you a maximum of two weeks to get a fully realized operational plan together along the outlines I've drawn up."

"Then I'll be going back into the West again."

The colonel nodded. "For the last time, I promise, my friend."

Again, a feeling of vague uneasiness washed over Lu. Not something that he could define, just a hollowness in the colonel's voice that haunted him.

"I'll need full support: forged documents, access to Center's computer data base as well as the updated files from the Gelding operation." He had reflexively, almost automatically, laid down the conditions because he wanted to spread the involvement and thus dilute the importance of his role if the thing went wrong.

The colonel nodded impatiently. "Of course. And I've provided a secure office for you on this floor. You'll work there, eat there, sleep there. No secretary will be assigned to you. All the initial planning will be done by you under my sole supervision. Otherwise, I'll get you what you need. There's a blanket authorization signed by me in the file. Use it sparingly and without any elaboration on what the mission is."

Lu fiddled with his cup, examining the bits of tea leaves which would foretell his future. They were clumped in the bottom of his cup, indicating the potential of good fortune coupled with danger. Still, he didn't like the overtones of what the colonel was saying because the plan sounded like the pet project of Politburo hardliners rather than a fully involved and unanimously Politburo-approved KGB operation. If something went wrong even in the early stages, he would be expendable.

"I want you to keep the operation extremely tight," the colonel emphasized. "Frame your planning to keep each separate task compartmentalized. I don't want any loose ends."

Standing up, Lu walked to the curtained window, staring down on the square below. "And will I be a loose end if something goes wrong?"

Behind him, the colonel gave a forced laugh which degenerated into a hacking cough. Finally, the colonel cleared his throat. "Louis, my dear, dear friend, you're becoming paranoid. I look upon you as my son. When this project is successfully concluded, I'll permanently retire you from the field. But for now I want you to give this your best efforts."

Working ten hours a day for six straight days, Lu had fleshed out the plan, then began to detail it.

A critical part was getting the Japanese industrialist's cooperation. Lu read through the dossier, then spent an afternoon browsing through Moscow Center's computer data base and microfiche records.

No, the old man would not be bought easily, he concluded. When a man owned an empire worth billions, a million or so would mean nothing. Like a dog digging for a bone, Lu scratched deeper. Sex, perversion, a personal background that was tainted? None of that. There was the war record, but it would be difficult to prove, and who in Japan would care? They still secretly revered their old warlords.

Hiroshi Katana was what he appeared to be: an old widower with a single son as heir, a man of simple tastes and yet wealthy beyond imagination. What was it that Lu could offer him that Katana didn't have? Until he tripped over Appendix Fifteen in Katana's dossier, and there it was, so obvious that Lu smashed the flat of his hand against his forehead in both elation of his discovery and exasperation for the stupidity of the time that he had wasted. Men like Katana would value only the invaluable and nearly unobtainable—like Getty, like Hammer, like Forbes, like any of the aging mega-rich.

It was too late for the last flight, but he had to know now. He cleared it with the colonel, then took the overnight train to Leningrad, holing up in a KGB safe house on Korablestroitelei. He was in the Hermitage's director's office by nine the next morning, only four hours of sleep and two cups of morning tea to soften his puffy face.

He placed his KGB identification on the man's desk. The director squinted up at him in annoyance, then perched thick bifocals on the beak of his nose and bent over to examine the card. In seconds, sweat glistened on the balding dome of the director's scalp. He slowly lifted his head to look up at Lu, real fear glittering from deep behind the lenses.

"There is . . . a problem?"

"With your cooperation and my authorization, I would hope not," Lu said, his smile controlled and controlling.

The next major element of the plan was transportation. Lu discussed his requirements at length with a KGB man in the technical section and realized the difficulty of what he was trying to accomplish. He would need the services of two separate vessels based in the Caribbean; the first, a large high-speed power boat, and the second, a smaller vessel, preferably a sailing yacht.

He made a scrambled call to a KGB liaison man in Cuba, calling in an old debt. "We generally have several sailboats that the Cubans have seized, but nothing the size or matching the specifications you require is available," Sudoplatov reported. "However, I think I might be able to fill the rest of your order."

"All right, but keep this out of official channels."

"No problem, old friend," Sudoplatov responded. He took two days getting back to Lu.

"It fits your requirements perfectly, Comrade," Sudoplatov said. "The former Nicaraguan dictator, Somoza's yacht, forty-seven meters in length, capable of very high speed, and with tremendous cruising range. It was traded to Fidel by the Sandinistas seven years ago in exchange for five MTB-4G coastal patrol vessels."

Which posed a problem. "Then it's Fidel's personal yacht?"

"No. The vessel's use is restricted to covert operations and some occasional drug running. The Cuban DGI have it registered in Panama and use it to clandestinely transport DGI agents and equipment to various Central American and Caribbean countries."

"Does it have a cargo hold?"

"Yes, but it's not large."

"How big?"

"Three meters square, barely high enough to stand up in."

It would be enough. "I owe you the very best dinner that Havana has to offer," Lu promised.

"Which will probably consist of black beans and rice," Sudoplatov responded. "But give me a hint, Louis, just what in hell are you going to use the vessel for?"

"What do you think, Sudoplatov? A pleasure cruise. What about manning?"

"Cuban navy special forces, well trained for . . . ah . . . pleasure cruising."

They discussed the financial details. The "charter" could be set up quietly, outside of "normal channels" through the deputy director of the DGI, who reported directly to Fidel's brother, Raul Castro, minister of defense. The cost was staggering—two hundred thousand American for the charter and another half million as a bond to be refunded on return of the vessel in good condition. Sudoplatov glossed it over by explaining that Raul had expensive tastes and that Fidel was willing to turn a blind eye to his brother's private enterprises.

There was a numbered bank account in the Caymans that Raul maintained for contingency fees. Sudoplatov joked that *blat* was as old a Cuban custom as it was Russian. It's the state's money anyway, Lu rationalized, and agreed without further dickering.

Surprisingly, the sailboat was much less of a problem. The colonel had already done his homework. Lu looked through the charter brochures of the two sailing vessels and then at the dossiers of their owners, both graduates of the Gelding operation. Either would do, but he vividly remembered one of the men and spent that evening watching films pulled from the dusty archives of Moscow Central, shot in Vietnam close to two decades before.

Penciled in the margin of the colonel's operational approval was his notation: "As the Americans say, 'The chickens have come home to roost.' *Our* chickens, Louis!"

6.

May 10

By Sunday the operational plan was firming up. Lu decided that he'd call it quits for the afternoon. After all, even God had supposedly rested on the seventh day. Why not the KGB?

He hadn't had any particular plan in mind, only to get out of the building and spend a few hours strolling in the sunshine, perhaps take in a film. He changed from his uniform into cheap slacks and a rough pullover, then slid out through the back door of the New Building.

He wandered without any particular plan and eventually found himself on Kutuzovsky Prospekt in front of *Dom Igrushki,* the "House of Toys." In one of the windows was a chess set, the white pieces sculpted from whalebone and the black from ebony. It would be a perfect gift for Sasha. He had planned to meet the boy the next weekend and then thought, I'll try calling right now. No school on Sunday and Sasha is likely to be home, might even answer the telephone, which was in the hallway of his apartment building. With luck . . .

But the old woman answered.

Lu tried to disguise his voice, simple tradecraft for a superspy.

"It's you again, isn't it?" she said in a monotone.

"Yes, it's me, the boy's father," he answered, exasperated. "Damn you, woman, put him on."

"You should know by now that your father doesn't allow it. Give me the telephone number of the place you're calling from. Wait for me to ring you back from a public call box."

"What's wrong?"

She ignored his question. "Give me your number. Your father's drunk like a pig that has eaten fermented apples—he'll never notice that I've gone out—but it will take me twenty minutes."

He gave her his number, bought a pack of cigarettes at a kiosk across the street, and chain-smoked as if he had never quit, waiting for her call.

The phone rang twenty-three minutes later. "There is something that you should know, but you will not tell your father that I talked to you about this. Is that agreed?"

His heart was hammering, its pulse pounding in his ears. He took a deep drag on the *papiroska,* the taste harsh in his mouth. "Agreed," he said. "Get on with it!"

"The boy had been complaining of fatigue and he caught a flu that wouldn't go away. I gave him hot packs and bitter root but he didn't get better. Then I pounded on the idiot director of the regional clinic and told him to do something. They took some blood, then a day later, a sample of bone marrow. The tests came back that he has the beginning stages of leukemia."

"Oh, God!" Lu's legs sagged.

The line was silent for a time, then she spoke again. "Yes, there is great need for God's divine help. I have prayed every day. The doctor says that Sasha, with luck, can live a normal life for a long time if he receives blood transfusions and antibiotics."

"How long?"

"She said that he had one chance in three of—I wrote the word down—remission. Otherwise, two years—maybe more, possibly less. There are other treatments that might help, but they are unavailable."

"In what clinic?"

"Not within the borders of our homeland. The doctor pointed to the west but wouldn't say any more, even though I begged her for more information."

"Sasha. Where is he now?"

"Sleeping. He's fine, just tired. Starting Wednesday, he'll receive regular transfusions."

"But he should be in a hospital."

"No, that is not the doctor's plan. Unless Sasha gets an infection, he can continue school. That's the way the treatment is handled, she told me."

Lu leaned against the side of the booth, his cheek pressed to the glass, his eyes closed, his mind numb. "What is the doctor's name, where does she live?"

"Dr. Raya Chebrikov. You can contact her at the number twenty-eight clinic only during weekdays."

"Is Sasha getting the right food?"

"The best I can manage. I steal from your father's purse to buy fresh vegetables out of season, but I can't take too much without him noticing."

He had always thought of her as his enemy in the fight for his son, never had thought of her as religious or compassionate, but now he saw her differently. "What made you tell me?"

"I've raised him from an infant. I never had my own children. I love your father, I don't know why, it's just that way, but I love Sasha much more—perhaps more than you do."

"Old woman, you have my thanks. Forever my thanks." He thought for a few seconds. "How often do you get into Moscow?"

"Usually once a month to visit my sister."

"There is a place on Sixteen Dzerzhinsky Street called the Stamp Collectors' Shop. There will be an envelope waiting in your name on the last weekend in each month. It will have two hundred American dollars in it. Keep half for yourself, convert the rest on the black market, and buy Sasha whatever he needs."

Besides being a stamp collectors' store, the shop was also a pay window for low-level KGB informants who worked as interpreters to the foreign press. With easy access to hard currency, Lu knew he could easily fiddle that much out of the discretionary account without raising any questions from the colonel.

The line was silent. Then, "You will talk to the doctor, you will do something?"

He didn't believe, not quite, but he said, "God will help us, old woman."

"I know what you do, the *svolochi* that you work for, but I also know that you love your son. So I will pray to God every day for your success, Louis Aleksandrovich."

The line went dead.

"Your son has acute lymphoplastia. Did his mother or any relative have any such disease?"

She was a youngish woman, her hair tied back in a bun, her face free of makeup. And she was not unsympathetic.

"No—rather, I don't know. She died very young of an infection."

"I'm sorry, Comrade Colonel." The woman checked her wristwatch. "We have little time before I must go on my rounds. I can assure you that we will do our best for him."

"There are special clinics?"

She shook her head. "It is a disease not well understood. There are many researchers working on a potential cure but—"

"Where?"

She eased back in her chair, looking into his eyes, measuring him. He now regretted that he had worn his uniform with its blue tabs of the KGB, but that had cut through the bureaucracy and scheduled appointments like a hot knife through lard.

"I want you to *tell* me! *Now!*"

She sat up straight, her face expressionless. "You demand an answer. Is your question made in an official capacity or otherwise?"

He bowed his head and put his hands to his temples. "Forgive me. This is only between us."

"There are hospitals beyond our borders that specialize in this disease. The chances would be excellent, perhaps as much as ninety percent in favor of remission and over sixty percent of complete recovery. But such treatment is not only expensive. It is unavailable to the average Soviet citizen."

"How much?"

She shrugged, then did a quick multiplication. "In English pounds sterling, more than one hundred thousand. It might be twice that much by now. I heard this figure from a Finnish doctor at a medical conference in Poland over two years ago." She pressed her lips together in apology. "My information is old."

"Where?"

She looked at him hard. "This information goes no further than you alone, because if it did, you must realize that I could get into a great deal of trouble."

"I will say it again. This is between just the two of us."

She wrote down five names and their locations, then got up. "I will do my best for him, Comrade Colonel. You have my pledge. The disease can be suppressed for many months." She picked up her medical bag and left the room.

For several minutes he sat in the chair, facing the empty desk. Then looked down at the paper.

Two of the clinics were in the United States, one in Great Britain, and the fourth in France.

The fifth was in Singapore.

The colonel had paid particular attention to constructing a cover, one that would allow Lu to move effortlessly in the West, that of Louis E. Kim, Canadian, financial software developer.

"But if I'm supposed to be selling financial software, I've got to have software to demonstrate and something to demonstrate it on," Lu said.

"The very best," said the colonel. From behind his desk the colonel removed a thick leather briefcase and opened it. Inside was a portable laptop computer. The colonel flipped up the screen and turned it on. "Not only essential to your legend, but because of the large amount of information that you must have continuous access to, an ideal means of accessing that data. This computer is the most advanced that our trading partners, the Japanese, make. It has twin floppy disk drives and a good deal of memory. It operates on any AC voltage as well as batteries." He tapped three keys and the display came up. LOUIS E. KIM ASSOCI-ATES FUTURES TRADING PROGRAM.

"The software was developed in England and is commercially available. Our programmers have made enough changes that give the program its own unique identity. If you ever have to demonstrate it, even an astute financial analyst would be impressed."

"But the other information—the radio frequencies, dates, timing, names, course information, navigational data?"

The colonel grinned like a father showing off a complicated toy to his son. He pressed some hidden catches on the inside lid of the briefcase. A thin, secret compartment folded out. "In here you will carry the actual mission's software program on a floppy disk as well as other material which would be suspect in a customs inspection." He inserted the floppy disk in the computer, then rapidly tapped in a dozen keystrokes. The screen registered the words: PASSWORD APPROVED, PHASE ONE. SELECT MENU ITEM.

The colonel hit the return key and a list of files popped up. "Select any file—telephone numbers, radio frequencies, background information, whatever, and you have the information that you need. As things change, you'll be able to conveniently update the data."

"What about password security? Surely it could be cracked if the software was examined by any Western intelligence agency. The whole mission would be exposed and me with it."

"A very small risk," replied the colonel, "because it would take many months for even a very sophisticated group of cryptographers with access to a mainframe computer to crack the encryption passwords."

"You just said passwords. There's more than one?"

The colonel poured two more tumblers of vodka, then dropped into his chair, trapped air hissing from the cushion.

"You and I, Louis, are like two specialists with different but overlapping skills. Let's say that I'm the engineer and you're the machinist. I design a part, tell you how it should function, what it should be made of, and you then take that concept and produce the finished part to my specifications. Phase one is your job. The concept has been tested twenty-eight times under realistic conditions at the Frunze Institute, and the success rate is approximately ninety-three percent. There are films of the results that I've scheduled to be shown to you. But a ninety-three percent success rate also implies the potential of a seven percent failure rate. Thus, phase two. If phase one fails for any reason, phase two is the backup. I need not elaborate on its details until the planning is finalized."

"I accept that. I'm only questioning why there are two different passwords."

"Marshal Khokhlov's idea. You handle phase one and I handle phase two. Those are his direct orders. He wants backups to backups."

"That's unclear."

The colonel sighed. "Independently, phase one has a ninety-three percent chance of working. Independently, phase two has an eighty-one percent chance of success. Combined, that means a statistical success rate projection of nearly ninety-nine percent. You see the problem, don't you, Louis? If anything happened to you and phase one fails and you're out of action, then, without me, there would be no backup at all. Therefore, I'll handle phase two. And if for any reason phase one doesn't work *and* something goes wrong at my end, *and* provided you're still operational, you'll be the backup to my backup. Forget the complicated statistics and take my word for it. We improve our chances tremendously by doing it this way."

Lu had made some discreet inquiries concerning Marshal Khokhlov. Nothing solid, but there were rumors within the KGB that he was trying to oust the general secretary by pushing for a much more aggressive foreign policy, possibly even a military confrontation with the West. But the rumor was also making the rounds that the general secretary wanted Khokhlov out of the Politburo. It had all the makings of a deadly internal power struggle. As such, there would be winners and losers.

The sun had set and the lights of Moscow were slowly winking on. Both of them sat in darkness, the illumination from the computer screen casting a dim amber glow on the colonel's desk.

"It seems like a reasonable way to handle the situation," Lu eventually said. "What are the passwords? I'll obviously need them."

"Both lines from poems. As you may know, I was second deputy KGB station chief in England just after the war. My English has always been good and I enjoyed reading English literature and history."

Lu tried unsuccessfully not to look surprised.

The colonel smiled. "Oh, yes, Louis, even I have a private life with private pleasures. Andropov built sailing-ship models and it's said that Stalin did crochet work. Can you imagine old Josef clicking away on the needles, somewhat like Madame DeFarge, forever detailing a list of his enemies? That afghan must have been large enough to cover half of Russia. And what's your private passion, Louis?"

"I collect small jade animals."

"And women, so I'm told." The colonel laughed.

"And women," Lu acknowledged. It was getting late and he wanted to get this over with. "The passwords . . ." he prompted.

"The password for phase one is the title of a Mother Goose rhyme, 'Humpty Dumpty.' You've undoubtedly heard it?"

"I think so. Yes," Lu answered

"Phase two's passwords are much more complex—actually several sentences—therefore almost impossible for a cryptographer to break. It's best that you don't know—simply on the basis of 'need to know.' When I meet with you in Cuba, then I'll give you the phase two passwords. For now, just concentrate on phase one."

The colonel took a puff on his cigarette and knocked back the rest of his vodka. Then he said, "Your report on the Leningrad trip states that under my personal blanket authorization you requisitioned three paintings instead of just one, as we had agreed upon. And you further state that they have already been forwarded to Cuba via the KGB pouch. Explain, Louis." His voice had a hard edge to it.

Lu set down his drink. "Do I have your confidence or not?"

"Don't play games with me. It would be unwise."

"My apologies then, Colonel, that I didn't first consult with you, but after talking with the Hermitage's director of Western art as to a collector's mindset, I had to make a decision on the spot. Katana, like any discriminating collector, surely has distinct preferences. In any collector's quest to acquire, the value of a painting is less important than how that painting complements his own collection."

He made a casual show of slowly sipping his vodka, not swallowing much, but allowing him time to pace his response.

"I'll first offer Katana the least valuable painting, a small Manet, as if it were the only one available. If he rejects it, I'll present him the second choice, a Renoir. If he rejects that one, then I'll be able to play my last and most valuable card—a Gauguin—because his dossier indicates that he owns two other Gauguins from the Tahitian period and this particular work would round out his collection for that particular era. It surely goes without saying that I'll return the other two works to Leningrad."

The colonel, his hands laced around one knee, leaned back, his eyes half closed. Then, "I accept what you did as justifiable, Louis. And, of course, you have my every confidence." Yet, his voice conveyed just a hint of doubt.

In the darkness of the office Lu felt a bead of sweat trickle down his neck. That night he wrote a hurried letter to Sasha. In the envelope he enclosed a five-ruble note and a map of Moscow.

Four days later, on Saturday, Lu left the New Building, dressed in working-class clothes. He strolled leisurely through Moscow, stopping at a street vendor's cart for mineral water, feeding the pigeons, occasionally resting on a park bench to check for the tail that he knew would be assigned.

Sitting on a bench, he noticed, as always, that Russians slid farther down the bench, away from him, as if he were contaminated.

Lu had finally come to accept the Russian disdain for Asiatics. It was a subtle bigotry, never overtly stated, but it manifested itself in many ways. In the KGB uniform he never had any trouble, but in civilian clothes, even though he patiently worked himself to the head of the line after hours of waiting, a counter clerk or ticket seller would often ignore him or find an excuse to shunt him aside. Something was wrong with his coupon, there wasn't the appropriate change available, or the supply of whatever it was was "finished." Yet Russians in the line behind him would be taken care of through "previously made reservations" or some magical "resupply."

It was now late morning. He checked his watch. Still an hour to go.

An old man shuffled by, his face ravaged by hard drinking, and he reminded Lu of his father. He wondered vaguely whether he would miss his father. He guessed not. Any bond that ever existed had been broken years before.

His father was Euro-Russian, a certified hero of the Great War for the Motherland, a train engineer who had once commanded the mammoth 4–10–4 steam locomotives on the Trans-Siberian Express. At the terminal in Nikolayevsk on the shores of the Sea of Okhotsk, Engineer Rogov had met Lu's mother.

She came from Sakhalin Island of parents Japanese on her father's side, and Chinese on her mother's side. After her parents died during the Soviet takeover, she had been sent to a state school for orphans in Nikolayevsk. From a bony girl she had grown into an extraordinarily beautiful and graceful woman. When Engineer Rogov had first met her, she was the lead dancer in an ethnic dance group which Intourist used to entertain the visiting client-state day-trippers. Rogov knew a good thing when he saw it and had casually moved in with her.

Once his father, in a rare letter, had jokingly referred to his relationship with Lu's mother as "layovers." The union was never formalized by marriage and lasted for only three years. Its only permanent by-product had been a blue-eyed baby with Oriental features.

Lu had been raised by his mother until age fifteen, his father just a yellowed photograph on a table. But after passing his secondary school exams with high marks, all of that changed.

Although not directly supporting his offspring, Engineer Rogov reluctantly agreed to give his bastard son his name and, as a loyal Party member, had been able to arrange a scholarship for the youth at the Lenin Institute of Political Science in Kiev. That fulfilled the obligation of father to son. From his teens, Louis Aleksandrovich Rogov had known that his Oriental features and illegitimacy were an embarrassment to his father, and no breach of that contract was ever to be made.

With admission to the institute secured, Louis recognized that this was his one chance to escape a lifetime of poorly paid manual labor, and he took it willingly.

In his first year at the institute he attended political meetings and could spout verbatim the words of Lenin's warped dialectic and Marx's flawed economics. It was only then that he fully realized how the naked power of Josef Stalin had been both molded and codified.

In his second year he was invited to join the Security Forces for the Defense of the Motherland as a noncommissioned officer. He turned down the offer because he knew that someone of his race could never rise through the ranks to officer status. Suddenly his grades plummeted, and other students, mostly of Great Russian stock, began to shun him. He quit trying to ingratiate himself with them or his teachers and signed his papers as Louis A. Lu, both to honor his mother's last name and as a sign of his independence. Forever after, he thought of himself as Lu because it became his talisman.

His third year at the institute was tenuous. He was placed on probation although he knew his work was outstanding. He immersed himself in his studies, completely digesting Soviet political science, able to regurgitate the words on demand. His grades edged marginally upward. A few overtures of "friendship" were made by student leaders. He was invited to join selected political study groups. Lu responded by accepting only the most influential of them.

In his fourth year his grades soared. More offers of "friendship," which he selectively accepted or ignored, but now politely. He capped his performance by denouncing several hack students whose parents lacked Party clout, delivering a blistering denunciation of their moral and political warts at a mass "self-criticism" meeting. Upon graduation, having received the coveted Lenin medal, Lu presented himself to the KGB as an officer candidate and was immediately accepted. It was then, in 1961, that the colonel, then a lieutenant-captain, became both his mentor and controller.

His first assignment was as a pipe fitter in a Mongolian steel mill. Lu infiltrated a mildly dissident group of workers who believed that wages and benefits equal to those of Great Russians should be paid to Soviets of Oriental extraction. Lu wiped out the cell, sending fourteen of his own race to Magadam. For this he received a promotion, the award of Hero of the Soviet Union, Third Class, and, more important, the attention of his superiors.

His second assignment was that of a Trinidadian exchange student at the University of California, Berkeley campus. His legend was that he had been born to emigrant Chinese parents and his passport and papers identified him as Louis An Lu, the name chosen jokingly by the colonel "to immortalize your naughty schooldays."

Lu prepared for that assignment by attending the KGB "illegals" school in Sverdlovsk, graduating again with honors. His mission was to refine his English and to study firsthand the newly emergent radical left but not to involve himself in its politics, an aspect which Lu found extremely difficult to avoid, given the American political climate of the mid-sixties.

Lu found the much-vaunted American way of life to be like the white bread sold in California supermarkets—an expensive, cellophane-wrapped, tasteless, colorless, nutritionless mush that neither filled nor satisfied.

Ten credits short of graduation, Lu was ordered to return to the Soviet Union, via Cuba. He brought back a list of eighty-nine American and twenty-two foreign students who showed future promise as being friendly toward the concept of "Universal Peace and Brotherhood through Socialist Justice and Prosperity."

His third assignment was as an intelligence liaison officer to North Vietnam, where he had the mission of interrogating American POWs.

Of the nine KGB officers assigned to the NVA, Lu achieved the highest "turncoat" rate and was therefore assigned as team leader. For his work he was promoted to full captain and given the award of Hero of the Soviet Union, Second Class.

Since then Lu had worked under the colonel's independent direction as an "officer, special projects." First in Singapore, next in Japan, a brief assignment in Canada and, finally, on the last mission, in California.

Lu checked his watch again. Twenty more minutes. A man in working clothes was sitting a couple of benches down across the path, flipping through the pages of a magazine. The clothes were authentic enough, but the man's face was well shaven, soft, and pale, as if the skin never saw sunshine or rain. The man's nails were clean, the fingers long and tapered. But the shoes were the giveaway. They were hard leather and of good quality, not what a working stiff could afford.

Of course, it was one of the colonel's predictable ploys: To sic one agent on the other, thus prodding his subordinates with the twin prongs of competitiveness and mutual distrust.

Lu stood up and strode down the path toward the toilet facility that was set in a grove of trees. As he turned up the graveled path toward the structure, he caught a glimpse of the tail off guard, just standing up, folding his paper under his arm, starting to follow him. Lu started to reach for the buttons on his fly, still moving toward the men's side of the facility, but when he was out of the direct line of sight, he broke into a run, keeping the structure between him and the tail. In a heart-pounding sprint of fifteen seconds, he gained a clump of trees a hundred meters away and sank to the ground, his lungs heaving.

The tail didn't go into the men's room, just stood casually

near the entrance, thumbing his paper, obviously ill at ease, betraying his inexperience.

Lu waited until the man turned away, then sprinted another hundred meters, swung aboard a bus, traveled two blocks, and got off, heading for Izmailovo Park. The tail would catch a blast of the colonel's wrath on Monday morning.

Lu was two minutes late. He could see Sasha standing near the flame of the Unknown Soldier. Young Komsomol members paraded up and down in goose step, AK-47s held at high port arms. A wedding party was just leaving after laying flowers at the base of the memorial.

The boy had sprung up like a weed, fully a head taller than when Lu had seen him two years before, but now terribly thin and pale. The boy's face was fully developed, with a hint of Yekaterina in the nose and mouth. He will be tall, Lu thought. Tall and strong and well.

He gently touched the boy's shoulder. Sasha turned suddenly, startled. They stood for several seconds, looking at each other, neither sure as to how they should react, but then the boy made the decision for both of them. He hurled himself into Lu's arms and breathed the magical word, "Father."

It was a splendid afternoon. The sun had come out, the weather warming, the wind still, the smell of growth strong in the air. All Moscow was out after the hard spring, and the sidewalks were crowded with old people, bounding children, lovers, and young couples pushing prams. An Uzbeckian street vendor of piroshki, little pastries stuffed with ground pork, sold them four of the delights. They wolfed them down, then stopped for cones of *morozhenoye,* the ice cream melting over their hands before they could sit down under the shade of a tree and eat them. They laughed together, licking and slurping the confection. All the barriers were down. Lu's heart filled, then overflowed.

"You have any trouble getting away from the apartment?"

The boy thoughtfully swiped his tongue across the ice cream. He looked up into his father's eyes, serious, a white mustache on his lips. "I didn't lie to Grandpa. I told him that I was coming to watch a famous Hungarian chess master of the first rank play at the Mayakovsky Theater." He held up a ticket. "You see. I didn't lie. I'm the best chess player in my school and I won the ticket as a prize."

He hated to share his son with others on this day but knew he would have to. "What time do you have to be there?"

The boy set his lips in a puckish grin. The ticket fluttered out of his fingers. "Grandpa tells me I'm a careless boy, and he must be right because I lost it," he said, then laughed.

After finishing the ice cream they strolled through the park. Lu finally asked the question that had been nagging him: "You're awfully damned thin, boy. Have you been sick?"

Sasha shrugged, his eyes averted. "Nothing serious. A flu that's going around. I'm starting some kind of dumb treatment next week, but knowing that you're going to be here in Moscow, I'm already better."

He knows, Lu realized. God in heaven, he knows. He quickly switched the subject. "And how are you getting along in school?"

Sasha shrugged. "I get top grades in mathematics, art, English, Chinese, and geography. Everything else is above average except for Socialist Realism. I'm sorry, Father, but it doesn't make sense to me."

Small wonder. "And do you have special friends?"

"A few. Chess players, mainly." He was twirling a blade of grass between his fingers, then pressing tighter, grinding it into green-stained filaments.

Lu cursed the stupidity of his question, for as it had been with him, so it would be with his son. "Do any of the other boys make trouble for you?"

"Some. The older ones. They call me 'the dumb yellow monkey.' " He set his lips in a determined, bloodless line. "They're wrong. My grades prove it. And I'm brown, not yellow. I see those same *duraks* lying on the river embankments in summer, burning themselves in the sun like chickens under a broiler so they can be the same color as me. So who is a dumb monkey?"

Lu knew what the boy was going through, would always go through, as long as he lived in this cold, alien land.

"So what do you want to be when you're finished with the university?"

"An artist, I think. A painter. But maybe a writer."

"And where would you want to live if you had your choice?"

The boy didn't hesitate. "With you."

They wandered crosstown toward Kalinin Prospekt. Stopping often, they examined the window displays in shops, the boy once laughing at a clutch of mechanical soldiers, beating on drums and tooting on trumpets. It was the first real laugh that Lu had heard from the boy, and it echoed Yekaterina's and the joy he felt in his own heart.

He guided Sasha through a glassed-in gallery to the Cafe Valday, and they settled into a back booth, sipping lemon-flavored tea, munching on sweet biscuits. It was getting late and the boy would have to catch the *elektrichka* in less than an hour.

There was very little time left. The planning for Excalibur was almost complete, and the colonel might order him to leave for the West within the week.

He had to do it now. "I am going to tell you a secret, Sasha. It is only for you, not for anyone else to know. If you tell it to anyone, it would put me in a very difficult position."

The boy nodded, his face perfectly serious and adult. "You're my father. Of course I wouldn't tell anyone."

Lu glanced around the room. Only two couples together at a table chattering. He leaned forward, his voice lowered. "I have been ordered on an overseas assignment by our government. I don't want the assignment, but I have no choice. It will be two, possibly three months before I can see you again. But if I do my work well, my superiors will allow me to retire with a large enough pension for both of us to live comfortably on. From then on, we will be together."

"Where would we live? In Moscow?"

Lu shook his head. "Not in Moscow. You said that you made good grades in geography. Where is Singapore?"

"Just south of Malaysia." The boy's expression was not smug, just proud that he knew the answer.

"What do you know about it?"

"It's an island nation, very beautiful. I saw a film about socialist trade unions in Singapore, and the film had a lot of scenes of the city and the countryside." His face clouded for a second. "Are we really allowed to move outside of the Soviet Union? They say in school that the Jews are both parasites and traitors when they apply to leave our homeland. Would we be traitors?"

Lu had made up his mind two days earlier. He wouldn't contact the Americans or British or French. And if he was ever picked up, he wouldn't give them anything. Let the white races fight their own wars. He just wanted to get out. "No," he finally answered, "we wouldn't be traitors." From his jacket pocket he withdrew a packet of documents and a small jade tiger.

He held up the animal to the light, then passed it to his son. "I bought this from a trader in Singapore three years ago. This little animal is over two thousand years old. If you like it, it's yours."

The boy held his palm out and accepted the animal, then studied it in the light. "It's very graceful. So exact and lifelike. See how his muscles are bunched up, as if he were about to pounce?" His palm closed around the animal. "I can even feel the heat of the sun in his body. Yes, I would very much like to keep him." He paused and regarded the package of documents on the table. "What do I do with these?"

"Nothing for now. Put them away in a safe place, where your tiger can guard them. In a few months you'll receive a telegram from Leningrad, inviting you to play in a weekend chess tournament, all expenses paid. As soon as you receive it, telephone your uncle Tsymbal from a public call box. His telephone number is in the packet. Uncle Tsymbal will set the date with your grandfather and travel with you to Leningrad. Once you get there, Uncle Tsymbal will put you on a train to Finland. I'll be waiting for you on the other side of the border."

The boy looked perplexed. "I don't think I can do that. I would have to have the proper papers."

Lu tapped the packet. "You have them. There is a seventy-two-hour transit pass in here with your name on it. The date is blank and all you have to do is to fill it in. You will be just another Soviet boy visiting his grandparents across the border for a weekend. After the 1939 war, some Soviet citizens chose to remain in Finland. Since the new general secretary has taken power, the authorities have made humanitarian allowances for visits to relatives across the border." He ruffled Sasha's hair. "Don't worry. Your uncle will rehearse your story, but see to it that you learn a little Finnish so it sounds good to the border guards."

"Why can't you meet me in Moscow?"

"I can't explain just yet, Sasha. Someday I will. Just trust me."

"But we'll be together?"

"Yes," Lu promised. For as long as we both may live.

Monday, Lu had his last meeting with the colonel.

His baggage had already been moved back to the Berlin Hotel and reservations made for a train ticket to Tallinn, Estonia, and a voucher for a cabin booked on the steamer *George Ott* leaving Tallinn for Helsinki May 21.

The colonel leaned back in his cushioned chair, scratching his chin. "You intentionally gave Kaarlo the slip. Why?"

"Because Kaarlo was as obvious as a bitch in heat. I thought it might be instructive to humble him a little."

"And what did you do that afternoon?"

"A man has certain needs that even the State doesn't provide for. Do I have to go into the details?"

Lighting a cigarette, the colonel leaned farther back in his chair, leering. "Say no more. I realize now that I was driving you too hard." He paused, scratching at his balding scalp. "So what do you think? Are you satisfied with our plan?"

"It could be improved, but not by much, and I like simplicity. The Helsinki part is critical, the Grenada part the most difficult. The rest of it is more or less under control providing that the Cubans are competent."

Swiveling his chair so that he could look out over the square, the colonel absently combed his fingers through his thinning hair, working slowly down to the nape of his neck.

"None of your tasks compare in difficulty to the problems that I will have in selling this project to the Politburo. But that's my end of it." He swiveled back and stood up, extending his hand. "Don't fail me, Louis. I mean it. Much rests on your efforts."

Eyes locked on the colonel's, Lu took the older man's hand and squeezed it very hard, very long. It was more than a handshake: it was a pledge. "I never think of failure, Mishka, only success. You'll get your money's worth." And he meant every damned word of it. It was just that he hadn't yet told the colonel the current rate of exchange.

7.

May 25

Lu half dozed in the dry Helsinki sunlight, not really listening as the loudspeaker system amplified the voice of yet another delegate.

The speaker from Angola droned on and on. Out of boredom, Lu shaded his eyes against the hard northern sunlight and looked above him. Sweeping upward on all sides were the tiers of the Finnish Olympic Stadium, flamboyantly draped with the banners of each national delegate group on this, the last day of the Peace in Space rally. Lu, despite himself, had doubled over in laughter at the unintended acronym when the colonel had briefed him and had received a frosty glare in return.

There were groups from Nicaragua, the United States, Great Britain, the USSR, Mozambique, Bulgaria, India, Mexico, France, Germany, Greece, and two dozen other countries. Most delegations were an eclectic mixture of age, ethnic background, and social position, yet all of them both enthusiastic and painfully earnest.

Sweat prickled on his brow, and his scalp itched. In the bowl of the stadium the air was stagnant. For Helsinki, it was an unusually warm day with only a light breeze blowing in from the Baltic Sea. Puff-ball cumulus drifted overhead, occasionally casting shadows over the stadium, and he momentarily wished that he was drinking Lakka in some downtown sidewalk café. But there was still one speaker that he had to hear, even though he had reviewed most of the man's videotaped speeches a week before in the archives of Moscow Center.

The three days since his arrival in Helsinki hadn't been demanding. Using the Louis E. Kim Canadian passport, he had been waved through immigration and customs, then had checked into the Hotel Presidentti and slept for sixteen hours.

On the following morning, still groggy, he had jogged in the Kluuvikasn and followed that with a sauna, then an enormous breakfast, casually shared at the same table with a charming

American couple and their not so charming brats. Sitting there, casually chatting about American politics, Lu confidentially sensed his fake Canadian identity locking smoothly into place.

His ongoing airlines tickets were delivered that afternoon in an unmarked envelope, and Lu completed his chores by hand-delivering a letter to the desk clerk at the Hotel Marski.

He had not planned to visit the stadium, but the videotapes had left him vaguely dissatisfied. He had to see the man before he met him—somehow to reach down through his skin and feel the bones.

The speaker from Angola finished, then raised his arms to the crowd in benediction. The bleachers thundered back their approval, then quieted in expectation.

Hiroshi Katana would now deliver the closing speech. The old man was carefully led to the microphone by an aide, then his hands guided to the edges of the podium. The aide lowered the microphone to the old man's height and tapped gently on the grillwork with his fingernail. Two great thunks reverberated within the bowl of the stadium. Katana bowed slightly to the audience and adjusted the dark glasses that covered his sightless eyes.

"I am a humble man," he began softly, speaking in lightly accented English, "and I am here to plead for peace in space." His voice gradually gained strength. "Even though I am a humble man, just as we are a humble group, our voices echo the oppressed of a war-weary planet." His voice rose even higher in volume, strong and resonant—"And we shall be heard!"

The initial burst of applause was like the snapping roll of a snare drum, then quickly grew to a thunderous drumbeat of stamping feet. Hiroshi Katana—who Lu knew could never be described as a humble man—slowly raised his arms for silence.

"This is a dangerous age we live in. There are two great powers who have the means to destroy the planet. One of them wishes peace; the other does not. Should nuclear war ever befall us again, all of us will be victims, as will our children and our children's children."

Again, a deafening crescendo of approval.

Katana signaled for silence, then touched a faint trace of scar tissue on his right cheek and said, "More than four decades ago, while standing in a courtyard with other workers waiting to donate blood to the victims of American bombing raids on our defenseless homeland, I was looking up at the clear morning sky, when the sun exploded and a wind greater than any typhoon swept the air. Around me I heard cries of pain and fear, but I could no longer see, nor will I ever see again."

All sound in the stadium suddenly ceased. Katana bowed his head slightly, then slowly raised it as if by great effort. His voice slowly gained strength, brittle and yet as hard as the tungsten steel produced in his Osaka mills.

"The dropping of an American nuclear weapon on Hiroshima was not just another thoughtless act in their inhuman war against Japan—it was a premeditated, senseless crime of the highest order, and that crime must never occur again."

The stadium exploded in a roar of anguished voices, then organized into a unified chant by delegate groups on one side of the stadium. Almost religious in its fervor, the chant was picked up, magnified, and echoed back by delegate groups on the other side.

NO . . . MORE . . . YANKEE WAR,
NO . . . MORE . . . YANKEE WAR.

Hiroshi Katana carefully groped for a bottle of mineral water and drank directly from it. The gesture was calculated, Lu realized, and he gave the old man credit for the common touch.

Katana then carefully put down the bottle and lifted his hand. The stadium fell silent as if a switch had been thrown.

"Arms control negotiations have been entered into by both East and West. Some minor progress has been made in the elimination of short-range missiles and in the reduction of long-range strategic arms. But there is much left to be accomplished. Proposals for nuclear-free space have been made in good faith by the Soviet government, but American inaction and their endless bickering about small details has put the whole planet at risk."

He paused for a few heartbeats, the stands frozen in silence. "The Americans claim that odious program is for their defense. But all the world knows that the American militarists' efforts are a thinly disguised preparation for war."

The stands howled, picking up the chant again, but Katana shook his head and the crowd quieted. He lowered his voice and, even with the amplification system, the delegates strained forward to catch the soft words, barely audible.

"I am also an uneducated man," he said. "Yes, I have some minor knowledge of how to build machines"—which Lu knew included a supertanker shipyard, a fleet of air cargo jets, an

She settled into the seat and looked at him as he slid in beside her. "You fly this route often?" she questioned.

He gracefully pulled his hands back through his hair and slipped the knot of his tie loose. "Thankfully, no. Normally when I go transatlantic I fly from wherever I am on the Continent to Paris or London and take the Concorde."

Awesome! This guy had juice. She modulated her voice. "Do you mind if I ask what your business is?"

He gave her a depreciative smile. "Not much of importance. I own a small firm in British Columbia which has developed a computer software program for specialized financial market applications. But now I spend most of my time traveling, servicing my international clientele."

"Hey . . . !" She caught herself, toning it down. "I mean, ah . . . fascinating. By coincidence, I'm in the computer software business myself—in Cambridge, Mass." Actually, she was. Sybil worked as a client representative for a computer dating service, Yuppie Love Unlimited, matching up-and-coming professionals by means of a sophisticated data base that dovetailed the multiple and diverse preferences of her clients.

He nodded. "I know Cambridge very well. I visit clients there frequently." Louis touched her lightly on the wrist. "Tell me what your computer software work actually entails."

Sybil folded her hands together, turned to him, and smiled professionally. "My computer work? Nothing very serious, really. The firm that I own uses a computer-generated data base to identify men with certain specific needs in hopes of fitting them into selected slots."

By the time Aeroflot Flight 39 was over Swedish airspace, they had finished one split of the duty-free Chablis and were working on the second.

8.

May 25

The in-flight meal had been superb, starting with caviar and a sweet Georgian champagne, then progressing to a lamb stew with pine kernels, some small unidentifiable fish cakes, black bread, and a salad. Dessert was ice cream that seemed to have a butterfat content approaching forty-five percent. The stewardess resupplied them with glass after glass of champagne.

Louis was a warm, charming man, obviously well traveled and with expensive tastes. The only personal background he had volunteered to her was that he was Canadian and had attended Berkeley in the sixties (a peace activist, he told her shyly, as if he expected a rebuke) and that he was single.

"Ever married?" Blindly following her instincts, she had asked the question almost automatically.

"Only once. She died shortly after childbirth. But she gave me a fine son."

"Oh, Louis. I'm so sorry for prying. Your boy . . . he lives in Canada?"

"With his grandfather. He's ill, but he'll be well soon and I'm working out my schedule so I can spend a great deal more of my time with him." His voice had dropped in tone, grown softer, almost distant. She glanced sideways at him and saw that his right hand had clasped his left, squeezing gently and repeatedly—almost as if he were actually holding the hand of his son.

She turned her eyes away, vaguely embarrassed, not wanting to intrude into his private thoughts, his own remembered agonies, his future hopes. He was vulnerable and therefore, in her mind, more than just a charming man—now a real human being with genuine dimension. In those few seconds she had so wanted to touch him, to tell him that his son would be all right, but those seconds quickly slipped away.

They were silent now, mental worlds apart. Curious, maybe stupid, she thought, how two strangers will reveal the most intimate aspects of their lives in the isolated cocoon of a long distance flight.

No more of this bullshit, she firmly decided. Lighten up. Life was *now;* she was trying to have some fun and she groped for a subject to break the mood of introspection that had fallen over both of them.

He had referred to his financial software business a couple of times. Just little tidbits of information that added up to an impressive bottom line. Stuff about an average of 183 percent annualized return on some kind of a computerized technical analysis of futures trading.

Not that she knew a lot about that stuff, but with a software program that told you exactly when to buy and sell pork bellies, silver, or copper, even a dummy could make a killing. Even a dummy like Eric.

She had met Eric at a PISR demonstration about six months earlier. Nice guy, good family, about her age, and they both spoke the same political language of commitment to peace. Recently, he had started trying to talk her into some kind of "meaningful relationship." She wasn't about to let him move in with her just so he could save money by splitting the rent, but she had seriously considered the possibility of marriage.

Pluses and minuses. He looked okay. Balding early, and he'd have a gut by forty, but she wasn't any princess either. So maybe he was a little retarded in the sexual liberation department, but she was working on that to their mutual satisfaction. Her real attraction to him was that he was a genuine sweetie. Sent her flowers, gave long backrubs, made a real attempt to like her friends, even scratched her cat despite his allergy. Only problem being that Eric was a financial disaster. He worked for a third-rate brokerage firm, his fourth job in three years on a career ladder that kept heading downward. The next step lower would be that of the world's first Harvard MBA mail clerk—that is, if he didn't get his act together.

Still, with a boost from her and a little luck, it could be a marriage that would work as long as she was on the helm and Eric was rowing hard with a good pair of oars.

Louis interrupted her train of thought, his mood also lightened. He passed her a glass of Armenian brandy. They clinked rims.

She turned to him, lightly resting her hand on his knee as if it were just a casual thing, the gesture of a small intimacy. "This computer program that you developed, Louis. It sounds fascinating. Tell me about it."

He had repackaged himself into the original bright wrapper—expansive, smooth, and, by now, a little drunk. "Easier to show you than to explain how it works." He reached up into the overhead bin and pulled down his briefcase.

As he thumbed the combination lock wheels, she watched casually, more because she was obsessively observant than for any other reason. First number to three, second to seven, but his hand was in the way and she couldn't catch the third number that he dialed in.

He snapped open the case. Nestled on the bottom of the case and cushioned with black foam rubber was a laptop computer. No identifying company logo but something very similar to the IBM laptop that her boss, Terry, used for field interviews with their clients.

Lu flipped up the screen and punched a couple of buttons. The screen came to life, displaying the words LOUIS E. KIM ASSOCIATES FUTURES TRADING PROGRAM.

More keystrokes. The screen cleared briefly, then was transformed into a maze of figures and symbols.

"Simple."

"Not to me," she answered, honestly perplexed.

"But it is. This computer has a built-in modem—a means of connecting it to a telephone. The client simply dials into any financial services data base, then loads the computer with all the futures prices that he's tracking. My software program computes a quality merit rating on the underlying value of the commodity, compares it to the targeted futures price, then gives both buy and sell recommendations."

"That's all there is to it?"

"Essentially. The program isn't always right, but if the client faithfully follows all the recommendations, he does very well."

Which had to be the understatement of all time. "But what does this software cost your clients, and why even sell it to them when you could just keep the program to yourself and make scads of money?"

Louis shrugged. "First of all, my clients pay me well. I restrict their total number to only fifty very wealthy investors because otherwise, a larger number would begin to disrupt the market and invalidate the underlying premise of the software program."

With a sinking feeling in her stomach she asked, "How much do your clients have to pay you?"

"Eighty thousand up front for starters. Then eight percent of their trading profits, all of which translates into a very nice bottom line." He tapped his briefcase. "But I'm beta-testing an even better version in my own trading account."

"And it outperforms the original one?"

Louis nodded. "*Outperforms* is not an adequate word. So far this year it's outperforming the standard version of the software by nearly three to one."

She felt as if she were going to melt. *Close to five hundred percent profit a year!* If Eric had the software, he could make a bundle. "Louis—I have a dear friend, a broker. Could he buy your program? I mean, maybe at a little discount as a favor to me?"

He laughed, shaking his head. "Sybil, I'd give you the program for nothing, but don't you see that it would soon turn into a disaster? Your broker friend would naturally use it to advise his clients. For the first few weeks the results would be spectacular, but as his customer base grew and the word spread, then my futures trading program would begin to dominate the market. It's like an alchemist who has devised a formula that turns lead into gold. So he unwisely decides to sell the formula to a large number of people. For a while they would all make huge profits, but eventually, the world markets would be flooded with gold and consequently, its value would tumble back to the price of lead."

As he talked, he shut off the portable computer, folded the screen down, then shut the briefcase, sliding it under the seat in front of him. Now she felt betrayed, angry. He was taking something away from her and yet it was there in his briefcase, so close, so very close.

"It's—it's really terrific," she finally said.

"Not really," he replied, leaning back. "Just a means of making a few more dollars when there are actually so many more pleasant things to do in life." Adding physical insult to financial injury, he casually placed his hand on her arm and lightly stroked it.

She removed his hand gently but firmly, turned away from him, adjusted the illumination of the reading light to its lowest level, and rockered her chair back to its reclined position.

Okay. Step by step. There had been a box of blank diskettes next to the computer in a small fitted recess, probably used for backing up data. The computer had two disk drives. Probably some new Japanese model because he would have the latest and greatest. But computers were computers. To copy the information from one diskette onto another, you put the working copy into drive A, a blank diskette into drive B, then punched a couple of keys. It took a matter of minutes to transfer the data, thus making an identical copy. She knew this from practical experience with her own computer at Yuppie Love. Went through the same procedure every night to back up data that she had generated during the day.

But she needed time. Time alone.

Louis, once mildly rebuffed, seemed to have cooled slightly. He had eased his chair back into the reclining position and was probably half asleep. The first class cabin lights were turned down, the other few passengers in the compartment immobile, pillows behind their heads, blankets pulled up around their chins. The stewardess had disappeared to that secret compartment that stewardesses always seemed to hibernate in during the latter stages of a long flight.

Ten or eleven minutes was what she needed. Better, fifteen. Sooner or later he would go to the john. Say two or three minutes peeing plus another thirty seconds while he stood there and shook his thing, like all of them did as if it were some kind of formal greeting. Then maybe a quick shave and a splash of first class Aeroflot cologne. Not enough time.

She could ask him to go get an aspirin from the stew, but that was a nonstarter. He'd use the call button and order the stew to bring it gift-wrapped.

Well, there was one other way. She edged up in her seat and looked at him carefully. His mouth was agape, his eyes closed. Occasionally, his body twitched.

Cautiously, she raised the armrest that separated them, then very very carefully lowered her head over his lap and stuck her finger down her throat. It had been a big meal.

"*Damn*, Louis! I'm sorry! I felt it coming and was trying to get past you so I could get to the toilet."

He was suddenly wide awake, at first disoriented, then realizing what had happened, furious. A large wet stain on his flannels spread from the crotch down his right thigh.

She mopped at the mess with a tiny paper cocktail napkin,

succeeding only in spreading it farther down his pants leg. "It was all the wine and champagne. Oh, Louis, I'm so terribly sorry."

"Keep your voice down, you silly bit—!" He bit the word off. Then more reasonably, "Keep your voice down, Sybil. This is damned embarrassing."

"I *said* I was sorry. Really!" she whispered. "Quick, go to the john and wash it off with soap and water. It'll dry in ten minutes."

Cursing under his breath, he stood up and headed toward the first class washrooms.

She looked carefully around. No one had noticed. Then she checked her watch. Eighteen after. She involuntarily shivered with anticipation. "This is for you, Eric baby," she whispered.

Retrieving his briefcase, she spun the first combination wheel to three, the next to seven and tried the lid. Still locked. Methodically, she moved the third wheel to each progressive setting until at nine, the lid snapped open.

She had already thought it through carefully: Power up the computer, copy the advanced software onto a blank diskette, shut down the computer, return the original diskette to its proper place, and keep the copy. It would be time-consuming and hazardous, but Louis would probably never know the program had been stolen.

Quickly, she twisted the two brass clips that held the upper compartment of the briefcase. Inside was a manila folder which she opened. She clicked on the reading light to its lowest setting and glanced at her watch. Twenty after.

Damn! No floppy diskette in the folder, but she still rifled through the contents. Nothing important in the first packet, which was bound with an elastic band: only charter brochures for two large sailboats, the *Pampero* out of Antigua and the *Panama Red* out of St. Thomas, Virgin Islands. "Sail South to the Sun," seemed to be the theme.

The other packet held a passport and a stack of airline tickets. Passport first. Canadian citizen—Louis Kim—engineer—blah, blah. Smudged entry stamps from all over the world.

The tickets next, a bundle of them, all with the passenger's name blank, all the flight dates open. Gander to Montreal, Montreal to Antigua, Antigua to Guadeloupe, then, oddly, a ticket from Bermuda back to Helsinki. Nothing else.

Frantically, she groped around in the compartment, but it was empty. The *shit!* He had lied to her about the advanced software.

She glanced at her watch again. Twenty after, two minutes gone. It had to be here. "We're talking about our future, kid," she chanted under her breath. Okay. Slow down. Let's say the diskette actually exists. It's valuable. So logically, it has its own compartment away from dust and dirt that could damage it.

Desperately, she moved her hand around against the back of the foldout compartment, pressing against the fabric-lined surface, feeling it yield a little as if it were hollow—possibly a false compartment. Pressed harder along the sides and heard a small metallic click, then another. The secret compartment lid flicked open.

Bingo! One floppy diskette, housed in its own protective cover and a manila envelope.

The envelope held three passports, two of them with a photo of Louis Kim, except that wasn't the name given and they weren't Canadian. Louis Sing (Malaysia) and Lu Duc Lee (Singapore). The third passport was also Singaporian, issued in the name of Sam Lee. The photograph was that of a young boy; close enough in features to be Louis's son.

Also bundles of thousand-dollar traveler's checks, unmarked, with no countersignatures filled in. She fluttered her fingers through just one stack. At least twenty thousand bucks per stack, and there were six more stacks. God! Here was a guy who was serious about not leaving home without it.

How much time had gone by? Another minute but it seemed like an hour. She checked the aisle but it was clear, the door to the toilet room still displaying the Occupied sign.

She removed the diskette from its compartment, then lifted the screen of the computer to its tilt-up position. On the right-hand side she found a switch and flicked it. The screen came alive.

Hurriedly, she slipped the diskette into drive A, then selected a blank diskette from its box and inserted it in drive B. A quick glance at her watch. Four minutes elapsed. Maybe enough time left, maybe not.

The screen looked fairly standard, a blinking cursor set to the right of the A PROMPT. Carefully, she pecked in the command: COPY A:*.* B: and hit the return key, holding her breath.

The screen flashed again, the disk drives started to whir. A message blinked onto the screen:

FILE COPYING IN PROGRESS. PLEASE WAIT.

God, it worked, but why in hell had she stupidly wasted so much time? Five minutes already gone. She peered down the aisle. The washroom still displayed the Occupied sign.

The little computer ground through its routine, dumb to her terror, dumb to time wasting away, dumb, dumb, dumb, just doing its own dumb thing in its own dumb sweet time.

The computer finally heaved a polite sigh and stopped whirring. The screen flashed a final message:

TWO PROTECTED FILE(S) COPIED. PASSWORD(S) REQUIRED.

FILE(S) INVENTORY:
FILE NAME: PHASE ONE
FILE NAME: PHASE TWO

Some early warning instinct caused her to look up. Louis was standing midway between the rest room and her seat, flirting with the stewardess, facing in Sybil's direction but obviously distracted by the conversation.

She snatched the copied diskette out of drive B and thrust it into the pocket of the seat in front of her. Then extracted the original diskette from drive A and stuffed it back into the hidden compartment, slammed the briefcase lid closed, and snapped the hasps shut. She glanced up again. He was no more than five rows of seats away, moving leisurely toward her, relaxed, smiling. She shoved the briefcase under the seat in front of his, much the way she had found it.

Sitting down, he said, "I sponged off my pants. Not quite dry, but they will be by the time we land. I'll change into clean ones at the airport once we've cleared customs. You're forgiven." He reached across and patted her knee. She didn't respond and he turned to her. "You don't look at all well," he said, concerned.

"Headache and an upset tummy. I'm no good at drinking." She found it hard to look at him. Involuntarily, a tremor ran through her body.

"I think you've taken a chill, Sybil."

She shook her head. "I'll be all right, Louis. Really."

"Tell you what. We'll stay at a hotel I know. They have a hot tub. Sure cure for a cold. What do you think?"

Not responding, she gave him a weak squeeze of her hand and lay back, eyes closed, feigning sleep. She listened to the hushed rumble of the engines, the occasional footsteps of people passing down the aisle, the hiss of the air-conditioning, now realizing that she had done an incredibly stupid and dangerous thing.

What was she really dealing with now? Louis would probably never miss the copied diskette. She would give it to Eric along with twelve thousand dollars that she had in a savings account but demand that he mustn't get greedy because if he did, the word would get out and Louis would come looking. But deep down inside she was beginning to suspect that all Louis's talk about his fantastic financial software was some sort of cover. Drug dealing maybe, or illegal currency transactions. Whatever it was, Louis was potentially dangerous and she would have to move very cautiously.

She opened her eyes to just a slit, looking at the seat pocket in front of her. She couldn't see the diskette but she could feel its presence just as if it were radiating a tremendous heat. She thought about leaving it when deplaning, then running back to the plane to claim it, but realized that she couldn't. As soon as the passengers deplaned in Gander, the clean-up crews would start servicing the aircraft and some damned efficient garbage gatherer would find it and turn it in to the flight crew. And for damn sure they'd identify the passenger who sat in that seat and proudly bring it to Louis while they waited for their onward flight to Montreal.

No way. She had to personally carry it off the plane. No problem if she could just somehow transfer it to her garment bag, but that wasn't a real possibility. Hide it under her dress? She wore just a flimsy white summer frock, and the stiff black diskette would stand out in the hard lighting of the terminal. Which left just one alternative. She would have to carry it off the plane in the folds of an in-flight magazine, then transfer it to her garment bag while Louis was changing into clean pants.

Suddenly, she realized that he had his hand on her arm, shaking it. With his touch her whole body tensed, her heart triphammering.

"Easy, Sybil," he said. "I didn't realize you were asleep. We're only about half an hour out from Gander. I thought you might want to refresh yourself."

Now. She had to implement the plan. "Good idea." She bent down, her body hiding her movements, slid her hand into the pocket and found the diskette, then shuffled it between the pages of a glossy magazine.

He stood up to let her pass. "*Soviet Life?*" He nodded at the magazine. "My God. You read that trash?"

She shrugged, giving him a limp smile. "I always read something when I sit on the can. It helps me to—y'know."

He smiled broadly back at her and put his face close to hers, pecking her cheek.

She headed up the aisle toward the first class washrooms. Before she got there, an older woman edged into the aisle, blocking Sybil's way to the washroom.

The woman, hitching up her girdle, waddled wearily up the aisle, then slid into the washroom on the right. The sign on the other indicated that it was already occupied.

She stood there, tapping her foot in agitation. Two minutes passed. Damn! How long would these people take? She looked back toward Louis's seat. He was gone! And then his head reappeared. He had been bent over, and she immediately sensed why.

She half ran back down the aisle. He had the briefcase in his lap, starting to open it. He looked up. "Feeling better?"

"Not yet. Both of the washrooms are occupied. I'll go back to the tourist class section." She gave him a weak smile.

He just nodded, resting his hands, palms down, on the top of the briefcase, waiting for her to leave.

She headed aft, into the tourist compartment, adrenaline pumping through her veins, kicking her reflexes into hyperdrive. He would find out for damn sure! Something out of order, something not replaced in its exact position. She had made a mess of it, and he would confront her when she came back to her seat. She was sure of that.

She was looking for Di (as in *Princess*), Kauckins (with a *K*) and spotted her halfway back, curled up across three seats, asleep. Sybil was sure that Louis wouldn't be able to see Kauckins's sleeping form and feigned a one-sided routine of old friends reunited, chums forever.

Waving her hand at the sleeping form, Sybil laughed aloud in delight, calling her name, mouthing an inane stream of senseless chatter. Kauckins frowned, face puffy with sleep, pulled the blanket up over her face, and mumbled something in a muffled voice about being left the hell alone, *dammit*. Still smiling, Sybil bent over her. "Listen up, airhead!" she whispered.

Kauckins didn't respond except for a moan, and Sybil ripped the blanket from around her face and savagely pinched Kauckins's cheek. Kauckins came fully awake, her eyes startled. "Hey!"

"The john," Sybil whispered. "I'm going there. I'll leave a computer diskette stuffed in the tissue box. You follow in after me. Hide it in your purse but make sure you don't bend it. When the plane lands, take the diskette through customs as if it were your own. I'll collect it from you in the baggage claim area."

"Why . . . ?"

"I'm with the Secret Service, airhead. Top confidential agent. Do as I say and you'll be on prime time, getting a medal from the President."

Kauckins's face brightened. "Really, I mean *really*?" Then frowned. "You're kidding?"

"We're dealing with a class-one emergency! Just *do it!*"

Sybil backed off and smiled. "Hey, good seeing you again," her voice overly loud, then pivoted on her Reeboks and made her way toward the rest room.

Once inside, she sat down on the john, her thoughts scrambled. She was winging it, taking chances, but if Louis found anything amiss, he'd probably search her. The airhead was her only chance.

She finished, then swiped some water across her face—which she realized was pale as pizza dough—kneaded her skin to restore some color to it, and finally stuffed the diskette deeply into the tissue box. She took a final look at the mirror—which assured her, even allowing for jet lag, that she was not the fairest of them all—and unlocked the door.

Kauckins was there, hovering. "This better be good, lady," she said, brushing by Sybil and pulling the door closed behind her.

Once he had watched Sybil traipse down the aisle, chatter with the redhead, and finally enter the rest room, Lu considered the immediate future. First he had to retrieve the Louis Kim passport and a few traveler's checks. No concern about the passport because he had used it before. The Documents Section at Center always did impeccable work.

Bending down, he started to set the combination lock to its opening position but suddenly realized that the numbers were already correctly dialed in, not the way that he had left them. He snapped open the hasps and frantically sorted through the contents of his briefcase, finally opening the false compartment. The floppy disk was in its folder but inserted backward and the files were out of sequence.

A sense of panic engulfed him. It had started with what he thought would be a pleasant overnight diversion in Montreal. He liked her, really did in the way that he liked a stray cat that would stalk up to him and rub its fur against his leg in return for a careless caress.

Of course he had overplayed it a bit. Had tried to impress her to make the conquest that much easier, but those simple lies had compounded into a disaster.

And now he wasn't sure of anything except that he had been very stupid, that he had betrayed himself and that he could already foresee the sure and messy outcome of his indiscretion. It also meant that he had to change his travel plans. He could not dare enter Canada, which meant that he would have to fly onward to Cuba, change planes there for Mexico, then make, through several connecting flights, his sweaty and time-consuming way to Antigua.

His mind was hazy, a combination of jet lag, lack of sleep, and alcohol. Possibly she was with some intelligence agency? Initially, he discounted the idea. A thief, then? He double-checked the traveler's checks. No sign that any of them were missing, although she might have slipped out a few.

Or was she just curious? The American woman's well-known compulsion to snoop into the background of a potential lover. Just plain curiosity perhaps, but that was what had killed untold generations of cats.

Then it came to him in a flash of absolute clarity. Someone in a Western intelligence service had photographed him at the Peace in Space rally—probably just a random shot—but those bastards had a compulsion to create files on all people even remotely associated with the left wing of the peace movement. Some lower-level clerk had routinely run a computer match with existing files and photographs, probably double-checked Finnish immigration records, and came up with his name and identity.

The Excalibur mission wasn't compromised because it was yet barely in motion. No, he reasoned, it was just bad luck. But they had sicced Sybil on him to learn what she could before arresting him on Canadian soil. Which meant that the CIA had a hand in the operation.

The more he thought of it, the more it made sense. It had been cleverly and yet casually done; he had to give them that much credit. She had known when she approached him in the passenger lounge who he was and what he was.

He made his decision quickly. Withdrawing his KGB identity card and pocketing it, he snapped the hasps shut and twirled the combination locks. He stood up and put the briefcase in the overhead bin on the opposite side of the aisle and then turned toward the cockpit.

He was almost to the cockpit door when the stewardess ambushed him from the first class galley.

"The door is locked," she said politely in English. "Please return to your seat. We will be landing in fifteen minutes."

He lifted the card and held it in front of her face. "I want to see the aircraft commander—*now!*" he said in Russian. "Not later, not in thirty seconds, but *now!*"

Her face went pale, but she nodded, ducked back into the galley, and picked up the intercom phone. A few seconds later the lock on the door buzzed and Lu entered the cockpit, latching the door behind him.

Both the flight engineer and navigator were bent over their desks, obviously briefed by the captain and not wanting to get involved unless commanded to.

Lu held up the magical card to the officer in the left seat. He was an older man, hair graying but firm-featured and with classical high Russian cheekbones, hair perhaps a few millimeters longer than regulations normally permitted. The pilot looked at the card and nodded as if he were unimpressed. He turned back and fiddled with some knobs on the radio.

"You have a passenger in first class," Lu said. "An American woman by the name of Sybil Ford. She wishes to defect to Cuba. How will you handle that situation?"

The pilot nodded to the copilot to take over, loosened his harness, and turned to face Lu. "It would be normal for her to disembark, make a statement to the authorities, and then reboard. We will, of course, be honored to have her as a passenger provided that—ah—certain agencies in our homeland pay for her fare."

Lu was close to exasperation. "You don't quite grasp the circumstances, Comrade Captain. The woman is shy. She wants no publicity, no contact with the Canadian authorities. Her desire is to simply remain onboard the aircraft during our refueling stop in Gander, then proceed on to Cuba. I was also scheduled to disembark this aircraft at Gander, but I must now submit to duty and accompany her. You will arrange it."

The copilot had his headphones clamped over his ears, imitating one of the troika of monkeys who saw, spoke, and heard no evil. Both the flight engineer and the navigator had their faces buried in their logs, seeing no evil. The captain glanced around the cockpit and, sensing no support, capitulated by speaking no evil. "It will be arranged," he said wearily.

She was already in her seat when he got back to the first class cabin. There was some color in her cheeks, but her expression was controlled and noncommittal with no hint of welcome in it.

He pulled his briefcase from the overhead compartment and then slumped down in the seat beside her. "We land in five minutes. Be good to stretch our legs on Canadian soil."

"You were up in the cockpit?"

"Of course. I just asked for the grand tour. Quite amazing place with all the bells, whistles, and flashing lights." He slid it in sideways almost as an afterthought. "Did you actually think that you would get away with it?"

"I didn't mean . . ." Her voice trailed off.

"Didn't mean *what*?"

"But I didn't take anything. Please, Louis . . ."

She started to get up, but he grabbed her arm and brutally squeezed it, making her gasp. "*Sit!*" he hissed in her ear. "You will sit and say *nothing* and do *nothing* unless I tell you to. Understood?"

Tears were streaking down her cheeks, eyes closed in pain. She nodded dumbly, defeated.

With his free hand he pulled an inflight blanket from the overhead rack and spread it over both of them as though to protect them from the chill of the air-conditioning.

He eased his grip slowly. "You have one choice, Sybil. Only one. You will sit by me quietly while the rest of the passengers disembark. After refueling we will continue on together to Cuba. You will be treated well. No harm will come to you as long as you give us the information that we require. In a few years you'll be released in one of the normal exchanges."

Her eyes opened wide, staring at him like a trapped animal, her expression reflecting both hate and fear. He slowly but inexorably increased the grip on her arm. "Don't," he said in a low, intense voice. "This is a Soviet aircraft manned by a loyal Soviet crew. Don't make this more difficult than it is."

A tremor passed through her body, and then she drooped back against her seat, all fight seemingly gone from her.

The IL-62 was on final descent now, the headlands of Gander flashing past under the wings, defined by the isolated patterns of scattered lights of individual homes and villages. Then, as the aircraft rolled onto final heading, they swept over the strobing approach lights.

He didn't think he'd need it, but he couldn't leave anything to chance. The wheels thumped down, the engines blasting into reverse thrust, brakes squealing. She was turned away from him, her face pressed against the window, watching the lights of the terminal blur pass in the night mist.

He lifted his briefcase from the aisle and reversed it, feeling for the bottom hinge pin. The briefcase was marked with the Louis Vuitton logo, but it had been made to exacting specifications by Russian craftsmen in Serpukhov, only a few hours south of Moscow. The only variance in its design was in the way the two halves of the briefcase hinged together. The Russian version had plates of brass screwed on either side of the division, meeting together at the hinge point in rounded ferrels, these joined by a long, continuous pin. Although an experienced customs officer would not notice it, nor would it register as anything other than part of the hinge mechanism on being passed through an X-ray machine, the pin itself was quite unusual. It was made of titanium, three millimeters in diameter, about half as long as the length of the briefcase and hollow-tipped with a spring-loaded needle that was released when a pressure in excess of three kilograms was imposed on the pin's nose.

Lu withdrew the pin and gingerly placed it, tip down, in his inner suit coat pocket.

There were the usual bumps and grinds as the aircraft slowed to a halt. Then the engines spooled up again as the IL-62 wheeled into a taxiway and trundled toward the terminal.

"Can we get off for a while?" she pleaded. "Someone's expecting me in Montreal and I have to call him. You can listen in on the conversation."

"Don't be stupid. How many of your associates are in there, waiting for me? CIA, Royal Canadian Mounted, MI5. *Who?*"

"*Nobody,* Louis. Really, I can explain, you have to let me explain, please. And you have to let me go. You can't keep me here against my will."

"Shut *up!* This is a Soviet aircraft, and it is therefore sovereign territory of the Soviet Union. The entire Canadian Armed Forces could be waiting for us and they still wouldn't be able to legally board this plane."

The aircraft had braked to a stop, the engines winding down, door depressurized and opening, overhead lights flaring up, background music of balalaikas strumming, and a throaty woman singing a Russian ballad.

He held her arm tightly beneath the blanket that covered them to their chests, both of them vibrating with tension.

The bulk of the Russian sailors on board herded through first class, followed by the remaining passengers, but some holdup at the passenger exit door temporarily clogged the aisle, each passenger reverting to an impatient queue shuffle, gaining or losing millimeters of territorial space as they uselessly checked their watches and adjusted their clothing.

Lu scanned the remaining faces, trying to catalog them. Nothing to worry about—until he saw the redhead bobbing around at the end of the line.

Under the cover of the blanket he slipped the titanium pin from his pocket and shifted it in his grasp until the pointed end was surrounded by his fingertips. Then moved it against her ribs, counting down two below the strap of her bra. He pressed the point firmly but carefully in the fleshy part between her ribs.

"Sybil," he said gently. "With your training you know what this is. Don't think about it. Close your eyes and relax. More than anything in the world, I don't want to hurt you. Don't force me to."

By small, almost immeasurable increments, she eased her body, the tension in her facial muscles going slack.

Lu relaxed his grip on the rod slightly, backing off on the pressure. It would be all right. The redhead was the last one in line, and she had passed by them, her glance overly casual and obviously guarded.

And suddenly Sybil exploded, thrusting herself forward, then twisting, trying to scramble past him. He felt the needle plunge into her, driven in deeply by the weight of her body slamming against it.

Deep inside her, somewhere in the vicinity of the left ventricle, the MPTP neurotoxin spurted from the tip of the hollow needle and instantly paralyzed her heart. She died shuddering in his arms within three seconds.

He instantly realized what had happened, knew the redhead had heard the commotion and would turn back. Damn! He should have realized before that they were working as a team. His hands sought Sybil's back, patting it, then stroking her neck. The redhead was just on the edge of his vision, asking something.

He looked up and shook his head. "She's still airsick," he said, the only thing that he could think of.

The redhead looked dubious, but before she could speak, the stewardess grabbed her arm and propelled her toward the exit.

He held her for a long time, wishing that the firm pressure of her breasts against him would throb with life, but she was still. It was such a waste.

Di Kauckins hovered near the baggage checkout area. For half an hour and then three quarters. The in-transit passengers for Cuba reluctantly started to straggle out toward the tarmac, toting plastic carry-on bags bulging with Beefeater and Johnnie Walker.

An engine spooled up, then another. Brakes squealed and the windows of the terminal vibrated with jet blast.

Di Kauckins frantically grabbed a pair of Mounties, trying to explain something that even she didn't understand. A man in plain clothes showed up within two minutes.

The men shrugged at each other as they followed the red-head to the window and watched the running and anticollision lights of the Aeroflot flight blur in the light fog, then disappear as the airliner thundered down the runway. They opened the door to the ramp and listened as the sound of the engines faded. There was a lingering smell of burned kerosene exhaust gas which finally washed away in the wet Labrador wind.

Sybil Ford's diskette was forwarded first to Toronto, then to Ottawa. A scrambled telex was transmitted. Eighteen hours later a polite call was received in Ottawa and two days following that the diskette was taken south to Langley, Virginia, in a sealed briefcase handcuffed to the courier's wrist.

9.

July 7

Stackhill pushed the manila envelope across the cockpit table toward Bracken, then leaned back against the coaming, capped teeth unnaturally white behind the thin wedge of his lips. "An attractive alternative," he said.

Legal-size manila envelopes had always created the same emotion in Bracken as had unopened telegrams. He hesitated and Stackhill bent forward, pushing it closer to Bracken as if he were encouraging a little kid to pick up forbidden candy. "Go ahead," he goaded. "Enjoy."

Slitting the flap with his fingernail, Bracken spilled out the contents. Nice paper. Well engraved with little confetti dots of color sprinkled over the crisp notes. The numbers indicated that each note was valid tender in the amount of one thousand U.S. dollars, and there were a lot of them.

"Thirty thousand," Stackhill said with the reverence that a village priest reserves for discussing matters of faith and morals. He poured some more Rémy Martin for himself and sipped it appreciatively, awaiting a reaction.

Bracken sat for a long time, looking at the pile of American Express traveler's checks. Neither the sample signature lines nor the endorsements lines were filled in. He flopped a book of them over and smeared the numbers on the left-hand side with a wetted finger. The ink smudged, just like it was supposed to. Soluble ink is supposed to be very difficult to print, and smearing it is a method of testing for forgeries, something that Bracken felt that Stackhill was eminently capable of.

"They're real enough," Stackhill said, as if offended. "And they're yours, provided . . ." He swirled the cognac around in the snifter, inspecting its color, just as they taught you to do in *Playboy*'s wine and spirits column.

The *Pampero* rolled easily in the slight beam swell of the outer harbor. Bracken leaned back, partially closing his eyes, listening to the small complaints that the old schooner made. A halyard aloft slatted lazily against the mast, and the topping lift creaked through a dry block. *Old wooden boat,* the sounds whispered.

"What's the money for?" he asked Stackhill, pushing the traveler's checks back to the no-man's land at the center of the table.

Even in the light trade winds Stackhill's silvered hair lay down in razor-cut perfection. His nose was a shade too broad, and the muscle tone, despite the face job, sagged a little around the eyes, but the overall effect would always be good for another fifty thousand on his margin account.

"Charter money for a couple of friends of mine," he answered, "plus enough left over to solve most of your problems."

"How much left over?" Bracken did some addition in his head. Twelve thousand for the Antigua Slipways yard bill, four thousand for back crew wages. And God knew how much to spread negotiable oil on troubled legal waters.

"This is just the down payment. When it's all over, another twenty thousand free and clear." He bent down and rummaged around in his Gucci attaché case with the paisley lining and the nifty red and green stripes. Colored tongues of folders lapped over their individual compartments. He yanked on one and slid the folder across the varnished teak.

"Moore, Spiegal, and Hinstock," he groaned with mock sympathy. "You can really pick a winner. My legal people tell me that the Cramer woman didn't have a case to begin with. But oh, no, you had to pick these assholes. You got what you paid for."

The folder duplicated everything that Bracken had squirreled away in the ship's safe. The complete file and then some: the U.S. Coast Guard report of the accident, the Cramer woman's complaint, court record, and judgment, more Coast Guard stuff, and a photocopied stack of unpaid legal bills.

Sweet Jean and Pam, Stackhill's current playmate, were down below in the salon playing backgammon. The rattle of the dice punctuated their laughter. Bracken knew that Stackhill would have briefed his toy to keep Sweet Jean below until the negotiations were over.

"How did you get these?" Bracken asked, trying to keep it cool. He lit a cigarette, shielding the lighter against the soft evening wind.

Stackhill propped up a leg on the cockpit cushions and formed a steeple with his fingers.

"Lawyers talk to lawyers. I have one of the best. He went down to Newport and got the case files in return for paying off half of what you owe them." He looked up, forehead creased and eyebrows raised. "You're in good hands now." As if he were God or Allstate.

Voices carried across the water of Shirley Heights. A woman singing a little off key. People laughing. Probably a party on the little plumb-stemmed English cutter that lay close inshore. From the cliff where the Inn clung to damp red soil of English Harbour, Antigua, Bracken could hear the tinny thump of a steel band. The night air swaddled the bay in damp cotton batting, and Bracken found himself sweating.

Stackhill was right about Moore, Spiegal, and Hinstock. His involvement with that firm had been a monumental fuckup from disastrous beginning to inconclusive finish.

Bracken watched Stackhill's eyes carefully, trying to read them. "How illegal is it?"

Stackhill picked up Bracken's Dunhill lighter and lit a menthol cigarette. Snapping it closed, he turned it over and over, allowing the fluted surfaces to reflect light from the cockpit oil lamp. "It depends on whose laws you're talking about."

Penny had given him the Dunhill sixteen years before on his birthday. Bracken knew that the lighter cost more than he brought in during a winter month's profits from charter flight operations. Recycled allowance from her daddy.

He examined the lighter, rolling it over in his hand, feeling the slippery gold with his fingers, then leaned down to kiss her upturned face. Even in February she smelled like spring wind.

He held it up to the winter's muted sun that poured through the kitchen window, watching the fluted surfaces catch the golden light.

"It's very handsome," he said. Almost unconsciously, he calculated what he could hock it for.

"So are you, old fart of mine," she whispered, and pecked him, then drew a pair of tickets out of her apron pocket. "Additional pearls lovingly cast before my favorite swine." She offered them up to him for approval. Boston Symphony. Solid Bach, Concertos for Harpsichord and Orchestra. It would be wonderful, he thought, like touching the face of civilization again. "You know I can't go," he finally said.

She jammed her hands deep into her apron pockets, something between anger and frustration on her face. "You know *damn* well you can, John. You haven't booked a charter flight in ten days. We have to get out of here, or we'll both be tearing each other's throats out by April." She kept her gray eyes leveled, not blinking.

Beyond the curtained window stretched the fields, smothered in a frozen sea of white. The winter days of New Hampshire stretch in an unbroken chain, shackling October to May. Bracken loved the place for its silent beauty, but sometimes the silent bit got too loud for him to think.

"I can't go," he repeated, his back turned to her, staring at the ridges of the White Mountains, jagged on the eastern horizon. "If I'm in business to charter airplanes, then I've got to be available. People count on me." His breath produced flattened globs of condensation on the pane, then laced into a tracery of frost. A door slammed behind him, and he heard her climbing the back stairs to the bedroom.

She left in the station wagon the following morning after dryly kissing him. She gave him a college classmate's number on Cape Cod and said that he could still fly down on Friday afternoon and she would meet him at Logan. Which they both knew wouldn't happen.

One week became another, then stretched into two months. During that winter Bracken kept the runway plowed and the hangar warm. As a peace offering he built her a four-poster from mahogany, carving crude grape leaves into the rich red wood.

She came back in late March, during mud season, and they made love for two days on the four-poster and she said that she had been lonely and miserable and sad because it hadn't been right without him. Dishes stacked up on the carpet and they left the phone off the hook. The timing was right, and yet she didn't conceive. The spring came early and there was a rush of business. They vowed to each other that they were still in love.

The second winter was harder. Waves of arctic cold fronts dashed over New England, leaving the countryside smothered with white foam set rigid by the cold. The storms broke, one by one, against the granite outcroppings of the White Mountains, and the countryside was locked in silence once more.

The money was running out. Bracken was two months overdue on his note for the Aztec. The lease on the airfield had gone four months without a payment and the aviation gas man would no longer cometh, pending payment of a twelve-hundred-dollar bill.

He quit plowing the runway and set the thermostat in the hangar back to thirty-five. For lack of anything better to do, Bracken rebuilt a Lycoming 0-200 engine on the kitchen floor. Penny left this time without tears, and it wasn't until June that she returned, silent and abstract. She set up a potter's wheel in the toolshed and spun out lumpy shapes of clay through four strained summer months, during which little love or talk passed between them.

The third and last winter broke both their relationship and his business. She talked one evening about a physician in Boston who was older but sweet. Sweet was the exact word that she had used. He had two children, was widowed, and he needed her. And that she would always love Bracken, but their relationship was over because it could never work.

Bracken tried to memorize her words as she spoke them, his head bent down, turning a ratchet over and over in his hands, his vision blurring. After she finished, he dropped the wrench into the toolbox and told her, inanely, that the wrench was busted. But that it had a lifetime guarantee. He then walked out of the kitchen and down the drifted runway, watching the shining mountains, which in February become opal as the twilight fades.

She must have been packed already. He heard the station wagon start but didn't turn. The tears were freezing on his cheeks, which is a painful thing in February on the edge of the White Mountains.

She pulled away and from the corner of his eye he could see the white plume of exhaust trailing down the lane, the car hidden by snowdrifts.

Ratchet wrenches might come with a lifetime guarantee. Love, he realized, did not.

He sold what was left of the business that summer, breaking even on the aircraft and making some on the land, which a local developer thought he could convert into a fly-in condo. Bracken sent Penny half the proceeds. The check was returned uncashed through her lawyer three weeks later without any written note. Bracken packed his tools in *The Thing* and headed for the Maine coast.

His dad was still living then. He had a place on a hill overlooking Boothbay Harbor. Bracken stretched out the days, talking about women, Vietnam, flying, and fishing. He avoided speculating about the future.

"So watcha think ya gonna do with the rest of ya life?" his father finally asked, not as if he were concerned—just curious. Bracken said maybe fishing on the banks like they had done together when he was a kid. It took his father two days of reflection before he said, "Nope, that ain't no good." He turned his hands over, working the joints, which were swollen and stiff, the raised blue veins a roadmap of his life. "Nope," he repeated, "that ain't no good atall."

Bracken knew the old man was right. Fishing wasn't a one-man business anymore, and the tax laws, the high cost of interest, and depleted fish populations were driving the small operators out of business. But sitting up there on the porch, some measure of peace returned, and it was partly his father's steady patience and partly the sea that lay shimmering in the haze to the east. Bracken had read somewhere that the analysis of spinal fluid conformed exactly to the chemical composition of seawater. So we are a part of it and somehow, he knew, that was where he had to return.

During that August he sailed his father's old Friendship sloop, working up the coast through foggy mornings and sunlit afternoons, feeling the southwest wind on his face and the taste of spray on his lips. He spent his nights on board, lying on the dew-soaked deck, watching stars wheel and listening to the waves forever grinding down the rocky ledges into sand.

By September the sun was in equinox, sliding south beyond the equator. Bracken loaded the pickup and came back up to the porch. The maples were turning early, the lawn littered in magenta and gold. The land wind smelled of cider pressings and burnt leaves.

The old man said, "Don't get one of them plastic things. Buy somethin' solid like they build down in Kennebunkport. And keep rock salt in the bilges. Stays the rot, ya see."

He handed Bracken a book, its cover jacketed in canvas, laced in tarred marline. "Just somethin' to read," his father said.

Bracken had never been very good at saying good-bye. He walked down through the carpet of dusty leaves, their rustling a mimic of the wind. He paused before getting into the truck and turned back. His father had settled into the bentwood chair, face otherwise expressionless but a smile formed in the corners of his mouth. He lifted his pipe as sort of a parting wave—nothing too committal, the way Mainers are. That was the last Bracken ever saw of his father, because he died the next spring.

That night Bracken untied the marline and opened the book while lying across a lumpy bed in a cheap motel room. The TV next door was turned up too loud, and he could hear the sounds of people wrestling on a bed and of a toilet flushing somewhere on the floor above him.

It was a journal of his father's passage aboard a Finnish grain ship, one of the last commercial voyages ever made under sail. He had shipped as a fore topman with a crew of eighteen other boys. The mate was twenty-one and the master on the shy side of thirty. It took them two hundred and twenty-eight days from Sydney to the port of Boston. The entries were terse and spoke of rotten pork and sodden bunks, of men lost and headlands weathered. There was mention of a woman in Valparaiso, but the journal spoke no evil of the ship or the sea. Only that it was hard but somehow fair. The last entry was penned in fresh ink, written in the shaky copperplate script of his father. It read:

> There's a schooner in the offing,
> her topsails shot with fire
> And my heart has gone aboard her
> for the Islands of Desire.

Bracken moved to the window. The sash had been sealed with tape, then painted over, the enamel checked and weathered. He felt stifled, almost claustrophobic. Using his penknife, he slit the seams and levered the sash open.

A stiff, wet northeaster was setting in, whipping the dead leaves into whirling dervishes. Below in the street a neon sign cast sick hues of coral and lime on the wet pavement, advertising factory outlet shoes. But beyond the reach of the harbor, the Monhegan Island light winked in the solitary darkness of the Gulf of Maine, a landfall for homeward-bound sailors for over two centuries. And an offing for those outward bound.

The frigate bird must have spanned over five feet. It rose in the first shards of morning sunlight, spiraling upward. Never moving a wing, it circled higher, blood-black but with golden light radiating from its swept wings, impervious to gravity, climbing toward the gray dome of the sky. Where the crest of the hill met the trade winds the frigate banked east, rising even faster through the chrome spokes of dawn.

Distracted, Bracken watched until the frigate was swallowed up by the clouds. A hard gust of wind pummeled the rigging, setting up a dull moan. It was overcast, and rain would come before noon. Leaning back against the standing rigging, Bracken absently sipped the cold dregs of coffee, eyes searching for the frigate. But it was gone, wherever frigate birds go at sunrise in the latitudes south of Cancer and north of Capricorn.

The *Pampero* surged against her anchor chain, fetched up hard, and came about on the other tack. He estimated that the wind was over thirty out in the channel and he could see the whitehorses kicking up, Guadeloupe just a thin, indefinite lump on the horizon.

Most of the other large charter yachts were tied up stern-to in the inner harbor with shore power plugged in and air conditioners switched on. Only two small cruising yachts shared the outer harbor with the *Pampero*, probably to save the expense of dockage and avoid the stifling atmosphere of the marina that, like all other marinas, were the most expensive slums in the world.

The water pump cycled below decks. The galley hatch cranked open and a hand appeared. Bracken passed his mug down, and it came up thirty seconds later filled with a muddy mixture of instant coffee and canned milk. Walrus appeared a minute later in the fo'c'sle hatch, mug slopping ink-black tea on the deck. He pulled himself up overhand on the hatch coaming and planted a foot on the deck; then levered himself up by an elbow and squatted down on his haunches, blowing across the rim of the cup. He was medium-short and inclined to be heavy around the gut. But his chest was full and his arms corded. He scratched at the ample mat of hair on his chest, swigged the tea, and looked aloft as if to find fault in the set of a nonexistent topgallant.

"Another shitty day in paradise, skip," he said, looking seaward. No answer required. He passed a wrist across his mustache and ran his fingers through ginger ringlets of hair, the completion of his grooming for the day.

Walrus was the *Pampero*'s first mate. Had been for seven years, since Bracken had bought the leaking old schooner for thirty thousand dollars and a wistful promissory note of more to come. Walrus had shown up on the dock in Essex that first winter with a

seabag slung over his shoulder. He had stood on the quay, looking over the rig and the decks, frowning.

"You hiring?" he had asked. Bracken had merely nodded.
Walrus then swung aboard over the lifelines, looked around, and
settled into the port berth of the fo'c'sle. He had never asked
Bracken what the wages would be, when he would get paid,
whether there was health insurance, a dental plan, or even if the
Pampero was likely to stay afloat.

Walrus turned out at five the following morning and proceeded to ream out the engine room, either reconditioning or
consigning rusted tools and corroded fittings to the shipyard's
dumpster. Once he finished that project, he had resewn all the
seams of the working sails, worked out the kinks in the plumbing
of the bilge pump, and rejuvenated two frozen sheet winches.
Bracken paid Walrus when there was anything left over, and
Walrus accepted his wages without comment or accounting.

Bracken secretly reckoned that Walrus was a reincarnation of
Melville's Billy Budd. He could serve and splice and hand and
reef. He kept to himself, rarely went ashore, played the squeeze
box, and sang sea chanties in a whiskey baritone. Walrus con-
ceded that ladies were something to *do* when you weren't sailing.
He drank only tea, Mount Gay rum, and Heineken beer.

Without looking aft to see whether Stackhill or his toy were
in the cockpit, Walrus hooked one leg over the fore staysail stay,
wrapped a fist around the wire rope above the sail's snap shack-
les, and urinated to leeward. There was a head in the fo'c'sle, but
it was Walrus's way of stating that he didn't give a damn for
charter guests and that this was his prerogative as a seaman: a
declaration of territory that was his—the foredeck. Or perhaps
just disdain for mechanical toilets when all you had to do was to
piss into the vast blue bowl of the Caribbean. Which never required flushing.

"Loop the loop to Guadeloupe?" he asked, shaking out the
last drops, tucking it into his pants, then looking out at the
whitehorses romping down the trades beyond the harbor entrance.

Bracken nodded. "You and the boys bend on the smaller jib
and we'll tuck in a single reef in the main after breakfast."

"Stackhill up yet?" He swirled the tea in his mug, depositing
bits of leaves on the perimeter of the rim. He squinted at them,
probably trying to read the portents of an uncertain future.

"No. He and I had a late night. He has a proposition."

Walrus turned to look at Bracken. His face was black from

the sun, but his nose, which stuck out of his face like a Baltimore clipper's beak, was forever peeling.

Fishing a Camel from his denim shirt pocket, Walrus struck a kitchen match on the underside of the mainmast's pinrail. He inhaled and blew out a twin stream of blue smoke. "Let me guess—turn the *Pampero* into a floating whorehouse for day-tripping commodity brokers?" His expression indicated that he didn't think much of Stackhill or commodity brokers in general or damn well anyone else who had to pay proper sailors running proper windships to ferry assholes from one island bar to the next.

Bracken pulled at his coffee. "He wants to charter the *Pampero*. My guess is that it isn't quite legal, but in his wisdom, he hasn't laid out the details."

"You gonna do it?"

"The money's good. Pay the yard bills and some crew wages. Maybe a little left over for the kitty."

"What about the Cramer thing?"

"Stackhill's lawyer claims that she shouldn't have been wearing heels when my brochure specified that guests must wear deck shoes. But it's going to take plenty bucks to solve."

"Hokay, skip, but you slipped the country. The Coast Guard, IRS, and other such bean counters don't take kindly to that kind of shit."

"Stackhill says that his lawyer can appeal the decision, and probably get the warrant overturned. And as far as the Cramer thing goes—it appears that despite complaints of grievous pain and suffering, she was playing tennis up in the Berkshires two weeks after the judgment, minus her neck brace."

Walrus blew his nose between two fingers, flicking his wrist off to leeward. He did it expertly and without thought.

"So what's in it for Stackhill?" Walrus asked, leaning back against the rail and balancing his empty mug on the bulge of his stomach.

"He didn't say."

Pulling back the fo'c'sle hatch, Walrus swung his leg down onto the ladder and then looked back up. "You know what they say, skip?"

"What?"

"There are a damn sight more sharks on the land than there are in the sea."

True, Bracken thought. So true.

*   *   *

Stackhill had Bracken between a rock and a hard place. In the first summer he had owned the *Pampero*, based in Newport, Rhode Island, Bracken had chartered, trying to pick up enough money to stay level with the yard bills and still lay in enough money for the trip south to the Antilles.

The media hyped it as the Summer of the Twelves. Take Newport, which Bracken thought of as a nice enough town, add fog, catatonic prices, middle-aged yacht groupies, half the population of East Side Manhattan, and four or five fragile toy yachts which chased each other around a twenty-four-mile course, and you had the America's Cup races. The prize, in theory, was an old, dented sterling mug. The real prize was big bucks to shop owners, hotels, restaurants, and kilobucks to sailmakers, yacht designers, shipyards, and yachtshit manufacturers. As Walrus had remarked that summer after surveying the Newport scene, it all had relatively little to do with men, ships, and the sea.

The Cramer woman and her party had been an average day-charter. She was mid-fifties dressed like late twenties with a companion who, because of his bald head, hanging earlobes, and furrowed brow, resembled Walt Disney's Pluto the Pup. Bracken's cook, a solid English girl with red cheeks and a good heart, had semi-seriously asked Bracken whether she should serve Mrs. Cramer's boyfriend a bowl of water and some K-9 Crunchies for lunch.

It had been a one-day charter and Bracken had taken them around the course, only once spotting *Australia II* and *Liberty* in the fog, the two twelve-meter sloops slogging to windward like old women in capes, leaning hard into a wet wind.

Back alongside the dock, the crew rigged the awning, and the charter party had started downing their final drinks as they sat beneath the dripping canvas and listlessly watched the spectator fleet straggle in.

The Cramer woman had consumed more than her share of gin-and-tonics. Going below to the head in her high heels, she had stumbled in the companionway and hit her head. Bracken ministered to her with a towel full of cracked ice, but she had told him not to bother, that it wasn't *anything*, Captain.

After that the Cramer woman was more subdued. She separated from the rest of her party, talking intently to Pluto and eventually, he hopped onto the dock and trotted toward Front Street at a determined gait. When he returned, two men in white

trundled along behind him with a stretcher. They carried the
Cramer woman ashore, a foam collar in place around her neck.
The last thing she said to Bracken was "Please do call your
insurance company, *Captain*." As if Bracken actually had one.

Bracken saw Hinstock, Malcolm G., of Moore, Spiegal, and
Hinstock that evening, simply because they answered their phone
after five P.M. Four hundred bucks of money that Bracken couldn't
afford went for a retainer. Hinstock took down the details in five
minutes, then asked Bracken the name of his insurance company.

Bracken told him that he didn't have any insurance. Hinstock
gave him a look that traffic cops generally reserve for those
driving under the influence, then leaned back in his nifty antique
chair, thumbs hooked into his nifty vest pockets.

"Do you have any other attachable assets in this country?"

"Everything's in the boat."

"Can you borrow anything? Say two thousand."

Bracken now had less than eight hundred in the bank, reserved for ship's provisions. But there was a rusty motorbike, a
decent guitar, and some odd gear. "Maybe another three hundred but not much more," he answered, trying to keep some part
of his financial future intact.

Hinstock, Malcolm G., stood up and walked around from
behind his oak rolltop desk. He stuck out his hand, which was
slightly sticky to the touch.

"That may be enough to get things going. I'll meet with Ms.
Cramer's attorney as soon as possible—that is, after we've received your additional good-faith money." He whisked an engraved card out of his vest pocket. Bracken was halfway to the
door when Hinstock added, "And if I were you, I would get my
vessel out of U.S. territorial waters as soon as possible unless you
want it attached." He gave a quick, professional smile. "My unof-
ficial opinion, of course, Captain Bracken."

By ten the following morning Bracken had the *Pampero* off
Breton Reef Light Tower fully provisioned with a three-month
supply of bangers and beans, a pickup crew of two seasick hip-
pies, a joyful Walrus and a marginally valid MasterCard. Once he
cleared the Tower and Block Island, he put the helm down, let
the compass settle on course, and steered southeast for Bermuda.

The muffled sound of the ship's clock chimed six bells, and
Bracken finished off the cold dregs of his coffee. A rain squall

swept in toward the coast of Antigua, blotting out the lichen-encrusted battlements of Fort Barclay. Bracken pulled the fo'c'sle hatch closed and walked aft along the *Pampero*'s deck.

The varnish on the cap rail was going spotty, and it would need to be rubbed down and recoated before long. The way of a ship—start at the bowsprit and work aft to the taffrail, and when you were finished, start again.

He caught a whiff of bacon and eggs from the galley stack and in sympathy his stomach growled. He was still halfheartedly trying to assess Stackhill's proposal, but deep in his gut he knew he had damn-all as an alternative.

10.

July 8

The *Pampero* shook her stemhead once more and plunged forward into the trough, smashing spray out to windward. Then, as the next sea rolled up beneath her, she lifted her forefoot, shedding a beard of white water, and plunged again. The sound and the motion of the wild waves transmitted their immense power through her every frame and strake. Her decks vibrated with raw energy. She was alive and running hard in the northeast trades.

Bracken stood just aft of the helmsman's seat, one hand keeping a purchase on the mainsheet. It was set rigid with the pressure of the wind in the mainsail, more like iron rod than Dacron line. Each seam of the sails strained. The shrouds and running backstays thrummed in a discordant resonance, the sound like a giant pipe organ being played by a madman. It was both wild and wonderful.

Far behind in the frothing green wake lay the dim mass of Antigua. It was lost from sight in every trough and then reappeared momentarily as the *Pampero* broke through the next advancing sea. To the south, thirty miles away over white water, shrouded in sea haze, lay Guadeloupe.

Until mid-morning, the sky had remained gray and broken, black squalls sweeping the sea with brooms of rain, but it had cleared by noon and the wind had picked up, blowing even harder from the northeast out of a polished sky.

Jean had the helm. She tracked down the course, feeding in additional spokes of helm as the seas hammered the hull, trying to slew the *Pampero* off her track.

"Yah-hoooooo!" she yelled, stringing out the sound like a rodeo cowboy astride a wild steer. Her hair was a tangled blond mass streaming off to leeward, and her face was slick with salt spray. A sea, larger than the rest, smashed against the hull, throwing a sheet of saltwater horizontally across the deck. She took it full on the face, not wincing, eyes closed and lips parted, like the acceptance of a kiss from a violent lover.

"What're we making?" Stackhill shouted against the wind. His skin was red and burnished white with salt. The hood of his foul weather jacket was cowled around his face, and he looked like a jolly monk.

"Twelve, maybe thirteen knots," Bracken shouted back, lying a little. She was doing a solid eleven and surfing on the backsides of the larger seas. He shifted his grip to the running backstay, feeling the mast surge against the rigging in the harder gusts, hoping like hell that the fore staysail wouldn't blow. After ten years in the tropics, the Dacron sails were brittle from exposure to the sun, and the stitching on the seams had been resewn so often that they were held together more by habit than by thread. One more thing to replace, he thought. Pam staggered to the companionway, bracing herself with the roll of the ship. In three minutes she returned with four beers and spread them around. The Heineken was a little warm and foamed at the mouth of the bottle. Bracken demolished half with one long pull and braced himself up against the topmast backstay, watching the seas pile up to windward. In the wind the bottle hummed a G above middle C. God, it felt good, he thought. The wind and the sea and fifty-six tons of schooner scalding down the trades, just as she was born to do.

Stackhill began to warble "Kingstown Market." It was good. Off key but good. He had a baritone with a hoarseness that made the lyrics reasonably honest. He had slung his arm around Pam's neck. She worked on the harmony, but her voice was thin and it carried away in the wind. Jean started whistling a counterpoint that even Brubeck would have given high marks to.

Bracken scrunched down beside her on the helmsman's seat. "Too much weather helm?" He touched her neck and she edged away. Not something definite as if she didn't want him to touch her. Just a subtle movement that was masked by the way she lay into the helm. Bracken figured that you could call it either way.

"No problem," she answered, keeping her eyes forward, watching the luff of the mainsail. Her gray-blue eyes were a reflection of the sea, her sun-bleached hair an echo of the salt-whitened sails. She rolled easily with the motion of the schooner, feeding in spokes as a sea broke under the counter. Releasing the helm, the wheel spun back, and she caught it exactly, repeating the process with each successive sea. She had a feel for it that a person either has or hasn't—not something that you just learned.

"Why—you want to take it?" she asked. The curve of her chin traced smoothly into her throat and flowed downward to her breasts. Bracken wished that he had the talent to draw that one classic line. "I'm trying to keep it straight, but I'm all over the place," she said. Which she knew was a lie. She steered beautifully, economically. A blind man below decks would have known that.

"No, you hang on to it. You're doing fine." He pointed to a lumpy smudge of gray about half a point to leeward. Guadeloupe was slowly spreading itself across the horizon, the mountains now separating from the lowlands. He picked out the mark: Mount Lamentin, a truncated cone, its top buried in cloud. "Come down about five degrees. You'll see the bluffs once we're closer in. Steer for them."

She nodded. Her hair was twisted in wet spirals, teeth precisely straight and white, lips wet, breasts swelling against the restraint of her bikini. She gave him the flash of a smile and leaned forward into the wheel, intent on steering. Bracken supposed that he loved her, not really understanding why. It certainly wasn't reciprocal, but then again, such things rarely were. Walrus, after a couple of straight-up rums, had once commented on his belief that all the beautiful bitches of the world went to the same secret finishing school where they were taught to be world-class cockteasers without being *overly* offensive.

Up forward, Walrus and the two deckhands from Bequia were swagging up on the fore staysail halyard. No decent winches on this Yankee bloodbucket, Walrus had bitched when he first came aboard. To Bracken, the equation was simple: If you had a winch with powerful gearing, the effort required to grind in a line under pressure was a simple function of taking longer to do it but with less effort. And yet Walrus had resisted every time Bracken had tried to bolt on a new winch. In a perverse way Walrus loved sweating the old ship, using only his hands and block and tackle. Now, with the Bequia boys trailing, Walrus scuttled across the deck, securing lines and coiling down, encased in his canary suit of yellow vinyl. The spray drove horizontally across the foredeck, rattling with the sound of shotgun pellets against Walrus's plastic foul weather gear. He wore a fierce scowl, but Bracken knew that Walrus was in seventh heaven, a man embraced by and embracing his chosen element.

Guadeloupe was more distinct, rising up out of the sea, rapidly taking on shape and definition. Bracken dropped down into the cockpit and lit a cigarette.

"What it's all about," Stackhill shouted in Bracken's ear. "One ride like this is worth the whole fuckin' charter fee." He nodded toward Jean, bobbing his cowled head. "She steers this bucket like it was on rails."

Bracken nodded, sorry that he had to share this moment with Stackhill. Hunkered down in the cockpit, out of the wind, the early afternoon sun was hot on his wind-burned face and he felt almost whole.

"What was the name of the cook you had on the last charter?"

"Nan Hogan."

"What happened to her?" Stackhill said it more as if he were asking what had happened to the relationship than to the woman.

"Just got a better job offer cooking on a stink pot up in the Virgin Islands. Thirteen hundred bucks a month she said they offered her. I paid her three hundred. Tough decision."

"She was a hell of a cook." Stackhill's stomach hung out over his bathing suit in testimony of his appetite.

"So what do you think of Jean's cooking?"

Stackhill rocked one hand in front of Bracken's face. "Sometimes great, sometimes iffy. I feel like she's the mad scientist and I'm the guinea pig. How long she been with you?"

The cigarette had taken some spray and had gone out. Bracken sucked on it, then threw it overboard, the taste of the wet tobacco biting on his tongue. "Two weeks. She turned up in Antigua during the broker's show. Said that she wrote cooking articles for some yachting magazine but wanted experience in the real thing."

Stackhill lifted an eyebrow. "So how's she in the sack?"

"Probably fantastic. Personally, I couldn't say." Bracken got up and slid down the companionway into the main cabin, hearing Stackhill's raunchy laugh compete with the shriek of the wind.

When Jean had first signed on, Bracken casually believed that the relationship would probably evolve into the seasonal bed-buddies bullshit that most of the yacht charter crews accepted as standard operating procedure. So be it, he thought, for he lusted after her perfect body.

In the first few days, like old friends, they had sat up until late, talking about the places they had skied and the seaports they had known in New England, then moved on to music and art, economics and politics. He began to realize that she had both brains and a body.

By the end of the first week, holding hands, tentatively, like shy teenagers, they had sat on deck in the evening, watching twilight gather, breathing the scent of the land and the tang of the sea intermixed. It was then that Bracken began to realize he was falling into something. Lust, certainly—love possibly.

But beyond touching and talking, nothing further had happened between them. Pragmatically, Bracken wanted to keep it that way; simple and uncluttered. But a deeper, emotional part of him wanted her—to fill a void, to give his life some kind of goddamn meaning. He began to find himself watching for signals, the way she touched her hair and looked at him, the small vital signs of love and desire.

Three nights before the Stackhill charter was to start, Bracken broke the bank and booked a dinner for the two of them at the Admiral's Inn. With Stackhill's charter deposit lining his account in Barclay's Bank, he felt further removed from poverty than usual. His blue blazer was slightly mildewed but presentable, and he had one clean shirt left whose collar wasn't frayed. He shaved carefully that evening, consciously inspecting the wrinkles around his eyes, knowing that they came from age and hard living, not the sun. "What the hell," he thought. "Forty-five isn't the end of the line." The cracked mirror mocked him.

That evening she changed outfits three times before she was satisfied with the effect. A simple white cotton summer dress with a single-strand gold choker won out. She decided against wearing shoes. The effect was a mixture of sexual sophistication and boardingschool innocence. Before they left the *Pampero,* they had some wine together. The pallor was gone from her skin, replaced by a deep tan. Her hair shone like molten platinum in the lamplight, enough to make his throat catch. She downed three glasses of the Riesling in quick succession, then took his arm, squeezing it. They sauntered across the darkened Dockyard, hand in hand, under a gibbous moon. Bracken was humming, happier than he had been in years. Before they reached the Admiral's Inn, she arched her neck and pecked him on the cheek.

The Inn was packed. Accents from Sydney and the Hamble, the Canadian Maritimes, New England, and the California coast. It was a place for offshore sailors, the few men remaining who still made their living from the sea in windships. The floors were brick, the rafters time-blackened oak. The place stank pleasantly of rivers of rum consumed by generations of sailormen.

MacKenzie, the skipper of a big Herreshoff ketch, flagged them down as they entered. He was slinging darts in a round of three-oh-one but broke away from the game, snatched three drinks from a waiter's tray, and herded them through the French doors and onto the patio. Bracken's idea of a romantic dinner for two was scuttled.

MacKenzie had named her Sweet Jean. No exact reason, just that she exuded pristine innocence, yet with strong overtones of suppressed sexuality, and the name fitted: Goldilocks caught with her hand on Papa Bear's crotch.

In his usual form, MacKenzie was charming, and he romanced her a little, putting Bracken down in an offhand way. And although she listened to MacKenzie, intense and responsive, beneath the table her bare feet played games with Bracken's leg. After finishing her drink, she finished Bracken's and by then her toenails were beginning to cut Bracken's skin.

Dinner was a vague blur of green turtle soup, snapper, and salad. MacKenzie bought a bottle of wine that he fussed over, sniffing and gargling until he pronounced the vintage "weak but amusing." Jean laughed often, tossing her hair, eyes overly bright, a thin film of moisture beading her upper lip. Bracken wondered what her ear would taste like. She caught his glance and blushed, squeezing his thigh.

After the dinner they stumbled back to the *Pampero*, laughing and weaving through the Dockyard, the lights of yachts riding to anchor mimicking starlight, the scent of bougainvillea heavy on the night air.

They sat together on the foredeck, the *Pampero* heaving gently beneath them. The moon had set, leaving the sky littered with stars. They held hands and kissed a little, then harder.

But then, as if an alarm bell had been preset to some level of emotional response, she pulled away from him.

"This isn't any good. We'll only hurt each other," she said. And went below. He heard her shower, then the light from the porthole of their cabin winked out.

Still sitting on deck, Bracken listened to the sound of the wind hollow in his ears. A metal fitting aloft clanked.

He had two more brandies and went to the cabin. In the darkness he could smell a faint trace of her perfume, and it tore his heart out. She breathed steadily, her face turned to the bulkhead, her body protectively cocooned in a sheet. He lay down naked beside her, not touching her, and stared at the black overhead, seeing nothing, wishing that he could feel nothing.

Bracken had been leaning over the navigational desk, staring sightlessly at the chart, rerunning the film of Jean again and again through the projector of his mind. He finally shook off the images, blinked, and focused his eyes.

He really didn't know much about her. Only that she was charming, gorgeous, educated, accomplished, and totally desirable. Slick city men, encased in three-piece gorilla suits and swaddled in Saabs, would fight to the death for her hand with theater tickets and weekend invitations to the Hamptons. And what in hell did he have to offer her? A low-paid job as a cook on a clapped-out schooner that earned just enough to keep both him and the crew in genteel poverty.

But with money, a lot of money, it might be a whole different story. Not the money itself, but what the money would buy: two years of running expenses for a cruise through the South Pacific. He had wanted to do the Pacific, had always wanted to do it since his father had first talked about it. Do it before the lovely atolls sank under the sheer weight of high-rise resorts, offshore banks, and three-mile-long jet strips.

He pulled a beer out of the cooler and flipped off the cap, then thumbed through the books, tabulating the charter income already confirmed for the winter. Stackhill's charter plus seven more weeks for a total of nine. He fished out the calculator and tapped in the essentials—forty-eight hundred a week less—tap, tap—expenses of eleven hundred a week times nine—tap—equals —blink—thirty-three thousand and change. Which he knew would barely get him through the summer with the repair work and replacement of equipment that he was going to have to fork out. But with Stackhill's blood money plus some paying passengers on the Pacific run, he could keep the old bucket going for three years on a reasonable budget. He couldn't believe that she'd turn down a deal like that.

Walrus thumped down the companionway and into the salon. He rolled with the ship, timing his movements between lunges. Giving Bracken a neutral sidelong look, he ducked into the engine room. A pump started, sucking air at first, then settling down into a steady gurgle. He reemerged, wiping his hands on some cotton waste.

"Smells like a pack of junkyard dogs been pissin' in there," he said, pulling a beer from the cooler. Walrus wasn't overly fond of engines or electrical things. All he figured a ship needed was kerosene for lighting, a little wind to keep her moving, and enough blocks of ice to keep the beer cold. He braced himself against the mast, one hand holding the teak overhead rail.

"I've been thinking," Walrus said. "About Stackhill's offer." He downed a good third of the bottle. "And it's okay with me but not for the boys."

"You didn't talk to them about it!"

He shook his head. "Hell no! But if we pulled off something like what I'm thinking Stackhill's proposing, they might. You know how Cousin is. Pour some jack iron rum into him and the next thing he'll start telling you his mantra."

"So who do we get? Besides Jean, you, and me, we need at least one other guy, better yet two."

Walrus laid back the rest of the bottle and chucked it into the gash can. "We'll be in St. Lucia day after tomorrow, right? Two English guys I know there. They work in the boatyard, live on a ketch they built. One was in the Special Air Services, the other speaks Spanish like a Spick. I figure linguistic talents might come in handy."

"Okay," Bracken agreed. "Feel them out. I'll pay four grand for the two of them and three for you. That suitable?"

Walrus shrugged. "I'm here to sail this leaking old bucket, not run dope, but if you can get the additional bread out of Stackhill, it's fine with me." He turned toward the companionway, hesitated, and turned back.

"It's none of my business, skip . . ." Lifting a fingernail to his mouth, he picked out a bit of meat between his teeth and wiped it against the sleeve of his oilskins. "But it's my advice as a friend to get rid of that lady you got cookin' for us."

"Bullshit," Bracken spat back. "That's my business!"

Shrugging, Walrus turned and climbed the companionway, shaking his head as if he had heard it all before.

Bracken rounded the *Pampero* up into Anse Des Hayes Bay just after five. Moments before, they had hardened up on the wind, the old girl laying her rail down, smoking to windward as the williwaws ripped across the bay, turning the surface into a froth of foam. Then under the lee of the headland, Bracken pumped his arm twice. The Bequia boys doused the main and foresail while Walrus and Jean dropped the fore staysail and headsails. The *Pampero* was still carrying seven or eight knots of way and Bracken used the momentum to round up into the head of the bay. When she was dead in the water, Walrus let the anchor go and twenty fathoms of chain ran out in a cloud of rusty dust as the *Pampero* fell off, then snatched up hard in good holding ground.

"That's all folks," Bracken said to the plastic Porky Pig that swung by a noose from the boom gallows. The pig didn't comment, just looked back with his cross-eyed stare and grinned stupidly.

Walrus, brushing by Bracken with a fistful of sail ties, gave him one of those looks that he reserved for idiots, landlubbers, and other inferior species. He peeled off his oilskins and started furling the mainsail. Keith and Cousin came aft, and in twenty minutes the three of them had squared away the deck and rigged the awning.

"You need anything else, skip?" Walrus asked. There was just the hint of defiance in his voice. Cousin and Keith stood behind him like two shadows.

There were a lot of things that Bracken wanted to get done. Like restitching a couple of seams on the staysail and Ajaxing off smoke stains on the hull around the exhaust, but he shook his head because Walrus had that look that said he'd had enough for the day. Not of sailing but of the crowd on board. Plus the immediate attraction of Madame Racine's bar, which served mind-bending rum punches and plump little shrimps in a creole hot sauce that would melt the armor plate off an M-1A tank.

"No," Bracken answered. "You going ashore?"

"You got it." Walrus pivoted on his heel, the two boys following him. All three evaporated down the fo'c'sle hatch.

Stackhill popped up out of the companionway hatch, an eight-ounce glass of scotch in his fist, tempered by only two ice cubes. "Will you take him if you do this trip?" He said it, obviously disapproving of the minor mutiny. Stackhill always wanted someone in the crew standing by at attention in case his glass was empty.

"Hell yes. I wish I had four more like him."

Stackhill lit a menthol, his periodic sop toward quitting the foul weed. He moved toward the rail. The sun was a distended red blob on the western horizon. "And the two local boys?"

"Probably not. They're good kids but not for something like this."

Stackhill didn't comment, and Bracken knew that both of them now knew that the deal was all but set in concrete with only terms to be haggled over.

The sun was almost gone, but the remaining light had the soft sepia tone that took the harshness from the landscape. The headlands of Anse Des Hayes enclosed both the town and the bay within two protective arms of land. The hills above, cut in stepped tiers of cultivation, resembled a wedding cake made of sunlight and shadows. A few mercury streetlights onshore flickered in the twilight. It was a perfect kind of peace save present company.

"I like it better each time," Stackhill said. This was his second charter on the *Pampero* in two months. He called it "recharging his batteries." Pam obviously had something to do with keeping his electrolytic level right up there.

"It's okay," Bracken said noncommittally.

The light was gone now, failing rapidly as it does in the tropics. Stackhill flipped his cigarette away in the wind, and it trailed a comet's tail of sparks that died in the sea. He turned back to face Bracken.

"You ever get tired of this?"

"Of chartering?" It was a question that Bracken had to answer with every charter party.

Stackhill dropped into the cockpit and lay down on the cushions, fingers lacing under his neck. "No," he replied. "The whole ball of wax—sailing, the islands, living out a fantasy."

"Nope."

"Lucky kid," Stackhill said, his voice betraying his disbelief. "You'll go far."

Smells were starting to percolate up out of the galley. Pam was down helping Sweet Jean. This was as good a time as any, Bracken thought.

"I've been working out the kinks in this Colombia run. I'll do it but with the understanding that it's only grass. No hard stuff."

Stackhill turned his face toward Bracken in the half light, his eyebrows twitching. "Who said anything about drugs or Colombia? I'm a consumer, not a seller. Shit, all I'm talking about is a charter. You'll have a couple of guests onboard plus some cargo they'll bring with them. You sail them up to the East Coast of the

U.S., drop them and their cargo off, and sail back down to the islands."

"I can't clear into the U.S. until the Cramer suit is completely cleaned up and I have a release from her."

"So true, buddy, but that wouldn't matter in this situation. The only thing even slightly illegal about this charter is that you're not going to clear the ship into and out of U.S. waters. Just mosey along some coast, drop them off in the dinghy, and bug out. No customs, no immigration, nothing. Just in and out."

"Who are these so-called guests?"

"I've got no idea, Bracken, and I don't want to know."

"Then what's the cargo? I'm not set up for heavy stuff."

Stackhill swigged at his drink. "I don't know that either. Not my end of things. I was only told that total weight is about six hundred pounds, some of it electronic gear which they'll leave on board."

"That's not good enough, Stackhill. I want to know what I'm going to be carrying."

"The people behind this obviously know what they're doing."

Bracken took a long breath and blew it out slowly. "And you're just a go-between and you don't have the slightest fucking idea of what the story is?"

"You got it."

"Why you?" Bracken watched him, trying to read Stackhill's expression.

Stackhill compulsively lit another cigarette. "Real simple. I'm being squeezed."

"Explain."

"I owe mucho dinero, a lot of bucks. Not too long ago I wrote some very large futures contracts on the Yankee dollar for a guy who's an Eastern European immigrant. Hungarian or Polish—who knows—Russian for all I know. Fascinating guy. Started as a taxi driver ten years ago but poured everything he made into an import business. He brings in a lot of stuff from the Eastern bloc countries—hams, dolls, crystal, and toys, you name it. And he has to pay for most of it over there in hard currency. So he uses the futures market to hedge against currency fluctuations.

"Everything that I knew about the currency market pointed to the dollar falling through the basement, so I never actually wrote the contracts—just kept the contracts on my books, figuring when the dollar fell far enough he'd cash out and I'd roll up a nice piece of change. You understand so far?"

Bracken didn't, but he nodded.

"So instead of the dollar falling, it went through the roof. And no way that I could cover the profits that were coming to him. I was short seventy big ones. He started pressing me, threatening to call the Securities and Exchange Commission, so I had to cut a deal with him."

"What kind of deal?"

"At first he didn't say. Told me not to worry, that he wouldn't press any charges and to stay cool, just that I should start to pay him back and maybe he'd ask for a favor sometime. About two months later I get a call from him. He gives me the name of two charter boats in the Caribbean, one of them yours, the other one the *Panama Red,* a ketch up in the Virgins. Sends me a pile of traveler's checks by messenger and tells me to charter both boats and report back."

"What did he want to know?"

"You name it. Seaworthiness of the boat, whether the owner was in financial trouble, whether he had a lot of charter bookings or was just breaking even, stuff like that. Plus layouts of the boat, photographs of the deck, rigging, snaps of the owner, drinking habits, girlfriend situation. I checked out this other boat in the Virgins but found out the guy's constantly watched by the narcs, can't move his boat ten feet without the Coast Guard swarming all over his deck. That left you. Before I boarded the *Pampero* in Antigua, some flunky flew in with even more traveler's checks. Told me to give you the pitch for this job. Believe me, Bracken, you're damn lucky to get the chance to make this kind of money."

Before, Bracken had felt a chill. Now his whole body had gone cold. "What kind of guy—a Colombian with gold chains and a bulge under his jacket?"

"Hey! This guy was laid back. English-speaking Jap, but like he had been to a good school. He handled himself real nice. No threats, no rough stuff. He just wanted to be sure that I understood I might end up in an intensive care ward unless you agreed to do the trip."

"I think this whole thing sucks. I don't need this charter, I don't need you, and I don't need the money."

Stackhill watched the shoreline as he spoke. "Didn't you ever ask yourself how I knew about the Cramer lawsuit? This Jap guy did a lot of checking on you. Said you were forced to resign your commission in the Air Force. Something about collaborating with the Vietnamese, which means that you'd have a damn hard time getting any kind of a decent job stateside. Even rumors that you gave the slopes classified information. Add to that the Cramer lawsuit and the fact that you illegally fled the country and have an outstanding judgment against the ship. I don't see that you owe the good old U.S.A. a thing, and you could damn well use the bread. The bank's within a hair of foreclosing on you. You painted yourself into a corner, Bracken. I'm the guy who can get you out."

Somebody deserved a gold star for their effort. A yacht was the least conspicuous and safest way to get a small cargo into the U.S. Just sail in from offshore on a Sunday afternoon, mix with the local boating gentry, and anchor out in the harbor, like you were just cruising coastwise. The Coast Guard was stretched thin by budget cuts, and they couldn't cover the whole coast.

And what kind of a yacht did that somebody look for? A boat that was in deep financial trouble run by an owner who had terminal legal problems. That easy, and Bracken knew that he fit the profile exactly. Stackhill had also tapped a pool of resentment that Bracken had tried to hide from himself for nearly twenty years.

"I'll think about it and then we'll talk some more," Bracken said. "But the money has to be more than you're talking about." He didn't give Stackhill time to answer, instead, walked forward to the fo'c'sle hatch, mentally mixing himself a large economy-size rum and tonic. He was sweating heavily, his nerves humming with tension, knowing that he was in way over his head.

11.

July 8–July 9

Bracken sat down with Jean, Pam, and Stackhill to a leisurely dinner. The women had made up a selection of condiments to go along with a beef fondue. Stackhill, relaxed, nudged the conversation along.

"Where you from, Jean?" he asked, refilling her glass. Bracken, slightly sloshed, realized that Stackhill wasn't drinking very much.

"Stone Harbor, New Jersey," she said, not even looking up. She speared another hunk of beef with her fork and plunged it into the boiling oil.

"How did you end up in the islands?"

She shrugged and stirred her fork in the pot. "I was tired of being a secretary," she answered. "Tired of doing the same things with the same people. I thought I'd make a change. A friend turned me onto the idea of cooking on yachts, maybe writing a book about it. Sounded like a neat idea." She looked up briefly at Stackhill, then dipped her chunk of meat into a dill-mustard sauce and popped it into her mouth. "So here I am."

"What kind of work did you do before?"

She hesitated for just the fraction of a second, looking up at him, their eyes meeting. "A food wholesaler. In D.C."

Bracken could almost hear the computer in Stackhill's mind whizzing away, saving that information in the permanent memory banks. "Interesting," Stackhill finally said, although it didn't sound as if he thought food wholesaling was interesting.

"Dull," she replied. "Bristol and Whitbriar. English jams and tea biscuits. Carriage trade products."

"How about you, Captain Hook?" Pam asked. "Where're your roots?"

Bracken detested that word. It seemed that everyone had to go digging around in graveyards and dusty registries to find their origins, but it didn't seem relevant to Bracken because most people didn't even know who they were in the first place.

143

"Grew up on the Maine coast," he said.

"Where you learned to sail, right?"

He thought about long-lining in the winter with frozen mittens encased in ice. And also about the days of autumn with the old man, sailing through Blue Hill Bay, hearing the seals bark and watching leaves putting to sea on the outgoing tide. "Right," he answered.

"You were married?" she asked, as if it had been a tragedy.

"Once."

"Miss it?"

Dinners together on the sun porch, watching Penny darning his socks, the night-long arguments or sitting on the lawn together in the evening dusk and watching the first fireflies of June ignite? It had been so long ago that he couldn't remember what it had been like, either the good or the bad, just that he still had this vague ache of love remembered he couldn't shake. "Not particularly," he lied.

"The ship's your lover," she giggled.

Jean shot Pam a look of pure hate. Bracken was lost. He couldn't figure where it was leading, what the little undercurrents of innuendo meant, but understood that he was drunk enough that it didn't really matter.

Some kind of silent communication passed between Pam and Stackhill. She nodded and got up, a little tipsy, heading toward the aft cabin.

"Either of you smoke?" Stackhill asked. There was a long silence.

"Grass, you mean?" Jean replied.

"Something like that," Stackhill answered.

Jean got up and went forward into the galley. Clanking of pots and pans commenced.

Talk about stupid, Bracken thought. "You took one hell of a chance bringing dope into Antigua. It's all in the same category down here—grass, coke, amphetamines."

"Pam carried it," Stackhill said, shrugging, as if it weren't his problem if she had been searched.

So who needed enemies when you had a friend like Stackhill, Bracken realized. Perhaps something to remember for the future.

Jean brought in a pot of coffee and settled down on a settee, away from the table. She flicked on a reading light and started thumbing through a magazine, agitated and withdrawn.

Pam came back into the salon wearing a short terry-cloth

bathrobe. She placed a small clay pipe and a silver tube in front of Stackhill and sat down next to Bracken. Jean gave Bracken a dour look, shook her head marginally, and then aimlessly resumed turning the pages.

Stackhill made a ritual of it, scraping the pipe with a gold penknife, then packing the bowl. He lit it and drew a long breath, holding the smoke in his lungs, then passed it to Bracken.

The smoke wasn't harsh like marijuana—more a ginger taste and vaguely sweet. Bracken puffed and passed it along to Pam.

"What is it?" he said, exhaling, the smoke already digging a hole in his skull.

She inhaled, drawing the smoke deeply into her lungs, causing her breasts to rise. The front of her bathrobe parted a little to reveal a glimpse of a white untanned mound tipped in pink. She exhaled slowly, her eyes closed. "Ha . . . ha . . . hash," she whispered, exhaling the smoke in little gusts.

Stackhill took the pipe and extended it toward Jean. "Your shot."

She got up from the settee, putting the magazine down on the stack in an overly precise movement. She went forward to her cabin and slammed the door.

Pam giggled. "Just the three of us." She took the pipe from Stackhill's fingers.

Bracken watched the second hand of the ship's chronometer sweep from one second to the next, then to the next. Precise, he thought, as if each tick were a millennium carved out of a great eternity.

The sweep hand made a couple of slow revolutions, and the pipe made a circle of the table. Pam stood up and lurched into the galley, returning with another bottle of Chablis from the fridge. Two bottles down. Bracken vaguely realized that he had been doing most of the drinking. She uncorked the bottle and refilled all of the glasses. As she bent over Bracken, the pressure of her breasts touched his neck and shoulders. Her fragrance had a musky sweetness, and from the corner of his eye he caught a momentary flicker of amusement on Stackhill's face.

"She wants to check out your equipment," Stackhill said.

"Whuzzat supposed to mean?"

"Professional interest. Get you in the sack and see how you perform. Think of it as a road test, old buddy."

Pam giggled again, ruffled her fingers through Bracken's hair, and headed back into the galley.

It was all very dreamy. Bracken watched the clock tick through another light-year. "This parta the deal? Benefit package on the side?"

Stackhill shook his head. "Nope. She's free to do what she wants and I'm not the jealous type. Based on personal experience, Bracken, I sure as hell wouldn't turn her down."

Bracken slugged down the remains of his wine and refilled the glass. He was tempted, like, *my God* he was tempted. Felt right now as if he were the sexual master of the universe, able to vault tall galaxies in a single bound. But something deeper in his cortex rang the alarm bell.

He finally stood up unsteadily, picking up his glass and the bottle of wine. "Let's keep it on a cash basis, Stackhill. Forget the fifty-thousand plus freebies. Seventy thousand and you've got a deal."

Reaching up, Stackhill offered his hand. "Deal, buddy. Actually, I was authorized to go to eighty-five."

Bracken sighed, visualizing fifteen thousand down the drain. He stumbled into the galley, leaving a grinning Stackhill behind. As he passed Pam, she smiled, showing a smudge of lipstick on her teeth and Oreo cookie crumbs on her lips.

Bracken patted her on the cheek. "Mighty tempting, Pam-lady. Some other time."

She giggled. "It'll keep, Cap'n Hook. It'll keep just fine." She mischievously flashed a corner of her terry-cloth robe open to give him a preview of coming attractions. The only word that he could think of was *awesome*.

Jean was lying on the bunk, stomach down, covered only by a towel. She had been playing with her laptop computer that she used to record recipes for "project cookbook," as she called it. Bracken pulled the door closed. She looked up, startled, snapped the computer lid shut, and slid it back onto the overhead shelf.

"Do you always have twits like these on charter?" Her towel was drooping slightly open, showing an untanned portion of her thigh.

Bracken turned away, placing the bottle on the dresser. "Stackhill was fine on the previous charter. Some other bimbo was with him but she was—you know—normal."

"Are you going to bed with Peter Pam? Sweaty bodies, Oreo cookies, hash, and all?"

He turned back to her, angry. She had pulled the towel

closed. "What big sharp ears you have, grandma," he said. There was some difficulty keeping her face in focus.

"In case you hadn't figured it out, skip, Pamela's a hooker. She says she's top-of-the-line, state-of-the-art—a thousand a night and no corporate discounts. You should be honored that she's willing to get it on with you for free."

"And what big sharp teeth you have, grandma." God, he loved it. She actually seemed to be jealous. He took another slug of wine.

"You know what I really think, Hook? I think Stackhill's trying to get you involved with Pam, figuring I'll do the jealous-lover bit and stomp off the boat."

He sat down heavily on the bunk, slopping a little wine out of the glass. "Oh-ho-ho—the lady actually cares!"

She shook her head. "I wouldn't count on it, Bracken. Just that I want to keep this job until the book's finished or I finally get really sick of watching you screw up."

The good news and the bad. She wasn't going to leave him, but she didn't sound like he figured significantly in her future.

He reached over and switched off the light, then sat in darkness, letting his eyes adjust, thinking about Pam. How would Stackhill list her on his tax return, customer entertainment, passive investment, or depreciable asset?

In the darkness he felt her fingers gently massage his back. "What goes on between you and Stackhill?" She ran her fingertips expertly down his spine, playing an arpeggio on his vertebrae.

"Nothing special. We're just talking about another charter for some friends of his." He told the lie automatically.

"Pam says that there's a lot of money involved. What is it, Bracken? Running drugs? Is this what you've spent your worthless life working up to?"

He pulled his shirt over his head and threw it into a corner, then dropped his shorts and rolled into bed with her, naked. "Pam doesn't know diddly-squat. She's guessing. Aren't any drugs involved."

They lay in the darkness together for a long time, not speaking or touching.

Her voice was sleepy when she finally spoke. "Whatever it is, Bracken, don't get burned." She tentatively sought out his hand and took it in hers and squeezed.

He leaned over and kissed her. At first there was some kind

of response, but then she gently, almost reluctantly, pushed him away. "Don't," she whispered.

"Why 'don't,' dammit?"

She inhaled, then exhaled, taking a long time at it. "Sensitivity isn't your strong point, Bracken. There was another man—a man in Washington. Things fell apart. It takes a long time to get over something like that. Maybe, someday, we might get together, but for now we'd both get screwed up in any sort of a nonprofessional relationship."

"I'm already screwed up and we've got bugger-all for a relationship."

"True, Bracken. Absolutely true. But I can't help you if you're not willing to help yourself. I've tried that before with other men, and it's always been a disaster. Nevermore."

It was the final straw and it triggered in Bracken the lines of an almost-forgotten poem. Edgar Allan Poe stuff:

Take thy beak from out my heart,
and take thy form from off my door!
Quoth the Raven, "Nevermore."

He damn well wasn't going to hang around until Jean unscrewed her head or tried to unscrew his; not when Pam was fluttering at his door. "Nevermore," he drunkenly whispered into the darkness, but Jean was already snoring softly.

He awoke late the next morning with the taste of sour wine in his mouth. The sun was high, crashing incandescent off the water with a scalding light and ricocheting through the porthole. He watched the reflections jiggle around on the overhead, nauseated. His head thudded unpleasantly, and his tongue felt as if it were a candidate for transplant.

Jean was up, of course. He could smell burned toast and bacon fat. Bracken rolled over, hugging the pillow, willing the world to take five.

Jean slid the door open. "Coffee, darlink. Everyone's been up for two hours and fed. They want to get under way. And, skip, you'll just *love* Pam's bikini." She banged the door shut against its stops. There followed sounds of pans rocking and rolling in the galley sink. Subtle, he thought.

He climbed into his shorts and drank the coffee, which was both cold and bitter—maybe her way of commenting on their relationship.

Stackhill and Pam were in the cockpit, folding the awning. Pam was wearing three minuscule triangular patches that looked as if they had been cut from a fishnet for minnows. Bracken croaked, flapped a good-morning wave, and dove over the side. The water was as refreshing as warm concrete that hadn't set up yet. For Pam's benefit he tried to simulate the typical bronzed Caribbean-yacht skipper, making a show of stretching out and grabbing fistfuls of water in smooth strokes, legs beating the water white, doing his Tarzan routine. He then surfaced, spouted water from between his teeth, grinned, and looked up. Pam wasn't watching. In fact, no one was. Bummer. By ten they got under way.

By early afternoon the *Pampero* was still in the lee of Guadeloupe. Protected from the full strength of the trade winds by the spine of mountains that form the backbone of the island, the winds of the western coastal waters are a maze of shifting, indolent, and contrary breezes. But by sailing well inshore, Bracken was able to keep the *Pampero* moving, although her speed never got much over four knots.

He downed two cold pork chops for lunch and cushioned their impact on his stomach's lining with three beers. By three in the afternoon he was feeling better, watching the mountains dip in and out of the clouds, the valleys, desolate and overgrown, shimmering in the damp heat. Birds, unidentifiable and pulsing with colors, paralleled his course. At times rain squalls would sweep through the clefts in the mountains, leaving rainbows in their trail.

Stackhill was eating up the scenery. He sat straddled on the bowsprit, firing off roll after roll of film. Then, both film and commitment exhausted, he lay back in the lubber's net, dozing in the sun. Pam was lying stomach down on the cabin top, her back, arms, and legs turning red. Bracken had designs in mind for this evening and made a mental note to waken her before the burn got too bad.

Stackhill must have had his antennae tuned in because he waddled aft and sat down in the cockpit. His tan was deeper now, erasing the lines around his eyes. Although on the short side, he had a good frame, well-muscled except for the flabby gut. He lit a menthol and blew the smoke out slowly. In the light wind it drifted up in the sunlight, haze blue.

"I'm kidding myself," he said to no one in particular. "About a lot of things—like these." He held the cigarette up and glared at it. "I think that because they taste like mint they're not killing me. Which we both know is a lot of crap."

"So what else bothers you?"

Stackhill lay back on the cushions and propped his feet up on the cockpit coaming, wiggling his toes. "About Pam. I was trying to buy you last night. Just a little additional inducement."

Leaning back against the helmsman's seat, Bracken felt the afternoon sun hot on his face, the wind cool on his neck. For once he had grasped control of the situation. "Don't concern yourself. Thanks to your generosity, Stackhill, I think everything will fit together neatly—no pun intended."

Stomping out of the cockpit on his flat sweaty feet, Stackhill made a show of being infuriated, which Bracken smugly figured he was. He didn't feel so smug half an hour later when Stackhill came on deck with Jean. They went forward together, Stackhill's arm around her waist. Bracken's stomach flopped over when she turned to Stackhill and favored him with a smile that would have turned glass molten. She briefly glanced back at Bracken, her face blank of expression, then slid down to the deck beside Stackhill, chin cupped in her palm, seemingly fascinated, listening to Stackhill's line of baloney. She was wearing her white cotton bikini, the one that Bracken had bought her in St. Barts. It didn't flaunt her body like Pam's did, but, rather, subtly hinted at the underlying mother lode.

He tried not to watch them, but he had a hard time keeping his eyes averted. Stackhill was animated, gesturing with his hands, laughing, and she responded, nodding, smiling back at him. He leaned over and whispered something in her ear, and Bracken watched as she first shrugged and then, her head lowered for a few moments, raised it and slowly nodded, as if she had considered something seriously and finally consented.

Signaling Walrus to take the helm, Bracken went below and slumped down in the navigator's seat, his equivalent of returning to the womb. He realized that Stackhill was probably propositioning her. It didn't matter that Bracken had already decided to dump her. It was the goddamn principle of the thing. He turned and looked up, examining himself in the reflecting glass of the liquor locker. It was the image of a man in his midlife crisis, face leathered by the sun and pouches under the eyes from too much drinking. Also a reflection of a man who had already failed in two careers and was about to throw away a third.

Seventy thousand. It wasn't a fortune, but it would clear his debts and leave him some breathing room. He just didn't want to consider the moral implications of what he was doing. Leave those sermons to the Sunday-morning televangelists.

The *Pampero* cleared the southern end of Guadeloupe just after four. Once abeam of the lighthouse, the wind freshened and veered into the east. Close-hauled for the Saints, the *Pampero* snorted in the freshening wind, picked up her gait, kicking out a creamy wake.

Walrus and the boys had sheeted in the sails at the first hint of a wind shift, and Bracken had slowly eased up on a course that lay to windward of Baline Rock and the channel into Ile de Bourg, already visible across the dusty six-mile gap.

Mid-channel, Keith came aft and relieved Bracken. He had a wiry medium build, compact and golden brown. Like a lot of the other Bequia boys, his great-grandfather had come from the New England coast on a whaling ship in the mid-eighteen hundreds.

"She going good," he said, sliding into the helmsman's seat.

"She's going good," Bracken corrected him. The Bequia boys were smart as whips, but they always dropped the contracted verb.

Keith nodded. It was likely that in his entire lifetime he had never been more than two miles from the sea. He gently curled his fingers around the spokes, easing in helm as if he were born to it, which he was. "Yeah, skip," he said, nodding. "Like I said, she going good."

Bracken dipped into the deck cooler and pulled out two Heinekens, popped the top on one and then went forward to where Walrus was sitting, his feet braced against the lee rail, working on a rat-tailed eye splice. He had a fid carved from whalebone, and he worked it carefully through the strands, taking each tuck, cutting off a few rebellious fibers of Dacron, then smoothing the lay of the rope by rolling it on deck under his hand.

Bracken sank down beside him, handing the Walrus the other can of beer. With the *Pampero* heeled down and moving fast, the sea rushing by was mesmerizing—sort of a giant Jacuzzi. The late-afternoon sun, low in the sky, reflected dazzling light off the frothing bow wave. Flying fish—startled—skittled off wave tops, leaving splatters of foam behind them.

"What's up, skip?" said Walrus. He jerked off the tab on the can and flipped it into the sea, then took a long swig.

"I've given it a lot of thought. I can't afford to pass up Stackhill's offer. I can drop you off in Martinique. I'll pick you up when I get back from the trip. It's your choice. I just don't want you to feel that you're obligated to come with me."

Walrus raked his lower lip over the bottom edge of his mustache, wiping off the foam. Bracken noticed for the first time that there were some gray flecks among the reddish-brown hairs.

Walrus breathed out hard, although it was difficult to tell whether he was agitated or satisfied. "Where do you think the dropoff point of the charter is?"

"South coast of the U.S.—probably someplace that's off the beaten path. We drop off two passengers and some cargo. Stackhill says there are no drugs involved. Just sail in and sail out, no clearance."

Walrus gave one of his rare smiles. "Shee—it. Think we'd have enough time so that I could go ashore and git me a mess of grits?"

Walrus's eyes were clear blue on white, unblinking, the smile still there. Waiting for easy acceptance.

"You're sure?"

"Someone has to be around to keep you from fucking up."

To Bracken, that seemed to be a recurring theme as of late. He stood up, bracing himself against the lee shrouds. "How come they don't make 'em like you anymore, Walrus?"

"I figure it's an environmental problem, skip, not a genetic one. It's the light beer they sell nowadays. Drink enough of that cat-piss and you get a limp dick."

The Saints were close. The passage through the channel was not tricky, but Bracken had to get the running rigging cleared away and be ready to tack. "Call out Keith and run the backstays. We'll use the fisherman to anchor with."

Walrus pushed the fid into its sheath. "Just don't try to teach granny how to suck eggs, skip," he said with just a trace of a scowl and padded forward on flat feet, then called down the fo'c'sle hatch to roust out the boys.

Ile de Bourg was opening up as the *Pampero* cleared the cut, the hillside homes and the small town spreading out before them. It was a one-off place, full of shops and little bars where the owners lived upstairs and the gendarmes played checkers under the shade of the trees. One home on the hillside predominated over the town, cast in concrete and shaped like the bow of a steamship, its stem jutting out of the raw dirt. The foredeck had awnings and the windows were cast round in concrete. A flock of flags fluttered from the halyard of a squatty mast. Bracken had heard that it belonged to a retired French ship's captain who compulsively paced the porch in foul weather.

The *Pampero* shot through the entrance of the harbor. Bracken bore off for a second to clear the reef, then brought her head-to-wind, the headsails and foresail luffing. The Bequia boys were good as usual, just this side of overdramatic. Keith leapt onto the fore-staysail boom, wrestling down the sail and securing the slatting halyard. Cousin was just forward of him, sail ties streaming from his teeth, whipping them one by one around the muzzled jib. It was, as the British say, a good show.

Putting the helm over, Bracken bore off and ghosted into two fathoms between a small plastic sloop flying the Barbados flag and a giant black power yacht under Panamanian colors. Walrus let the hook go, the anchor chain rumbling over the gypsy.

"Good sail," Stackhill said. Pam had closed up behind Bracken, her arms possessively over his shoulders, saying nothing but not leaving much space between their bodies.

Bracken had rehearsed his little speech to Stackhill all afternoon. "Last night you said you were authorized to go up to a maximum of eighty-five thousand. Somebody else is shelling out the dough so it's no skin off your hide. I want the full price."

Stackhill's eyes weren't connecting. He looked across the water at the power boat that was launching a large inflatable Zodiac dinghy. Three men in slacks and sport shirts edged down the gangway to the boat that was held in place by two paid hands, both in spiffy crew uniforms.

"Talking with me is all over. Now you talk to them," Stackhill said, nodding toward the launch that was already thundering toward the *Pampero*.

Edwardo X. Sanchez of Sanchez y Vierro, S.A. (Panamanian Exporters of Refrigeration Equipment to Latin America, the business card proclaimed in finely engraved print) settled back into the cushions of the settee. His fresh-off-the-rack Lacoste sport shirt suited him as well as it would a devout Mennonite. His head was melon-shaped without wrinkles to mar its otherwise seamless surface. The eyes, nose, and mouth were grouped tightly in the center of his face, leaving large surrounding areas of sun-reddened flesh as a kind of contrasting and yet featureless landscape. He smiled, favoring Bracken with a passport photo grimace that was as genuine as a politician's promise. He repositioned the majority of his bulk on the cushions, leaned down, and examined a yellow legal pad.

"It is my understanding, Captain Bracken, that you have agreed to undertake the charter." Sanchez spoke nearly perfect English, only slightly accented.

The other half of the dynamic duo of Sanchez y Vierro sat on a folding chair near the entrance to the *Pampero*'s salon, his body relaxed as a coiled spring. Vierro was mid-thirties and lean with wiry muscles, as if he played a great deal of squash or did a lot of serious arm wrestling. His elongated face was pitted with acne scars, his hair wispy brown and thinning, his eyes hidden behind mirrored aviator glasses.

"The charter fee isn't settled yet," Bracken said flatly.

Sanchez smiled again. Not really the way that most people smile. There are variations of smiles, ranging from a wispy grin to a twenty-one-tooth salute. But Sanchez had only this one smile—lips together and slightly turned up at the corners of his mouth, which he clicked on and off as the occasion required.

"I would like to avoid endless negotiations, Captain Bracken. Seventy-five thousand is satisfactory to us, provided you're willing to accept this generous charter fee without further bickering. If you're not, then there is a complication that you should consider." Sanchez sailed a document across the table to Bracken—U.S. Coast Guard Form CG-1348; titled First Preferred Mortgage of Vessel, held by the Seaman's Bank of Thomaston, Maine, but recently transferred to Sanchez y Vierro, S.A. of Colon, Republic of Panama.

Bracken glanced at it. "Okay. So I'm behind by two lousy payments. You'll get your money. The charter fee is still negotiable."

Sanchez gave an elegant Latin shrug. "Our firm has paid the funds necessary to purchase this note from the bank in Maine, a very common business practice. So you see, we own the *Pampero*. Since you are sixty days in arrears on payments, you will note on page three that the owner of the mortgage has complete authority to repossess the vessel and to sell it for whatever it will bring at auction. Any money left over after satisfaction of the outstanding balance, accrued interest, and legal costs would be returned to you, of course."

Despite the lateness of the afternoon, the sun was still hard, the light glaring off the water, framing the portholes in a hot glare. There were the familiar things that he had collected over a lifetime—the books of some twenty years, well worn and smelling of age and mildew. A photograph of Willie, set in a tarnished frame and yellowing. The oil lamp which his father had given him, which his grandfather had given his father, originally stripped from a Dutch barque driven ashore on the coast of Maine in the winter of 1893. The brass lamp gleamed like newly minted gold, throwing off splinters of afternoon sunlight.

The *Pampero* was rolling slowly, almost imperceptibly, transmitting its motion to the lamp which creaked in its gimbals. The schooner was Bracken's home and, papers or not, it was *his* and, more important, a long, long way from any American port where the vessel could be legally seized. The thought gave him confidence.

"You're in Iles des Saintes," he said. "Not U.S. waters."

The muscles under the smooth skin of Sanchez's face momentarily jumped and then relaxed. "I'm well aware of that, Captain Bracken."

"That mortgage was originated and signed in Maine. The *Pampero* is a U.S. documented vessel, regardless of who owns it."

"I anticipated that might be a problem, Captain Bracken." He flipped a page of the legal pad and ran his finger down a paragraph of compact writing, then closed the pad. "That is why we have had Mr. Stackhill order the cruise to include Les Saintes—specifically because Les Saintes is French territory."

"So what?"

Sanchez made admonishing little shakes of his head, his jowls flopping sideways like a beagle's. "Your knowledge of Admiralty law is lacking. Les Saintes *is* a dependency of Guadeloupe, which, in turn, *is* a department of France. The essential point is that Panama and France have a mutual treaty which respects and enforces each other's maritime laws."

"So?"

"I can bore you with legal technicalities, but under Panamanian law, if payments on a vessel are seriously in default, the Panamanian holder of the mortgage may obtain a writ transferring the ship's registry to Panama and thus obtain full protection of Panamanian maritime law. The significant point is that the

French are willing to respect and enforce Panamanian law in French waters."

"You didn't—"

"But I did, Captain Bracken. My associate, Mr. Vierro, has the papers necessary to impound the Panamanian sailing vessel *Pampero,* and unless you are prepared to immediately pay up the full amount of the loan's principal plus back interest and substantial legal fees, the vessel will be sold at auction in Guadeloupe in two days time." Sanchez glanced up at the beams overhead as if appraising her value. "I doubt that she would bring very much down here, Captain Bracken. Perhaps some local would want her to carry cargo. Of course, it would be a shame. Such a classically beautiful vessel . . ."

Vierro came in on cue. His fingers were interlaced and he bent them back, cracking the knuckles. Like he was dead bored. "You read the French, Bracken?" he asked in heavily accented and halting English. He pulled a document from the briefcase and scooted it across the varnished surface of the table.

It was, as far as Bracken could determine, a French court order. The *Pampero,* John Bracken, and the firm of Sanchez y Vierro were mentioned. There were no less than nine signatures of various witnesses and officials. The document was stamped with the mark of the Palais du Justice, Guadeloupe, sealed with red wax and bound in red ribbon. Bracken had heard it said that legal paperwork created by the French bureaucracy is a dead language rivaled only in complexity and unreadability by the Dead Sea scrolls.

Bracken pushed the papers back toward Vierro. "You realize that I can up anchor and be out of here in five minutes?"

Sanchez took over. "I think not. Panamanian law gives its citizens the right to protect their property. By force, if necessary, you understand? And French law would sanction our actions." He motioned toward the deck. "Raul, our associate, is prepared to make sure that you do nothing disrespectful of the law." He smiled. "For the sake of our continued friendship, I suggest that you don't make him angry."

Sanchez had effectively presented the stick. He now leaned forward, chin cupped by hand supported in turn by wrist, arm, and elbow, and dangled the carrot. "All of this is very unpleasant, Captain Bracken, but we felt it was necessary to make our position clear. However, the bright side is that in addition to the seventy-five thousand that we have agreed to pay once the charter is completed, I will sign over the vessel to you, free and clear of its fourteen-thousand-dollar encumbrance. I am also assured that the lawsuit you face will be cleared up by Mr. Stackhill's attorneys at no additional cost to you. At that time you will be free to transfer the vessel back into U.S. registry if you so please."

Bracken rose, went to the liquor cabinet, and poured himself a stiff whiskey. "And who's paying for all this?"

Except for the sound of a grunt from Vierro, there was a profound silence.

Some sage had once said that there is a time to reap and a time to sow. To waffle in the decision between doing either meant that you were likely to get run down by the tractor. "Let's make a deal," Bracken finally said.

Keith and Cousin had their seabags packed. Bracken slipped down the fo'c'sle ladder just as the sun was setting. He peeled off a thousand-dollar American Express check for each of them; six weeks of back pay, travel expenses, and another fifty thrown in.

"How come you paying us off, skip?" Keith asked, obviously distressed.

Bracken had a hard time looking either one of them in the eye. "I'm not paying you and Cousin off, Keith. Just bringing your salaries up-to-date and giving you a vacation. I'll be back in Bequia in about a month. In the meanwhile, take some time off and go fishing in the Grenadines." Keith smiled, but Cousin looked doubtful.

"You taking those men on charter?"

Bracken shrugged. "Something like that."

Cousin slowly shook his head. "Bad news, skip. That man on deck is packin'."

West Indian vernacular for carrying a weapon. Bracken just shrugged. "No problem. Raul's got a thing about sharks. Likes to keep a gun handy so he can shoot them." He glanced down at his watch. "Get going. Walrus is waiting in the dinghy. You've got only fifteen minutes to make the mail boat over to Pointe à Pitre. You can catch that LIAT flight out to St. Vincent at seven tomorrow morning."

He watched them go, a glass of scotch in his hand. Keith waved back, Cousin didn't. Hard to explain to them. Bracken hoped that they would keep their mouths shut and had briefed

Walrus to impress on them that this was all in the family and no one else's business.

She was standing beside him before he realized she was there. "You're hitting the sauce a little hard, John," she said softly, her eyes avoiding his, following the dinghy.

"Nice that you care, but none of your business, lady."

She held out her hand, palm down. "Don't I get a ruler on the knuckles as well?"

He blew out his breath. "Okay. Sorry. I didn't mean that, Jean. Just that I've got a lot on my mind."

"So what, if anything, *is* on your mind, John?"

He turned to her. She had on the same white cotton dress that she had worn in Antigua on the last night before the Stackhill charter, and he felt a catch in his throat. He had to look away. "Vierro and Raul No-Known-Last-Name are moving aboard. They'll take the aft cabin. Stackhill and Pam take the starboard guest cabin. Sanchez has given me my sailing orders—a straight shot to the Mona Passage and then up through the Old Bahama Channel."

"And just where is the Old Bahama Channel?"

"Between Cuba and the Bahamas. Somebody did their homework. Sanchez brought all the charts, including a list of navigational aids." He sipped at the scotch. "You still sure you want to come? I can run you ashore when Walrus gets back. There's a seven A.M. flight out tomorrow. And you've got salary coming."

"I'm staying," she said flatly, "but I'd damn sure like to get ashore this evening so that I can spend some time by myself. This whole scene stifles me—people slinking around, double-dealing, that bitch of a woman and now guns."

"I'm afraid that won't be possible." Sanchez was standing in the companionway, his fist wrapped around a glass of ruby port. He climbed the last three steps and slid his bulk onto the coachroof. "As they say in the movies, 'All shore leaves are canceled.' " He nodded toward the returning dinghy and turned toward Bracken. "When your first mate gets back, you will get the anchor up immediately. Our launch will guide you across the bay and around to the anchorage in the western cove of Terre-de-Haut." He nodded to the black power yacht. "The *Victoria* will follow you. Both vessels will anchor there for the night and get under way in the morning."

"Why the change in anchorage? It's fine in here. No roll, good holding ground."

Sanchez regarded the port, sniffed at it, and then took a

small sip. Its quality obviously wasn't up to his standards. He sloshed the contents overboard.

"I would remind you that my firm now owns the vessel. If we want it moved, you move it." He slid off the coachroof and nodded to Raul, who was scowling from his position near the wheel. "Raul and Vierro will assist you in moving the vessel. You are both invited for supper on board the *Victoria* this evening. Your first mate, who is also invited, will be served his supper in the crew galley of the *Victoria*. Eightish."

"I already have a roast in the oven," she objected.

"Then let me put it another way," Sanchez said, looking out across the bay at the *Victoria*'s approaching launch. "My invitation falls into the category of compulsory attendance. Reasonably formal dinner dress would be in order for the occasion."

The sun had been down for more than an hour and a half. Bracken and Walrus had reanchored the *Pampero* in two fathoms, just off the deserted beach, and the *Victoria* had eased in astern of them. Bracken had changed into chino slacks and his mildewed blazer, then motored over to the *Victoria* with Jean and Walrus. Sanchez, Stackhill, and Pam had taken the launch over to the power boat an hour before.

Bracken felt uneasy, as any ship's master does, leaving his vessel unattended. For what it was worth—and in Bracken's mind, it wasn't worth much—Raul and Vierro had remained aboard, playing dominoes in the salon, swearing hotly at each other in Spanish, a rapidly diminishing bottle of rum on the table between them. For luck, Bracken had switched on the automatic bilge pump.

Close up, the *Victoria* was larger than Bracken had first estimated, probably more than one hundred and forty feet overall, black aluminum hull and huge exhaust ports in the transom that hinted at three high-speed turbo-diesel engines. The bloody thing could probably do forty knots, he guessed.

A Latin crew member, decked out in a striped jersey and a pompon hat, took their painter and wordlessly guided them toward the deck salon, then ushered Walrus forward through a passageway toward the crew quarters.

The salon was expansive, carpeted in deep white pile and enclosed by smoked-glass windows. The furniture was a crazy mixture of velour-cushioned couches and chairs constructed of thick Lucite rods covered with leather seats and backs.

Sanchez, dressed in a white linen suit, waddled through the carpet toward them, extending his pudgy hand. "Welcome aboard my vessel."

Bracken took the extended hand and shook. Sanchez then kissed the back of Sweet Jean's hand, lingering a bit too long for Bracken's taste.

Then Sanchez signaled a waiter, who immediately responded by drifting silently out of the gloom of the dining area. Bracken's eyes, adjusting to the light, saw two more waiters, both in white mess jackets, their faces indistinct, lined up like cigar store Indians against the bulkhead. And they said that good domestic help was hard to find.

"A malt whiskey for Captain Bracken," Sanchez ordered. "And for the lady . . . ?" He had turned to Sweet Jean.

"Chablis," she answered negligently.

Sanchez waffled his hand toward the waiter. "A glass of the Chablis Grand Cru les Clos. Domaine de la Maladière, the 1981, I think." The waiter faded into the gloom. There was the sound of a door being discreetly shut.

"And how do you like the *Victoria,* Captain Bracken?"

"Exporting refrigerators to South America seems to pay."

"If you say so, Captain Bracken." Sanchez slid back a smoked-glass panel and turned on the stereo. A string quartet played Mozart through hidden speakers.

As the drinks were produced on a silver tray by the waiter, Stackhill and Pam made their entrance. Stackhill wore a dinner jacket which didn't fit him very well but probably fit Sanchez perfectly. Pam, on the other hand, wore a glove-tight dove-gray silk gown that fit her extremely well. Her hair was softly glossy, her face painted with a minimum of makeup. As she moved across the salon, Bracken realized that she wasn't wearing anything under the gown except her marvelously constructed body.

"Evening, Hook." She extended her hand as if she expected it to be kissed. Bracken settled for a quick pressing of the flesh. "Hi, Pam. Terrific outfit."

She illuminated the salon with her smile. "I'm so pleased you like it. It's so hard to get into, but, actually, it comes off quite easily." She gave him the barest flicker of a wink and Bracken felt himself flush from the knees up.

Sanchez ordered two more bottles of the Chablis as he guided them to the table. Once seated, he nodded to the waiters. In the dim light Bracken saw that two of them were fairly young Latinos, but the third one was older and wore dark glasses, features Oriental—the majordomo, Bracken guessed. The two younger ones quickly scuttled off toward the galley, but the older one just stood there, his face hidden in the gloom, immobile. Bracken, for no good reason, felt uneasy about the man, as if he had met him before. Possibly Stackhill's contact in Antigua? But that was improbable, wasn't it, and his mind turned to the meal as the food was set before him.

It was one of the finest meals that Bracken had ever eaten. The fish course was freshly caught bonito sauted lightly in lemon butter and shallots. Delicately forking up a chunk of the fish from his plate, Sanchez placed it on his tongue, savoring the taste before chewing. "Don't you find the fish exquisite, Mr. Stackhill?"

"Yeah, mind-boggling. Pass the grape juice."

One of the waiters immediately filled Stackhill's goblet, and Stackhill sloshed it down in a series of noisy gulps. "Not half bad," he said, and held it up for a refill.

As the two younger waiters cleared away the fish course, a man entered the salon from an alleyway which presumably led forward to the bridge. The man was mid-forties, mustached and Latin: an Errol Flynn type dressed in white trousers and a white shirt, three gold stripes on his epaulets. He spoke in a low, rapid-fire Spanish to Sanchez. Bracken caught just a few of the words—something about *electrónicas*.

Sanchez approved the request and waved the man away with an impatient flick of his wrist.

"Problems?" Bracken asked.

"No problems," Sanchez replied. The next course was arriving and the waiter first offered Sanchez the plate. Sanchez examined the chicken and sniffed appreciatively. "Suprêmes de Volaille Printanier," he announced. "My own version." He reached over and patted Pam's hand as if he were reassuring a little girl that her braces didn't *really* spoil her smile. "Enjoy, please." Pam shivered visibly.

He turned to Bracken. "All of you will stay aboard the *Victoria* tonight, including your first mate. Guest accommodations have been prepared. Overnight, my engineering officer and his men will be working on your vessel, fitting certain equipment. They should be finished with their work by sunrise."

"Wait a minute, Sanchez. No one goes aboard the *Pampero* without my permission."

"Don't be tiresome, Captain Bracken. Your ship is ill equipped for this passage. You will need a great deal more than a sextant in order to determine your position. And Señor Vierro must stay in contact with the *Victoria* by high frequency radio. Consequently, under the supervision of my first mate, my men are installing radar, a satellite navigational set, and a single-sideband radio. You will be free to keep the equipment once the charter is over, with my compliments."

Bracken was stunned. Sanchez was talking about ten, maybe fifteen thousand bucks worth of gear.

Jean kicked his shin lightly. "Close your mouth, Bracken," she whispered. "You're drooling." A few seconds later he felt her leg nudge his. Accidental or intended? Either way, arousing. Still, he couldn't take his eyes off Pam's cleavage. The cut of her dress invited exploration. As he was staring at her, she glanced up, making momentary eye contact, and sealed the unspoken promise by briefly running her tongue over her lips.

Sanchez signaled the waiters to clear the plates. The dessert was peach sorbet, followed by a variety of liqueurs. Satiated and fatigued, the five diners lapsed into silence, no common ground of conversation left to prolong the dinner party.

Stackhill's eyes were drooping, his head nodding. On the other hand, Pam exuded all the elements of being switched on— overly bright eyes, flushed cheeks, and a wonderful, fascinating sheen of perspiration on the swelling mounds of her breasts. "The food was fabulous," she cooed.

Sanchez returned the compliment with his click-on smile. "It has been my great pleasure, Pamela. I would love to have you— again." He smiled, meaningfully, Stackhill not catching the innuendo. "But for now . . ." He reached in his jacket pocket and extracted keys. "I have ordered four cabins to be prepared. I would imagine that you all look forward to a shower and a calm night's sleep. Breakfast will be served in the salon at six A.M." He pushed back his chair and stood up. "Would you require one stateroom or two, Captain Bracken?" Sanchez gave an amused smile, as if it were more of a challenge than the innocent question of a host.

Jean made the decision for Bracken. "We'll take separate accommodations." Bracken caught Pam smiling in triumph.

One of the young waiters ushered them down the spiral

staircase into a long corridor that serviced the guest cabins. Stackhill, dead on his feet, took the first stateroom on the port side. He made a grab for Pam and tried to pull her into the cabin, but she twisted out of his grip. Stackhill turned away from her and slammed the door behind him. Flouncing her hair, Pam entered the stateroom opposite Stackhill's. "How nice," she said, her voice overly loud in the confines of the corridor. "Stateroom A. *So* easy to remember." She waved to Jean and Bracken. "Nighty-night."

The waiter offered the two remaining keys to Bracken. Bracken unlocked one door and stood there, looking at Jean, not sure of what he was trying to silently convey to her—or what she might be conveying to him. She seemed on the verge of following him, hesitated, looked into his eyes, then pressed her lips firmly together and held out her hand. Reluctantly, he handed her the other key.

"Nighty-night, Cap'n Hook," she whispered, mimicking Pam's cloying voice, then entered her stateroom, pulling the door firmly closed behind her.

Bracken bit down hard, grating his teeth. Damned bitch! Seething with anger, he opened the door to his stateroom, then slammed it.

The room would have rivaled a cabin on the first class deck of a cruise ship. There was no hint in the decor that the stateroom was in a ship. Two queen-size beds bracketed the opposite sides of the room, thick carpeting smothered the deck, the kind of nap that instead of vacuuming, you mowed. At the far end of the stateroom a door opened into a large bathroom.

He explored the rest of the stateroom. The drawers of the bureau were empty, as was the hanging locker, except for a terry-cloth robe packaged in cellophane. A television was set into the bulkhead. He switched it on and was rewarded by the sound of static and scraggly white lines. He snapped off the knob.

But the tiled bathroom yielded treasures. The shower was large enough to accommodate a Senate subcommittee, and on the counter was a wicker basket that held all the goodies: shaving cream, deodorant, shampoo, hair conditioner, a disposable razor, body talc, various soaps, skin bracer, and a loofa sponge. The toilet was matched by a bidet, both pale rose. Spanning across the bathroom was an expanse of mirror, also rose-colored, and flecked with gold. The faucet handles and spout on the sink, head, and bidet were gold-plated dolphins.

Bracken moved to the porthole. Like all the other ports in

the ship, it was smoked Lexan plastic. He could just make out the vague profile of the *Pampero* as she rode to her anchor more than a hundred yards away in the faint moonlight. Her spreader lights were on and he could see men moving on her deck, but it was impossible to make out what they were doing. Not something he could control, and why bother? It was their money.

He scrubbed down in the shower, luxuriating under the hard spray of hot water, dried off with a fluffy towel, then shaved. He combed back his wet hair, scrubbed his teeth, and applied talc.

Climbing into the tent-size terry-cloth bathrobe, he succumbed to a momentary temptation and eased his body down onto the bed. His wimpy cerebral cortex argued that he should sleep the sleep of the righteous, but the insidious glandular part of him kept nagging that Pam was up the corridor in cabin A, similarly showered, perfumed, and horny. Gradually, his glandular cheering section began to gain the upper hand.

Despite his fatigue, he tried to conjure up some lusty enthusiasm for his forthcoming main event with Pam. But his cerebral cortex valiantly fought back: Pam was a chocolate Easter bunny— undoubtedly delectable in small nibbles but cloying if you ate the whole thing.

The decision was made for him. There came a tap-tap-tapping at his door.

He turned down the comforter, rumpled the sheets into an inviting but casual state, turned up the air-conditioning a notch (some liked it hot but Bracken definitely preferred it cool), slicked back his hair with a single stroke of the comb, and opened the door a crack.

"What's the password?" he whispered to the figure silhouetted by the corridor light, her features indistinct.

"The Shadow." She glanced over her shoulder, then pushed by him, pulled the door closed.

She sank down on the opposite bed, her *Victoria* unisex terry-cloth robe overly large on her body, partially revealing, without apparent malice aforethought, inviting cleavage. But it was the wrong body. Bracken's glandular cheering section groaned at the prospect of a time-out.

Jean's hair was still wet and glistened like goldenrod after a summer's shower, her tanned skin pinkened and moist from the shower. She smelled wonderful. Bracken's glandular cheering, having second thoughts, rose to their feet, screaming for resumption of play.

"The *Victoria* isn't Panamanian—it's Cuban."

Bracken pulled a chair from under the dressing table, sat on it backward facing her, then realized that his terry-cloth robe undoubtedly revealed the magnitude of his rapidly swelling degeneracy. He quickly stood up, shoving his hands into the deep pockets of the robe, the shape of his hands hiding the betraying bulge, trying to look attentive. But some flicker of distrust licked at his brain, and his glands were now howling in protest for satisfaction which would probably be found only in cabin A. Jean obviously knew that he and Pam were planning a sexual challenge match, and yet Jean had intentionally intervened. Envy, territorial protectionism, or just plain bitchiness?

"How do you figure that?"

She pulled a penlight and makeup mirror from her pocket. "Okay, Bracken. Squat down and check out the mattress label."

He did. Of course the label read upside down and backward, but he eventually spelled out Garcia y Garcia, Industria Cubana.

"Now check this out." She produced a matchbook. "One of the waiters used it to light the candles, burned his fingers, and accidentally dropped it."

Bracken examined the matchbook. The advertisement was for Crystal Polar beer. "So . . . ?"

"Cuban beer, *mon cher*."

He had to persuade her to leave. Soon. "What's the point?"

She slid off the bed and levitated over to the dressing table, pulled off a recessed lid which revealed a sunken refrigerated cabinet. In the cabinet were several bottles of champagne and two moisture-beaded glasses. "Didn't you notice, or were you saving it to share with Pam?" She gave a wolfish grin, danced her fingers around the wire, then eased the cork out so that it gave just a polite cough. She poured generous glassfuls for both of them.

"The point is, Hook, this gin palace is owned by Cubans but registered for convenience in Panama."

"That's pretty thin. A matchbook and a mattress tag don't prove a damn thing."

She clinked her glass against his and swallowed. "Not conclusive either way, Bracken, but it still makes damned good sense."

"So maybe you're right and maybe you're not. Rather than jump to conclusions, let's see how this thing plays out." He made a point of yawning. "We'll hash this over tomorrow." He stood up and walked over to the door, opened it a crack, and looked up and down the corridor. "Okay, Shadow, the coast is clear."

Reluctantly, she headed for the door, then turned, her arms sliding like Eve's snake around his neck, pulling him tight against her. She gave Bracken a long, thoughtful kiss. " 'Night, Hook. Don't bend it." She pulled the door closed behind her as if she were reluctant to go.

Damn her! he swore. Damn, damn, damn her! Because in just those few seconds of contact she had proved to him that he still desired her (loved her?), and it wasn't something that he was going to get over that easily. Agitated, he stalked back to the bathroom, furiously brushed his teeth again, and applied body lotion to his armpits. Then went to the bulkhead nearest Pam's stateroom and rapped. There was a pause, then an answering rap.

The glandular cheering section that had been dozing in the back bleachers came to life again. From the hidden cooler he extracted the other bottle of champagne. No more fresh glasses, so they would drink it from the bottle. Cary Grant and Katharine Hepburn stuff. He checked the mirror before leaving, trying to comb back his now-dry hair, but the thinning strands were unruly and his cowlick wouldn't lie down. What the hell, he thought. At least I smell clean.

He opened the door. Jean was standing there, her hand raised as if she were about to knock.

"Jean ..." he said, flustered. "I was ... well, I was just coming over to ... ah ... see you. Nightcap. Cozy chats about the Cuban enchilada theory, stuff like that."

She glanced down at his robe. "What you really need is a cold shower, Bracken." She gently pushed him back into the stateroom, then pulled the door closed behind her and turned the key. She took the bottle from him and guided him toward the bed. She pulled the belt loose from his robe.

"Up and down," she softly commanded.

"Whatdayamean?"

"Lie down. I'll take care of the rest."

She woke him just before dawn, the porthole haloed in a creamy light, her body just a suggestion of tan skin against the white silk sheets.

At first she kneaded his back with her hands, doing marvelous things to his muscles, then gently rolled him over and bent down, the nipples of her breasts just touching his skin, sending tiny electric shocks through his body.

"You're a rogue, Bracken," she whispered. "A rogue and a scoundrel. You're also sweet and naive and incredibly transparent. And for what it's worth, I love you dearly."

She planted a moist kiss on his lips and he felt his whole body responding with a hum, as if some powerful motor had been switched on and was coming up to speed.

She raised herself up on her knees, straddling his body, and then lowered herself onto him.

"The last was a seven," she whispered, smiling, and started to move gently, the pleasure, the pressure within him excruciating. "But now we go for a nine point three."

"So go for it, Shadow," he said, semi-conscious, his voice thick.

She paused for just a second, taking a strand of her hair, drawing it over her upper lip, making a mustache of it.

"Who knows," she said in a husky voice, again rising and falling in a gentle gait, "what evil lurks in the heart of a loving woman?" She picked up the pace into a canter, her head arching first forward and then back, her long hair swishing across his chest and face like an incredibly soft mane.

"The Shadow knows," she said, answering her own question, although Bracken could no longer hear her.

Overhead in the blue dome, the sun, still below the horizon, illuminated stringy wisps of cirrus which converged in an arrowhead toward the north. The wind brought with it the smell of inland cooking fires.

A parrot cawed in the brush, and seconds later exploded into the air in a flurry of red and green, screeching in birdtalk at the predator who threatened it.

Lu leaned against the varnished rail of the flying bridge of the *Victoria*, a mug of coffee cupped in his hands. He had stripped off the waiter's jacket and now wore a *Victoria* crew Windbreaker.

Sanchez slid back the glass-paneled door to the bridge and joined him. "It is the best time of day."

Lu silently nodded. He would have preferred to spend this time alone and resented Sanchez's presence.

"You have seen Bracken. Is he the same?"

"Certainly older—but nevertheless the same." He turned

slightly, leaning his weight against the rail. "Nearly two decades ago I broke his spirit, Sanchez, then mentally castrated him. Is that too profound for you at five-thirty in the morning, Comrade?"

"Still, he is a dangerous man, an unpredictable man," Sanchez answered testily.

"The solution to controlling Bracken and other men like him is exploiting a mixture of the elements of greed, guilt, revenge, and vulnerability. He is greedy for money. He feels guilt for a wasted life. He wants revenge for the treatment that he suffered from his country, and he is vulnerable to women. The first three elements are already proven. As to the last, I believe that he slept with his cook last night, because her stateroom was empty. At any rate, his infatuation with her is evident. If he gets out of line, then we will use her as a lever."

"Then Stackhill's whore was unnecessary?"

What a waste, Lu thought. There was a woman who had been born to please men. He shook his head. "She was the primary bait. Bracken didn't nibble, but his cook has voluntarily solved the vulnerability problem for us." He blew across his still-steaming mug of coffee and then looked south across the channel toward Dominica. "You will instruct Vierro to take care of Stackhill when it is convenient. We have no further need of him."

Sanchez nodded as if he had expected this.

Across the water where the *Pampero* lay anchored, two inflatable dinghies were motoring toward the *Victoria*.

"They're finished?" Lu asked.

Sanchez nodded.

"Then send your stewards down to the staterooms to wake our guests. Serve them breakfast and get them under way as soon as possible. Once they're gone, I'll want the *Victoria* headed south."

"Where to?" Sanchez asked cautiously.

"Grenada," Lu replied. "We have a plane to meet."

12.

July 10–July 11

Bracken was the last to leave the *Victoria,* chauffeured over to the *Pampero* in the launch by one of *Victoria*'s crew.

Already six-twenty, the sun up, the wind freshening with the dawn. He sat on the launch's thwart, looking back at the *Victoria.*

Her profile was more that of a sleek Corvette than wallowing, tail-finned Cadillacs that the current breed of yacht builders were producing. The only thing that marred her looks was a satellite dome that had been tacked on just aft of the bridge, its bulbous fiberglass hemisphere now pinked by the morning sun. Still, for a power yacht, Bracken thought, she was handsome.

He ran his eye along her sheer and superstructure, trying to trigger some firmer recollection, and as he did, a man moved from within the smoked-glass bridge and onto the wing deck. The distance was more than fifty yards, but Bracken thought he recognized the thin face of the Oriental that had presided over the previous evening's dinner as majordomo. He was now wearing chino slacks, a white T-shirt, sunglasses, and a Windbreaker.

For a moment frozen in time, they stared at each other, then the Oriental slowly lifted his hand. Somehow Bracken realized that the gesture was more than just a casual greeting. It implied intimacy, as if they were old acquaintances. Hesitantly, Bracken lifted his hand in silent reply. The Oriental nodded, smiled, then turned away and retraced his steps back to the bridge. Something about him, the way he moved his body, the shape of his face that Bracken couldn't place, yet was somehow familiar. From the past? Bracken asked himself, unable to make the connection.

The launch driver throttled down and shifted into neutral, swinging in alongside the *Pampero*'s boarding ladder.

Bracken turned around, ready to board. Walrus helped him up the ladder, his face purpled with anger.

"You actually authorized those bastards to do this?" Walrus shouted at him. "Not only does it looks like shit, but how in hell do you think we can set the fisherman staysail with that thing hung up there?" He jabbed his finger upward.

Glancing aloft, Bracken saw the bulging blob of a plastic radome jutting out from the mainmast, the cables leading from it crudely stapled to the mast. Where the cables reached the mast boot, a hole had been bored in the deck to lead the wiring through to the salon, then plugged with globs of brown mastic putty as temporary waterproofing.

"You don't want to go below just yet." Jean had come out of the fo'c'sle hatch, a mug of coffee in her hand. "I put some rum in it." She passed the mug to Bracken.

She was wearing a pareu, wrapped back on itself, the upper crescents of her untanned boobs slightly flattened but peeking cheerfully out from beneath the folds of the fabric like the whites of two eggs sunny-side up.

Bracken thankfully sipped at the rum-spiked coffee. "What's going on below?"

She ticked off her fingers. "They've installed a radar, a satellite navigational unit, and a long-range single-sideband transceiver."

"So what's wrong with that?" Fifteen thousand worth of gear. If he didn't want to keep it, he could clear at least eight thousand by flogging it off.

"They didn't take much trouble installing it, skip," Walrus answered.

Bracken flung the coffee overboard and headed for the companionway.

They had installed the equipment all right. Bored holes through the teak dressing table in the aft cabin, using straps of aluminum bolted through the top of the dresser to secure the equipment. Wires in spaghettilike bundles were secured to the overhead with cable clamps and lag bolts. Dirt, sawdust, shavings, grease, and bits of stripped cable insulation littered the cabin sole. He wanted to weep.

"Nice, yes?" Vierro was standing behind him, grinning, a bottle of beer in his fist.

"*Nice? Nice my ass!*" Bracken shouted. "You have any idea what it'll take to repair this damage to the woodwork?" Bracken had thrust his face to within a couple of inches of Vierro's, yelling at the top of his lungs, spittle spraying Vierro's sunglasses.

Vierro backed off, unconcerned. "A few hundred dollars in materials, a week of work. You will send me a bill, of course."

Bracken slumped down on one of the berths, his head in his hands. "You fuckers."

Vierro froze, his voice going flat and hard. "That is not a nice thing to say, Captain. A good deal of money has been invested in this equipment. There was not much time to install it. When you are near the reefs of the Bahamas in the middle of the night, you will praise the firm of Sanchez y Vierro for our forethought." He chugalugged the rest of the beer and dropped the empty bottle on the cabin sole, leaving a dent in the wood.

The insult was so obvious, so premeditated, that Bracken at first couldn't *believe* it was intentional. Vierro helped to dispel that illusion by kicking the bottle across the cabin sole, where it ricocheted against a molding, leaving another gouge.

"I truly wish you would keep a cleaner ship, Captain," Vierro said. "Glass bottles rolling about the floor are dangerous to the safety of your guests. You could be sued—again." As he said it, Vierro smiled, challenging Bracken.

Halfway to his feet, bunching his fist, Bracken froze. Vierro had produced a small .22-caliber automatic.

"I would advise you to control yourself, Captain Bracken. This weapon is not large but it is lethal. And if I missed, which I would not, the result would be more holes in the woodwork and no captain left alive to send me the repair bill."

As Bracken hesitated, he saw Walrus slide silently up behind Vierro, the whalebone fid reversed so that the blunt end was poised over Vierro's head. And behind Walrus, moving with equal silence, was Raul.

"Back off, Walrus!" Bracken shouted. Simultaneously, Raul hit Walrus on the temple with the butt of his revolver. Walrus slumped, eyes rolled back, mustache twitching.

Vierro didn't even bother to turn. "Stupid, Bracken. Both you and your first mate would be dead now if I had wished it." He motioned with the barrel of the .22. "Sit down. We will discuss the chain of command aboard this ship."

Bracken's anger had evaporated, replaced by fear. He dumbly nodded.

"This little exercise was intended to make a point," Vierro said evenly. "Raul and I want to be assured that our commands are carried out by you and your crew without question. *Claro?*"

Bracken nodded.

"It is satisfying that we understand each other so clearly. I would now like you to get the ship under way. You will sail a course to the Mona Passage, which is west of Puerto Rico. All headings and distances are already laid out on the charts. I will monitor your progress with the satellite navigational unit. If you deviate from that course, I will know it, and then there will be further unpleasantness. Raul has taken a liking to your cook, and it is all that I can do to restrain him. But I will do so providing my commands are obeyed. *Claro?*"

Bracken's stomach lurched. Looking up, Vierro's face was expressionless. He had holstered his .22, but his feet were slightly spread, his body tensed. *"Claro?"* Vierro repeated more insistently.

The Walther 9mm semi-automatic was there in the engine room, along with a clip of eight cartridges. Bracken had owned it for years, keeping it as an insurance policy against the improbable. He had no doubt that he was in way over his head, that his actuarial longevity was measured in days if he did nothing.

"Claro?" Vierro shouted.

"Claro," Bracken finally answered.

The barometer was down over eight millibars since dawn as Bracken came off watch at sundown. He wrote up the log. Ninety-two miles in the last eleven hours, an average of just over eight knots. The old girl was rolling along on a broad reach, streaming out a creamy wake, sails rose-red in the twilight of the setting sun. But the fall of the barometer nagged at him. Too early in the hurricane season to be potentially serious, but sure enough there had to be a depression thumping around somewhere out to the east of him. He entered the wind-, sky-, and sea-conditions columns with "northeast at twenty knots, high cirrus, and nine-foot swells." But that didn't tell the whole story. The wind was steadily building, but it wasn't shifting in direction, which meant that *if* there was a depression overtaking him, it was on a collision course. But how far away?

Bracken bent over the chart, spread the dividers along the latitude scale, and walked off 92 nautical miles along his course line. Then he spanned off the remaining distance to the Mona Passage. Only 272 miles to run, which would put the *Pampero* in the entrance to the passage by sometime late tomorrow night. By then, and with luck, he would be out of the way of the storm.

The light was just about gone. Bracken switched on a reading light and was rewarded with a dim glow. *Dammit,* he swore. The batteries were just about flat. He lurched his way to the engine room amidships and peered at the voltmeter. The needle sagged below eleven volts. Already knowing the likely result, he tried to start the generator. It turned over sluggishly, then wheezed to a stop. And Bracken could guess why. Vierro's toys; the radar and radio must still be on, sucking up what little remained of the charge in the battery banks.

He pulled a flashlight from its clip on the bulkhead and examined the generator. It was a single cylinder Onan. A sturdy beast when it decided to run but cursed with a surly temperament when it decided it wouldn't. In theory and according to the manual, which was probably written by a factory engineer with clean fingernails, it could be started manually by swinging a cranking handle, but that required both the strength and agility of an ape. Admiration for the prowess of endangered species aside, Bracken didn't think he had it in him. He had busted his knuckles twice before trying to start it manually, both times in a calm harbor. And when he had asked Walrus to give it a go, Walrus had started making mutinous noises. In the end, Bracken had to humble himself and borrow a St. Lucia taxicab's battery to effect a jump start.

"The electricity is very weak," Vierro said from behind him. Bracken had never heard him coming. He turned.

"You stupid sod. You've used up all the juice in the batteries with your damned radar."

Vierro frowned. "I do not like to be called stupid. What does this other word mean?"

"It means pal, friend, buddy. That's just a loose translation, of course."

Vierro was still frowning. "I am not stupid, nor am I your buddy." He pulled a penlight from his shirt pocket and flashed it around the darkened engine room. "What is the problem?"

"The problem is that the batteries are flat. Therefore, the bloody generator doesn't have enough juice left to start it. Your radar pulls too much current."

"And how will you correct this problem?"

Bracken's brain finally began to function.

Despite the ongoing moral dilemma in the yachting crowd as to carrying firearms aboard yachts, Bracken had long ago decided that it was worthwhile insurance. There were crazies, druggies, and common thieves in most of the ports he had visited, and the 9mm Walther semi-automatic that he had purchased long ago was wrapped in a cushion of cotton waste and hidden behind the battery banks of the engine room. It would take at least ten minutes to dig it out and clean off the cosmoline grease. But if he could subdue Vierro with a wrench, then he could nail Raul with the Walther when Raul unlocked the aft cabin door in response to evening chow call.

The generator was mounted on a bench. The starting handle was swung from the forward side of the generator, but in order to get a proper grasp on the knuckle-buster, one had to crouch like a primate on top of the battery banks. In port it was theoretically possible, but at sea and with the *Pampero* rolling heavily, it was a task that called for single-minded dedication, agility, and the willingness to break one's back.

Chewing on his lip, trying to look both serious and competent, Bracken first held his fingers to the injection pump and then to the decompression lever of the generator, as if he were taking its pulse. "Difficult but not impossible," he said almost to himself, then looked up into Vierro's eyes. "First step is to squirt some starting fluid into the air intake manifold. Then someone has to swing the handle while the other person first chokes the framis valve, then pulls out the flagentia and finally, when the generator begins to fire, tightens this nut on the flibbertijib." He selected the largest adjustable wrench from the tool rack and backed off the injector nozzle nut. The wrench weighed over six pounds, and Bracken had already picked an inviting streak of gray hair just above Vierro's left ear as the target.

"Good," Vierro responded. "You will show me the sequence of the things to do and you will turn the handle."

Bracken shook his head. "Not that easy. Wish it were, but the timing is very delicate." He stuffed the wrench under his belt. "Okay, now assume that I'm cranking the handle. *You* would squirt a shot of starting fluid in here for about eight and a half seconds. Then you have to feel the framis valve until it starts to get a little bit warm—you know—just a couple of degrees. . . ." He fluttered his right hand over the decompression release valve and jittered it up and down in a syncopated three-quarters beat. "Then give the old flagentia a couple of licks. . . ." He then whipped the wrench from beneath his belt, fitted it to the injector nozzle nut, and gave it half a turn. "And last of all, screw down on the flibbertijib. Got all of that?"

Vierro looked doubtful. "Yes, I see how difficult the process is. You are the logical person to handle the delicate matter of the controls, but you will excuse me first. I need some gloves to protect my hands." He pushed past Bracken, closing the engine room door behind him.

In less then three minutes Vierro was back, Raul behind him, revolver in hand.

"You'll crank, Bracken," Vierro said, ". . . and I'll handle the controls. Raul will watch with intense interest." All the phony-accented Spanish was gone. The inflection was almost American and the tone of his voice didn't leave room for argument.

Bracken, his plan a shambles, climbed up on the battery bank and grasped the cranking handle, Raul's weapon trained on him.

Vierro looked at Bracken with contempt. "It's a stupid Yanqui flaw that you treat Latins as if they were idiots. I grew up on a farm where the only electricity came from diesel generators. I've run them, maintained them, even rebuilt them. I have also lived in Miami for several years, so you might understand that I know the meaning of the word *sod*. Now, swing that cranking handle, Bracken, as if your life depended on it, because it does."

Bracken was sweating now. He swung the crank several times, predictably skinning his knuckle on the bulkhead as Vierro depressed the decompression release lever. Slowly, Bracken's hand-cranking brought the generator up to a starting speed. Vierro squirted the ether starting fluid into the air cleaner, advanced the throttle, intently watching diesel fuel spurt from the nozzle, first in bubbles and then in a steady stream. He quickly tightened the nozzle nut with the wrench and dropped the decompression release lever. The engine fired erratically, picked up speed, faltered again, then finally gained rpms. The voltmeter climbed to a healthy thirteen volts. Vierro clicked on the engine room light. The bulb glowed brightly.

Almost as an afterthought, Vierro swung the wrench, smashing it into Bracken's ribs. Bracken gasped in pain and straightened up, his head colliding with an oak beam. Then his knees buckled. He screamed and rolled off the battery banks onto the engine room floor.

Vierro placed his foot on Bracken's ribs and swiveled it, exerting increasing downward pressure, as if he were eradicating a cockroach. Bracken screamed again.

Vierro spoke softly. "You're fighting the system, Bracken. Do it right and you'll live to spend the money. Try to fuck with me just once more and you'll end up fish food."

*   *   *

Bracken woke just after 0200, groggy, his whole body throbbing. He lay in his bunk for a few minutes, his senses slowly beginning to pick up on the motion, sounds, and vibrations from *Pampero*'s rig and hull. He measured them against his past experience with the old schooner. She was moving damn fast, the sound of the sea hissing past her hull, but she was laboring under too much canvas. The masts were groaning in their steps, the wind load in the sails causing the ribs, stakes, and frames to complain with the effort. Water in the bilge sloshed heavily. The old girl always leaked, but she leaked more when driven hard. He had to get the bilge pump started.

He snapped on the reading light and tried to sit up. A red hot poker skewered him through the chest. He collapsed back on the bunk, took a long count, eyes squeezed tight with pain, and then sat up again, much more carefully, worming his way upright with his elbows.

As he did, he heard the cabin sole creak in the corridor outside his cabin. The door slid open and Jean came in, her oilskins dripping, hair plastered into a tangled mess.

"What's up?" he asked.

"Walrus asked me to wake you up. Wind's up to thirty-five, gusting forty. He says the mainsail has to be reefed. Too much weather helm. I tried to relieve him, but I can't handle it and he's dead on his feet."

"What about Stackhill and Pam?"

She fluttered her hand. "I rousted Stackhill out and he's getting his foul weather gear on. Forget about Pam. She's out for the count."

"What about the Gold Dust twins?"

"Vierro's locked in the aft cabin, probably in the sack. Raul's in the salon, scared out of his wits and slugging down straight shots of rum. No help there."

The *Pampero* lurched as she fell off a wave, plowed down into a trough, then rising slowly, sluggishly shook off tons of water. With the shock of the impact, Jean fell against him. He grunted in pain, but she tightened her hold on him as if she were unwilling to let go. "Bracken—I'm scared out of my wits. Not of the storm—but of what you're getting us involved in."

"It's going to be okay, babe. I've got everything under control." *Lie*, his brain cells screamed. "Tell Walrus that I'll be up in a minute."

She backed off a little, doubt etched in her face, seemed about to say something knowing that he had lied, then finally nodded.

Avoiding any deep probing of his psyche, Bracken dug into his shaving kit, found the tin of aspirin and swallowed three of them whole. Then slid the door open and lurched down the corridor, bracing himself against the roll of the ship. He paused and ducked into the engine room, then flipped the switch that started the electric bilge pump. It sucked air for a second, then settled down into a steady gurgling pulse.

Raul was in the salon, body braced against a corner opposite the dining table, feet planted against the liquor locker, seemingly mesmerized by the oil lamp that was swinging in insane arcs. His eyes were glazed over, the pupils contracted pinpoints of black. His hands grasped an almost empty bottle of rum as if it were the only link left to a normal, rock-stable world. His face glistened with sweat.

It wasn't seasickness or intoxication, Bracken realized, it was fear. He dredged up the few Spanish words that he knew. *"Malo —muy peligroso."* He shook his head, frowning, his expression fatalistic.

"How bad . . . how much is the danger?"

It was the first time Raul had spoken English. Heavily accented but understandable.

"Bad, very bad," Bracken answered. "A storm of the worse kind." Actually, it was a helluva sailing wind, but without a full crew it would be damned difficult to reef. Bracken made a big deal of tapping the barometer. It had stopped its free fall and stabilized at 982 millibars, a good sign that the depression had either stalled out or was recurving to the north. But Bracken played the part of a ship's master looking death in the face and flinching. *"Bloody hell!"*

Raul's eye's narrowed. "What is the problem?"

"Don't be concerned. Ships the size of the *Pampero* have made it through hurricanes like this before without much damage."

The blood drained from Raul's face, replaced by the color of spinach fettuccine. *"Huracán?*

"Si, Señor Raul. Huracán es sicko-malo-grosso-tempesto-elshito. Now you fucking *comprende?"*

"May the Holy Mother save us!" Raul rapidly crossed himself. "What will you do?"

"The only thing that I can do . . . pray," Bracken replied,

trudging painfully up the companionway as if he had a destiny
with death. From behind him he heard Raul gagging.

Once on deck, Bracken realized that the storm was still building but it had a raw beauty to it that was nearly indescribable.
The *Pampero* was shouldering through heavy seas, reaching off at
hull speed. Black curtains of rain squalls hung on the eastern
horizon, backlit by the moon and electrified with jagged smears
of lightning. The sea roared and the wind howled. The night had
a Winslow Homer quality to it, the living enactment of what every
blue-water sailor both loves and fears—driving a big wind ship to
the very edge. Still, on this particular night, Bracken would have
much preferred to have experienced the thrill in an art gallery
with a glass of wine in his hand.

Using the running backstays and rigging as handholds, he
scrambled aft to the cockpit and sank down on the thwart next to
Jean.

Hunched down behind the helm, Walrus was totally encased
in his yellow foul weather gear, the hood drawn up around his
face so that only his eyes and mustache, lit by the dim red light of
the compass, were visible. He looked like a red-eyed, waterlogged canary.

Stackhill was squatting in the protection of the cockpit, hugging himself, his teeth chattering with cold although Bracken
figured that the temperature of both wind and sea was in the
high seventies. So scratch Stackhill as a player.

"You enjoying yourself, Walrus?" Bracken yelled.

A sea, larger than the rest, rolled up behind the *Pampero*,
spitting and hissing as its crest broke off, cascading in an avalanche of seething white water against the transom. The impact
sent a shudder through the whole ship. Raul will love that one,
Bracken thought.

"Pretty goddamned interesting," Walrus shouted back. "Except that she wants to broach. On the big ones, I've got to get five
or six spokes of helm into her to keep her straight."

Bracken looked astern. A squall, black as soot, covered the
horizon from north to south, advancing down on the *Pampero* like
the final curtain of *Macbeth*.

He had been through a lot of tropical squalls, and they all
had a common factor to them. Before they hit, the wind picked
up. Then the rain came down like a cow pissing on a flat rock.
Eventually, the wind would moderate and sometimes even fall

slack as the squall passed overhead. And finally, the wind resumed with its former force.

It was blowing forty now, and the squall would add another fifteen knots to the average wind velocity, but what Bracken wanted was that one brief lull as the squall passed directly overhead.

"Can you hold it through the next squall and then we'll drop the main when the wind backs off?"

"Why not? I've got nothing better to do except drink a little rum, get outta this wet gear, and grab some sleep."

Jean sought out Bracken's hand with hers, watching the blackness begin to envelop them, the breaking waves streaked with foam and lines of phosphorescence. She squeezed his hand and, unthinking, he squeezed back.

"Can the sails take it?" she asked, her face only inches from his.

"Sure," he replied, but he wasn't. What worried him more was whether the rigging and spars would take it. The pressure generated by wind is proportionate to the square of the velocity of the wind speed. An increase of wind speed from 40 to 55 knots would nearly double the pressure on the sails, and yet he couldn't drop the main on the run even in a wind speed of 40 knots because once the main halyard was slacked away, the belly of the sail would plaster itself to the mast, spreaders, and rigging. The alternative was to round up into the wind, but with 15 to 20 foot seas running, it would be tricky to get the *Pampero* around without broaching, and the force of the wind would surely flog the sails into ribbons before he could lower them. It was a classic case of waiting too long in a rising wind to reef.

The frontal squall was on top of them. The first icy blast of rain hit with the fury of a volley of musket balls, the wind first picking up in erratic, pumping gusts, then steadily increasing until it was almost impossible to breathe. Bracken's eyes stung from the rain, impossible to see, his eardrums popping with the sudden pressure change.

The *Pampero* groaned, then lurched through seventy degrees and lay down on her beam's ends, seas coursing along the deck, spreader tips normally fifty feet above sea level skimming the water, the schooner broaching, totally out of control.

Six days before and west of the Cape Verde islands, a small kink in the isobars of the Bermuda-Azores high developed. In that small patch of lifeless sea, perhaps only a hundred miles in diameter, the trade winds had fallen quiet and the heat of the subtropical Atlantic set up a small low pressure system in the fold of that minute barometric anomaly. Without the cooling effect of the trades, the temperature of the subtropical sea superheated the air above. And once heated, the air began to rise, continually renewing itself with warm, moist air which was sucked into its base. As this invisible column of air rose, the rotational forces known as the Coriolis Force slowly began to rotate the rising mass. A small, very localized, and as yet unnamed tropical storm began to develop.

A Liberian tramp freighter transited the area, plodding her way north from Capetown to Liverpool with a cargo of dried fish, plastic toys, and soybean oil. There were a few squalls, some rain, but within six hours the tramp was steaming under clear skies with the off-watch crew sunning on the decks. The captain, a prudent mariner, noted the small disturbance in his log and reported it to a coastal station in Senegal. His report was filed, but due to an error by a young clerk was never forwarded to the National Hurricane Center in Miami.

In two days the tropical storm increased its dimensions so that its effects were felt out to a three-hundred-mile radius. The steering winds aloft began to move the depression on a westerly course, tracking slowly across the southern North Atlantic, an area once frequently traversed but now, in an era of steam turbines, unsinkable hulls, and shipping company accountants who viewed the bottom line as the ultimate arbiter of ship management, was nearly vacant. The old trade wind route was seldom used except by the occasional yacht or low-powered tramp steamer. Now, only Sargasso weed, plastic trash, frolicking dolphins, and the occasional bosun bird frequented those silent seas.

The next vessel to experience the storm's effects was a thirty-three-foot New Zealand sloop en route from the Canary Islands to Barbados. It was a small yacht, well-found and crewed by a retired New Zealand dentist and his wife. Having come halfway around the world without difficulty, the dentist handled the depression as routinely as he would have an extraction. Except for an old jib which blew out and wet bunks from deck leaks which he had neglected to caulk in Gibraltar, the passage of the tropical storm was a minor nuisance. The two of them toasted the resumption of sunny skies and mild trade winds with two bottles of warm Spanish beer and a dinner of canned beef.

Normally, a U.S. weather satellite would have picked up the swirling cloud mass in the Atlantic. A few years before, two weather satellites, namely *Geos West* and *Geos East* were always on station in geosynchronous orbit, covering tropospheric weather formations from the middle of the Atlantic to the middle of the Pacific. When *Geos East* finally died from a diseased power amplifier stage, it was to be replaced with a technologically ungraded sister satellite, but that replacement was lost in the catastrophic launch of a Titan II/34D, leaving only *Geos West* to cover the entire hemisphere. During this particular week, *Geos West*'s tunnel vision was focused on the Pacific basin and the mainland of the U.S. The cloud mass, generated by the tropical storm, slowly gaining strength in the largely untraveled waters of the Atlantic, went unnoticed.

Thirty miles to the east of the *Pampero* was another vessel, a heavily laden native schooner out of Tobago, poorly ballasted and burdened with a deck cargo of hardwood from the coast of Guiana and thirty tons of Venezuelan cement stowed in the forward hold. The cargo was destined for a resort developer in St. Martin, still seventy miles to the north. The schooner was laboring in confused seas and squally winds only thirty miles to the southwest of St. Kitts.

It was not a situation that worried the experienced master and part owner of the vessel. The weather report from Radio Antilles on the island of Montserrat had not mentioned any tropical weather systems. Barbados, an island to the southeast, reported light northwesterly winds, a bit of lightning, and drizzling rain. The weather report was followed by Lord Invader's latest reggae hit, "Rasta Man Got Mighty Sword." The master of the schooner had smiled and relaxed, tapping his fingers to the Jamaican beat. It would be a wet and windy night, but he would be in port by tomorrow afternoon. And it would be a profitable passage.

He had prudently ordered the crew to shorten sail at dusk and cranked up the diesel engine to assist the sails in making headway through the confused seas. His considerable prior experience told him that by dawn he would probably be clear of this weather. He lay down in his bunk for a few hours of restless sleep.

Except for the helmsman and one deckhand, only the cook

was on duty. He was brewing up a batch of cou-cou for the midnight watch. His pot was strapped down on the stove by wire ties, and yet the contents slopped over onto the stove top and instantly vaporized, adding to the already oppressive humidity of the galley. Condensed moisture beaded the portholes of the galley, and he was sweating profusely. Muttering to himself about the condition of the ship in general and the sea in particular, he threw another three pounds of rice and six more bluggers into the pot. He then poured himself a cup of cocoa, pulled on his rain slicker, and went out onto the deck, leaving the galley door open.

The vessel, a ninety-six foot wooden schooner which had been launched in the fifties with the overly optimistic name of *My Hope*, was lurching northward in confused seas. The cook, a man who in his earlier years had fallen overboard from a small fishing vessel and had spent ten hours thrashing through shark-infested seas before he reached the shore, was a born-again Christian. His name was Damian Collie and he had nine children and a faithful wife who sang in the Baptist church choir. He had saved his pay for nearly forty years, and after two more trips he planned to retire to a plot of land that overlooked the Bocas. In his remaining time on earth he would raise mangos for sale in the Saturday market, watch younger fools put out to sea, and hold his wife to him in the stillness of hot summer nights.

As he sheltered in the lee of the galley sipping at his cocoa, he watched the windward horizon. Lightning, never actually visible but illuminating the interior of clouds with dull flashes, flickered over the eastern horizon.

Damian was not alarmed. He had seen weather like this before. He didn't understand it but he knew its effects—a little of God's thunderbolts playing up the sky, His hard breath messing up the sea, His tears soaking both sinning and pious sailor alike. He mildly resented God's will in weather like this because it made the work of an honest and devout man like himself just that much harder. And he was distressed because he knew how irritable the common sailors became in this kind of weather. Not just from the exhaustion of continually changing the sails and heaving on the ropes, but from the fact that below decks their sweat never evaporated and they couldn't sleep. They grew irritable and argumentative. Then arguments and cursing would break out in the fo'c'sle, resulting in fistfights. And that was an affront to both God and peace-loving sea cooks.

As he stood there sipping on his cup of cocoa, the wind suddenly changed. A gust blew out of the north, almost frigid, bearing on it a splattering of rain. Damian shivered, tossed the remains of his mug into the sea, and was about to turn to reenter the galley door, but for some reason that he couldn't fathom, hesitated.

The wind died, replaced by hot stagnant air that enveloped him in its clammy shroud. His scalp prickled as he heard an odd thrumming in the atmosphere.

Lightning flashed closer, this time the bolt sharp and hot and hard like the devil's pitchfork. Its flash crackled and lit up the whole eastern horizon, followed by two near-simultaneous blasts of thunder.

"It gonna rain plenty, man," he said aloud to himself, the last coherent words he spoke.

A wall of wind from the frontal squall of the storm hit the schooner broadside, heeling it over until *My Hope*'s decks were buried in seething foam. Damian was thrown violently against the bulwarks. He heard his spine fracture, which he immediately realized would be a terrible inconvenience in his old age because one had to reach up to pluck the mangos from the tree and he started to cry out to his God with the question of why a devout Christian should be punished like this, the words forming on his lips. But God must have been busy looking after the other tenders of his many orchards, because there was neither help nor answer except for a black comber of seawater which swept him from the deck and into the stinking wet blackness, erasing all the uncertainty of Damian's future.

My Hope's hatches crushed under the weight of tons of seawater that inundated them. The old boat, 40,000 board feet of greenheart lumber, 600 bags of cement, and twelve souls slipped beneath the sea in less than sixty seconds.

Eleven miles to the west, ten minutes later, the *Pampero* lay over on her beam ends, the sea breaking across her, seething green water coursing down the deck, filling the cockpit, cascading in a roaring flood past the shattered teak washboard, and down the companionway. There were shouts from below, the sound of crockery breaking, things smashing. Stackhill screaming something incoherent, the fear in his voice like the squeal of a wild animal caught in a steel trap. Walrus, with the helm hard over to the stops, was trying to bring her back down onto her course, but the schooner lay over almost perpendicular to the seas, wallowing like a gut-shot elephant with no will or strength to rise.

Bracken scrambled across the cockpit to the recess in the coaming and switched on the spreader lights. They lit the deck with a pale, flickering light. The rain from the squall was pummeling down with the ferocity of bullets, each one glinting briefly in the light like a tracer before splattering onto the deck or into the sea. So intense was the deluge that the sea around the vessel was beaten down flat into a dull, heaving sheet of lead.

"Forget the goddamn helm! We've got to get the mainsail down!" Bracken screamed, but Walrus was already crawling forward, bracing himself against the deck boxes and cabin trunk, a soggy human fly trying to negotiate a surface that was normally horizontal and reasonably dry but now tipped over at a seventy-degree angle and slick as ice. Somehow he got to the main halyard winch and tripped the brake. A few feet of the halyard ran out, then stopped, the sail plastered against the mast and rigging by the pressure of the wind.

Bracken, clutching onto the aft cabin dorade could see it, hear it coming. A sea, much larger than the rest, spitting and snorting, a green mountain of liquid eternity racing down from windward. Before it the surface of the water was a cascading froth of boiling white water.

"Hang on!" he screamed, and dove into the cockpit, pinning Jean down, bracing his legs against the opposite bulkhead, grabbing fistfuls of the mainsheet, which trailed through the cockpit like a wet, whipping anaconda. He heard the sea break in a thunderous shock against the side and decks of the ship, then was hammered under tons of seawater. It went very quiet, very peaceful; just warm and wet and then the sucking rush of sea sluiced out of the cockpit accompanied by the cacophony of the roaring wind and sea.

He spit out a mouthful of seawater, swiped at his eyes, stunned. Jean was still beneath him, vomiting, wiggling under his weight, swearing.

They come in threes, Bracken knew. Big waves always came in sets of three, and generally, the second mother was the biggest and most dangerous. He looked out to windward but his eyes were smarting from the salt water and he couldn't see much more than a confused blur. Two more like that one and she would go down. How many tons of blue water had gone below, filling the bilges? The period between the seas had been running about seventeen seconds, and most of those seconds were gone.

He looked forward. Walrus wasn't at the mainmast halyard winch, and Bracken felt a stab of panic, then was relieved as he caught sigh of Walrus grabbing the leeward shrouds, leaning out almost horizontally like a monkey on a string, trying to reach the jib sheet. He had his K-Bar knife out of his boot and in one stroke sliced through the Dacron line. The jib, no longer restrained by the sheet, started to flog violently, the force of the sails snapping shaking the whole vessel, the rigging twanging like the string on a gigantic bass fiddle. In seconds the jib flogged itself to death, ribbons of torn sail streaming in the wind, tearing off, then flying away to leeward. But with the jib gone, the *Pampero* was no longer balanced, and now the mainsail, still taut under the press of the wind, began to exert leverage, slowly rounding the schooner up into the wind. And as she rounded up, she righted herself, shaking off tons of water, the seas gushing out of the freeing ports and streaming from the scuppers like water from a fire hose.

"Jean—start the engine! Bring her up and hold her dead into the wind."

He didn't even bother to look back to see whether she heard him, let alone could do it. Half scrambling, half crawling, he headed forward. Walrus met him at the mainsail and as the *Pampero* staggered up head-to-wind, the mainsail luffed, then flogged. In fistfuls, they both frantically hauled down the sail. They swore, ripped fingernails, smearing the flogging canvas with their blood, then somehow wrapped three turns of the mainsheet around the boom and canvas, muzzling the sail.

The spreader lights dimmed momentarily, the batteries obviously under heavy load. Bracken felt the vibration of the engine turning over, catching, then dying, then catching again.

Like an elevator, the *Pampero* started to rise to the advancing sea, the wind momentarily blocked by the wall of water. His knees buckled under him. Out of the corner of his eye he saw Walrus leap over the main boom, clutching it with both arms and legs like a sloth clinging to a branch in a high wind.

Higher they rose, the sea hissing on either side of them, the bow of the vessel now dead into the wind. Then they were over the top of the wave, the decks frothing with broken water from the crest of the breaking sea, heading down on the back side of the wave.

The *Pampero* slid down into the trough of the wave, accelerating, buried her bowsprit in white foam, rose again, shaking off the water like a wet dog. The third wave was still dangerous but smaller than the preceding two. The *Pampero*, even under full engine power, was almost dead in the water, a cork. Except for some slop, she rode the third wave easily, but Bracken knew that the only hope was to run her off before the wind.

And after three big waves, there was always, almost always, a calm patch. Bracken knew that it had to be now. His voice raw, he yelled back toward the cockpit, trusting her because he had to. *"Put the helm hard over! Now!"*

The old bucket responded slowly, but he could feel her coming around, the biting force of the wind now on the forward quarter, now on the beam, now on the aft quarter, the ship rolling heavily. By the time he was back in the cockpit, she had steadied the ship out on a course dead downwind.

The wind momentarily slackened. It started raining again, but this time not as hard. Up forward, Walrus was getting the fore staysail on. It flogged briefly, but Bracken sheeted it home, then nudged the helm over so that the wind was on their stern quarter.

The *Pampero* stopped her violent rolling and settled down, slowly accelerating. Bracken threw the gearshift lever into neutral and pulled back on the throttle. The transition was magical. Now, instead of thrashing through the seas, overburdened, the schooner meshed into her environment, running off, easing through the broken water, trailing a slick wake that quieted the seas still humping up behind her.

Bracken took over the helm. Jean retreated to the cockpit sole, hunched down, her face pale in the dim lights of the spreaders.

"Was that it?" she asked.

"Just the frontal passage of the storm, but that's generally the worst of it." He paused, watching her. Hair scraggly, a rip in her foul weather gear, one sea boot missing. "It'll be rough for a while. If the wind picks up again, we'll drop the staysail and just jog along under bare poles. But we're okay—for now."

He was dying to get below. It would be a mess, possibly worse. "Can you hold it for another fifteen minutes?"

She nodded dumbly, mechanically, too strung out to care.

The salon was a shambles. All kinds of junk was strewn over the cushions, and the cabin sole was awash with salt water, two feet deep, sloshing back and forth as the *Pampero* rolled. Locker doors hung open, swinging with the roll of the ship, banging against their stops.

No Raul, no Vierro, although Bracken could hear voices yelling at each other in the aft cabin. Stackhill's stateroom door was closed. Bracken tried it, but it was locked. From within he heard muffled sobbing and a man's querulous voice. Stackhill had deserted the deck just when he was needed most. It figured.

He lurched with the roll of the ship, hanging on to the overhead grab rails and headed for the engine room. Walrus was already there.

The diesel was still pounding away although it sounded rough. Walrus was refitting wooden wedges into the battery bank. He had already cut in the engine-driven bilge pump.

"Not good, skip," Walrus shouted over the howl of the engine. "Three batteries with cracked cells. The refrigeration compressor took a lungful of salt water and the engine starter motor is still submerged."

"Is the level of the bilge water going down?"

Walrus shrugged. His wet mustache drooped like a Mexican bandit's. "Too damned early to tell."

The refrigeration compressor was the least of his worries. The electrical motor could always be replaced. The battery status was bad news. With some of the cells cracked, they would have to be isolated from the system, leaving the *Pampero* with half her normal battery capacity. But it was the starter motor that had Bracken concerned. Submerged in salt water, the windings in the motor would short out and fuse if he tried to start it again. There was only a slim chance that he could save it. Unbolt it—always a knuckle-busting routine, even in port—flush the starter motor with lots of fresh water, remove the brushes, and bake it in the oven at 110 degrees. Like as not, even with immediate corrective care, the starter motor would probably have less than five or six starts left in it. And without the starter motor operational, Bracken would be up the creek without a motorized paddle.

Walrus was dead on his feet. Bracken pushed him out of the engine room and toward the galley. There Bracken pulled out the bottle of rum that Jean had tucked away, and both took a long slug, bilge water sloshing over the tops of their boots, the remains of a shattered jar of strawberry jam drooling down the bulkhead.

Walrus fished out a damp Camel from his jacket and lit it, leaning back against the sink, exhausted.

"It was a bugger that I had to cut the jib loose."

"No sweat. I'll take it out of your pay."

Walrus give him a tired smile. "What pay, you turkey."

They both laughed a little.

The bottle made another round.

"Get a good kip, Walrus."

"Might just do that, skip," Walrus responded, sloshing forward to his berth already half asleep. "And don't forget to call me if it gets deeper."

"Semper Fi," Bracken said under his breath. And meant it.

13.

July 12–July 13

Through the rest of the night and into the morning, Bracken ran the pumps, the level of bilge water slowing receding until by mid-morning it was sucked dry.

The wind was still hard, but it had lost its bite, settling down to a steady thirty-five knots and veering more into the east—a promised resumption of the trades. Under ragged gray scud, the horizon no farther than the next wave, the *Pampero* thundered northwest on a beam reach.

He was dead on his feet as he wrote up the log. Barometric pressure up slightly to 990 millibars, also a portent of clearing weather. Bracken plotted a tentative position: fifteen or twenty miles off the Dominican Republic, somewhere in the middle of the Mona Passage.

Vierro, stinking of body odor and bad breath, was suddenly standing over him.

"Move your position more to the east." He dropped a scrap of paper on the chart with the coordinates of his satnav fix.

Bracken plotted it. Made sense, but he would check it out with a celestial line of position, assuming the sun broke out. "I suppose you got the weather report as well?"

"It was a tropical storm called Hannah. We caught the tail end of it. Forecast is for moderating winds from the east." Vierro lit a cigar. "Tell the woman that we want breakfast. Now."

"She's been up half the night and she's just taken over the helm."

"Then you fix it yourself, Bracken." Vierro touched the leather of his shoulder holster.

There was no arguing with sweet reason, Bracken realized.

Just before noon, the sun squinted out between fractured clouds and Bracken got a reasonable line of latitude with his sextant which roughly agreed with Vierro's satnav position. The wind had further fallen to twenty-five knots, the seas diminishing to fifteen feet, and the barometer up another two millibars. Bracken called Walrus out of the sack and together they bent on the spare jib and a single-reefed main.

Bracken slept through the afternoon, oblivious. He woke about sundown, took a sponge bath, admiring the black, blue, and yellow bruises on his body. Look like the flag of a banana republic, he thought, trying to grin back at his image in the mirror. After retaping his rib cage, he took four aspirins, pulled on his foul weather gear, and stumbled aft to check the chart.

Walrus and Jean had both made entries for their watches. There had to be a good current behind the *Pampero,* and coupled with a nine-knot average they were halfway up the Mona Passage.

He swung the dividers over the chart, up through the Mona, along the north coast of the Dominican Republic and Haiti, then up the Old Bahama Channel between Cuba and the out islands of the Bahamas.

That was the part he was nervous about. To stay in deep water, he had to avoid the shoals of the Bahamas by hugging the coast of Cuba. The prospect didn't appeal.

Bracken heard the sound of a match striking and looked up. Vierro stood in the doorway to the aft cabin, smoking a cigar. He blew a thick cloud of blue smoke toward the overhead. "So Captain Courageous is finally awake?" He tipped the ash on the soggy carpeting. "I have received radioed instructions from the *Victoria* to put into port. I also note that you have inflicted damage to the ship. I need to know what replacement equipment you will need for the safe operation of the vessel. Give me a list by nine tonight with the names of the items, their manufacturer, and part numbers."

"I . . ."

Vierro didn't wait for an explanation. He turned and headed into the aft cabin, slamming the door behind him.

So where would it be, Bracken asked himself: the north coast of the D.R., Haiti, or—Cuba? He could guess.

After climbing the companionway, Bracken balanced briefly against the coach roof, squinting up at the sails, the rigging, and then at the eastern horizon. The sun was just going down. He watched it for a few minutes, shading his eyes. A blink of green followed the sun; a forerunner of fair weather.

The wind down to eighteen or twenty knots. A long storm

swell still rolled in from the north, but the wind was back in its old easterly quarter. There were still some scud clouds overhead, but on the eastern horizon the sky was clearing. He guessed that it would be a calm night with smooth sailing.

Pam was at the helm. The wake of the *Pampero* looked like a drunken snake's trail. But at least her trick on the helm had bought Walrus, Jean, and himself some additional sack time.

Before, Bracken had thought of her as glamorous, chic, sexy, and upscale, but now, without makeup, designer clothes, and meticulous skin care, her face clearly showed wear and tear. For the first time he noticed the wrinkles under her eyes. Amazing how a man's lust was a woman's best cosmetic.

She looked up from the compass and smiled, noticing him, then self-consciously pulling her hand through her hair. "Capt'n Hook himself!" She tooted on an imaginary trumpet. "Tah-tah."

"None other." He slid down onto a cockpit thwart and bunched one knee under his chin, arms clamped around his leg. "So how do you like life on the rolling sea?"

"Like last night? It sucks! I wanna get off this tub as soon as it's physically possible. I want a bath and a facial. I want dry clothes. I want a king-size bed with satin sheets in an air-conditioned room. I want a pitcher full of martinis. But mostly and mainly, Hook, I want some rock-solid land under my feet."

He didn't want to pursue this conversation. Her voice had a whine in it, something that he couldn't abide. He shifted the subject. "See any shipping?"

"If I had, I would have swum for it. But Stackhill did in the mid-afternoon when he was on watch. Some kind of small tanker passed us about five miles off, heading south. He tried to use your VHF radio. Raul didn't like it, atall, atall, atall."

"So what happened?"

"Whacked Stackhill in the chops. Said something about 'radio silence.' Told Stackhill that if he tried it again, he would be shark bait."

No doubt about that, Bracken thought.

Jean appeared on deck, juggling two plates of baked beans and sausages. In contrast to Pam, she had changed into clean, bun-hugging jeans and a Red Sox T-shirt one size too small which did marvelous things for her superstructure. She had combed her hair. No lipstick, no eye shadow, just a good suntan and a terrific body, which to Bracken's way of thinking qualified her as the most physically desirable of all women: thirty percent Miss

Universe and seventy percent the girl next door—the one that, as a pimply-faced teenager, you spent interminable hours spying on, trying to catch her parading around in the raw through cheap binoculars from your darkened bedroom window.

"I'd suggest you go below for din-dins, *Pam dear,*" Jean said. "Stackhill's down there already stuffing his face. Send him up when he's finished. He's taking Walrus's watch."

"Thanks, *honey,*" Pam said with acid sweetness. She handed the helm over to Bracken, pecked him on the cheek, and dropped down the companionway with "Later, Capt'n Hook, if not sooner."

Jean stewed in silence for several minutes, demolishing the bangers and beans with jerky swipes of her fork. Bracken knew enough to keep his mouth shut.

Dark now, the twilight gone. He flipped on the compass light, eased up to windward four degrees, found a star hanging in the rigging, and settled on it as his course. The wake hissed from beneath the transom, a light thrumming of wind in the rigging, blocks creaking, the slow roll of the ship in response to the softly heaving sea. A pair of longtails flew together over the ship in the last twilight, circled it, and then headed west.

For several more minutes they sat silently, not speaking, just watching the sea and sky. It was the thing that he loved most about offshore sailing—both the best and the worst of it—each extreme accentuating the other, closely coupled to a suspension of time where every moment was too short or an eternity. He put his hand out, seeking hers in the blackness, connected and squeezed. *"I only have eyes for you,"* he crooned softly off key, doing a very bad imitation of Willie Nelson.

"Damned right, Bracken. If you don't, you won't." She squeezed back hard, very hard.

Venus poked her light up out of the eastern horizon. The few scattered clouds in that quadrant of the world were backlit, rimmed in silver, their hearts darker than the sky around them. Reaching off under full sail, the *Pampero* eased up the long black hills and then slid down them, a ponderous but gentle rolling corkscrew of motion, giving back the sense of restrained but unlimited power. As if she could go on forever, beyond any horizon, to the far corners of the known universe.

"I will always remember this night, Bracken," she said finally after a long silence. "Bury it deep in my memory to call up again and again when things are wrong, knowing that eventually they'll be right." She slid next to him on the helmsman's seat, her arms around him.

He wanted to say something, something that would reassure her that he understood, but couldn't find new words. She had already said it. He could only nod.

"Where from here?" she asked, snuggling her face into the hollow of his neck, her hair soft on his cheek.

"Vierro told me that we're putting in somewhere to fix his goddamned radar. My guess is Cuba. And after that, assuming that they don't lock us up, probably Florida or the Keys thereof."

She absorbed this information in silence, her only comment the tightening of her arms around him. Then she started to say something, but Stackhill appeared in the companionway, first belching, then farting in a gassy accolade of the bangers and beans dinner.

"Stackhill on deck," he announced, working his way aft into the cockpit. He lit a menthol, settling down on the cushions. "Great fuckin' dinner." He belched again, putting his best efforts into it. "Basic high-carbohydrate food is what I need for the demanding life at sea. Nothing fancy. Just plenty of it."

Jean squeezed Bracken. "Do you need me," she breathed into his ear.

"On deck, no," he answered in a whisper. "Otherwise yes."

"Ten minutes," she promised, getting up, stacking the plates, putting the forks into the pocket of her jeans.

"I didn't get that," Stackhill said, leaning forward.

"You're not likely to," she replied.

Bracken checked his watch, feeling his manhood, or whatever the romance novelists called it, come to life. Ten long, very long, interminably long minutes to go.

Jean threaded her way forward and went down through the fo'c'sle hatch. The galley light switched on for a second, then switched off. Bracken heard the water pump cycle in the forward head.

"You think you can hold a heading?" Bracken asked.

Stackhill slid behind the helm. "Shit, Bracken, I've sailed to Bermuda with really hot sailors on a Swan 51—not a bucket like this."

Bracken had heard that one before. One offshore passage does not a seaman make. "Okay, Stackhill—nothing fancy. Just hold a northwesterly heading, somewhere around three-four-zero. About 2100 you should pick up the light on Cabo Engano. When that's abeam, call up Walrus and he'll take the watch."

Grabbing Bracken's arm, Stackhill said, "Hey, buddy—last night—I did all right?" His voice pleaded for absolution.

Last night, when the frontal squall had hit, Stackhill had dived below like a rat headed for the safety of the sewer. "You got it, Stackhill," Bracken white-lied. "You did fine—just fine."

Robert Stackhill was bored out of his skull. He was also cold and his buns had atrophied from sitting on the hard helmsman's seat for more than—he glanced down at the luminous hands of his watch—three hours. He estimated that he would still be sitting on this same goddamned seat for another agonizing forty-five minutes. Seemed to him that he had been intentionally nailed by Bracken's watch schedule for the second night in a row on the midnight to four in the fuckin' A.M. watch.

The lighthouse on the north coast of Ile de la Tortue, Haiti, now less than twenty miles away, blinked on the horizon.

He had the *Pampero* cranked up hard on the wind. Bracken had given him a course and he held it, plus or minus ten degrees, but it was damned tedious. The red-lit compass silently mocked him by capriciously swinging past the desired heading. Cursing the schooner, the sea, the wind, and Bracken, he countered with a turn to port, overshot the heading, then put in opposite helm, compounding the error.

"Shit on it," he muttered to himself. He let go of the helm and fished for a menthol cigarette in his Windbreaker, then pulled out his Zippo lighter. He tried to snap the flint, but his hands were cold and the lighter skidded out of his hands, clattering to the cockpit sole.

Stackhill seethed with dumb rage and frustration. Everything, but damn-all everything had gone wrong. Far from a nifty little cruise with a terrific piece of tail for a bunkmate, the charter had turned into a certifiable Stephen King nightmare. For damn sure, Raul and Vierro scared the piss out of him. The fuckin' boat leaked and leaned over most of the time, he had almost crapped in his pants during the storm, Pam had cut him off, and he hadn't had a decent meal or eight hours of sleep in the last four days.

He glanced down at the compass. The heading was a little off but holding fairly steady. Magically, the schooner seemed to know where she was going, the helm moving lazily as if steered by a phantom helmsman. So take five, he told himself.

Heaving his bulk out of the helmsman's seat, Stackhill groveled around on the cockpit sole, searching for the lighter, and finally found it.

He lit a menthol and sucked in the candy-mint smoke, glad to be down out of the wind. Actually, not blowing that hard, he figured. Maybe twelve, fifteen knots. And, swear to God, not a bad night compared to recent history. He looked up.

Stars smeared the sky from one horizon to another. Occasionally, a meteor streaked in at an oblique angle from far space, burning white and green, then winking out in a little burst of light like a kid's Fourth of July sparkler. A sliver of a moon was up; not much, but enough to make it all nice and cozy.

He plopped himself onto one of the cockpit thwarts, pulled his Windbreaker closer around his neck, and dragged on the cigarette. The helm turned lazily, completely unattended. He had seen other yachts steer themselves to windward, but he hadn't even thought it was possible that an outdated tub like this one could. But, by Christ, she did. And he could shoot Bracken for not letting him in on the secret.

Stackhill, now relaxing a little, let a satisfying fart go. He moved farther forward in the cockpit until the aft cabin hatch sheltered him from the wind and lit another butt from the stub of the first one. Freed from the demands of steering, he started to absorb the scene. Astern, phosphorescence from the wake left blinking light specks trailing behind the schooner like a formation of fireflies swirling in a darkened field. His dad had loved the countryside, and Stackhill still remembered the fireflies of a long-ago summer vacation in upstate New York.

He glanced aloft. The sails formed overlapping triangles against the heavens, heaving softly in the press of the wind, the mast making slow arcs against the night sky as the *Pampero* dipped and curtsied to the swell. Shit, he was now actually starting to enjoy this!—driving fifty-six tons of boat through the black of night—captain-of-my-ship master-of-my-soul stuff.

A little drink would be nice—no, terrific. A toast to his old man and to warm up the creaking bones. He had a bottle of Wild Turkey stashed over his bunk, and he had to get another pack of butts.

He stood up and checked the compass. Off a couple of degrees, but she seemed to be averaging a better course than he had steered. Problem was whether Vierro or Raul was playing watchdog. Neither one of them would take kindly to him boozing on watch or leaving the helm. One of the twin set of pricks took turns staying up while the other slept, no exceptions. Raul was probably up now, but he liked his rum, and more than once Stackhill had seen him dozing.

What the hell! He rechecked the compass—close enough to heading—then crept to the top of the companionway.

The aft cabin door was closed. So much for one of them, probably Vierro. However, there was a thin shaft of light from the salon, but Stackhill couldn't hear movement. He eased down the companionway stairs, one step at a time.

Raul was stretched out on the salon settee, eyes closed, mouth agape. He had been reading some kind of a manila-bound folder which was now spread across his chest like a flattened tent.

Stackhill watched him for a full minute. Except for the creaking of the ship, the hush of wind in the rigging, and small rattles of unsecured gear, the ship was quiet. He slowly rotated the starboard cabin doorknob, lifted it up to keep the door from creaking, and ducked into his cabin.

Pam was snoring, sprawled out naked across the bunk. He reached over, ran his hand along the shelf, and connected with the bottle. He tucked it inside his Windbreaker, then took a pack of menthols from the dressing table. The *Pampero* rolled a little more than usual, just a wave larger than the rest, and Stackhill bumbled against the edge of the bunk, his belt buckle grating against the lee board.

Pam snorted in her sleep, maybe sensing his presence. He froze and a short time later was rewarded by her even breathing.

Quietly backing out of the cabin, he eased the door shut.

He was ready to go up the companionway but turned back to check Raul. He had rolled over, now facedown, his arm flung out, feet braced up against the cushions, snoring. The folder or whatever it was had fallen onto the salon carpet.

Stackhill knew the feeling. Experienced it only three or four times in his lifetime, sitting there in his New York rabbit warren that passed as an office, watching his computer tick through the worldwide commodity trades, sensing that some major shift was quietly gathering steam. Not definite and not a reaction to hard news, like blacks taking over a gold mine in South Africa or a killing frost in the Brazilian coffee groves. Nothing quite that exact. Just the sense that something *big* was about to happen, accompanied by a couple of ticks in the tape that indicated an uneasiness or optimism by a few savvy traders. Never heavy, big-volume movement, but steady, as if they were spreading their orders through a lot of small brokers in Hong Kong, Zurich, London, and Chicago. And not enough to generate a major price movement but still, a trend if you keep your eye on the tape. He had made a killing on platinum a year earlier just because of that feeling. Bought on a combination of pure hunch and by watching the tape for hours after detecting a quiet but persistent buying trend. On that one alone he had racked up a sixty thousand profit. And Stackhill had that feeling now, looking at the folder on the salon floor.

Damning himself but unable to restrain the impulse, he took two steps forward, picked up the folder, and retreated to the companionway. A look back. Raul still zonked out, almost vulnerable in sleep.

He climbed the companionway like a kid sneaking to the forbidden attic and silently eased into the cockpit, then checked the compass. Like a rock, just three degrees below course. The light on Ile de la Tortue had edged aft, but it would still be half an hour before it would be abeam and he could call out Walrus.

Complete asshole, he silently swore at himself. The hairs on his neck rose at the thought of what Vierro would do to him if he discovered the folder missing. Still, it was Stackhill's compulsion to discover secrets and exploit them. Something to be used to advantage, maybe now, maybe later, or maybe never, but he accepted that snooping coupled with intuition was part of survival.

He first slugged down a big shot of Wild Turkey, letting it burn hot in his gullet. Great stuff, Christ, the best. Felt a little ripple of courage flowing through him, things coming off the knife edge of pure chance, flowing to his advantage. Humming softly, he pulled out a penlight from his jacket pocket and began to leaf through the pages.

It was typewritten in Spanish, and his fluency in the language was limited to dealing with Mexican restaurant menus and Spicks in the car wash. Exasperated, he flipped through the pages. Some photos of a flat landscape with a couple of complicated towers in the background. Looking closer, he recognized that the foreground of the photo was a beach of some sort— mainly marsh grass and sand with small breaking surf. Inked on the photo were arrows and numbers—probably compass headings.

He quickly flipped through the rest of the folder. Page after page of typed Spick instructions, a couple of cutaway diagrams of some kind of grain silo with bands around it, each band marked with numbers, and finally a couple of pages that were obviously a timetable.

Dull reading and yet Stackhill had that feeling. This was hot stuff, heavy-duty shit, but he didn't have a clue as to what the hell it meant.

Suddenly, a light snapped on in the aft cabin, its glare illuminating the frosted glass of the skylight. *Vierro was awake!* Which meant that he would be relieving Raul in a few minutes. No damn way he was going to go back down to the salon and ditch the folder. Thought about throwing it overboard but somehow sensed the thing was essential to his survival. Shit—no place in the cockpit to stash it. Couldn't drop it through the closed hatch over his own cabin or the main salon because they were shut.

Seconds were clicking away, now maybe half a minute. His skin prickled. More movement in the aft cabin, the light going out, a door banging open, voices in the salon, at first conversation, then arguing.

Stackhill couldn't think straight. Had to get rid of the folder. Like a flash he had a partial answer, not fully formed, but he acted on it. He pulled off his deck shoes and tiptoed forward, then dropped the folder through the open engine room hatch. If it was missed, he would deny seeing it, having been on the helm for the whole watch. If blame was dumped on anyone, it would fall like a ton of bricks on Bracken's head.

Within seconds he was back on the helm, shoes back on. He took a quick shooter of the Wild Turkey, then with deep sadness in his heart tossed the bottle overboard.

When Raul and Vierro stormed up the companionway, Stackhill was dozing over the compass, the spokes of the helm held tightly in his sweaty palms, humming softly to himself.

They came aft and squatted down on either side of him.

Vierro's voice was soft, insistent, without inflection. He strung out the words, enunciating them very carefully. "Where is the book, Robert?"

"What book?" He tried to lighten up on his voice a little. "Oh, the log book." He shrugged. "Probably on the navigational table. Least it was there when I came on watch."

"I do *not* mean the log book," Vierro's voice emphatic. "I *do* mean the book that you stole from Raul."

Stackhill shrugged again, trying to compound his innocence.

"Don't know what the hell you're talking about. Shit, I didn't even think he knew how to read."

Raul clamped his hands around Stackhill's throat, his thumbs seeking nerves, then pressing. Bolts of lightning sparked through Stackhill's brain, red coronas forming on his retinas.

"*The book*, Stackhill. The one Raul was reading."

Fear had replaced guile, and Stackhill, unaware of his fatal error, panicked, letting both his tongue and brain slip out of gear.

"He—wasn't reading. Asleep. Fucker was—asleep."

The fingers tightened around his throat, thumbs pressing harder. Red was going black, sounds fading, senses numbing. Stackhill's feet beat an involuntary tattoo on the deck.

"*Where, Robert, did you hide the book?*" Vierro's voice came from a great distance, metallic words overlaid with static, like a fading long-distance telephone call.

"Overboard . . ." Stackhill croaked.

The pressure relaxed, replaced by a sharp point digging into his body. He looked down, still gasping for air. The point was the business end of a six-inch blade held by Vierro against the fat of his own gut. Vierro snapped an order in Spanish to Raul, who scuttled below. Seconds later Stackhill heard Pam's terrorized voice whining, the sound of drawers being pulled out and dumped on the cabin sole, screeching, a cry, and then Raul was back up on deck with a powerful flashlight. He searched the deck boxes, the cockpit locker, the lazarette, under the cockpit cushions, methodically moving from aft forward.

He came back, shaking his head.

"How much of the book did you read, Robert?" His voice was vaguely distant. The pressure of the point relaxed slightly.

"Come off it, man," Stackhill answered, trying to keep it light. "You know I don't read a word of Spick—ah, Spanish."

"But like a dirty little boy, you looked at the pictures, Robert, didn't you?"

"No." The point of the knife dug sharply into his gut. "Okay, okay. Yeah. I mean, a little. Jus' one. Some kind of beach. Thought it was something about a resort development. Always looking to invest in hot property. It's the businessman in me." He tried to sound humble. "You know, curious but no harm done, right?"

"And you threw it overboard when you heard us coming. Don't you think that implies that you knew the book was more than just the outline of a resort development?"

"Hey—back off. I had it only a couple of minutes. Sorry

about throwing it overboard. Panicked. I mean, I'll pay to have it replaced. Couldn't be all that important, right?"

"Wrong, Robert. Very important, but I can get a replacement. Relax. I just wanted to know the truth."

Sweet relief flooded Stackhill. Shit, these dudes were tough, but they weren't all that bad. Could see how they might be a little upset, but what the hell—everyone makes mistakes.

"Call out the first mate in ten minutes," Vierro said to Raul. He turned back to Stackhill, withdrawing the knife. "You can let go of the wheel, Robert," he said calmly.

Stackhill felt buoyant, light-headed. He stood up, stretching. "Gets cold on watch, doesn't it?"

"Truly," Vierro agreed amiably, his body language signaling that it was the end of the confrontation. He looked astern thoughtfully. "Actually, the water must be a good deal warmer than the air. Bracken says it's almost skin temperature. Pleasant for swimming, I would think."

"Yeah, maybe so," Stackhill replied. He scratched at his armpit, then hawked and spat overboard. "Think I'll turn in." He started to move toward the companionway, but Vierro took his arm. Gently but firmly.

"Robert, there is one thing that you can do for me."

Stackhill put a smile on his face. "You got it. Anything."

"Please go get the book for me. It will be most embarrassing for me to explain to Señor Sanchez that I lost it."

Puzzled, Stackhill was mentally and physically off balance. "Well, you know—I mean—like I told you, I threw the damn thing overboard."

He tugged, trying to pull away from Vierro. There was an explosion of pain in his gut. Shit! Damned beans. Gas attack. Probably have a case of the runs the rest of the night. He looked down in disbelief. Vierro's knife no longer had a blade because Vierro's hand was holding the handle of the knife against Stackhill's stomach but there wasn't any blade showing, and only then did Stackhill realize that not only was the blade still attached to the handle but it was now sheathed in his own intestines.

"Go find the book, Robert," Vierro said softly, forcing the blade upward, then twisting and withdrawing it. "When you find the book, you can come back and all will be forgiven." With a gentle push he toppled Stackhill backward over the lifelines.

The sea was warm, as Vierro had said, nearly skin temperature. At first the pain was intense, then rapidly faded until, oddly enough, it wasn't bad. He was leaking buckets of blood but he didn't know it. His body was beginning to shut down, the senses in the extremities going first.

It would be a great little swim, Stackhill was thinking, his body going into deep shock, his mind numbing. Like the pool in the spa on the East Side that he visited once a week. Five laps without even getting winded if he took his time. Always had been a hell of a good swimmer. Smiled, because fat made staying afloat easy. Hell with diets. Gas from the beans would help too. Pictured a balloon called Stackhill floating on the tops of the waves. A little weak maybe, a long day (or was it night?), but the old bod was like a cork. And corks didn't need energy to float, right?

He languidly started to stroke toward the coast of Haiti, feeling sleepy, relaxed, as if he were just putzing around in some giant hot tub. He noticed that his hands, as they scooped the water aside, left trails of sparkling phosphorescence, as if he had stars dripping from his fingers. Terrific, he thought. And remembered Pop and that long-ago summer and the showers of fireflies that mimicked the starry night sky.

Two hundred yards behind him, another trail of phosphorescence streaked forward, tasting the blood, vectoring in on the body of Robert Stackhill, a former futures commodities broker who, had he been coherent, might have understood that he now had very little future left.

"You catch any fish on your watch?" Walrus asked. Bracken had just come on deck and was snugged down in the cockpit, drinking coffee before the change of watch at 0600. It was just after sunup, the haze of Haiti's peaks to the south, the Windward Passage ahead, the west coast of Cuba beyond that less than eighty miles distant.

"No. Why ask?"

Walrus eased in a spoke, checked the luff of the main, and pondered the heaving horizon. The sun was up but it cast a cold light, high clouds filtering out the warmth. "Some blood on the deck, skip." He nodded down at the dark brown stains on the teak planking.

"Stackhill probably has piles." Bracken was listening to his own voice, not quite believing what he was hearing, seeing, saying. "You relieved him, didn't you?"

Walrus shook his head, the tips of his mustache lifting in the freshening wind. Bracken had often suggested a training bra or wax to keep them glued in place.

Walrus dropped his voice a couple of decibels. "Raul called me out a little before 0400. Vierro was on the helm when I came up. I didn't ask why the change in the watch schedule."

Bracken felt uneasy. "I'll be back in a couple of minutes."

First he checked the logbook. No entry for Stackhill's watch. He checked the heads. None of them occupied. The aft cabin door was closed and locked. Briefly checked the engine room. Checked the galley. Raul was wolfing down a bologna sandwich and a beer, his back turned to Bracken, leafing through a girlie magazine, his mind closed down to any intrusion.

Bracken opened Stackhill's stateroom door. Pam was awake, lying in her bunk covered by a sheet, leafing through a dog-eared copy of *Vogue*. She looked up, blinked, and automatically combed her hand through her hair, smiling a real Colgate salute.

"The infamous Captain Hook!" She edged over in the bunk, making room for Bracken, the sheet sliding down, coyly exposing half a breast. "What's up, I hope?"

"Where's Stackhill?"

"Feeding his face, in the head, reading in the salon, pulling his pud, who knows? Come on, sit down for a minute." She rolled over, exposing her back and tightly muscled buns. She arched her arm behind her back and tapped a finger in the hollow between her shoulder blades. "Scratch here, Hook. Allah reserves a special place in paradise for backscratchers. So do I, except you'll get to my special place a lot sooner."

"Did Stackhill come down last night after his watch?"

She moaned. "Gimme a break, Hook. When I'm out, I'm out. If Stackhill laid his body down on this berth last night, I'd never know. Only thing I do know is that Raul Pit-Face busted in, looking for something. He punched me up a little, nothing special." She turned her face to him. "Come on, Hook. Just a quickie. It's a better waker-upper than orange juice."

He knew that she was putting him on, but he couldn't stop the glands from reacting because they didn't listen to logic. She rolled over and slid a pillow under her butt, her hand dragging him down onto the berth. "Come on, Cap'n. Gimme your hook."

Bracken had never figured he was in the stallion category. Enthusiastic pony class, maybe. "Thanks, but not now. Stackhill's missing." His groin was aching, trying to hold his attention.

Bracken squeezed his legs together, trying to crush his testicles into obedience although they were still clamoring for action.

Her eyes suddenly clouded and she sat up abruptly. "Whatdayamean missing?"

"Gone. He's not on board—at least I can't find him."

She snatched the sheet up around her neck. "That—that can't be! Robert knows how to get around on boats. He's a stupid shit, but not stupid enough to fall overboard."

"What is the problem?" Vierro pushed open the door. He wore Jockey shorts with a *Victoria* terry-cloth bathrobe draped over his shoulders. He had obviously heard the raised voices. His face was still puffy with sleep.

"Stackhill's missing," Bracken answered.

"Of course. You knew that he was going to leave the vessel once we were north of the Dominican Republic. He had to get back to his business in New York. That was part of his deal with Sanchez."

"Nobody ever said anything about that to me. Anyways, we've already passed the Dominican Republic. We're off Haiti."

"There was a delay," Vierro said smoothly. "His transfer to shore took longer to arrange than I thought. Through much of yesterday, I was in contact with my associates by radio. A fast sport fishing boat came alongside last night." He glanced at his watch. "He should be in the Dominican Republic by late this afternoon. From there he will fly to Puerto Rico in a private plane. And from there to New York by commercial jet. Do you have any problem with this arrangement, Captain Bracken?" It wasn't a question but more of a challenge. Vierro's shoulder holster made a bulge under his robe.

"He didn't even take his passport, for Christ's sake," Pam wailed. "Didn't say good-bye to me, didn't leave me any money!"

Vierro shrugged. "There had been delays. It was a last-minute thing. Please be assured that he sent his regards. The last glimpse I had of him, he was waving a fond good-bye." Vierro matched Bracken's stare. "Does that answer your question, Captain?"

Remembering the bloodstains on deck, Bracken nodded.

Through the morning and into the afternoon, the *Pampero* romped across the Windward Passage at close to hull speed on a broad reach, all working canvas set. The high deck of clouds had dissipated by noon and the sun was hot, the decks dry. Porpoises played in the bow wave, and shoals of flying fish, startled by the passage of the vessel, broke from beneath the surface and skimmed the wavetops, their rainbow colors dazzling in the sunlight as they skipped from crest to crest. It was glorious sailing.

With the exception that no one spoke much. Bracken could still feel Stackhill's presence everywhere, but there was now no doubt in his mind that he had been deep-sixed by Raul and Vierro.

Pam had gone into mourning, wearing a black bikini to signal her sorrow, heavy into a bottle from Stackhill's stash of Wild Turkey. Whether she believed Stackhill was dead or just a deadbeat, she didn't say. She lay on an air mattress forward in the lee of the dinghy, her head propped up on her elbow, expressionlessly watching the sea from behind a pair of black-rimmed two-hundred-bucks-a-shot Porsche sunglasses.

Jean had taken her turn at the helm, but Bracken hadn't been able to talk to her because Raul had also been in the cockpit, picking dirt out from under his nails with a knife, drinking rum, leafing through a *Soldier of Fortune* magazine, but otherwise incommunicado.

Walrus, now in the sack, had scrubbed off the bloodstains with soap and seawater, but a dark residue remained embedded in the grain of the teak decks, an enduring reminder to those still living that there were finite limits to mortality.

By five in the afternoon, through the binoculars Bracken could pick out the peaks of El Yunque de Baracoa and Mt. Majayara rising through the coastal haze, marking the northeastern coast of Cuba, no more than twenty miles off. He took a bearing on both of the peaks, handed the helm over to a semi-fried Raul, and then slipped below to plot a fix. On the chart table lay a sheet of paper with Vierro's fluid handwriting on it, giving a satnav fix for 1630 hours, a course to steer, and their destination: one mile to seaward of a small inlet off Cuba named Cayo Mambi. Bracken spanned off the distance with the dividers: about fifty-five nautical miles. With the winds probably lighter along the coast, say about seven hours, which would put them abeam of the inlet by midnight, at the latest 0100 hours.

As usual, Vierro had soundlessly slipped up behind him. Bracken knew he was there only when he heard the match strike, followed by sucking sounds. Vierro was clothed in khaki pants and shirt, creases pressed to a knife's edge. He wore no badges of rank, but the outfit was obviously a uniform.

"You have an estimated time of arrival?" Vierro asked, puffing on the stogie.

"Midnight would be the earliest. Maybe an hour later. It depends on whether the wind holds up."

Vierro puffed on the cigar again. "That would be my estimate as well. We will be met by a pilot boat. I'll be in radio contact with them as we approach."

"What then?"

Vierro shrugged. "Nothing much. Some rest, some repairs, some additional equipment."

"I was hoping that you and Pit-face would be disembarking. Not that I haven't enjoyed having the two of you on board."

Smiling thinly, Vierro regarded Bracken for a long while. "You should watch your mouth, Bracken. It is sometimes too big as compared with the limited capacity of your brain."

Bracken let it pass. "Was Stackhill's mouth too big?"

Vierro shrugged eloquently, the absolute embodiment of a Latino's acceptance of things as they are and will be. "That is history, Captain Bracken. He made his choice. As do you."

Bracken thought it best to drop that part of the conversation. "How long in Cuba?"

Vierro nodded. "At a minimum for a few hours but perhaps as much as a day. I don't know exactly."

"And from there?"

"West northwest, Captain. That is, approximately." Vierro snuffed out the tip of his cigar on the chart table and left the salon, climbing the companionway.

Bracken laid out a rough course to the west northwest. It could take in the coastline anywhere from the Florida Keys to Fort Lauderdale, maybe even farther north. No way of knowing except that everything pointed to Vierro keeping the crew alive to make the delivery.

He doodled over the log for a few more minutes, playing guessing games. With Vierro and Raul still on board, there wasn't a chance of physically overpowering them. But with a little time to get ready, the odds could be evened.

Bracken popped up the companionway and edged his nose over the sill to see what Vierro was doing. He was aft, setting up a yellow feather lure on the deep sea trolling rig, then easing it out.

It was good country for hooking into tuna. Jean was on the helm, Pam still forward. Raul had turned in five minutes earlier, the aft cabin door closed and undoubtedly locked. Bracken figured that he had a clear ten minutes.

He eased forward into the engine room, wedging a crowbar into place to prevent the door being opened from the passageway.

The Walther was there, all right, except the cigar box that housed it was crushed from the weight of shifting batteries. Bracken pulled the weapon out. It was badly corroded, the bluing eaten away by spilled battery acid, the action frozen. He tried to chamber a shell, but the slide wouldn't budge. *Damn it to hell*, he swore under his breath. Tried to eject the clip, but it was also frozen solid.

He had pinned his faith on the damned Walther, but that was symptomatic of his whole approach. Flawed planning, no balls, and too little too late.

For the next five minutes he scoured the surface of the Walther with deck bleach and steel wool to get rid of the rust. Then emptied a gallon jug of distilled water, cut off the top of the jug, filled it with diesel fuel from the day tank, and immersed the entire weapon in the fluid. He was reasonably sure that the action would loosen up but wasn't sure whether the delicate springs inside the trigger mechanism would be operable.

He slid the jug under the battery bank and, as he did, his fingers met an obstruction. He pulled it out. It was a manual, oil-stained, soggy with seawater that had sloshed up from the bilge, pages folded over each other and stuck together.

He began to read.

14.

July 13–July 14

Lu lounged against the navigational desk of the *Victoria*, listening to the afternoon weather from Radio Barbados. The announcer reported that at first light this morning, the National Hurricane Center had dispatched a hurricane-hunter C-130 from Puerto Rico. The crew had radioed back that a small but intense low pressure system, now named Hannah, was drifting slowly north through the Leeward Islands. The winds in the eye measured sixty-five knots. The Barbados weather bureau's forecast was for light winds in the local area, rain tomorrow morning but clearing by midday. Perfect, Lu thought.

He flicked off the switch and ambled back out onto the wing deck. The Grenadine islands were abeam to the east, the peaks of Union Island and Carriacou just visible, Grenada only seventy miles to the south.

Aft on the boat deck, Sanchez, clad in Bermuda shorts, his naked torso glistening with sweat, had a crew member flinging empty beer bottles overboard. Sanchez tried to shatter them in flight with an AK-47 machine pistol, but he rarely connected. Once the bottle hit the sea, Sanchez would then burn through the remainder of his forty-round clip, turning the sea into white froth. The bottles seemed to have a charmed life, and Sanchez was obviously frustrated, yelling at the crew member to throw the bottles higher and somehow make them drop slower, as if the man had it in his power to dictate the laws of gravity.

Lu watched, amused, for several minutes. The sun was hot but the speed of the vessel created a breeze as the *Victoria* cleaved through the calm, transparent sea. He leaned his chest against the rail, feeling the vibrations of the engines rumble in his chest cavity, relaxed.

So far it had gone well. Both the *Victoria* and the *Pampero* were well-suited to the mission. Bracken had been his main concern, but that worry had evaporated. He was the same man with the same self-centered mindset, easily manipulated. It was just a matter of pressing the right buttons to make Bracken perform on cue. But now, as the operation intensified, the risks and unknowns would multiply. Still, Lu felt confident.

He glanced at his watch, then turned and ducked into the deckhouse to check the chart. The helmsman, a taciturn Cuban, puffed on a cigar and ignored Lu's presence.

Another sixty-eight miles to go, he calculated. Which would put them abeam the southern end of Grenada, about five miles offshore by sundown.

Sanchez, puffing from his exertion, lumbered into the deckhouse. "This piece of Soviet-made junk has faulty sights." He tossed the AK-47 onto the cushioned bench, then squeegeed the sweat off his chest with his hands. He pushed the intercom button to the galley and ordered up a rum and Coke. "Have you heard from Vierro yet?" Sanchez asked. His skin was splotchy with sunburn.

"He reported in at noon. They had heavy weather from the tropical storm up north, some minor damage, but everything is now under control."

Sanchez shrugged. He drained the glass and then chewed on the ice cubes, the sound as grating on Lu's ears as chalk screeching on a blackboard. "And what next?"

"We will take the *Victoria* around the south coast of Grenada into l'Anse aux Pines. It's a yacht anchorage and has customs and immigration services. I have all the necessary clearance papers from Guadeloupe. When we clear in, we'll also obtain clearance papers outbound for Panama with a departure scheduled for tomorrow morning. It will appear to the authorities like a normal refueling stopover."

Sanchez nodded. He liked explicit instructions.

Lu tapped his finger on the desk for emphasis. "Once cleared, you will assemble your entire crew and take them ashore to the Red Crab restaurant. It's a short walk from the docks. Our local contact has rented the place for the sole use of *Victoria*'s crew. Your men will stay together at all times, no individual excursions. They may have a maximum of two beers each—no liquor, Sanchez—and that means you as well. You will leave the restaurant at 0300, no sooner. Four hours later, the *Victoria* will depart l'Anse aux Pines on a heading for Panama. When we are thirty miles out, I will give you further instructions."

Sanchez pressed the cold glass against his cheek, watching Lu's eyes. "And what will you be doing in the meanwhile?"

"My assigned mission without questioning my orders. I would suggest you do the same."

Just after sundown the *Victoria* slid past Point Saline at twelve knots, then cautiously reduced speed to six knots and headed east in the shallow waters along the south coast of Grenada. Lu could see the reflected glow in the sky from the lights of St. Georges more than eight kilometers to the north. Scattered over the hillsides were a few individual lights of houses and the occasional flash of car headlamps.

He stood on the wing bridge, tense, watching the dark shore slide past through his night glasses, then ducked into the bridge to check the radar. The sweep painted a series of small indentations in the coast as well as the hangars and the control tower of the airport just a hundred meters inland. Another shape showed up on the scope, located on the eastern edge of the tarmac. He switched the range down to its lowest setting. The images on the scope leapt in size. The shape was so large, had such a hard return, it had to be the aircraft. Involuntarily, Lu breathed a sigh of relief.

He picked up the portable VHF and moved back out onto the wing bridge. He toggled the set to low power and depressed the mike button. "Two, this is One. Over."

Long pause then, *One, this is Two. Flash your running lights for positive ID.*

Lu moved back inside the bridge. He nodded to Sanchez, who flicked a switch off, waited a few seconds, and flicked it back on.

See you, man. All set here. How soon?

"Four hours," Lu replied. "You've seen the aircraft?"

Came in about two hours ago. Some kind of problem with the hydraulics. They're unloading now so that they can get at the problem.

Lu nodded to himself. "Your equipment?"

All set, buddy.

"Very good. Monitor this channel. I'll call you on our way in."

Two clicked his transmit switch twice.

Lu relaxed a fraction.

*   *   *

The *Victoria* slowly powered up the south coast of Grenada against a one-knot current, cleared Glovers Island, then executed a slow turn to port into l'Anse aux Pines Bay. The bay was dark, but a few anchor lights of yachts moored farther inshore flickered. Still far out in the bay, much farther out than any yacht would normally moor, the *Victoria* dropped anchor in eight fathoms of water. Within six minutes the inflatable dinghy was launched, a twenty-horse Johnson outboard attached, and the first officer at the helm. Through the infrared night scope, Lu could see the lights of the immigration and customs office blink on, and a man, a cigarette glowing in his mouth, standing on the porch.

The first officer was back in half an hour. The *Victoria*'s crew were lined up in white sweaters and pompon hats, all silent and disciplined. On Sanchez's command they scrambled down the boarding ladder into the ship's whaleboat.

Sanchez was the last to leave. "Three in the morning?"

Lu nodded. "And not sooner. Keep your men under close control and watch them. I don't want any incidents."

Wearing a white captain's uniform which was beautifully tailored, Sanchez shrugged, his gold braid glittering in the glow of the decklights. "As you say, Comrade."

Lu waited until the whaleboat had disappeared into the darkness, then went into the salon, down the spiral staircase, and into his cabin. He changed into a dark blue boiler suit which had an embroidered gold cormorant. Within the circle of the wings were the letters KSAC—Katana Shioji Air Cargo.

Over the boiler suit he drew on a black foul weather suit. After worming his feet into sea boots, he donned a wool watch cap, then spent three minutes brushing his teeth.

Finally, he dug into his duffel bag and removed two half-liter bottles of Cuban Gold Label rum. He checked the labels carefully, then broke the seal of one and poured a third of it into the sink. Into a canvas flight bag he placed both bottles of rum, a pair of wire cutters, a small package wrapped in plastic, a bail of galvanized wire, his VHF radio, and a flashlight.

Heading forward on deck, he made his way to the small cargo hatch and examined the lead seals. They were unbroken. He severed them with the wire cutters, then drew back the clamps. Next, he went to the bridge, switched on the crane winch circuit breaker, and climbed to the boat deck. Holding the flashlight in his mouth, he manipulated the controls so that the crane, normally used to launch and retrieve the twenty-five-foot whaleboat, swung inward and over the hatch. The cable counter reeled off until it reached twenty-three feet, and Lu was rewarded by a dull *clunk* as the forged hook hit the top of the cargo hatch.

Back down to the forward deck. Lu withdrew a spiderweb of steel cables from the bosun's locker and attached the hooked ends to welded tangs on the cargo hatch and mated the lifting eye to the hook of the winch cable. Then back up to the boat deck to lift the hatch.

It was a time-consuming process. A couple of the *Victoria*'s crew could have done the job in a fifth of the time, but that would have exposed yet another layer in the security of the operation. Lu had practiced this routine eight times in Mariel Harbor before the *Victoria* had left Cuba. By his sixth, seventh, and eighth try, his average time had been nine minutes. Tonight he timed it at slightly under eight. The adrenaline factor, he thought. It always worked for you, but later, he knew, his nerves would be burning like a shorted electrical circuit.

He engaged the clutch and lifted off the hatch cover, swung the cargo boom through ten degrees of arc, and gently lowered the hatch cover onto the deck. There was a muffled clang. He then set the brake on the reel to *Run*. The cable eased out a few feet, then went slack.

He checked his watch. Only five minutes behind schedule.

When he got to the opened cargo hatch, the space below was black, silent, and reeked of body sweat and human waste.

"Privyet! Zdrah's stvosite!" he called softly into the blackness.

The beam of a powerful flashlight blinded him for a second, then switched off.

"There is a ladder to the right of your hand, Comrade Major," a voice replied in Russian. A dim overhead light switched on, illuminating the hold.

It smelled like a cave where animals went to die—only a few meters square with just enough overheard clearance for a man to stand. Lashed in one corner was a chemical toilet and three plastic drums of water. Three inflatable air mattresses were spread out on the opposite side of the hold. A crate lashed near the mattresses contained the tins and foil wrappers of consumed field rations. Completely isolated from the crew, without air-conditioning or a place of exercise, three men had existed in this sweatbox for seven days. The stench was almost enough to make him gag.

Lu inhaled the night air deeply and descended the ladder, pulling the slack cargo cable behind him. At the bottom he turned to examine the men. They were slick with sweat, dressed in rumpled gray engineering overalls, complete with grease stains. The one on the right saluted him.

"All present and ready for duty, Comrade Major."

Feeling like a fraud because Lu had never actually commanded real troops, particularly elite *Spetsnaz* commandos, Lu returned the salute awkwardly.

In the center of the cargo hold was a white fiberglass container, lashed down with heavy lines to rings which were bolted into the deck. Based on the paperwork, Lu knew that the container was exactly 1.9 meters high, 1.73 meters square, and weighed a bit more than 1,500 kilos. The sides of the fiberglass container were unmarked except for a few Japanese kanji letters and a detachable plastic envelope containing the shipping invoice. Orange arrows indicated the universal symbolism of "this side up."

"The contents of the container have survived the trip in good order?"

The lieutenant nodded. "There are no apparent faults."

"And the watertight seals are pressurized?"

"They have been thoroughly checked, Major."

"We're running slightly behind schedule. You have your papers?"

The lieutenant nodded. "Norwegian passports, seamen's papers, and a few kroner each."

"No other identification?"

"Of course not, Comrade Major." From the tone of his voice, the lieutenant seemed miffed at even the suggestion of possible incompetency.

"Very well. Unlash the lines on the container and strap on the padding. Then attach the hook. I'll man the crane."

It took the four of them another thirteen minutes to offload the container. Using the *Victoria*'s inflatable Zodiac dinghy, one of the sergeants motored forward until he reached the anchor chain of the *Victoria*, looped a line over it, then drifted the Zodiac back alongside the ship. The lieutenant and the other sergeant stripped the tiedowns from the container, wrestled a padded black canvas jacket around it, and attached the cargo hook to the lifting eye. From the boat deck Lu cautiously hoisted the container through the cargo hatch and lowered it into the sea, where a towline was attached to it, then replaced the cargo hatch, locked and sealed it.

With the three *Spetsnaz* commandos hunched down in the

inflatable, Lu snicked the gearshift lever into forward and started the three-kilometer journey, the line towing the container twanging taut. Keeping the bulk of the *Victoria* between the inflatable and the shore, Lu headed out of the harbor to sea, and once well clear, steered down the coast three hundred meters offshore, retracing *Victoria*'s inbound journey.

The sea air was warm—the smells of hibiscus, bougainvillea, wet earth, and growing things thick on the night wind. The moon had just set below the western horizon, but the higher clouds were still tinged with silvered light.

He turned the steering over to the lieutenant and pulled the VHF radio out of his flight bag. "Two, this is One. You copy?"

There was a hiccup of static, then, *Copy.*

"We're inbound. Estimate one hour, fifteen. Any patrols?"

No smokies, man. They're all hibernating.

The *Spetsnaz* lieutenant nudged him. "He's referring to police militia—that they're not present. Tell him 'ten-four.' "

"Ten-four."

No sweat, man. I'm primed and ready. Gimme a call when you're past Glover's Island and inbound for the beach.

Lu clicked the mike button twice in acknowledgment and shut the radio off.

Vierro had selected this man from three candidates, once Grenada had been chosen as the transfer point. Nothing complicated in his makeup—a drifter, a record of minor drug arrests but no convictions, now just scratching out a living in the islands as a custom's warehouse security guard. Lu had read the man's file many times. No wife, no mistress, no particular friends; a young, wasted kid who spent his spare time sniffing around for nickel and dime drug deals. The world would not miss Lennie C. Gluckman.

Reaching into his flight bag, Lu felt both bottles of rum. One of them sloshed slightly, the cap turning easily. He brought it out and passed it to the lieutenant. "There is time. We will all share a drink in anticipation of our success."

The lieutenant's teeth gleamed in the darkness. It wasn't often that an officer thought of his men. He lifted the bottle in a silent toast, took a swig, and passed it to the senior sergeant, who swallowed, then passed it on to the junior sergeant, who took an even longer pull. Lu sealed the pact with a final sip, putting the bottle to his lips but swallowing very little.

The container, towed by the steel cable, was half submerged, creating its own small bow wave. Lu kept the throttle on a setting that would keep an even but not excessive strain on the tow. Additional power was a waste and created too much noise. Still, with the current behind them, he was averaging better than two knots. He checked his Rolex. Less than another forty minutes to run. They had made up some time.

Grenada had been the logical choice for the transfer. It was within an easy two days run from Cuba in the *Victoria*. The runway, long enough to accommodate a Boeing 747, was located on the south shore of the island. No local settlements, no security patrols or fences, no aircraft traffic after sundown.

Through binoculars Lu could now pick out the outlines of the control tower, terminal building, and hangars. He smiled to himself. The fitting part of it was that the airport had been built with Soviet funds and Cuban labor before the Americans had strangled the revolution. The colonel had loved the irony of using Grenada as the transfer point. "Our investment there is going to pay off after all," he had commented.

Another twenty-five minutes ticked by, the dim bulk of Glover's Island growing larger. Inshore of Glover's, Lu swung the boat toward the mainland and keyed the transmitter.

"Two, this is One. Copy?"

This time, no delay. *Five by fiver.* The strength of Gluckman's transmission was much stronger.

"We're off Glover's, inbound, about five hundred meters from the beach."

Stand by.

At first he didn't see them, then a light winked on, followed by another, slightly lower in elevation.

You got 'em?

Lu maneuvered the boat and the container, swinging back to the east, finally lining up the range lights, one over the other.

You got 'em? Gluckman's question was more insistent.

Lu thumbed the mike button. "We're on the range."

Make damned sure you are. There's a coral outcropping off to your right.

The lights grew steadily brighter, the elevation between them increasing. The darker horizon of sand dunes blotted out the skyline. The dinghy was suddenly in light surf, the skeg of the outboard motor thumping along the sandy bottom, pebbles grating under the bow.

In the darkness Gluckman was just a thin shadow. He splashed through the shallows to the dinghy, grabbed the painter, back-pedaled inshore, and secured it.

Then awkwardly scrambled back through the soft sand to the waterline, a penlight in his hand, shining it briefly on the four men. He stuck out his hand. "All *right*! Name's Gluckman. Where's the load?"

Lu didn't take Gluckman's hand. "In the surf on a wire towline. It's heavier than we agreed on. There'll be another three thousand in it for you."

"Hey, man . . . terrific! What kind of stuff you got in the container?"

"A rocket booster engine for a satellite."

"You're shitting me!"

"And packed inside that are fifty kilos of refined heroin." Lu had thought this through a long time ago. Gluckman vaguely understood drug trafficking. That was what he expected and that was what he would believe.

Gluckman's knees almost buckled. "Fifty *kees*? That's got a street value of . . ."

"Not your business, is it, Gluckman?"

"But custom narcs in Florida—if they found the stuff, they'd trace it back here."

"The container that was shipped from Osaka was precleared by U.S. Customs because it contains equipment built under contract by a Japanese firm for NASA. There will be no inspection of the container by American customs. We're wasting valuable time. You have the truck?"

Gluckman headed into the darkness. A diesel engine coughed into life, gears growled, and Gluckman backed a wrecker truck to the water's edge.

It took them eleven minutes to move the container ashore on inflatable rollers, then another fifteen minutes with the truck's crane to lift the container onto the cargo bed of the truck.

"This is your truck?" Lu asked.

"It's a rental. Paid a garage seventy bills to rent it overnight. Told them that I had a contract to haul busted engine blocks down to the marina to be used as moorings."

Lu got into the passenger seat after first pushing aside several empty beer bottles and the remains of a sandwich. Gluckman got behind the wheel. The *Spetsnaz* lieutenant vaulted onto the bed of the truck.

"How 'bout them other two dudes?" Gluckman asked.

"They stay here. Get going. We're slightly behind schedule."

Lu knew exactly what to expect. Three weeks previously, two KGB illegals posing as honeymooning Danish tourists had worked up a report, complete with detailed maps, photographs, and a background and personality profile of the six candidates. Gluckman stood out as the obvious choice. Once the decision was made in Moscow, Vierro had flown into Grenada as a Venezuelan tourist, ambushed Gluckman at his favorite rum shop, and recruited him for what was to be a simple drug transshipment deal.

Now Gluckman, enriched with twelve thousand dollars in low denomination bills, drove along the perimeter road that paralleled the runway. His lights were off and he had to move slowly in his lowest gear, steering by starlight. As he drove, he cursed with such detailed dedication that his foul mouth grated on Lu's nerves.

There was no light in the control tower. The runway and taxiway lights were switched off. Only near the hangars at the opposite end of the runway, where the SP-747 was parked, were lighted. Lu could see a few maintenance trucks parked around the aircraft and the occasional figure moving around the plane.

"There are no inbound flights this time of night?" he asked Gluckman, testing.

"Shee-it no, man. Nothing till eight tomorrow A.M."

It took another eleven minutes for the truck to rumble to the graveled parking area behind the bonded warehouses.

"Who's on duty now?"

"Buddy of mine—a guy named Zeke. He goes off duty in about ten minutes."

"And you relieve him?"

"Yeah. I go on at midnight. Zeke and I generally sit around for ten minutes, shoot the shit, blow a little ganga, and then he takes off. I hold down the fort until eight in the morning. Forty bucks Beewee a night—that's sixteen Yankee greenbacks for eight hours of work. Man, like I can really use the bread from this job. Get the hell out of here, go down to Colombia and buy a couple of kees of coke. Then head up to Florida and score. You got tight connections there?"

"It would seem that way, wouldn't it?"

Gluckman turned to him and beamed. "You think you could use me again on another run through Grenada? Just like this time, I'll set things up real neat. No mistakes. I'd like to ease into the big deals, learn the trade from a pro, get my feet wet, understand?"

"That can be arranged," Lu answered.

"Cool," Gluckman responded, moving his tongue over his upper lip. He parked the truck behind the bonded warehouse. "Give me fifteen minutes for the shift changeover, then twenty more to get the cargo."

Lu grabbed Gluckman's wrist, squeezing hard. "Don't rush the man you're replacing. Nothing unusual—just the way you normally do it."

"Gotcha!" Gluckman replied, giving Lu a big O with his thumb and index finger. He retrieved a Walkman from the glove compartment, pulled out a lunch pail from beneath the driver's seat, and bopped into the darkness toward the darkened hangar.

The lieutenant had silently dropped off the cargo bed.

"Follow him at a distance," Lu ordered. "Once the other guard has left, secure the area. Monitor channel 131 with your earphone. Call me if there is any problem."

The lieutenant saluted and followed Gluckman into the blackness.

Gluckman, the Walkman headphones plastered over his ears, jogged along to the music, swinging his lunch bucket in time, feet crunching over the gravel in beat with the percussion. Singing brain-dead lyrics by the Down and Out under his breath, Lennie was high, bouncing along, the music in his brain pan blowing white hot. Twelve grand. Plus three more. In SnowLumbia, he could peel off big bread and buy two kees of cocaine. Trip up to Miami Viceland and multiply that ten, fifteen times over.

Thing that kept eating at his brain was all that prime Asian skag packed in the container. Fifty kees. He couldn't even begin to calculate the wholesale, let alone the street price of a load like that. Thought about how, maybe, just maybe, he could do a little discreet unpacking. Five kees maybe? One-stop shopping and he'd be an instant megabucks winner.

But deep in his gourd he knew that people like the Chink wouldn't take kindly to a guy like Lennie Gluckman shaving the load. No way, Hose-A. He'd play it straight up, real cool, and super-dooper careful. Professionalism—that was the ticket. You got a rep in the dope business and that rep stuck forever. Good rep was good and bad rep was gonzo in a dark alley with a bullet in your brain.

He checked his Timex, pulsing the little light button. A little past twelve straight up, ol' midnight-madness time.

Zeke, the security guard that Lennie relieved at midnight, was stationed down in front of the second warehouse in the guard shack. He was a fat, older guy, fuzzy-gray haired, loved his food, and big on playing the football pools. Had won a thousand pounds sterling sixteen years before and had already gone through five times that much trying to duplicate his luck.

Lennie loved to scare the shit out of Zeke. He snuck up on the shack and pounded on it with both fists and was rewarded by the sound of Zeke falling off his stool.

"Zeke, my man!" Lennie stuck his head into the open window. "What's happenin'?"

"You late, you fish-belly-white son'abitch. Like always. And I keep tellin' you, don't freak me out like that!"

Zeke invariably complained, but he was a good-humored bastard and they had a deal. They covered for each other. And they shared. Zeke almost always had a spare slice of banana bread that his wife had made wrapped up in a cloth napkin which Zeke left behind for Lennie. And Lennie almost always had a joint to share with Zeke at the shift changeover. And sometimes on their days off they would down a few beers together at Zeke's house or watch cricket matches on TV at a local rum shop.

"Who you like?" Zeke asked. "Blackpool or Manchester?"

"Who's favored?" asked Lennie, pulling two joints from his pocket and lighting one of them with a flourish.

"Blackpool by three goals."

"So take Manchester, asshole. You know that the bookmakers always buy off the tipsters. Figures."

Zeke nodded, lips pursed together and Xed in his selection on the betting sheet.

They shared the first joint. Then Lennie lit the second one. It was thirteen minutes after midnight.

"So what's up?" Lennie asked, huffing out puffs of smoke.

"Usual stuff due custom's clearance tomorrow, all stashed in warehouse two. Other warehouse"—he sucked on the joint, held it in his lungs, and jerked his thumb over his shoulder toward the outlying warehouse—"has six, seven containers in-transient storage from the Jap plane that flew in about suppertime. Got some dumbass mechanical problem and had to offload all the cargo to get at the access panels inside the cargo hold. Stevedores had to work overtime, offloading the shit and storing it in the warehouse. Maintenance been workin' on that bird all night." He tapped a cargo manifest sheet on the desk. "All here. I checked it off."

Lennie took a big hit on the ganga, holding it in his lungs too long, then coughing. The Trinidad stuff was good but rough as a cob. "Terrific—like you mean they're gonna want me to open the warehouse in the middle of the frigging night to reload cargo?"

Zeke wagged his head back and forth as if he were watching a slowly orbiting mosquito. "Don't worry your head, honkyboy. Crew shagged out for the Spice Island Inn right after I gave them the gospel according to Zeke. Not due back until eight. Told 'em that there wouldn't be no ground handlers to reload their cargo until two hours after the roosters crow unless they was willing to pay triple overtime."

Lennie scooped up the cargo manifest. Eight containers in warehouse number one, in-transit for KSAC charter flight 14. Item number six, container LL-B-119 (1,500 kilos, 5.66 cubic meters), expendable transition state vehicle Pam-G445-M-5R, cargo invoice item 006/2-113, class A2 inflammable materials: special handling required. He quickly compared it with the slip that the Chink had given him. That's the sucker!

"Okay, Zeke my man. You're outta here. Take care the jumbies don't grab your big black ass."

"No way, white boy. It's *you* that gotta watch out 'cause they can't see us black folks in the dark, and 'sides, jumbies sure do *pre*-fer white meat." Zeke rumbled a laugh up from his belly, punched Lennie amicably on the shoulder, and headed out for his motorbike. As usual, he had left the banana bread wrapped in an immaculate and freshly ironed napkin. A good man, a very good man, Lennie thought, munching on the bread, watching the feeble headlight beam of Zeke's motorbike wobble over the lumpy tarmac toward the exit road. I'll buy him a new color TV, Lennie promised himself. Twenty-six-inch with remote control. Absolutely blow him right out of his skull.

He let ten minutes tick by. Called the security officer in the terminal. No, man, of course no inboun' traffic and why you callin' me in the middle of the night, man? Your brain fried on dope again? Then the slam of the receiver. So it was safe.

He unlocked the access door to warehouse one, then punched the door switch. The panel rumbled along its tracks. Next he checked the containers with his flashlight. The one marked LL-B-119 was the third one in line. Looked the right size. Weight stenciled on the container was right, everything but everything perfecto.

He fired up the propane-fueled forklift, wheeled it around to the container, and expertly slid the forks under the pallet, then steered the machine with its load out of the hangar and toward the truck.

The switch went smoothly. Within thirty minutes he had the replacement container positioned within warehouse one right on the chalkmarks he had left. He carefully erased the chalkmarks, wiped off the container with a dry rag, parked the forklift in the corner exactly as he had found it, and then closed, locked, and resealed the doors.

The Chink and the industrial-strength dude were waiting in the truck. Payday. Three more big ones. Lennie tried to keep his movements calm, not show signs of fidgeting or nervousness. He had watched videotapes of *Miami Vice,* and he was hip to the scene that came with the payoff, but he kept telling himself that he wasn't worried because this was small potatoes to big operators like these guys.

The Chink handed him an envelope. "Three thousand dollars U.S. currency in small bills."

Lennie breathed a sigh of relief. Nice working with professionals. No pain, no strain. Trying to be real hip about it, and although he was dying to count the money, he casually slipped the envelope under his shirt, then stuck out his hand. "Pleasure doin' business with you. It went down slick as whale shit, right?"

"You were very efficient," the Chink answered. "We will take the truck back to the coast, offload the container, then bring it back. Where do you want it parked?"

"Leave it back of hangar one, keys under the seat. What about the tire tracks in the sand? Not many local spooks go out to the coast much, but once in a while some fishing guys put in there. Netting sprats is good in the coves when the wind's in the south."

"The tire marks will be filled in and swept over with brooms by my men. The Barbados coastal marine forecast indicates that there will be heavy rain through most of tomorrow due to the tropical storm up north. That should eliminate any remaining marks that they miss."

For a few more seconds the Chink and Lennie stood there. It was a little uncomfortable, as though there was something more to be said. "So when do we do the next load?" Lennie asked.

"I'll contact you. It might be soon." The Chink then pulled a small package from a pocket of his jump suit. "Just a present from one friend to another as a token of my appreciation. You did a fine job, Lennie." The Chink turned without further comment and got in the truck.

Lennie watched it back up, turn, then disappear slowly into the darkness.

He trotted back to the guard shack, the package clutched in his hand, the envelope against his chest burning with a pleasant warmth.

He replaced the phone on the hook and settled down. No notes on the door, no one had been there, all cool as ice cream. He'd pulled it off! Fifteen grand for one night's easy work, more money than he had ever seen in one pile.

Lennie tore off the wrapper of the package. More bucks, he hoped, but was at first disappointed because the container inside was a little rectangular tin marked with the brand of a Dutch pipe tobacco. He pried off the lid carefully. Inside, the tin was filled with a white crystalline powder. He licked his fingertip, then touched it to the powder and tasted it. The *real thing*—more than an ounce. He had snorted coke once before, but that was at a party in Long Beach years earlier where he dragged just half a line; enough to be interesting but not really enough to get up on.

An ounce was worth how much in Grenada? But he immediately discounted the idea. With the money he'd made tonight and from the bread he'd make from another couple of runs with the Chink, he didn't want to blow the whole deal by being busted for nickel and dime dealing. No way, Hose-A. This was for personal consumption: a gift.

He checked his watch. One-eighteen. No one would be around to bother him, no hassles. First the cash. He counted it. Three thousand on the nose, all well-worn tens and twenties. He tucked the money away in his shirt. Then munched on the banana bread, popped the lid on a Tab, and took a sip. He felt up, really up. Pulled it off with no glitches. And now for dessert.

He took out his Swiss Army knife and dipped a blade into

the coke. He fussed with the quantity, tapping the blade on the paper, then adding a bit more. It was a generous amount which he laid out on the page of the telephone book, and he spent a lot of time gently massaging it with the knife blade into a nice fat line. Then took a bill from his pocket, rolled it into a thin tube, and snorted up the entire line.

Woo-eeeee! He was immediately into a rush the magnitude of a major bombardment, artillery shells going off in his head, the shrapnel bursting through his brain. His heart was screaming up through ten million rpm and then started to seize. He clapped his hands over his ears to shut out the noise, doubling over with the unbearable pain in his rib cage. Then, just as suddenly, the noise started to fade, the pain diminishing, and he realized that he was slip-sliding away.

Unable to control it, motor coordination gone, heart no longer pumping, his head flopped down onto the page of the telephone directory. The ad, under his eye, distorted by his contracting vision, was an advertisement for takeout Cantonese food from the Yoo Too Chinese Restaurant. "The bastard Chink" was his last thought, unable to finish the sentence in his dying mind.

The lieutenant, having delivered and unloaded the container into the surf, drove the wrecker back and parked it as instructed. He then stood at the back of the warehouse and waited silently for five minutes, listening. Then moved carefully down to warehouse two and waited another five minutes. Edging sideways in the overhanging darkness of the warehouse roof, he observed the guard shack for several more minutes. He tossed a pebble against the shack, but there was no response.

He crept up to the shack and looked inside. Lennie was slumped over the desk, his mouth open, his eyes sightless. A thorough man, the lieutenant felt for a pulse on Lennie's neck. He would have been very surprised if there had been one.

Next he retrieved the payoff envelope and pocketed it in his overalls. Other than the VHF radio, Lennie's lunch pail yielded nothing except a ham sandwich, an orange, and a second can of Tab. With luck, Lennie's dead body would not be discovered until after sunrise.

The lieutenant hooked Lennie's VHF on his belt, then took the opened can of cocaine laced with prussic acid and substituted a small cloth bag, this one marked with the label of an English cough drop manufacturer. Inside the bag were three small plastic pouches of unadulterated cocaine. One of them was open. Using tweezers, the lieutenant took the open bag, spilled some of the white powder on the page, and pressed Lennie's still-warm face into it. On a tropical island where there were no facilities for embalming, Lennie would be six feet under potter's field by sundown.

The lieutenant spent a few more minutes going over the guard shack and the surrounding grounds. There were no tracks and no trace of footprints. He checked the locks and seals on warehouse one. All was as it should be.

Humming a Red Army marching song, "Battalions Forward!," the lieutenant double-timed on the road back toward the beach.

Lu, along with the two sergeants, was already in the inflatable dinghy when the lieutenant arrived, the towline to the container attached, the motor ticking over.

Taking off his boots, the lieutenant walked across the sand backward, scuffing out his footprints. He waded through the light surf and pulled himself up into the dinghy.

"All is in order," he reported. He handed Lu the envelope and tin of cocaine.

"An excellent operation, Lieutenant. You and your men will be mentioned in my report, including a recommendation for advancement in rank." He was rewarded by three sets of grinning white teeth. It was really too bad, he thought. Really fine men who had done their duty.

Lu dropped the gearshift lever into forward and headed away from the coast, laying a course past Glover's Island, heading out to sea.

As he cleared Glover Island, the sea became a bit rougher but not really uncomfortable, just a light chop. The stars were out, but to the north a high, thin overcast was beginning to dim their light. As forecast, Lu thought, it will certainly rain.

He reached into his flight bag and retrieved the partially empty bottle of rum. "To the success of our mission, Comrades." He took a swig, wiped his lips, then stretched forward to pass the bottle to the lieutenant, but before the bottle was in the lieutenant's grasp, Lu dropped it. The bottle bounced off the inflatable tube and into the sea, bobbing away into the blackness.

"Damn!" he swore.

The lieutenant made a flying leap, trying to grab the bottle, but he missed.

"No matter." Lu laughed. "Like all well-prepared Soviet campaigns, we have replacement troops waiting behind the lines to fill in for our fallen comrades." He fished out the second, unopened bottle of rum and carefully, ceremoniously, handed it to the lieutenant. "Comrade Lieutenant, you have strict orders from me, your superior officer, to toast the conclusion of our successful mission. I trust my order will be obeyed without question." The three *Spetsnaz* men laughed in unison.

The lieutenant twisted off the sealed cap of the bottle, raised it on high in a salute, and took a long pull at the bottle. He then passed the bottle, according to rank, to the senior sergeant, who drank deeply and offered it to the junior sergeant. Then the bottle was passed back to Lu. He put the bottle to his lips but didn't drink.

The bottle went through a second round, nearly finished. It was passed back to Lu, who put the bottle to his lips, then tossed it into the sea.

The outboard engine droned on, Lu heading over the outer banks into deep water. The coastline of Grenada was now over a kilometer to the north. To the west was over 1,800 kilometers of open water.

The lieutenant started up a soft chorus of *"Battalions Forward!"* and was joined by the men. One by one their voices faded, then trailed off into silence.

Two of the *Spetsnaz* men were nodding now, the senior sergeant's chin already resting on his chest, beginning to snore heavily. In another two minutes the junior sergeant slumped over, his body curling into the fetal position on the Zodiac's floorboards.

The lieutenant was the last to go, having had less of the rum than his men. He made no hostile moves, probably couldn't; just sat there, his head heavy on his shoulders, nodding toward sleep, unable to fight off the effects. But he had put the pieces together in his drugged mind. He kept snapping his head upright, trying to stay conscious.

"The rum . . . ?" His speech was slurred, his tongue thick.

"Yes," Lu answered. "The rum. It's very strong. Don't worry. I will not report this. Sleep well."

Still heading south, Lu waited another ten minutes, reluctant to act. All three of the men were curled up on the floorboards, their breathing rapid and shallow. They were good men, all dedicated, a tribute to the State and their own determination. Hundreds of thousands of rubles had been invested in their training. He had not wanted to learn their names or to know them as comrades. He tried to think of them as bullets fired from a gun—expendable but well used in a difficult battle—but he couldn't. Rather, these were brave, dedicated men with families and a love of country and he had used them like toilet paper. Still, the colonel had ordered their deaths under the all-encompassing mantle of operational security. So be it, he thought, except that he knew when he got back to the *Victoria* he would drink himself senseless.

This part of the mission was nearly done. Nearly.

Slowly turning to port, he rounded the dinghy up into the wind and shifted the outboard engine into neutral.

All three of the men were comatose but still alive. Lu hoped they would feel no pain.

He used the bailing wire to bind their ankles together, then retrieved the container's tow wire, unshackled it from the eyebolt on the transom, and wired the ankles of the three bodies to the loop.

Depressurizing the container was more difficult than he had expected. Using the wire cutters, he cut the seals, but it was difficult to undo the four access plugs because the container was bobbing around in the sloppy seas. It took him nearly twenty minutes.

A duplicate container loaded with a duplicate mock-up of the rocket engine had been fabricated in the Soviet Union and tested in the towing tank of the Aurora Naval Institute. With all pressurization ports open, the container had taken an average of thirty-seven minutes to sink.

The current was running down to the west at over a knot. Coupled with that, as long as the container was still above water, the wind would propel it to the west at an even faster rate. Some nameless engineer had probably expended two days of calculations to come up with the estimate that the container would track downwind for 3.4317 nautical miles before actually sinking. It didn't really matter. Lu knew that his rough location was in water well over five hundred meters deep.

The container was already visibly lower in the water. He

rolled the three men over the side of the Zodiac and then stood there, his knees braced against the side of the inflatable, watching the container slowly drift away from him until it was lost in the darkness. Like Vikings, he thought; the warriors consigned to the deep with their sinking ship. He saluted them.

It was beginning to drizzle, the stars gone. He sat down in the bottom of the Zodiac, shifted into forward, and increased the engine speed until he was planning off the tops of the seas, the few lights of l'Anse aux Pines growing steadily brighter over his bow. They were just bullets fired from a gun, he kept telling himself.

15.

July 16

The colonel slouched back against the Thai-silk cushions of the settee, his legs crossed, slowly rotating the glass of chilled vodka between his palms. His face was haggard from jet lag and his body was bloated by a heavy lunch. And he was slightly drunk.

Beyond the smoked glass of the *Victoria*'s salon, Lu scanned the muddy stretch of water enclosed on either shore by mangrove swamps. A Cuban patrol boat was moored up on the far side of the inlet. The *Pampero*, which had been piloted in during the previous night, was anchored out of sight beyond the bend in the inlet but was due to be rafted up alongside of the *Victoria* before sundown.

Lu approved of the location. Desolate, completely protected from the weather, a Cuban military-restricted area which insured security and yet was only three kilometers from the sea through a narrow and unmarked channel. Through his KGB contact in Havana, Lu knew that the Cubans used the inlet of Cayo Mambi as a transshipment point for South American drug shipments headed north and for arms headed south—a profitable sideline that earned both hard currency and political credits to be repaid in some future time.

He had arrived on the *Victoria* less than two hours earlier after hammering up through the Caribbean Sea from Grenada to Cuba at full throttle, the passage of 1,094 nautical miles made at an average of nearly thirty-five knots. Lu would never have believed that a yacht could make that kind of speed in such punishing sea conditions. Grudgingly, his estimate of Sanchez had gone up a notch.

"From reading your progress report, it seems that your end of things went well," the colonel said.

"As planned," Lu answered. "The Grenada operation came off without any problems."

"As did the rest of the M-5R substitution." He looked up at

Lu, holding eye contact. "Successful in all respects. Our contact at the cape reported that the rocket motor arrived safely in Florida. It checked out perfectly and is being mated to the Japanese GINGA sometime tomorrow." He glanced at the calendar on his watch. "It will be loaded into the shuttle cargo bay along with the Excalibur satellite by tomorrow with the launch scheduled in four days."

The Patriots had won, Lu thought, relieved. "So I take it that the project has been fully approved by the Politburo and we have permission to continue the project?"

The colonel downed the remaining vodka and held out his glass to Lu. "Just a touch more, Louis."

Which meant a full one. Lu took the glass to the bar, opened the freezer, and withdrew the bottle of Absolut vodka. It was so cold that the liquor had a slick, viscous texture. He carried the brimming glass back to the colonel, who took it, then held the glass up to the fading light in a toast.

"You have the heavy hand of a good host, Louis. *Na zdahrovyeh!*"

He knocked down a third, then leaned back against the cushions, his eyes heavy. "There is a problem, Louis. The project has been unconditionally rejected by the general secretary and the pacifist members of the Politburo, who hold the majority vote. In very clear language, they cite global political considerations, progress in arms negotiations, the threat of discovery, blah, blah, blah. Choose from any of the reasons given by these revisionist rat-brained apparatchiks but understand that the real reason is they're scared shitless to risk a little even with the prospect of winning a lot." He lifted his glass. "So a toast to our faint-hearted leaders, my friend. In fraternal and socialist solidarity, may they roast in the capitalist hell they've created."

There was a sudden chill on Lu's skin. He had come so far, had taken great risks, exposed himself, wasted good lives, and gambled the future of his son and himself on success. Now the project was being yanked out from beneath him. Worse, with the mission canceled, there would be blame assigned, and blame, like horse dung rolling downhill, would gravitate to the lowest level—his. It was likely that the colonel would now order him to fly back to Moscow immediately. Lu calculated that he would be fortunate to serve out the next fifteen years commanding some KGB garrison on the Turkish border—or worse. As for Sasha, there would be no future.

Still, somehow he sensed that the colonel wouldn't have taken the time to fly out to Cuba when he could have sent a simple cancellation order, distancing himself from failure. Lu recalled from his mother that the Chinese ideogram for "problem" is a combination of the symbols "danger" and "opportunity." As in this situation, it was a question of emphasis.

He turned away from the colonel, leaning against the sill of the salon window, watching gulls wheel over the garbage dumped by the patrol boat. Two young Cuban seamen, their heads shaved to regulation baldness, swam naked in the tidal water, laughing and splashing each other like carefree children. If life were just that damned simple.

"Have you found anything lacking in my performance, Colonel?" he finally asked, keeping his voice level.

Silence.

Exasperated, Lu turned to face the colonel. "Do you?"

The colonel placed the cold glass against his cheek, half closing his eyes. "No. I find no fault, Louis," he said softly. "No fault at all."

"Then, with the project terminated, you will enter that statement on my record?"

"You disappoint me, Louis. Is that all you can think of— covering your ass?" The colonel shook his head. "Of course I'd give you the highest commendations for your performance and would necessarily have to accept some blame as your superior, but it's not that simple. Nothing ever is."

Lu was puzzled by the response, but at least the colonel was willing to share in the equation of responsibility, thus decreasing the possibility of danger. The question now was one of opportunity. "And what does the colonel have in mind?"

The old man lay back against the cushions, his face slack but his eyes carefully surveying Lu's. "To carry out the project as *we* planned it, Louis."

We was a word which implied co-conspirators to treason, Lu realized. Therefore very deep and extremely dangerous water. "It was my understanding, if I heard you correctly," Lu said, "that the Politburo has canceled the mission."

The colonel got up and ambled over to the bar. He found a can of cashews under the counter and munched a handful, then pulled the Absolut from the freezer and topped up his glass.

"The situation is that for several months the project has already been in motion; 'approved in principle' as our superiors euphemistically say. It will be easy for others to pin the cause of failure on us, but consider that the most difficult parts have already been successfully accomplished. We both now know the plan has an excellent chance of success."

"Even supposing that it does, we would be defying a Politburo directive. Failure to obey carries the death penalty."

The colonel marginally shook his head. "You're so frightened, Louis, that you're myopic, only focusing on your nose and not realizing what the horizon looks like. Consider this—two factions within the Politburo have hotly debated the merits of this project. The pacifists won by a slim majority, but there is still a powerful minority within the Politburo, mainly Red Army, Ministry of Defense, and KGB—all of whom clandestinely support the project, provided that the results we have projected can be fully realized."

"But it was still a majority Politburo decision. That makes it final."

The colonel shrugged, not deterred by that line of reasoning. "I would have surely received instructions to cancel the project *if* I had hung around Moscow for another day. But Marshal Khokhlov called me on a secure line five minutes after the Politburo decision was made and ordered me to get my ass to Cuba before anyone in Moscow Center got wind of what had happened. Khokhlov had a military aircraft on alert for me in case the vote went the wrong way. So, officially, I haven't received the cancellation order."

"But they'll contact you here in Cuba."

"That's why I canceled our meeting in Mariel and switched it to Cayo Mambi. Center doesn't know where I am, what I'm doing, so how could they contact me? Our original orders were to keep the details of the project absolutely secret, the specifics of the project confined to you and me alone. Even Khokhlov never received any of our paper planning, just verbal briefings, because he wanted the cloak of 'deniability.' And no one except Khokhlov knows where I am. Moscow might be able to figure it out given three or four days of sniffing around, but by that time the project will have been either successfully completed or it will have failed."

Quite suddenly, the colonel's speech was no longer slurred. "I have one question, Louis. Are you with me in this? I want you to carefully think about the ramifications and then answer without any qualification. No hedging. Total commitment if you join me or your guaranteed silence if you don't."

Lu knew that the colonel would never feel secure with just a verbal guarantee if he tried to pull out. His silence would be insured with a bullet in the head. "I have always been loyal to you, Colonel," he said, his eyes averted.

The colonel smiled broadly, dipped his fingers into the glass of vodka, and splattered Lu with drops of Russian holy water. "Bless you, Louis, both for your loyalty and your intuitive sense of self-preservation. It takes a man of faith to accept things as they are and might be."

"What happens to us if the operation succeeds? There'll still be the stigma that we disobeyed orders."

"The Politburo pacifists who opposed the project will find it convenient to forget their opposition if they want to keep their heads. The patriots who support the mission will gain an enormous amount of credibility and, potentially, controlling power. You know the old saying: Both wise men and good results speak for themselves. For my reward, Khokhlov guarantees me immediate promotion, control of the KGB within three years, and within five, a candidate membership in the Politburo. As I am raised in power and position, so will you be."

"And if the project fails?"

"It won't, given our joint and total commitment."

"But if it does?" Lu insisted.

The colonel thumbed his nostrils and sniffed slightly. "Marshal Khokhlov would be instantly removed, probably executed. We would also be at great risk, undoubtedly recalled to face charges. I'd be willing to turn my back and let you disappear— let's say 'killed in the line of duty, body not recovered.' I know that you probably have some money hidden away in the West, plus that gigantic pack of traveler's checks you're carrying. I'm both your friend *and* a loyal officer of the KGB. Splitting the difference for as long as possible, I'd do nothing either to help or harm you. You'd be on your own. As for me, Louis, I'm old. I wouldn't make it through a rigorous interrogation. And there's nothing that they could take from me that I'd miss—other than liquor, food, women, and the privileges of rank. I'd resign by blowing my brains out. And without me to interrogate, you'd be safe in whatever hole you crawled into."

"You'd let me disappear?"

"But that's what you've been planning, isn't it, Louis?" The colonel's voice had dropped, now barely audible, and brittle as a willow twig after the first hard freeze.

"No, of course not. I—"

The colonel cut him off. "Don't you fucking dare lie to me, Louis. I received a report ten days ago. Kapitonov from the illegals documentation section called me and asked about a transit pass and a passport that you had procured under my blanket authorization. It was a routine inquiry, but I did some checking. The stuff was for your son." He laid the miniature jade tiger on the coffee table.

Lu couldn't answer.

The colonel stared at him for a long time and then his expression slowly softened. He fluttered his hand casually, spilling cigarette ashes over his trousers. "Don't worry, Louis. The boy's fine. I had a little talk with him, although it was rather one-sided. He denied knowing anything. However, under pressure, your brother-in-law was more cooperative." He studied the glowing tip of his cigarette and shrugged philosophically. "All field men think of getting out at one time or another, Louis. They just never talk about it, and most don't have the balls to try." He stood up and moved to the windows. "It first occurred to me that you might be planning to cross the river—to some Western intelligence service." He looked back, his eyes hard as marbles. "Is that what you plan?"

There was no point in denying anything because he had known that this discussion would eventually have to take place—just that he had wanted to initiate, then control it. "You know I wouldn't. They'd take three years to suck me dry, then throw me away. That's their style. And if you can still believe me, I'm loyal to the State." He shook his head. "No, I wouldn't turn. But I'm burned out. I want to retire to someplace where my bones will be warm and where I don't feel eyes on my back, but primarily because my son is ill and he needs expert medical help—something that our country can't provide. It's that simple."

The colonel finally nodded after a long silence, as if he had made up his mind. "Stupid and short-sighted, Louis. That describes what you're doing. But I can smell the truth. I should have realized your problem in Moscow and never put you on this project." He tentatively stroked his chin with a fingernail. "I don't need to remind you that the boy would die if you ever went over. I might not be able to get to you, but I would get to the boy. You understand that?"

"You have to believe that I would never turn, regardless. I made the decision for purely personal reasons."

"I believe, Louis. I believe. It's just that I want us to understand each other very clearly."

Lu probed gently. "So whether the project succeeds or fails, you'll let me and the boy go?"

"I didn't say that, did I? It's a new arrangement, this relationship between you and me. You're no longer my trusted subordinate and a loyal Soviet officer. You're now working for your own interests, so the rules must be changed to accommodate this new reality."

"So what *are* the new rules?"

"You will still be in charge of phase one—the destruction of the shuttle in the early phases of launch. Regardless if phase one is successful or not, you will meet me and the *Victoria* in the Bahamas as planned. When you get there, you are responsible for destroying the *Pampero* and her crew. We can undoubtedly arrange it so that it appears you died with them. I'm sure that you've already worked out your exit."

"My son—?"

"If you carry out your end of the mission to my satisfaction, he will be released. He's now staying with your brother-in-law in a Moscow apartment under the supervision of my men. My orders are that if I do not give instructions to the contrary, your son and your brother-in-law will be released from custody in ten days' time."

"And if phase one is not successful?"

The colonel nuzzled the glass of vodka against his cheek. "Not as easy, Louis. If you fail, then you must accept that your son and brother-in-law are hostages to your failure. I don't think it's necessary that I spell out the consequences."

"You said that there was only a ninety-three percent chance of success but a seven percent chance of failure, regardless of how well the operation goes."

"True, Louis. Ninety-three percent provided that you can deliver Raul and Vierro to that beach fifteen minutes prior to launch. So the odds are with you. But from my distance, I won't be able to distinguish between a bungled operation and bad luck. Either way, you will have failed."

He didn't have any latitude to negotiate, had to accept the seven percent risk of failure. "But what if the launch is canceled or delayed?"

"I'm not an unreasonable man, and I've made allowances. As best as we can determine, the launch is scheduled for the morning of the nineteenth. If it's delayed for no more than a day, then you'll stay in the area and try again, but not for longer than that. To keep the *Pampero* in the area beyond the twentieth would entail too great a risk of exposure to security sweeps by patrol craft. So if the launch is delayed for more than twenty-four hours, you will sail for the Bahamas and phase two will be the only option left."

"And you'll run phase two?"

"Yes." The colonel crushed out his cigarette.

"And I'll back you up?"

"That's the plan—if for some reason I'm incapacitated, but as of now, I don't think that's even remotely possible."

"After phase two—whether it goes or not, provided I perform as expected, then I'm free?"

"Freedom is an illusion, Louis, but yes—you and your son can go and I'll turn my head the other way."

The sun was low in the western sky, and its light, transformed to a golden haze by the darkened glass, tinted the interior of the salon with muted bronze tones. The colonel exhaled a stream of smoke, and it stratified in the ancient light, swirling lazily like some nebula of a distant galaxy.

"So the original project profile remains operational," Lu said.

Waving his cigarette, watching the swirls of smoke in the light, the colonel leaned back deeper into the cushions. "Exactly. And to pave the way for the disaster, we have launched a *dezinformatsia* campaign. The supposed purpose of this launch was leaked to the world press by Japanese aerospace engineers controlled by Moscow Center. The results have been quite gratifying. I take it, Louis, that you haven't had a chance to read the news lately."

"No, of course not."

Opening a briefcase, the colonel laid out a photocopied clipping on the coffee table from *The Washington Post,* under the by-line of a Pulitzer Prize–winning investigative reporter. Lu picked up the clipping, switched on a reading lamp, and read it carefully.

U.S. Star Wars Nuclear Weapon Satellite Rumored
to be Payload for Upcoming Shuttle Launch

WASHINGTON, D.C.: Two independent and highly reliable sources in the Japanese defense industry have recently revealed that the upcoming launch of the space shuttle will carry two satellites to be used in the first American nuclear weapons space test of the Strategic Defense Initiative program, often referred to as "Star Wars."

A number of arms control experts have pointed out that such a test would be in clear violation of the U.S. Administration's pledge to the Soviets that Star Wars research will be confined to the laboratory and also that no nuclear weapons will be launched into space.

Although categorically denied by Pentagon and NASA spokespersons, the test is rumored to involve a U.S. satellite which will carry a three-megaton nuclear device. It is alleged by the Japanese sources that this U.S. experimental satellite code-named Excalibur will test the feasibility of a nuclear device as the "pump" for an ICBM-killing X-ray laser weapon.

Lu looked up from the clipping. "You haven't briefed me on this aspect of the operation. What in hell is an X-ray laser?"

"The X-ray concept is simple, Louis, yet the most effective space defense system devised. Picture a tube four meters long and two meters in diameter. Place a three-megaton nuclear device at the bottom of the tube and surround it with a bundle of metallic rods, all of them independently aimed by actuators. Ahead of the nuclear device, place a tracking infrared telescope. Once the telescope detects a cluster of ICBMs rising from the missile fields of the Soviet Union, small thruster rockets will roughly align the entire satellite tube in the direction of the missiles. A self-contained computer will then independently aim each rod at each separate missile. Then the nuclear device, referred to in the article as the 'pump,' detonates. In the billionth of a second before the lasing rods vaporize from the nuclear detonation, they will gather and focus powerful streams of X rays on the missiles." He splayed out his fingers in a mock explosion. "Puff! No more ICBMs."

"But such a weapon would be a one-shot affair."

"True. The Americans would need to launch about two hundred Excalibur satellites. Roughly fifteen could be deployed in one shuttle launch, so it would take only fourteen shuttle flights to put the full complement of the American Star Wars defense system in place. At any given moment, enough would be positioned over the polar area to seriously degrade any Soviet attack. Our planners estimate that the American space defense system would be somewhere between fifty-three and sixty-eight percent effective, increasing as more were added. For our strategists, it is an unacceptably high attrition rate."

The colonel lit another cigarette and nodded toward the clipping. "Read on, Louis. It gets more interesting."

> The other satellite to be used in the experiment has been manufactured under an S.D.I. contract, funded by the U.S. Department of Energy and built by a consortium of Japanese electronic and aerospace manufacturers. This satellite, code-named GINGA, will act as a "target," simulating a large but unspecified number of Soviet SS-18 intercontinental ballistic missiles, considered by many American defense analysts as being a dedicated Soviet "first-strike" weapon. Unclassified Department of Defense data on the Soviet SS-18 missile indicates that the payload of the SS-18 ICBM is fourteen one-megaton warheads.

Lu raised his eyebrows. "How much of this is true?"

"Enough to give the rumor credibility," the colonel answered, smiling. He pushed his glasses up on his brow and hunched his body forward. "As we both well know, in the art and practice of dezinformatsia, the most believable lies are those that include some fundamental element of truth." He stubbed out the butt of his cigarette, caught up in his idea. "We have a fair idea of how the space experiment will be conducted. The Excalibur satellite is superficially similar to the X-ray laser weapon except it has no nuclear device. Instead, it has a cluster of commercial lasers of a type used in long-distance range finding. Once the Japanese GINGA satellite passes over the Soviet Union in low earth orbit, multiple flares will be ejected to simulate the heat patterns produced by twenty of our SS-18 ICBMs. The mission of Excalibur will be to detect the heat signature of these simulated missiles, align itself, then simultaneously fire the low-powered laser beams. The Japanese target warheads will each have sensors to detect whether they have been directly and precisely illuminated by a laser beam, and this information will then be reported by telemetry back to the American Mission Control."

"Then no nuclear weapon is actually involved in this launch?"

"Of course not. They're not that stupid. But this is a crucial step in the development of the weapon system, the purpose of the experiment being to determine whether the tracking, aiming, and discrimination mechanisms will work."

Lu nervously plucked at his ear. "But even if the test was successful, the Americans would ultimately have to verify the capability of the entire weapon system in space. An actual test of the X-ray laser pumped by a nuclear weapon would be a clear violation of the Soviet-American accords concerning interpretation of the antiballistic missile treaty. World opinion, the outcry from the American public, our own protests in the U.N. would—"

"A nuclear space test is desirable but may not be necessary." The colonel said it flatly, definitively. He ran his hand over his balding scalp. "Starting back in 1977, the Americans believed that they had achieved a theoretical breakthrough in the design of an X-ray laser, something we still haven't been able to achieve. They've tested nuclear-pumped X-ray weapons under the Nevada desert for over a decade, perfecting the design. That's why we initiated the unilateral underground nuclear test ban. We wanted to pressure them through world opinion into stopping the testing so that we would have time to work out the same physics that allowed them to achieve their breakthrough.

"But they didn't stop and their series of tests have finally perfected the weapon's configuration. If the Excalibur test is successful, the American military is going to push hard to deploy an operational system. Reagan funded Excalibur. The present administration seems to be quietly following through, despite the current President's anti-nuclear rhetoric during his election campaign. Because of the treaty, the Americans can't test a nuclear-pumped Excalibur in space, but if both the nuclear pump and the aiming mechanisms work independently, why shouldn't both parts work when mated together? It's a gamble but a logical one."

"Then any first strike that we throw at them would be neutralized?"

"Not neutralized. Not entirely, but enough to throw the credibility of our attack planning into serious doubt. Eventually, we could work out a defensive system or an Excalibur weapon of our own, but given the present Politburo leadership, I'm not sure that will happen. And at any rate, it would take us years and billions of rubles to catch up, and we can't afford either of those luxuries. So you now understand why the success of this project is so critical?"

Critical to whom, Lu wondered. Critical to the survival of the Soviet people or the Kremlin hardliners and their dream of a world under the red banner?

The colonel was waiting for an answer—more than that—a commitment.

Lu slowly nodded. "I understand the importance of stopping Excalibur," he said, giving the expected answer, not sure that he fully believed in what he was saying but no longer able to afford the luxury of questioning it. He had his own priorities.

The colonel grunted his satisfaction, then, digging deeper into his briefcase, handed Lu a second sheet of paper, a verbatim transcript of a broadcast by the BBC World Service.

Five thousand peace activists had mobilized at the gates of the Kennedy Space Center, violently protesting nuclear weapons in space. There had been rock throwing and baton-bashing scuffles between police and activists. Four hundred arrests had been made. There were widespread charges of police brutality clinically documented by network TV. One particularly gory sequence was of a woman protestor who had doused herself with lighter fluid and flicked her Bic. She was reported to be in serious but stable condition.

"Impressive," Lu finally said. "But does this have any effect on phase one planning?"

"Yes. It helps. The authorities will probably throw most of their security resources into keeping the protesters off the bridges leading from the mainland to the launch pads, making your job that much easier." The colonel leaned forward, his voice lowered. "Up until now, Louis, I've kept you in the dark about many things. But now I want you to have a greater appreciation of what's going to happen." Pulling a pen from his shirt pocket, the colonel sketched a cross-sectional outline of the Japanese rocket motor on a napkin.

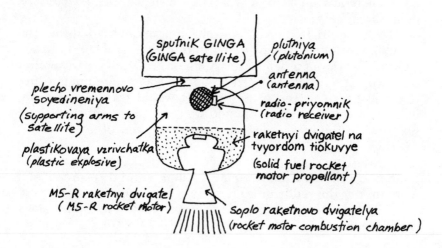

The colonel tapped his pen on the sketch. "With the exception of some modifications that were done by the Frunze Ordnance Works in our labs at Alma Ata indicated by the cross-hatched area, the rocket motor is an exact duplicate of the Japanese one you sank off Grenada. It's nothing more than a sophisticated skyrocket—a combustion chamber that contains solid rocket propellant, an ignition device, guidance control, and a swiveling rocket exhaust nozzle."

Lu bent down, studying the cross-hatched area. "What's different?"

"There are a few electronic mechanisms hidden within the housings, but the main difference is that instead of solid rocket fuel, we've filled most of the rocket motor housing with plastic high explosives. The weight is the same for both materials, and short of taking test samples, which is prohibited, the unit would pass—actually has passed prelaunch checkout.

"Once Raul does his work, a shock-sensing device will trigger over a thousand kilos of plastic explosive. The shuttle, instead of being engulfed by slow-burning liquid fuel, will explode in a shattering microsecond. There won't be a scrap of debris left that's larger than a tin can."

"But the *dezinformatsia* campaign has led the American public to believe that there's a nuclear weapon aboard. If the shuttle explodes, there would probably be some residual radioactivity."

Leaning back in his chair, the colonel smiled. "That's been taken care of, Louis. The explosive is salted with seven kilos of granular plutonium compressed into pellets, exactly the weight of the radioactive fallout had a three-megaton nuclear weapon been aboard. Nothing of the shuttle will remain, but the entire area of the Space Center will be contaminated for a very long time, completely unusable. The spectators, scientists, and technicians will breathe this dust, as will thousands more in the fallout path, which will stretch inland as far as the Florida-Georgia border. If you don't know this piece of trivia, plutonium has a half-life of twenty-four thousand years."

He realized that he was staring at the colonel, his mouth slack, no words coming.

"You understand now?" asked the colonel. "When the 'accident' happens, the *dezinformatsia* leaked by the Japanese engineers will be automatically confirmed and obviously, there will not be any substantial evidence left to contradict them. And even if there was a conflicting government report, the public would never believe it. They're cynical from all the cover-ups of previous American administrations, from NASA, and from the military. Based on the public's outrage, Congress will force the Administration to dismantle not only its Star Wars program but even possibly a large segment of its nuclear arsenal. In one throw of loaded dice, Louis, the Soviet Union has the chance to win the game."

Lu slumped down in a chair, the light of the setting sun hard in his face, his mind numb. He wanted a cigarette, badly. He took the colonel's pack from the table and lit one. He almost gagged, but then the old nicotine craving came back to him. The second puff was better, making him light-headed, the third one almost soothing. He looked down at the cigarette and realized that his hand was shaking.

"It leaves a bad taste in the mouth, doesn't it," the old man said.

"How many deaths?"

"Many, Louis. Thousands in the immediate vicinity, perhaps hundreds of thousands all told. The plutonium will be blown into dust fine enough to be inhaled. The material lodges in the lungs. Fatal cancer results in all cases." The colonel looked up at Lu. "You are, perhaps, having second thoughts about your involvement?"

He knew that he couldn't back out now. Lu shook his head.

The colonel smiled. "I'm pleased that you see it my way. I realize that the project has its distasteful aspects, but the end justifies the means."

Which is what Lenin had preached, what Stalin had practiced, what the colonel had perfected.

"Raul's equipment. Is it ready?"

The colonel nodded. It will be placed on board the *Pampero* tonight.

Lu had seen the films taken at the Frunze ordnance range. Although the scheduled launch time was never predisclosed on U.S. military shuttle launches, once the main engine of the shuttle fired, there was a six-second delay for the liquid-fueled engines to stabilize at full power. If the computers reported normal performance parameters by the end of those six seconds, the two solid boosters would be ignited, and almost immediately, the shuttle would lift off. The culmination of Lu's efforts was to place Raul and Vierro on the beach at Cape Canaveral, approximately 1.5 kilometers from the shuttle launch pad and within fifteen minutes of the projected launch time. Using a custom-made, telescopically sighted bolt-action 23mm cannon, Raul had to fire no later than three seconds after the main engine started because the projectile would take nearly two seconds to travel to the launch pad. It was a tight time framework, but Raul, practicing in Cuba, had been able to hit the mock-up booster just above the field joint ninety-three percent of the time.

The colonel had commissioned other studies as well. At the Frunze Works, high-speed films had been taken of a 23mm projectile striking a Soviet-duplicated section of the solid booster rocket. Only a puff of smoke appeared on the surface of the booster rocket, but after the projectile penetrated the 12mm steel casing, it broke up into thousands of high-velocity fragments, fracturing the rocket's solid propellant. It took another twelve to fifteen seconds for the engine's flame front to reach the fractured rocket propellant, but when it did, the propellant burned at an uncontrolled rate, melting a hole in the side of the booster rocket, which then burned through the thin skin of the main engine oxidizer and fuel tank. The result was total disintegration of the shuttle, engines, and fuel tanks—a near replay of the *Challenger* disaster. The American people expected another shuttle failure because they'd been thoroughly conditioned to believe that it could and therefore *would* happen again.

He tried to avoid the vision in his mind's eye of thousands dying. "Phase two. How does it work?"

"How it works, what it does, is no concern of yours. How it is implemented is your *sole* concern and only in the event of my incapacitation."

"How is phase two implemented?"

"By a coded radio signal sent by the *Victoria*'s satellite tracking and communications antennae. In the event that Raul misses, there is a small receiver in the duplicate Japanese kick stage motor housing which will automatically activate and listen for the signal."

"This radio signal—you transmit it from the *Victoria* during liftoff if Raul misses?"

"No. That would be an ideal backup, but it's operationally impossible. The two satellites are carried in the cargo bay of the shuttle. The cargo bay is enclosed by the cargo bay doors which are made of a composite metal and plastic matrix. Any radio signal transmitted while those doors are closed would be blotted up by the metal. It's roughly the same principle as listening to a broadcast on your car radio when you pass through a steel bridge— the signal fades or disappears because the steel of the bridge soaks up the radio broadcast station's signal. No, the signal can be transmitted only *after* the shuttle is in orbit. Only then will the shuttle roll inverted on its back and open the cargo bay doors. One other critical criteria is that the satellite must be in radio signal line of sight of the *Victoria*."

"How will you know the exact time to transmit the signal?"

"We won't be able to determine that until after launch. The time that the signal should be transmitted is presently unknown because the U.S. military doesn't reveal the exact time of a military launch. But once the shuttle is in orbit, Soviet over-the-horizon radars will be able to track it and predict the times of all subsequent events. In addition, there is a manned *Soyuz* in an approximately similar orbit which will participate in tracking the shuttle. Once the orbital and launch time parameters are established, Moscow Center will send a command to the *Victoria* for me to transmit the signal."

"Why the *Victoria*? Couldn't this be done from one of our submarines or trawlers?"

Giving him an exasperated look, the colonel shook his head. "If this were a fully sanctioned operation, I could use any transmitting facility that the Soviet government commands, but this, Louis, is not a sanctioned operation. Khokhlov can't risk involving elements of the Soviet armed forces, GRU, or the KGB too deeply in this operation. The firing signal *has* to come from the *Victoria*."

"How will you get the information from Moscow?"

There was a long silence, the colonel toying with his empty glass. "In the most reliable way possible. Khokhlov has access to the deputy director of Radio Moscow. Radio Moscow, which transmits in the English language on thirteen different frequencies at any given time, will break its transmission for exactly forty-three seconds. The announcer will then come back on the air and apologize, saying 'We regret that due to technical difficulties a portion of this broadcast has been interrupted.' When the announcer finishes the word *interrupted*, I will start a stopwatch.

Two minutes and ten seconds later I will transmit the radio signal. There is a twelve-second leeway either side of the two minutes and ten seconds to transmit the signal."

"What happens when the signal is received?"

"That would be telling, Louis."

Long after the old man had left, Lu stood at the salon windows, looking out into the blackness.

16.

July 16, 2330 hours

Jean Hutchinson danced a slow pirouette under the shower head, letting the hot water cascade over her body, her eyes closed, her pores singing under the needle spray. She turned, yet once more, slowly, imagining that she was a sleek otter under a waterfall, thrilling to the sensuous rivulets of water pulsing over her body. God! It was an unbelievable experience to be clean again.

She stepped aside from the spray and soaped her hair for the third time, working the lather up in a mound, then ducked under the spray, her head and body bent forward, letting the water massage her scalp, neck, and back. She was almost drunk with the sensation.

For a long time she remained in the position, the heat of the water pummeling her skin, seeping down into her bones, not thinking about the muddled past or not-yet-seen future. Just the now.

Reluctantly, she shut off the shower and stepped out onto the bathmat, toweling down and fluffing her hair.

Still pink from the heat of the shower, she paused, regarding herself in the fogged mirror. A little past the leading edge of the "dirty-thirties," but her body was still firm, her breasts generous and uptilted. Bracken had once called them "perky" while they were showering together on the *Pampero*. Secretly pleased, she still had told Bracken that he was a male chauvinist piglet. He turned around to face her, his whatsis shriveled after their long session of lovemaking.

"What's this piglet crap?" he had challenged her.

" 'Cause, Bracken, you aren't equipped with enough pork to make it into the big leagues." With that he twirled her around and slapped her none too gently on the rump. God, she wished he were with her now because she needed to talk to him. But she was on her own now that they were onboard the *Victoria*—in a locked cabin separate from Bracken's.

He still didn't know her background and why she had signed on to the *Pampero*. But she had made up her mind. She would tell him as soon as they were alone together again. She had to believe that he would understand.

She padded from the head into the spacious cabin and sat down on the bed, first combing and then blow-drying her hair, her mind fogged with fatigue but still running back through the events of the last day.

The *Pampero* had been met by a Cuban naval patrol boat off of Cayo Mambí, then led down an unmarked channel into a swampy inlet and directed to anchor. Then, after nightfall, men in military fatigues had boarded the *Pampero* from a launch and rafted the old schooner up alongside the newly arrived *Victoria*.

When the lines were secured, Sanchez appeared on the bridge of the *Victoria*, resplendent in a white dinner jacket and plaid Bermuda shorts, a loud-hailer in one hand and an open bottle of champagne in the other. Obviously bombed.

"Welcome, my dear friends, to the People's Democratic Republic of Cuba. All crew of the *Pampero* are to gather their things for an overnight stay on the *Victoria* while repairs are effected. You will be escorted to the same cabins that you used before in Les Saintes. A buffet will be set in the salon for your dining pleasure after you've had a chance to clean up." He belched into the amplification system, laughed, and lurched back to the bridge.

Jean had gathered up a few things—the toilet kit, undergarments, and the white cotton dress that Bracken had bought in St. Barts. And her Walkman tape player. Then had stuffed them in an airline flight bag and presented herself on the *Pampero*'s deck. An older Oriental man in a steward's mess jacket had met her at the gangway of the *Victoria*, bowed graciously, and escorted her to her old cabin.

"The buffet will be set in a few hours, miss," he recited politely. She almost giggled, but he was so *sincere*, his face void of expression, the perfect Oriental man Friday. God—what her mother wouldn't do to hire a guy like this to tend her place in Arlington.

She now sat in the chair, her hair dry, the terry-cloth robe cocooned around her, wondering what her next move would be. Assuming that there were moves left to make, which seemed unlikely. They didn't cover situations like this in the Drug Enforcement Agency training. And it all revolved around that damned floppy diskette.

When the floppy diskette had been sent to Ottawa from Gander, the Canadians had tried to crack it, then had thrown up their hands and passed it on to their CIA cousins in Langley, Virginia. The CIA had tried their hand, finally matching Humpty Dumpty as the password to the phase one file only after seven days of decryption efforts on a CRAY III, the best and the brightest of the CIA's computers. Phase two seemed to have a more complicated password, and the CIA acknowledged that it might take months to crack. They had allowed as how they might be willing to try except that all the information revealed in the phase one file indicated some kind of a Caribbean drug-running operation. So the CIA passed the diskette to the Drug Enforcement Agency with a sweet smile of relief and the intention of calling in a future favor. And that is where Jean Hutchinson came in.

She had majored in romance languages at Bryn Mawr, graduated with her bachelor's, and expected that there would be enough grant money floating around to finance her way through grad school. But Reagan had axed most of those grants, and she was reduced to applying for translation work. First with the State Department. No work there, but they gave her a telephone number to call. She thought it was going to be the U.N., but it turned out to be the DEA, who wanted translators capable of speaking both Spanish and Italian.

For the next three years Jean sat in a stuffy cubicle, headphones clamped to her ears, and transcribed tapes recorded by electronic surveillance devices of suspected drug pushers in the Washington, D.C., area. Nothing very technical, just phone taps and bugs planted in pizza parlors and Mafia-run junkyards. No arrests, no convictions, but she could now swear fluently in Spanish and was an expert on where the best and cheapest Italian restaurants were between Miami and Boston.

Her personal life was okay if not overwhelming. Fletcher, her boyfriend, who worked at the Treasury Department, had occupied a lot of her life over the last year. Charming, talented, good family, and very proper. Dinners, concerts, the theater, long drives down to the Maryland shore, but never any close encounters of the best kind. She took his hesitation to be some sort of old-fashioned morality and found it refreshing. And she had more or less convinced herself that she loved him. Her friends assured her it would be a good marriage.

After a year of hand-holding but otherwise sexless courtship, she had finally taken the initiative. She invited Fletcher for dinner: wine, swordfish with a honey-mustard sauce, artichokes, a tossed salad, and flan for dessert. She had replaced the light bulb of her bedside reading lamp with a pink-tinted one of much lower wattage, bought a sexy lounge dress which nicely outlined her nipples, and put aside some scented bath oil for them to share in her tiny tub after the dirty deed was done.

From the beginning of the evening she felt his unease and, as the evening progressed, his growing distress. Then he finally confessed that he was hooked on a terrific fellow over at the Office of Management and Budget. Fletcher was sweet and he was kind, but when he declared his sexual preferences, she wept and, goddamn him, he had *patted* her hand and told her that he would always be a sincere and caring friend.

For three insane months after Fletcher had opted out of her life, she had gone through two boyfriends and innumerable Brie and Chablis parties, populated almost exclusively by that special breed of Washington yuppie. The talk was not political or about the Meaning of Life, but rather centered on upward mobility, stock options, dental plans, progressive day schools, and which garage gave the best deal on Honda repairs. Finally exhausted, she quit that routine, went through a cycle of seeing all the old Bergman movies by herself, and knew that if she ever ate Brie again, she'd probably gag.

Four months and one day after Fletcher had tiptoed out of her life, Byron, her DEA supervisor, had dangled an assignment in front of her: Go to the Caribbean and try to sign on a charter boat called the *Pampero,* the object being to find out what kind of a drug deal a certain Captain John Bracken was up to. Bracken, whom her supervisor had painted with a very black brush, was the probable kingpin of a drug-smuggling ring.

He then had explained about the stolen floppy disk and promised to equip her with the latest gadgetry. He trotted out a laptop computer which was loaded with the phase one and two programs, as well as word-processing software. Together, they concocted the cover story of the aspiring authoress who was putting together a seagoing cookbook.

Then he had equipped her with a miniature wireless microphone that would transmit back to a receiver hidden in a modified Walkman tape player. "A hundred-yard range and state-of-the-art," he had proclaimed.

The phase one file had been cracked, but phase two was still locked. Bracken, being a degenerate character of the worst sort, according to her supervisor, would probably know what phase two was all about and would undoubtedly know the password. If Jean could find out what the password was—at that point, her supervisor raised his hairless eyebrows and winked, ho ho ho, you sexy lady—then she would be able to plug the password into a laptop computer and thus crack the case.

Except for the sexual innuendoes, it had seemed to be just right: a big career step upward if she uncovered the deal with the personal plus that it offered her a strategic withdrawal from her own crumbling personal life. She snapped up the assignment, saw two James Bond films to fortify her knowledge of secret agent tradecraft, bought a bunch of bikinis and a book on sailing with government money, and headed south for Antigua on Pan Am.

When she got to English Harbour, Antigua, the *Pampero* was in port and Jean haunted the docks until Nan Hogan, Bracken's cook, came ashore to pick up the ship's mail. It had been relatively simple to get rid of Hogan. A cozy conversation over rum punches revealed that Hogan never paid any taxes to the Internal Revenue Service. "Like, who does down here? You gotta be kiddin'!" she said. Jean had flashed her DEA identification card and offered Hogan immunity from prosecution, which she really couldn't offer, in return for Hogan disappearing over the horizon. Hogan took the hint and quit her job the next day. Half an hour later Jean applied as the best chef this side of the Four Seasons and was hired by a bewildered but grateful Captain John Bracken.

She glanced at her watch. Still half an hour before the buffet but nearly midnight. And still some serious thinking to do.

Bracken, of course, wasn't involved in a drug deal. That much was abundantly clear after Les Saintes. Naive, yes. Inclined to take stupid chances, yes, and certainly in hock up to his ears. But she knew that she loved him—God help her—because she had found a man who could give as well as he could take.

Her mind had strayed from the immediate and she pulled it back, blanking out a future which might not be. Sanchez, Raul, and Vierro had to be running some kind of smuggling operation, and although they had brought no drugs aboard initially, Cuba might be where they would load up.

Of course, Bracken had bought into it, then finally realized that the stakes were a great deal higher than he had been willing to play for—but now he had no way to back out. It was up to her to solve it.

There weren't a lot of options; in fact, there was only one.

She had to hide the bug and hope that Sanchez, Vierro, and Raul would have some final meeting in which the password for phase two or some of its details would leak out in their conversation. Then, when the *Pampero* was within radio range of the U.S. Coast Guard, she could tip them off if Bracken and Walrus could overpower Raul and Vierro.

She stood up and slipped on bra, panties, and dress, then combed her hair and touched up her throat with perfume. Terrific plan, Not-So-Special-Agent Jean Hutchinson. On a scale of one to ten, hardly more than a two. She slipped the bug into one of the cups of her bra and waited like a good girl to be let out to play.

Just after midnight the Oriental guy unlocked her door. She followed him to cabin A, where Pam was waiting. Pam was dressed in a white body-hugging nylon jump suit which obviously displayed her body's attributes without the detraction of superfluous undergarments. But her eyes were hollow. As they followed the man up the stairwell to the salon, Pam reached across and gripped Jean's arm fiercely, her eyes straight ahead.

"Give Sanchez what he wants, honey," she whispered. "Vierro told me the score when I came on board this evening. That's what it's going to take to keep you in one piece."

It didn't make sense to her until they reached the salon deck. No Bracken, no Walrus. Just Vierro, Sanchez, and an older man who was already snoring, his head thrown back on the couch, his yellowed teeth displayed like rows of ancient tombstones. The Oriental took up a position behind the buffet, a towel draped over his forearm.

She studied them. Sanchez and Vierro were drunk but still dangerous. Both wore standard-issue *Victoria* terry-cloth bathrobes but probably nothing underneath.

Sanchez staggered to his feet, making an awkward bow. Matted black hair and a gold chain with a cross peeked out from within the V of his terry-cloth robe. "*Buenas noches, Señoritas!* We have an assortment of lobster, shrimp, black bean paste, tortillas, and sliced avocados garnished with my own special dressing. And, of course, champagne."

"Where's Captain Bracken and his first mate?"

Sanchez did his Latin shrugging routine. "They are tired and preferred to eat alone in their cabins. Impolite of them, but I understand their need for rest."

Which was pure horse-hockey. Jean turned to Pam for support, but Pam had already slipped into her role. She had ignored the buffet, poured herself a glass of champagne, and settled down next to Vierro, her arm thrown over the back of the couch and around his neck, stroking his hair.

Jean slowly turned back to Sanchez and understood that she was his for tonight. He smiled at her, showing teeth, and the look on his face told her that it could be gentle or it could be violent, and he would like it either way—preferably the latter.

She was trembling. Overlapping her arms, she hugged her body, trying to hide her fear. Sanchez brought her a glass of the champagne, pressing it into her dead hand.

"You are cold," he said, mock concern in his voice. "You need to be warmed. How thoughtless of me." He toyed with her hair, picking up the strands with his fingers, running them through his palm. "You would rather go back to your cabin perhaps? I will personally bring you some shrimp and wine. We will talk. Nothing more, of course."

She was about to tell him to go to hell, but she didn't, not if she didn't want to be bloody meat by morning.

"That would be nice" was all she could manage.

Sanchez nodded. "Good. Our friendship starts well. Captain Bracken wishes you and Pamela to stay aboard the *Victoria* for the next few days. He feels that you both will be safe in my custody while he conducts important business." He lay his hand on her arm and squeezed it. "We will be friends, Jean," he said. He moved his face close to hers and smiled, a real close-up. Bits of lobster were lodged in the gaps between his teeth, and his breath smelled like a fish-packing plant. "*Momento, por favor.* I must give my servant instructions."

Sanchez turned and waddled to where the Oriental stood behind the buffet. Sanchez spoke to him in Spanish and she strained to pick up the words.

"I'm bedding her. What time is our meeting in the morning?"

"You're making a fool of yourself, Sanchez. And I want no harm done to the woman."

"Shit on you, the people that sent you, and that drunk Russian pig you work for. I'm running this vessel and we're in Cuban territory, so I call the tune. She wants me. It's written all over her face."

The Oriental leaned forward, his face flat of expression, eyes hard. "You're drunk as well and you're talking too loud, Sanchez. She might understand what you're saying."

"No! She's a dumb *norteamericana*. Vierro told me she doesn't speak Spanish."

"What you do with the woman is your business, but you better be damned sure that she's not harmed. She's the lever that we have on Bracken, and we need his cooperation. If she's marked, you could jeopardize my plans."

Sanchez lifted his hands a little, relaxing. "Hey! It's no problem, my friend. She wants me, understand? The only mark on her tomorrow morning will be the love shining in her eyes."

The man stepped closer to Sanchez. "So play your games, Sanchez, but be sure that you don't play too hard. Eight in the morning, cabin F, the colonel's stateroom, final briefing. I want you there and I want you sober, understood?"

"Comprendo." Sanchez backed away from the Oriental, giving him a sloppy clenched-fist salute. "At great personal sacrifice, Comrade, I do this for the glory of the Party and in the cause of Cuban-American relations."

Jean had been turned away from them, feigning disinterest, but she caught most of the conversation, carefully keeping her face blank of understanding. She moved to the buffet and sampled the goodies, moving closer to the two men. Just as Sanchez broke off from the Oriental, she took an opened bottle of champagne from a bucket and turned to meet him with an inviting smile.

"Would you bring some shrimp and another bottle?"

He smiled, his sunburned skin wrinkling into an expanse of spiderweb lines. "Of course, my dear woman." He started to pile up a plate, and she put her hand on his arm.

"Give me the keys. I want to go down to my cabin and—ah, to make myself ready, you understand?"

"But I will help you. That will be my greatest pleasure." He slid his arm around her waist, drawing her hard up against his body, squeezing her.

She was burning through ideas and throwing them out just as quickly, nothing really making sense. Then it came to her, fully formed. She twisted out of his grasp. "But I have a favor to ask of you. Something that would make it all so much more wonderful."

His eyes lit up. "You only have to ask."

"Would your chef have a bottle of cooking oil?" She rubbed her fingers together and smiled. "It's so slippery, you see?"

His eyes widened, his lips moist, practically drooling. "But yes, I understand. To love with true abandon is to taste the gods' nectar."

Leaping lizards! What grade-B movie had this pig gotten his lines from? She managed a sultry look. "Five minutes." She held out her hand and he gave her his key ring.

Pam and Vierro had already left, undoubtedly to her cabin. The old geezer was still snoring. He looked harmless, almost pathetic. Yet they had referred to him as a "Russian" and then again as a "colonel." A whole new ball game.

As she turned to descend the stairs she looked back. Sanchez was already headed forward for the galley, but the Oriental was still there, looking at her curiously. She flipped him a wave of the hand and walked down the stairs. Five minutes.

She fumbled for the key marked D, opened the door, and went immediately to her cosmetic case. She had brought along a few capsules of Nembutal in the event that she couldn't sleep. One of the caps generally knocked her out in ten minutes and guaranteed a dreamless sleep for eight hours.

The bottle of champagne was still three quarters full. She gulped a little, then emptied most of it into the toilet, leaving only a few inches sloshing in the bottom of the bottle.

Only a couple of minutes left. She opened three of the caps and emptied them into the bottle of champagne, then sloshed it gently. It would knock a horse out, given enough time to act. And she knew she had to buy that time.

She took off her dress. The bra and panties were apricot and semi-transparent, something that she had hoped would be a special treat for Bracken. She swore that after this night she would burn them.

She brushed her hair with quick strokes, then sprayed on perfume. When she opened the cabin door and peeked around it, Sanchez was just arriving, his face florid.

He held up a bottle. "Olive oil, from Spain and very slippery."

So she would end up smelling like a tossed salad.

She backed into the cabin, moving her hips the way she thought a stripper would, and Sanchez suddenly sucked in his breath. "Take off your robe and lie down on the bed," she softly commanded.

His face clouded. "I will decide how it is done."

She took her jeans from the back of the chair and withdrew the leather belt from its loops, doubled it, then smacked it against her open palm. "You are being very bad. If you don't obey me, then I will spank you."

His eyes gleamed.

She tore off his cloth belt and stripped away his robe. A paunch overhung a second paunch that overhung a third— cascading waterfalls of fat. She tried to focus her eyes out at infinity, blurring the details of his lower anatomy. "Down on your stomach," she commanded, taking the bottle of oil from his grasp and opening it.

The bed springs groaned, Sanchez's body almost quivering with anticipation.

She handed him the bottle of champagne. "First drink. You will need to be fortified for what is ahead."

He gulped down some of the champagne, then made a face. "It has gone sour."

"Finish it! I will not start your discipline until you drink the last drop."

Obediently, he chugalugged it in noisy gulps.

She bent over him and poured the olive oil, then spread it in broad, greasy strokes across his skin. Then kneeled down and pummeled his muscles with her fists as hard as she could.

"*Cristo!* That hurts!"

She laughed wickedly and swung the strop of her belt hard across his buttocks. "It will hurt even more if you disobey me, wretched slave."

She was winging it, trying to draw on the scenes of some weirdo X-rated videotape that she had seen at a dumb party. He loved it. She stropped him some more, starting at the soles of his feet and working up to his shoulder blades, leaving red welts on his skin in a cross-hatched pattern. He writhed with ecstasy, his fists beating a tattoo against the mattress, his head rolling from side to side, moaning with pain and pleasure.

"Now," he croaked. "I must have you now."

She lashed out harder with the belt on the already-reddened flesh of his buttocks. "*Bad . . .*" Slash. "*Boy.*" Slash. "It is I who will determine when, not you. But first I will ease your pain before you join me." God! Where was she getting these lines from? She poured more olive oil over his skin and worked it in.

He started to turn over. "I want the whole bottle over my manhood. It is crying out for relief."

She roughly shoved him back down. "Not yet. Oh, no, not yet, my naughty little boy," and desperately kneaded his back muscles. Maybe five minutes had gone by and she didn't know how long the Nembutal would take to work. Surely not more than another five minutes.

He still moved his head from side to side, but the movement became slower and slower. She backed off on the massage, easing her fingers up along his spine, then down again, bumping along his vertebrae.

His head slowly stopped moving, as if he were an electric doll whose batteries had gone flat.

Once, he snorted awake and she resumed rubbing. "Soon," she cooed in his ear. "Soon, my lover." He smiled in a dreamy way.

She waited for another fifteen minutes, then poked his skin with her fingernail. He didn't stir. She poked harder and harder, then slashed across his legs with the belt. The blubber didn't even quiver.

She checked his heartbeat. Rapid but strong. He would have a hangover to end all hangovers in the morning.

Checked her watch. Close to one A.M. She took a shower and got back into her robe, not even bothering to dry herself.

Opening the door to her cabin, she checked the corridor. A crewman was slumped down asleep at the foot of the stairs leading to the salon, a machine pistol lying on the carpet next to him.

She selected the key to cabin C and softly unlocked the door. "Bracken—you there?" she whispered.

A grunt.

She closed the door and felt for the light switch. Bracken was laid out on the bed, bound at both hands and feet with plastic ties. He had surgical tape over his mouth. She peeled it off and stuck the tape on the nightstand, then started to work on the ties.

"Don't," he said. "If you get them off, you won't be able to get them back on and they'll know you were in here."

She sat down on the side of the bed and stroked his face. "Bracken—we're in deep trouble." She told him about the conversation between the majordomo and Sanchez which referred to the "Russian colonel."

He wrinkled his forehead. "You sure you heard right? Your Spanish isn't that good."

"It isn't good, Bracken, it's excellent," she shot back. Then told him the whole story of her DEA involvement, the floppy diskette, the laptop computer, and the reason for her coming on board the *Pampero*.

He closed his eyes, his voice dead. "So you came down to the West Indies with the idea of nailing me on drug charges? Everything you've said and done was part of your job description?"

She buried her face in his chest, shaking her head. "No, Bracken, no. Don't try to make me feel cheap. From that evening we had dinner in Antigua and onward, I loved you, but I was still positive that you were involved in a drug deal. It was tearing me up until that night in the Saintes when we made love on board the *Victoria*. Even then I wasn't positive that you were clean, but it didn't matter anymore. Bracken—you have to believe me, I love you—no reservations and no holds barred."

They both were silent for a long time, the minutes ticking away. But Bracken could feel the wetness of her tears on his chest. He couldn't move much, couldn't hold her, felt powerless. Which recently seemed to be the norm.

"The major domo—" he finally said. "I never saw him up close, but you did. Anything special about him that you noticed?"

She shrugged. "Definitely in control of Sanchez. Fifties, plain, thin—you know—nothing unusual, except—"

"What?"

"Well, his eyes. The lights were dim in the salon, but his eyes were strange, different. Gray, maybe blue-gray, sort of."

Bracken unconsciously sucked in his breath. It was improbable but not impossible. He thought back to the morning in Les Saintes, the man standing on the bridge of the *Victoria*, the face and body motions, familiar and yet not.

"Did Sanchez address him by name."

"No. Just 'comrade.' "

"The guy Sanchez referred to as a Russian colonel. What about him?"

"I saw him for just a few moments. Older. Overweight, bad teeth, balding, and dead drunk. But his features were kind of Slavic." She hesitated. "Dammit, Bracken. I'm not sure of that. Just an impression from a second's glance."

His mind was numb, images of Lu, Willie, and Vietnam flooding back, the humiliation, the pain, the defeat that he had never shaken off. With a sudden clarity he realized that his life since 'Nam had not been an elective but rather a compulsory course. And Lu had written the textbook.

The first priority that came to his mind was escape. There

wouldn't be any way that he could get the *Pampero* out of there, but he did have the Zodiac inflatable dinghy. With enough fuel they might get far enough off the coast of Cuba to reach international waters and flag down a passing interisland freighter. But logic told him that was a dead end: literally a dead end. The Cuban patrol boat would be fast and it would have radar. Even if they could find Walrus and get off the *Victoria* in one piece, they'd be lucky to make it to the inlet without getting blown out of the water.

And there was this dark thing, deeply imbedded in his brain, nagging at him. If this was a Cuban-Soviet operation, what were they up to? It had to be important, because the expense of the operation would be enormous. But for what purpose? He thought about it, then realized that Stackhill had given him the answer: Land men and their equipment on the coast of the U.S., probably Florida. So it had to be some kind of military target. He mulled over the manual of photographs, cross-sectional views of cylinders and timetables, tied in with the contents of the phase one file Jean had described. Something cylindrical, something big. Fuel tanks, maybe. Possibly a SAC bomber base, or maybe Jacksonville Naval Air Station or—oh, God!—he knew suddenly and with absolute conviction where the dropoff point would be.

He had a headache where Vierro had clouted him, spikes of pain stabbing into his skull. His ribs still ached. His body was drained of energy, stomach empty, wrists and ankles raw from the plastic ties. But there was something else now as well, something that he really hadn't felt for twenty years—the will to win for a reason other than his own self-interest. Patriotism and loyalty? Not exactly, although that had to be a part of it. Dumb nationalist conditioning? Stuff that, mate. No, he finally realized, it was a mixture of pride and revenge, not the most noble of human attributes but certainly the most powerful.

"Jean?"

She nodded against his chest.

"This bug you've got. Do you know which cabin the meeting's going to take place in?"

She hesitated, thinking, then, "The Oriental guy told Sanchez it was going to be in F."

"I'm asking a lot, but you've got to plant it there. Take your time, but don't take chances. If the Russian's as drunk as you thought, he'll be out for the count. If he begins to wake up, freeze. Take it from one who has a lot of experience with booze—drunks have a very short attention span."

"What then?"

"Get back to your cabin. Make sure you're up by eight. Monitor what goes on."

"If it's in Spanish, fine. But what if the conversation is in Russian?"

"Can you tape it?"

"Yes."

"Okay. They'll probably wait until after the meeting to move us back on board the *Pampero*. Keep the tape separate from the Walkman just in case you're searched."

She lifted her head and looked down at him, her hair brushing his face. "I haven't told you yet. Sanchez is going to hold Pam and me hostage on the *Victoria*. He said we'd be going out to the Bahamas and you'd meet us there."

"Damn!"

She touched his nose with her finger, tracing down its ridge. "Bracken, what's going on?"

"I think it's a Soviet operation with the Cubans somehow involved. My best guess is that the target is Kennedy Space Center. God knows what they're up to, but the best guess would be that they're trying to pick up classified information on one of the test launches of military hardware—maybe the Trident D-5 SLBM. That's the hot ticket these days. The Soviets are calling it a 'first strike' weapon."

"But how could you stop them?"

He bit his lip. "Together, Walrus and I could have taken Raul and Vierro any number of times. But we didn't because I was too goddamned concerned with the charter money, with your safety, with protecting my own hide, fear of failure—shit—I can make a thousand excuses but they don't hold up. That's over. I've got a handgun on board the *Pampero* that the Cubans don't know about. Walrus and I will work out some kind of plan to take out Raul and Vierro, then come to the Bahamas to get you and Pam." As he said it, he realized how vague a plan it was. "But we have a big problem—getting the tape cassette from your cabin to the *Pampero*. If I can get ahold of it, I might understand enough Russian to get an idea of what they're planning—possibly even the phase two code words."

"My cabin is on the side that the *Pampero* is rafted up to. I have a porthole. So I tape the meeting, pull the cassette out of the recorder, open the porthole, and throw it on the *Pampero*'s deck just as you're pulling out."

"Too risky. There'll be crew from the *Victoria* on deck helping to cast off the lines. Chances are someone would see the cassette and then we'd really be in the caca."

"Okay. Plan two. I've got a roll of dental floss. I'll tie one end of the thread to the cassette, drop the cassette into the water, and tie the other end to one of the ropes that hold the rubber fenders. After you've pulled away from the *Victoria* and you're out in the channel, have Walrus take in the fenders like he normally does. He can get the cassette aboard without much likelihood of being detected."

"Better, but the tape would be saturated with seawater."

"So you rinse it in rubbing alcohol. Three, four hours of drying time and it will be usable. Fast-forward and fast-reverse it through the ship's stereo system to get the tape unstuck." She glanced at her watch. Nearly 0200. She leaned over and held his head in her hands, then kissed him. "Have to go."

"You think you'll be all right on board the *Victoria*?"

"Don't worry. I've got it under control."

"Sanchez is a real sleaze. Watch out for him."

"I'll take care of him."

"How?"

She smiled and shut off the light. "Trust me."

Sanchez was sprawled all over the bed, the sheets saturated with olive oil, grunting in his sleep. He had rolled over on his back and at first she averted her glance. Then peeked. And she had been afraid of *that*? It was hard to believe that there was such a thing as penis envy, but she also realized that it was the 270 pounds of flab behind that thing that would do the damage.

She checked his pulse again. Slower, more normal, but he was really out. Checked her watch again. Not much sleep tonight.

She dug the bug out of her tape recorder and checked it. Got her little penlight. Then checked the corridor. Guard still zonked out. Difficult part now. If some of the crew had brought him down to his cabin, how deeply did the Russian colonel sleep? Opened the door of cabin F. Shielded her light and played it around. Empty, praise be to Allah. She laid the bug on top of the mirror frame, then stepped back to see whether it was visible. It wasn't.

Tippy-toed back to her cozy cabin. Her heart was beating like a timpani. Calm down, lady, calm down. She returned the key ring to Sanchez's bathrobe pocket.

One other problem. Sanchez hadn't gotten any relief, and it was likely that he would be even hornier tomorrow.

There was a bottle of mercurochrome in her toilet bag which she used to dab on small cuts. She dug it out of her toilet kit and painted Sanchez's shriveled penis a deep yellow. He never winced. A little dab will do ya, she hummed as she applied a second layer to the withered appendage, turning it a deep orange.

She had set her wristwatch alarm for seven forty-five. The irritating peeps dragged her awake after only four hours of sleep. Her body was exhausted, her eyes gummy, her mouth thick with the taste of sour wine. God, she wanted to roll over and forget everything. But couldn't. She staggered out of bed and had a cold shower, then dressed in her jeans and polo shirt.

Now seven fifty-three. She shook Sanchez. Hard, harder, then violently. His eyelids fluttered.

"Lover—wake up. You said you had a meeting at eight."

He wrinkled his face, trying to focus. "Eight? Eight what?" He rolled over and in seconds began to snore.

She gently slapped his cheeks. "Wakey, wakey. Eight o'clock. You told me last night to make sure that you were up by then. Some kind of meeting, you said."

"I did? Where? Who said . . . ?" then lapsed off again.

It took her another minute to drag him out of bed. He tottered on his feet, still half drugged, three quarters asleep.

"Shower," she said, and pushed him toward the bathroom. Turned on the faucets. *"In!"* she commanded, and shoved him.

At first he stood like a half-dead animal under the shower head, not moving. She increased the velocity of the spray to full blast and slowly turned up the heat. Sanchez started to show minute signs of life. He rotated mechanically under the shower head, opening his mouth, filling it with water, then spitting it out. Then flapped his arms like a chicken, dousing his armpits. Charming. Satisfied with the revitalization process, she then twisted the controls to cold and watched with satisfaction as he danced a jig under the icy needles of spray. She finally let him out.

"Eight o'clock," she repeated. "Don't blame me. You insisted that I wake you." She let him towel off, standing behind him, kneading his shoulder muscles. "You were so good, lover. Last night—it was incredible, wasn't it?"

"It was?" His face scrunched up and he looked at his fogged reflection in the mirror. "Yes, of course it was." A smile came to his lips, and his metabolism seemed to pick up a couple of degrees. He shook his head as if to clear his brain. "Yes. Of course I was incredible."

"All I can think of is tonight." She put her heart into it. All the while watching his eyes in the mirror, waiting for the inevitable. And finally, he looked down.

"*Nuestro Señor!* It's gone yellow!"

She reached around his body with both hands, clasping them over his soft gut, drawing him against her. "It's nothing. A small infection that I have. But it goes away as long as you take the pills. It doesn't mean anything. Just a nuisance."

He wheeled on her, throwing off her embrace. "This infection, what is its name?" He was on the verge of panic.

"Nothing. Really, nothing. The specialist told me that it's a mutant form of something that's going around. There's only a small chance of anything serious happening."

He was backing away from her. "The name of the disease. *What is it?*"

She lowered her eyes. "I'm bad at remembering medical terms. The doctor called it genital something-or-other. Like warts." Then looked up, smiling. "Best thing for a man who gets the infection is to wrap his thing in a mustard plaster. Hurts a little but . . ."

He backed away from her, pulling on his bathrobe. *"You filthy little puta!"* he screamed at her, then slammed the door in her face.

"Don't forget the mustard plaster, Sanchez," she said under her breath, smiling in sweet satisfaction.

Bracken came awake in the dark cabin to the sound of the door opening, then closing. The drapes over the porthole filtered out most of the light, but he could see a man standing at the side of his bed, watching him. The man reached down and ripped the surgical tape from his mouth.

"Good morning, Captain John R. Bracken, U.S. Air Force, serial number 29574A. It's been quite a while, hasn't it?"

The man leaned down and turned on the bed lamp, then

took off his sunglasses. He was dressed in the same outfit that Bracken had last seen him in; a *Victoria* Windbreaker, khaki pants, and a polo shirt. Older, of course, lines around his eyes, balder, but still the same face from nearly two decades and a million miles ago.

Amid the powerful and conflicting emotions welling up within him, Bracken focused on one and asked the question. "Did you give Williams a decent burial?"

Lu moved over to a chair and sank into it, crossing his legs. "Yes. We buried him in a soldier's grave with three of our own men who died in a bombing raid. Somebody once said—I forget exactly who: In death, all men are comrades." Lu's words invited cynicism, but he said them as if he believed them.

"Untie me," Bracken said.

"You'd love to kill me, wouldn't you? Oh no, not quite yet, Bracken. Not until we come to some kind of understanding."

"What's to understand other than you screwed up my life."

Lu stood up and went to the porthole, drawing back the drapes. Early morning light spilled into the cabin. He dropped the drapes and turned back to Bracken. "I didn't screw up your life, Bracken. You screwed it up through a combination of greed, self-interest, and by consistently placing yourself in the wrong place at the wrong time."

"That was 'Nam. But there are fifty boats like the *Pampero* in the Caribbean and probably ten percent of their owners would have done it for the money."

"Perhaps. That is if money were the primary motivation, but sometimes, when a person does something for just money, they're unreliable when things get unpleasant." He drew in a deep breath and slowly released it. "You killed Williams, didn't you, Bracken?"

Strange question, but the answer leapt to his lips. "I had to."

"Yes, you had to. That was clear to me. I would have done the same in the circumstances, but if Hanoi released that information to your government, would they view it in the same perspective? Your authorities might call it murder. And what of the information that you gave to me concerning nuclear weapons? You see your problem?"

"You'd really do that to me, wouldn't you?"

"Nothing less than you would have done were you in my position. We had a talk a long time ago, remember? Both of us were instruments of our states then. I still am. What matters now is how you react to what I propose."

"You're working for the Soviets."

Lu nodded. "Who are working for world peace."

"Which we both know is absolute bullshit!"

Lu exhaled, agitated. "What do you and your country really want, Bracken? The Soviet Union to disarm itself, lie down, and roll over. Unless you're deaf, dumb, and blind, for the last three years the world media has been talking about glasnost and reform in the Soviet Union. We've released tens of thousands of dissidents, initiated sweeping arms control measures, and instituted far-ranging internal political reform. We are seeking accommodation and peace with the West, and it is the few like you and those within your military who either distrust us or are trying to destroy this progressive commitment to peace."

Bracken groaned. "Christ, Lu, I've heard all this crap before. You guys just keep grinding it out and expect that the big lie will finally be accepted as the truth."

First glancing at his watch, Lu shook his head. "We don't have much time, and I didn't come here to argue politics. I came to offer you some options." He touched a shape behind his jacket. "I have an automatic, Bracken. I wouldn't hesitate to use it. Do I have your pledge of good conduct?"

Bracken couldn't do anything trussed up like a chicken. Pledges were perishable based on circumstances. "Why not."

Withdrawing a penknife, Lu cut the plastic ties on Bracken's hands and legs. "Stay on the bed. Nothing sudden—agreed?"

"It's your show."

"I'll explain what's involved," Lu said. "A treaty was signed last fall which prohibits either the Soviet Union or the United States from engaging in the development, production, or testing of Star Wars technology outside of the laboratory. The Soviet Union has faithfully abided by that treaty. The U.S. has not." He withdrew the newspaper clippings from his Windbreaker pocket. "Read this."

Bracken read. Rumors of a nuke satellite being launched by the Department of Defense in violation of the treaty, protesters being bashed, the Administration denying the rumors and yet not allowing inspection teams to examine the satellites.

He looked up. "You could have faked this stuff."

"Not likely, and if you want confirmation, then you only need listen to the radio. Our intelligence reports confirm that the rumor is valid, and if the true purpose of the launch is not exposed, then it will be your country, not mine, that is breaking the treaty. I am acting under orders to expose the true nature of this mission and thus prevent your military from testing the weapon. If that's possible, then the matter will be taken before the World Court in the Hague. The Soviet Union will take the position that as long as those responsible for this violation of the treaty are punished and that on-site inspection is open to Soviet technicians for all future satellite launches by the U.S., then this incident will not stop the progress that both our countries are making toward peace."

"And how do you propose to fit me in?"

"You are going to take the *Pampero* to the coastal waters off Cape Canaveral. Raul and Vierro will go ashore prior to the launch of the shuttle and set up telemetry monitoring equipment just inshore of the tide line. The information beamed down in the launch phase will allow us to prove to the world that the launch is an illegal test of Star Wars technology."

"That sounds like pure bullshit. Your trawlers could do the same thing."

"If they could, it would be a lot simpler for me, but it's not possible. The telemetry for this particular shuttle launch is being beamed down in the initial launch phase by a very selective high-gain antenna. Only a receiving antenna on the Cape itself will be able to capture the signals. I'm no engineer, Bracken. That's what I've been told, and it's obvious that for the Soviet Union to go to this extreme, our engineers know what they're dealing with."

So it wasn't just an ICBM launch. Lu was talking about the shuttle. "And my options?"

"You and your first mate will take the *Pampero* to the Cape. Your cook and Pamela will remain on board the *Victoria* as insurance of your cooperation. Once the *Pampero* is off the Cape, at the appropriate time Raul and Vierro will be taken in to the beach in the dinghy by a third man, who will join your vessel here in Cuba while I remain on board the *Pampero* to supervise you and your mate. Raul and Vierro will set up a portable telemetry antennae and record the data, then be retrieved. After the launch you'll sail the *Pampero* to North West Cay in the Bahamas, where the *Victoria* will be waiting. My men and I will transfer to the *Victoria*, and in exchange your woman and Pamela will be allowed to transfer back to the *Pampero*. At that point we all go our separate ways."

"What prevents you from welshing on the deal once we get to the Bahamas. Why wouldn't you kill me and my crew?"

"Why would I? Once I have evidence of U.S. illegal Star Wars activity, I turn it over to my superiors. Whether you talked or not wouldn't concern me. In fact, I think that if you did talk, Bracken, the American authorities would probably be very unhappy with you—perhaps charging you with espionage against your own country. And I would arrange for Hanoi to release the interrogation tapes we made in Vietnam. Don't you see that there is no reason for me to harm you or your crew as long as you perform in the way that I've outlined? In and out, Bracken. Clean, with no long-term repercussions. And, if you can believe me, a great service to the cause of peace."

"And if I don't agree to go along with this Mickey Mouse deal?"

"There are other men here in Cuba who could sail this vessel if they had to, though that is not my preference. Too much is involved for me to do anything by half measures."

If he agreed, it would buy him the time he needed. If he didn't agree, he knew he was dead. Bracken carefully sat up, rubbing his wrists. "Okay, Lu, the whole thing stinks, but you haven't left me much choice. You're on."

Surprised, Lu smiled.

But I'll also bust your ass in the process, Lu Duc Lee, or whatever your name is, Bracken thought, smiling back. My word on it.

17.

July 18, 1100 hours

She seemed to feel new life in her ancient oak bones, strength surging through her mahogany sinews. The *Pampero* was nearly sixty years old, but the old girl picked up her skirts and flew.

Twenty-six hours out of Cuba, she had edged the Great Bahama Bank, then ran through the Santaren Channel and hardened up into the Straits of Florida. The Gulf Stream was nipping at her heels, adding two and a half knots on top of her eleven and a quarter.

The wind was snorting up from the southeast, blowing a rock-solid thirty knots, whitehorses breaking heavily on the crest of the bigger waves. She rolled and screwed and pitched and plunged through the seas, straining her guts out, right up to the fine edge of being overpowered. But it was grand sailing.

Except for the line of Gulf Stream puffball clouds, the *Pampero* drove through the seas under a clear blue dome that edged down to a more misty pastel on the horizon. Her bowsprit dipped and lifted, her dolphin striker creasing the seas, her wake sprawling out behind her in a smother of white froth.

In the late afternoon a bunch of porpoises escorted her for more than an hour. They dove and crossed and recrossed under her bow, occasionally rolling their bodies sideways to grin, then to dive again. They would occasionally skirt off abeam to snack on a yellowfin or a dolphin, but they came back, just for the sheer damn fun of it all, playing their games again under the thundering bow wave.

She had been conceived in the owner's mind, germinated under the pen of Sam Crocker, and brought to birth on the ways of Reed's Shipyard in Winthrop, Massachusetts, on a blustery morning in May of '31.

Her specifications had been laid down in 1929, before the Crash, and the full contract price had been paid in advance. There was to be a diesel engine, butternut paneling, leaded glass cabinet windows, brass doodads, and the latest in gadgets. She was to get full-length Honduras mahogany planking, a lead keel, and Sitka spruce spars. The deck was to be teak, two inches thick with the grain laid vertically—good enough to last a lifetime.

The salon cushion coverings were custom made from unborn-calf hide in Costa Rica, and she carried hand-carved trailboards and a transom nameboard crafted in Haiti. Bronze fittings for the hounds, the boom bails, cleats, and steering gear were custom-cast and machined in Lunenburg, Nova Scotia.

The trailboards were long gone now, and the transom's carving was blurred from over half a century of sanding and revarnishing. The bronze fittings were worn thin or replaced with galvanized iron. But it didn't matter now, because all the men who had a hand in building or designing her and who had sailed on her would have cheered their lungs out on this day at the sight of her, careening up the Stream at hull speed.

Bracken was on the helm, sweating. He had to pay close attention, because if he slipped off the course by much, he would jibe her. Or blow sails, or broach. Or any of the above.

He knew that the bilge pump was running steadily. She was taking water like a sieve under the hard press of sail, but he had expected that, knew the pumps could keep up. Nowadays, people who owned plastic boats panicked at the thought of a teacup of salt water leaking into their bilges, but wooden boat owners figured that a lot of salt water leaking in, then pumped out, would keep the bilges "sweet." At least that's what they told each other at the yacht club bar when reality was blurred by a couple of gin and tonics. In truth, a wooden boat is a collection of planks floating in formation, pretty much held together by habit. The pressure of the seawater presses the planks against the frames, making it more difficult for water to leak in. But it does, particularly in old boats with spiked fasteners when pounding through rough seas. Over the years Bracken doubted that there still remained a quart of water in the Caribbean Sea that hadn't been pumped through the *Pampero*.

Walrus, bags under his eyes, his fist wrapped around a can of beer and a frazzled look about him, took over the helm just after noon. Bracken hadn't been able to talk privately with him since they had pulled out of Cuba, both because of the watch schedule and the presence of Lu or one of the other men in the cockpit. Raul, who generally took noon-to-four guard duty, hadn't shown up yet, and Vierro was still below playing navigator. It gave them their first chance to talk since leaving Cuba.

"What course, skip?" Walrus settled into the helmsman's seat.

"Steer three-forty. Vierro's getting a satnav fix and will probably give you a course alteration in about twenty minutes."

"You figured out where we're headed?" Walrus kept his eyes on the compass, not making contact with Bracken's.

"Cape Canaveral."

Walrus raised his eyebrows, frowned, then scratched at his unshaven jaw. "Fits together. That photograph of the beach—the tower in the background—could be a launch gantry. Read through Raul's manual a bunch of times, and all I can figure out is that it's a timetable with other information on compass bearings from the sea into the beach. Question is, what the hell are they up to?"

"Intelligence gathering, Lu claims. They want telemetry data on a satellite launch." He filled Walrus in on Lu's explanation.

"The shuttle?"

"You got it."

Before coming on watch in the morning, Bracken had picked up a talk radio show out of Key West that confirmed the authenticity of the newspaper clippings Lu had shown him.

A shuttle launch was scheduled sometime early the next morning, a classified Department of Defense mission with no specifics given. Driven by the organizers of half a dozen peace groups, six thousand protesters had set up squatter camps on the NASA Causeway, which leads over to the Shuttle Launch Complex. The National Guard was threatening to clean them off the causeway with bulldozers. Over six hundred arrests had been made within the last twenty-four hours, but ever-increasing numbers of protesters kept pouring into the area, replacing their depleted ranks. There were howls of protest in Congress. Both the White House and Pentagon were stonewalling. And the media was having a field day.

"Know what I think?" Walrus said. "Lu's trying to sell you a load of crap."

"Meaning what?"

"This guy's the same one who worked you over in 'Nam, right? So he manipulates people for a living. Why believe him now?"

"I'm not saying that I believe him. Just that the telemetry thing makes sense when you tie it in with the newspaper reports. It sounds like some kind of an illegal payload and God knows, neither NASA nor the Administration has been up front with the public in the past. What else could they be up to?"

"If you want my worst case scenario—sabotage the shuttle."

"Yeah, sure. They just sneak ashore with a bomb, climb an electric fence, avoid detection by the choppers, tiptoe over a mile of swamp filled with rattlesnakes, duck past security patrols, then blow the shuttle."

"Not quite. They could use something like a Stinger hand-held missile."

Bracken shook his head. "Already considered that, but it doesn't wash. A Stinger or something like it would leave an exhaust trail. For damned sure, it could destroy the shuttle but NASA security and the Coast Guard would be swarming all over the beach in minutes. And if the government figured out that it was a Soviet operation, then you're talking about instant World War Three." He took Walrus's beer and swigged on it, then handed it back. "No way—it has to be one hell of a lot more subtle than that, and the telemetry thing still makes the most sense."

Walrus wasn't buying it. "Maybe it sounds plausible, skip, but the Russians could have enlisted some antinuke organization like Green Peas to put Raul and Vierro on the beach with the so-called telemetry gear, provided it's that bloodless an operation."

His eyes gritty from lack of sleep, Bracken tried to think straight. Lu had scheduled him and Walrus as the only helmsmen, both of them standing two-hour back-to-back watches. With sail changes, navigation, maintenance, and cooking, the schedule left them both exhausted and isolated from each other. "But if sabatoge is what Lu's planning, then how would they do it?"

After taking a last swig of beer, Walrus crushed the can in his hand and heaved it overboard. "Beats the shit out of me."

Half-Ton, the hulk that had trundled on board the *Pampero* with Lu just before they left Cuba, popped his head out of the companionway and watched them with intense interest. Undoubtedly Cuban and spoke no English. In fact, never said anything except the occasional grunt. Although close to three hundred pounds, Half-Ton was light on his feet and seemed to play the combined roles of gun-for-hire and surveillance camera. Hired meat, Bracken figured, but competent. More than competent. All the hallmarks of being both deadly and professional. And with Lu, Vierro, and Raul also on board, the ratio of bad guys to good guys had increased from reasonable to nearly impossible.

Half-Ton wore shorts but was naked from the waist up, glistening with sweat, wearing only a shoulder holster with a revolver nestled therein. He flashed the dead smile of a mortician to Bracken, then, raising his hands, knuckle to knuckle and spreading them, motioned Bracken and Walrus to separate.

"Any luck on the Walther yet?" Bracken said under his breath.

"I've moved it to the paint locker in the fo'c'sle. Trigger spring is eaten through by the battery acid and the firing pin's jammed, but I'm still fiddling with it. Might take two or three more hours of work, and even then I'm not sure whether it'll fire."

"It's all we've got, Walrus. By tonight you've got to have it functioning."

"I hear you loud and clear, skip. Just that we won't know if it will work until the trigger's pulled. And if it doesn't fire the first time, it could be real embarrassing."

True, Bracken thought.

Bracken went below and slumped over the navigational table, studying NOS chart 11484. Based on Raul's manual, Bracken estimated that the pad the shuttle would be launched from would be at least a mile and a quarter away from the point on the beach that Raul and Vierro would land on. There was probably a chain-link fence just above the surf line, undoubtedly festooned with security sensors and spiked with high voltage. So no way could Raul get near to the shuttle to do it any damage. The interception of telemetry data still made sense, despite Walrus's misgiving. Still, the real answer was probably on the cassette tape, provided that he could play it back.

Jean's rough plan for transfer of the tape had worked well enough. Walrus had been able to retrieve the tape without being detected, and Bracken had immediately dunked it in rubbing alcohol, sloshing it around for five minutes in the fluid, then stashed it behind the generator to drip-dry. Twice in the last thirty hours he had rewound the reels with a pencil, and there was no apparent sticking of the tape. He guessed that it might be possible to play it back by this evening through the *Pampero*'s stereo tape player, but the problem was that if he played it, even at low volume, Lu or one of his buddies would surely hear it. Neither Bracken nor Walrus had a portable Walkman, and Jean had taken hers with her, so the ship's stereo was the only available option.

The ship's clock struck and, without looking, Bracken reached up to the VHF radio to switch it on in order to pick up the update marine weather forecast for the Straits of Florida. His hand fumbled through empty space. The bracket that held the radio was still there, but the radio was gone, as was the wiring.

He got up and clumped aft, then banged his fist on the cabin door.

A couple of seconds—the sounds of voices—then Lu opened the door, a pair of wire cutters in his hand. "You're off watch. Get to bed," he said in a bored voice.

"What about the VHF radio?"

"I'm installing it back here."

"Why? I need the damn thing!"

Lu breathed out a tired sigh, irritated. "I wouldn't want you to transmit on the radio without my permission, so I've removed the temptation. I'll get your weather reports." He slammed the door in Bracken's face, like a housewife stiffing a vacuum cleaner salesman.

Bracken threw his weight against the door panel and it swung open with a bang. Lu was caught off balance and stumbled backward. Through the open door Bracken saw Vierro rising from the port bunk, pushing the sheets aside, now sitting up, his revolver out of its holster. Lu turned to him, pushed the barrel of the revolver roughly aside, and said something in Spanish, too quick and in too harsh an accent for Bracken to catch. Vierro spat back something but holstered the weapon, glared at Bracken, then lay back on the berth.

Turning to Bracken, Lu said, "In the salon. It seems we have to talk. I'll be there in a few minutes."

Bracken went back to the salon and slumped down at the navigational table. He had missed it before: a slip of paper with the noon satnav coordinates that Lu had written. Bracken plotted the fix. Mildly surprised because they were already abeam St. Lucie Inlet, well past Palm Beach. The Gulf Stream had to be stronger than he had estimated. He laid off a course and distance to Cape Canaveral. Course three-five-one magnetic, about seventy-nine miles. He tapped that into the calculator and estimated arrival about 1900 hours, just at the end of twilight.

Lu appeared in a boiler suit carrying a bottle of rum. "You want to share a drink, Bracken?"

"I wouldn't mind."

Lu poured into two plastic cups and handed one to Bracken. "To our respective futures," he said, raising his glass, then drank the amber liquid in small sips. He sat down on the salon settee, his hand cushioning his chin. "I thought we understood each other, but if you have a problem, then tell me about it."

"The VHF radio."

"That is definitely not your problem. What else is bothering you?"

"One helluva lot."

"Then tell me." Lu was patience personified.

"Besides you, there are three other men on board, all armed. At least two of them are on guard all the time. Walrus and I can't turn around without someone pointing a gun in our direction. I want you to back off."

"What else, Bracken?"

"Walrus and I are dead on our feet. I want Vierro and Raul to take watches once the wind gets lighter."

Lu smiled. "Is that it?"

"No. I want to see this telemetry equipment before Raul and Vierro go ashore. Just to be sure it's what you say it is."

"And that's *all*?" Lu lifted his eyebrows in question.

"Yes—for starters."

"Indulge me, Bracken. Try to understand where I'm coming from. This is my last field assignment, and it's terribly important, because it affects world peace. And on the personal side, I have a teenage son. I want to live with him, raise him, see that he gets the right schooling and the benefit of a father to guide him. But most of all, I'm tired of the game and I want to retire. For all those reasons I want this operation to be safe and clean for all concerned without any problems—an old man's swan song. Boring, isn't it?" He paused. "You had a wife as well?" Part question, part statement. Clever, even. The humanizing bit.

"It didn't work out. She left me."

"Yes. Penny was her name, as I recall from your dossier. And Jean? Is she important to you?"

Even more clever. A reminder of what he had to lose. "We get along."

Lu got up and poured himself another drink, raised the bottle at Bracken, who shook his head. "No? Then I'll have to drink alone." He remained standing. "You understand what's changed, Bracken? We both lived dangerous lives but we lived them for our own amusement. Now each of us has made the mortal error of commitment to another person. That makes both of us human, vulnerable, and subject to external pressures. What you ask for is reasonable. But I have a job to do. You're being paid well, you agreed to do the work, and I'm footing the bills. Therefore, things will be done my way. Your requests are denied."

Bracken got less than an hour's sleep. His alarm clock shook him out of a black, dreamless stupor. He got up, doused his face with water, gobbled down two caffeine tablets, pulled on a Windbreaker, and headed for the cockpit.

Walrus was nodding at the wheel, the sun getting lower in the west, just after four in the afternoon.

"Get enough sleep?" Walrus asked.

"Not long enough." He traded places at the helm, checked the compass and the sky to the northwest. Obvious signs of a cold front approaching, and he guessed that tomorrow would be rough.

Half-Ton was on watch but not in the cockpit, stretched out forward, sunning himself, probably dozing. The security was slowly breaking down into predictable patterns.

"You run the cassette tape yet?" Walrus asked softly.

Bracken shook his head. "No opportunity. The tape's fairly dry and the reels turn freely without sticking. But the only way that I can play it is through the stereo system."

"Vierro's got headphones for his boom box. You know that?"

"You're sure it's the same size jack plug?"

"Think so. Looks like the standard rather than the miniature size."

Half-Ton was sitting up now. He thumbed at Bracken to get below, then started to get to his feet.

"I'll give it a go," Walrus said. He gave Bracken a thumbs-up sign and eased down the companionway.

Walrus found Vierro spread out over the salon settee, dozing. He slid a Miami Sound Machine cassette into the stereo tape player and flipped the circuit breaker on, then cranked up the volume. The speakers were big, the amplifier fifty watts a channel. Panes of glass in the liquor cabinet began to vibrate to the beat.

Vierro jerked straight up, startled, banging his head on the bulkhead. "Shut that damn thing off! I'm trying to sleep."

"What's your problem, man? Gimme a break."

"Then turn it down."

Walrus fiddled with the controls, lowering the volume but turning up the bass. Bulkhead panels began to vibrate in sympathy with the beat.

"Enough!" Vierro shouted.

"Raul's got some headphones, doesn't he? Let me borrow them and we'll both be cool."

Three minutes later, Walrus was plugged in.

Through the evening twilight, the *Pampero* angled in toward the Florida coast until she was ten miles offshore. The strong southeasterly wind was dying, and the light aged to the color of burnt umber as the sun sank into the haze.

Past Vero Beach, Sebastian, Palm Bay, and Melbourne. Even from ten miles at sea Bracken could see the tops of the towers of Gold Coast condos gleaming white in the last sunlight, their windows dazzling with the reflection of the setting sun.

The wind had eased off to twenty knots by the early afternoon, fell to fifteen by twilight, then dropped to under ten as darkness fell. Farther inshore he had caught an occasional glimpse of sportfishermen headed for harbor. In his mind's eye, skippered by stereotypical guys dressed in gaudy sport shirts with heavy gold chains clanking from their necks and hued with deep copper tans; their stereotypical ladies graced with even deeper cocoa coloring (their suntan lotion laced with secret and exotic emollients) and decked out in blinding white bikinis that sold for $50 an ounce. With lots of gin and tonics being splashed around and the promise of evening fun and games to follow. Bracken, like every other rag sailor he had known, both loathed and secretly loved the idea of such a setup. And right now he figured he would gladly swap places.

Lu had just called up a course change to parallel the coast. Half-Ton was sprawled in the forward part of the cockpit, picking his teeth and fingering his revolver as if it were some private part of him.

High overhead in the dome of the sky, cirrus clouds had begun to reach out from the north with long, lacy tendrils, foretelling the approaching cold front. Tomorrow would not be the kind of weather that the Florida State Chamber of Commerce liked to brag about. Ladies with blue-tinted hair who were currently stuffed into designer swimsuits two sizes too small would be cloaked in their ankle-length minks by mid-morning tomorrow, frantically being tugged toward trendy boutiques by similarly blue-tinted poodles as temperatures plummeted into the frigid fifties. It would not be the kind of mid-July weather that the Flordia Chamber of Commerce liked to brag about. Smug New England newspapers would give the freak Florida weather a few lines on page three, probably coupled with a puff-piece about the greenhouse effect, as if that had anything to do with it, which it probably didn't. But Bracken also knew that the norther would blow like hell, churning the Gulf Stream into a gigantic washing machine.

In the dying wind, the *Pampero* crept up the coast, hardly moving through the water and yet still boosted by an inshore tributary of the flooding Gulf Stream. Past Indialantic, Satellite, and Cocoa beaches, clumps of multicolored lights marking each town, illuminating the bellies of dissipating coastal cumulus. On the far northern horizon, with the sun down and the twilight gone, Bracken first picked out the lighthouse on Merritt Island and beyond that, a dazzle of floodlights from the Kennedy Space Center.

Lu came up the companionway, nursing a mug of coffee. For a moment he was silhouetted by the lights from below, then moved forward on deck, sniffing at the wind and studying the horizon. He stood immobile for several minutes and Bracken wondered what the man was thinking.

Lu finally turned and moved aft into the cockpit, motioning at Half-Ton to go below.

For minutes he sat there in the darkness, his profile a dark, unmoving cutout against the lighter background of the horizon.

"Did you get the weather report?" Bracken said for openers.

Lu turned back, the sound of his voice a little agitated at being broken off from his thoughts. "They're calling for moderate southeasterly winds until mid-morning tomorrow, then frontal passage with the wind switching to the north and blowing hard. Temperatures falling into the mid-fifties. Does that present a problem?"

"For us, no. A northerly wind will give us a favorable shot across the Gulf Stream on our way back to the Bahamas. It'll be rough and wet, but fast. And the timing makes it mandatory for NASA to launch the shuttle as soon after dawn as they can, particularly before the frontal system arrives. Otherwise they'll have to delay the launch for twenty-four hours because of the high winds and low temperatures. O-ring seals, wind shear, stuff like that. Too risky to launch."

"Like the conditions that led to the *Challenger* disaster," Lu said, a statement, but said it reasonably without inflection, as if it meant nothing.

"Yes, like the . . . *Challenger*," Bracken echoed. The television sequences came vividly back to him: the flowers of fire unfolding against the deep blue backdrop of the Florida sky, pieces of shuttle, tank, and booster rocket engines cartwheeling through billows of smoke like petals unfolding in time-lapse slow motion. He had cried for the first time in years when he had seen the film clips. So many dreams destroyed in that one terrible instant. More than just individual dreams. Eventually, the dreams, confidence, and the trust of a whole nation.

It suddenly struck him like a blow to his heart. The destruction of this shuttle would shatter the American space program. Not for another few years—but forever. Walrus was right. His skin went cold despite the warm dampness of the Florida night. Somehow he knew what would happen tomorrow. Not exactly how, just knew it would happen, saw the same awful film footage repeated in his mind's eye, still guessing but really knowing deep down in his gut that Lu was out to destroy it. He breathed four or five times, in and out, deeply. "This thing about telemetry?" he asked.

"Yes . . . what about it?"

"I still want to see the equipment."

"Why should I, Bracken. I can't unpack it. It's sealed in a watertight container."

"Let's just say I'd feel better, all right?"

Lu stood up slowly, stretching, turning toward Bracken. "I've personally seen the equipment demonstrated. It's just a small receiver, a tape recorder, and a foldout antenna. About twenty kilos, packed in a plastic tube with watertight seals. I'd like to accommodate your curiosity, but I don't have the authority to open it up."

Which was terribly convenient. Bracken backed off a little, not wanting to stir up Lu's suspicion. There was still the cassette tape for all that was worth, but Lu had now added to the element of doubt.

He shrugged, then switched subjects as if he were marginally satisfied with the answer. "What's our schedule?"

"When I receive the launch time from the *Victoria,* I'll calculate our course and heading to make sure we'll be two miles offshore from the Cape an hour and a half prior to launch time."

"You just don't mess around off the Cape, Lu. Not when a shuttle is scheduled for launch. The rules are laid in *U.S. Coast Pilot,* volume four. Everything to seaward of the Cape, out to about ten miles, is a prohibited zone."

"The prohibited zone is closed off only an hour before launch. Until that time any vessel can pass through the area."

"But NASA doesn't advertise launch times for military shuttle launches."

"But they do, Bracken. Right now instructions are going to tracking stations worldwide, to camera and telemetry crews, to technicians on the Cape. We have ways of monitoring this transfer of information. Once it's known, the *Victoria* will be informed. Then they'll relay the time to me by single-sideband radio."

"You've got it all organized."

"As well as anything can be with all the variables involved." His voice had just the tinge of pride.

"One thing puzzles me, Lu. Why do we meet the *Victoria* in the Bahamas? I'd have thought she'd stay in Cayo Mambí and we'd meet her back there for the hostage swap."

"It's obvious. Neutral territory. If the exchange were done in Cuba, I couldn't guarantee that the Cubans would let you go. It's for your own protection. Bracken. I owe you that much."

Sweet, Bracken thought. It was good to have friends. "But your superior's aboard the *Victoria.* The 'colonel,' Sanchez called him. I'd have thought he wouldn't want the exposure to possibly being boarded by the Coast Guard in a country which is basically pro-Western." The part about Sanchez was a lie, but Lu had no way of checking.

"It was at his insistence," Lu said, distracted, obviously displeased with Sanchez's supposed indiscretion.

Not definite, Bracken thought, but still it pointed to the possibility that there *were* two parts to the operation, maybe each in support of the other but, possibly, each with a separate objective. He knew that he was treading on dangerous ground and switched the subject. "You said you have a son?"

Lu's voice thawed a few degrees. "Fourteen, nearly fifteen. He lives in a suburb of Moscow."

So the kid was post-Vietnam. Had to be part Asiatic. "Your wife—she there too?"

"My wife is dead, Bracken." Lu's voice had a coating of frost.

A complex man, Bracken thought. What you see is not what you get. But he kept it up, probing tentatively into Lu's psyche. "Dammit—I'm sorry. Hard on you, even harder on a kid, growing up alone without either of his parents." It could pass for sympathy or a mild accusation of negligence, and Bracken had intended it be interpreted either way.

But Lu didn't respond except with silence. Bracken realized that he needed a few minutes of casual talk to thaw out Lu, to bring him up out of the well of memories. "What's the boy's name?"

No hesitation. "Sasha. He's chess champion of his school. Very bright." He paused, again caught up in his private thoughts, then, "You'll never know what you've missed until you have a son of your own." Lu's voice had a detached quality to it, the chain of private memories triggered.

"What does he want to be?"

"An artist, a writer. Something like that. He has the mind, the will, and the ability to do almost anything."

"Like work for the KGB?"

A dark silhouette against the lighted shore, Lu turned to him. "I'm a military officer, Bracken. I swore to defend my motherland. Some officers use weapons to achieve their national purpose, much as you did. Others, like me, collect information." He softened his voice a little. "Still, we're an older generation, you and I: part of the problem, not realizing that there was a solution. Because of men like us, neither of our countries learned their lessons soon enough, and for that reason we have fought a senseless cold war for over four decades. You and I can help rectify the past mistakes if we complete this mission. And perhaps our sons will be friends. I'd like to think that, Bracken."

Was Lu trying to con him, or was this for real? It sounded so damned convincing—enough so that Bracken *wanted* to believe, but he knew from experience that he couldn't. He checked his watch—almost time for Walrus to come on. He needed hard specifics. "So how's the actual operation set up for tomorrow?"

"I'll tell you when the time arrives. No need for you to know as yet." Still trying to stay in control.

Bracken blew up in a calculated manner. "You stupid shit! I want to get this thing over with, collect my paycheck, my woman, and get the hell out in one piece. We may not share the same politics, but we share the same immediate objectives. Unless I know, I can't anticipate problems. There's just Walrus and me to run this ship, keep the systems going, keep her sailing. I need to know exactly what's going to be happening so I can stay on top of it."

Lu sighed as if he had just broken his shoelace—something aggravating and minor, but something that he could deal with. "All right. I suppose you should have the broad outline. We'll continue north until I receive the approximate launch time from the *Victoria*. From there on in I'll time our turn inshore and head back toward the Cape so that we're abeam Titusville one and a half hours before the launch. At that time you'll anchor."

"They probably have radar on the Cape. They'll spot us, probably send out a crash boat to investigate."

"Unlikely. The prohibited zone will not be closed off at that time. Also, consider that one of the reasons we chose the *Pampero* is that both the hull and the masts are made of wood. It will present a very poor radar return, and even if it's picked up, there will be no reason for suspicion. We'll be more than two miles offshore, perfectly legal. Your stationary position will roughly match the profile of a vessel drift-fishing, something common in these waters according to my background briefings."

"What then?"

"The man that I brought on board in Cayo Mambí, the man that you so appropriately refer to as 'Half-Ton' is a Cuban marine, very experienced in amphibious operations. He'll take your inflatable boat and, using compass bearings and other navigational markers, motor to within two hundred meters of the beach. At that point Raul and Vierro will ease out of the dinghy and swim to the surfline, then descend to the bottom. They will each be wearing a three-tank scuba pack. Resting on the bottom and conserving their air, they'll wait until fifteen minutes before launch time, then drop their tanks and move ashore with their equipment. Even with some minor delays they'll be set up in the dunes ten minutes prior to launch."

"What about shore patrols and the choppers that sweep the Cape right up to launch time?"

"There are security patrols and helicopters, but they're withdrawn fifteen minutes prior to launch for safety reasons. Raul and Vierro will have between eleven and twelve minutes to get ashore, set up their equipment, cover themselves with a camouflage net, and wait for the launch."

"And if the launch is delayed?"

"Lying on the bottom, conserving their air, they have over nine hours of endurance. In general, if a launch is delayed beyond three or four hours, it's scrubbed and rescheduled. And when a mission is scrubbed, the prohibited zone is reopened almost immediately. We would then sail back into the area and pick them up two or three miles offshore. We would recharge the scuba bottles and try again the following morning." He glanced up at the night sky, the stars now veiled by the cirrus of the approaching cold front. "But I think that they will make every effort to get the launch off as soon after dawn as possible, even if NASA has to compromise on safety. The protesters and the press . . ." He made a throwaway gesture with his hand.

Yes, indeedy, Bracken thought. The protesters and the press. If there was a delay, they would use it to gather additional support from Congress to delay the launch indefinitely until a full investigation of the shuttle's payload could determine exactly what was contained in the suspect satellite. And if NASA and the military were lying about the payload, it would be a replay of Irangate without an eloquent Ollie North to carry the ball.

"And what happens if a Coast Guard cutter stops us?"

"My associates and I have valid Panamanian passports. We have a valid charter contract for this vessel. There would be no great problem—just that we might be delayed, although that could possibly prevent the successful completion of my part of the mission."

Slip of the tongue, Bracken thought. Lu must be tired. But there it was again. Lu was running just part of the mission and the colonel was running the other part from the *Victoria*.

"So they board us. You're free and clear, but what about me and the *Pampero*? There's still a seizure pending on her."

"On the American-registered *Pampero*, Bracken, but this vessel is now under Panamanian registry. The Coast Guard has the right to search a foreign vessel but not to seize it without evidence of some wrongdoing. Certain powerful politicians in Panama are ready to lodge a diplomatic protest should the Coast Guard try to pursue the matter too far."

"But with the delay the whole deal would be for nothing."

Lu didn't answer immediately. He glanced at the shore and then moved to the compass, bent down, and checked the course. His facial muscles were set hard in the dim red light. "The consequences of failure would be very difficult for me to personally deal with, Bracken, regardless of whether it was a bungled operation or just bad luck. But if we keep to our timetable and stay outside of the prohibited zone while presence in it is restricted, there should be no problems."

The pieces of phase one were beginning to come together. It had to be sabotage. But what did phase two entail? The answer to that was hopefully contained on the cassette tape. In a few minutes Bracken would know.

Lu yawned, stretching. "When does your first mate come on watch?"

"Fifteen minutes or so."

"Good. When you change the watch, I want you to check the scuba tank pressures and top them up to their maximum with the compressor we installed in Cuba."

"Shit! I'm short of sleep and with two hours on, two off, plus maintenance and keeping the ship running, I don't have the time. Let Vierro or Raul take care of it. They damn well don't do anything else."

Impatience in his voice, Lu snapped back, "Vierro and Raul have a strenuous day in front of them. I want them at their best. Therefore, you will take care of the tanks."

Bracken had seen the nest of air bottles strapped down in the engine room: nine of them. Plus an air compressor which had been installed during the stopover in Cuba. It would be a simple job but it would eat into his sack time. "Let Half-Ton do it."

"He's not familiar with the procedures but your dossier indicates you are. You will do the work, Bracken. No arguments."

"Okay, okay—it's not a big deal. I'll check the bottles and fill them if they need it. How about letting me off watch right now. You take it until Walrus comes on. That gives me a fifteen-minute start on the job." Bracken had finely tuned the tone of his response to somewhere between mild protest and wheedling.

Lu rapped on the aft cabin hatch, and three minutes later Half-Ton trudged up the companionway. Lu spoke to him in Spanish, then Half-Ton nodded silently and went below. Three minutes later Walrus was on deck, bitching under his breath about not even being given time to brew a cup of coffee.

"Watcha steering, skip?" he grunted, settling down on the helmsman's seat, yawning.

"Parallel the shore about eight to ten miles out. A good course would be about three forty-five." He moved in closer, peering over Walrus's shoulder as if he were watching the compass. He dropped his voice, looking at Lu, who was turned away, scanning the shore. "What was on the tape?"

"The audio is godawful: a lot of hissing and I couldn't run it all the way through because Raul grabbed the headphones back and I had to eject the tape. But there was some interesting stuff. . . ."

Turning back toward them, Lu obviously realized that some sort of private conversation was taking place. "I thought I had made it abundantly clear that I don't want any contact between the two of you without either Vierro or myself present!"

"Don't try to bust my balls," Bracken shot back. "In case you didn't realize it, you *are* present."

"What was that conversation all about, Bracken?"

Walrus answered for Bracken. "Just that the refrigeration compressor was running rough. It took some seawater in the knockdown and probably fritzed its bearings. Sounded like someone put a load of rocks through it. The sucker's completely *bust*." Emphasis on the last word.

What the hell was Walrus talking about? The refrigerator compressor had been shut down ever since the bilges were flooded during the storm.

"We've got plenty of ice," Lu said. "More than enough to see us through the next few days. I take it you shut the unit off?"

"Just did," Walrus answered. "Thought maybe I could fix it, but the maintenance manual is too technical for me. Maybe you can make something of it, skip."

"I'll give it a shot. I've got to check out the scuba tanks anyway."

Apparently satisfied, Lu nodded. "Then get on with it, Bracken. The air tanks first, then if you want to play with the refrigeration, don't complain to me about lost sleep."

Half-Ton came up the companionway, stuffing his face with forkfuls of refried beans from an open can. Lu motioned to him to take over surveillance and started to go below, then turned back. "You too, Bracken. No more chitchat." He stood there, waiting.

First squeezing Walrus's arm, he followed Lu, pausing to check the barometer, then heading for the nav table. Lu was already bending over N.O.S. chart 11484, studying it.

"Thin water up there," Bracken commented, pointing to Ohio and Hetxel shoals.

"Deep enough," Lu replied, his voice flat. "Leave the navigation to me. I want you on those diving bottles. Now."

Bracken sighed as if it were a great imposition. "If you say so, boss." Lu ground the muscles in his jaw but didn't bother to comment.

He walked forward to the engine room and flipped on the lights. Nine air tanks were stacked in a pile and lashed down. He checked their pressure gauges. Presumably, they had been filled in Cuba, but all the pressure readings were short of maximum— probably because whoever had filled the tanks had not bothered to cool them down before pumping compressed air into them. Basic rule: Place scuba tanks in a bucket of cold water because the air which is crammed into them has been heated by the air compressor, thus reducing maximum tank capacity. If the tank, and thus the compressed air, is not first cooled down, then the amount of air pumped into that tank will be a couple of hundred pounds short of its maximum capacity. Not a big deal, but enough to reduce the tank's capacity by ten or twelve percent.

But the tanks weren't what he was interested in. Rather, the time alone in the engine room. Walrus had mentioned the refrigeration manual. The point was that there wasn't one. But there was a general maintenance log that was stowed in the top of the toolbox. He desperately wanted to read it but not just yet.

Just as Bracken had expected, Lu slowly eased the engine room door open. Hadn't heard him, hadn't seen him, but knew that he was there, his eyes boring into Bracken's backbone.

"What's wrong?" Lu asked, leaning over Bracken's shoulder.

Bracken did a quick about-face, showing an appropriate degree of surprise. "Nothing. The air pressure in the bottles is a little low but still in the green. They're fine." He eased out of squatting position, wiping his hands on his jeans, putting the flashlight back in its bracket. "I'm off to the sack. Have Half-Ton call me out fifteen minutes before Walrus's watch is over." He stood before Lu, shifting his body restlessly, waiting for Lu to unblock the doorway, trying to appear reasonably loyal and yet with the look of grievance on his face that a worker has when the boss wants him to stay on the job without the compensation of overtime pay.

"Get on with it, Bracken," Lu said flatly. "I want those bottles pumped up as high as they'll go."

It was not just the line and the sinker that Lu had swallowed. Now it was the hook. But it wasn't set. Not quite.

Bracken twitched the rod, setting the drag on the reel, holding his breath in anticipation. "Look, Lu. These tanks average about 2,800 pounds per square inch of pressure. Full up, they'll hold 3,000 pounds, maybe 3,200 pounds if they were iced down. But those last few hundred pounds takes for bloody ever on a compressor of this size."

"How much more time on the bottom does it give a diver— those last few hundred pounds of compressed air?"

"Depends on how hard he's working, how deep he is, but it's not much. Say twenty minutes per tank maximum. With three tanks, about an extra hour."

The imaginary fishing rod was almost yanked out of Bracken's hands as Lu swallowed the lure, sank into it, and ran to the depths, the line whining out, the reel smoking.

"*I want those damned tanks filled to maximum!*" Lu's eyes were hard and black as a deep-water predator's.

Bracken scratched at his scalp, shuffling his feet, avoided eye contact, as if he had come up against the real boss. A lot of seconds ticked by, and finally he shrugged, acquiescent. "All right. No big deal. I'll get another couple of hundred psi into those bottles, but it'll take ice. Every cube we got, plus all the cold water in the fridge."

"Get on with it." Lu actually sounded as if he were disappointed with the capitulation but also compelled, like a fair-minded manager, to acknowledge good and faithful service.

Lu turned and was halfway down the engine room passage leading into the salon when Bracken called after him. "Hey! I need some help. I want you to dig ice out of the fridge while I get the compressor going."

The sweetest sound Bracken ever heard was Lu, in a fit of terminal vexation, slamming the door to the salon. At a minimum it guaranteed Bracken a reasonable time to work in peace. He set to work, humming the theme song from *Rocky VII*.

Almost all of the scuba compressors Bracken had seen were powered by a gasoline engine. But this one was run electrically. Not very efficient, not very fast, but he realized the logic behind its selection. Unlike gasoline-powered units, which had to be mounted on deck due to the danger of explosive gas fumes, this compressor, being electrically driven, could be mounted below decks, protected from the corroding effects of salt spray.

Bracken read the power rating on the compressor's motor. Two horsepower, which would demand one hell of a lot of juice.

He checked the Onan generator for oil level, a full coolant system, then pushed the start button.

The machine rumbled over a couple of times, coughed, and caught.

The plumbing on the compressor was simple. There was a flexible hose that sucked in clean air through a fitting on deck. That air was ducted to the compressor intake, raised to 3,300 pounds, filtered through chemicals to remove any smell, then pumped through high pressure pipes to the scuba bottles.

Bracken connected the high pressure hose to the first air tank and turned on the compressor valve. Then made a quick trip to the fo'c'sle, found a large plastic bucket, and filled it with ice from the fridge. On his way back to the engine room he noted that Lu was absent but that the starboard stateroom cabin door was closed. Obviously, catching a catnap. Aft cabin door closed as well, where Raul and Vierro would be beddy-byes, leaving Half-Ton on deck to monitor Walrus.

Back in the engine room he set the first air tank into the bucket. Ten minutes a tank to top up, he figured. He then took an assortment of wrenches out of the toolbox and laid them around the engine room floor, then, with his back turned to the engine room door and facing the seized refrigeration compressor, he slid the maintenance log out of the tool box. If Lu or any of the rest of his buddies looked in, Bracken would have the appearance of a legitimate tradesman bent to his work.

There wasn't much that Walrus had written in the log's last page. The paper was smudged with oil, the ink smeared, but Bracken could read it well enough.

Tape still damp but runs free. Bad audio with a lot of hiss and some missing stuff. Needs more drying. I restowed it behind generator.

Conversation first in Russian between Lu and some other guy. No capito, skip. Then Vierro, Sanchez, and Raul showed up. Conversation in English with some Spanish thrown in, but I got the gist of it. Plan is for Raul and Vierro to go by dinghy with scuba gear and lie on the bottom just off the beach until fifteen minutes before launch.

"Telemetry gear" is some kind of large caliber rifle.

*Raul referred to it as a "ZSU." ZSU is a 23mm cannon—
same caliber that the Soviet chopper gunships used in Afghani-
stan and Nicaragua. Raul mentioned a telescopic sight. Range
would be over two miles and projectiles could be either armor-
piercing or incendiary shells.*

*Timetable looks like Raul shoots just after the main
engines fire but before the solid boosters fire. Something like
about six seconds between those two events so the sound of the
gunshot would be masked by the roar of the main engines
startup. Target is just above the first field joint on the solid
booster rocket engine—exactly like* Challenger *in '86.*

Bracken was sweating profusely, his hand trembling as he
turned the page.

*Missed about a minute's worth of conversation due to
a section of the tape that was still wet. Just squeal and hiss
stuff. Then slowed down again and readable. Just Lu and the
old guy—everyone else split. All in Russian except one phrase—
jabber-something. Might be able to make it out once the tape is
completely dry.*

*Sorry couldn't get more, but I'll try it again when I have
the chance.*

Walrus

The pressure-relief valve on the compressor blew off. He
turned, startled. Thirty-four-hundred pounds per square inch on
the pressure gauge. He cut the supply valve off, unscrewed the
fitting, and reached for another tank. Only one done, eight to go.
Then stopped to think. He had to stop the operation but stop it in
such a way that Lu would think that the operation on the beach
had gone wrong, not attributable to sabotage. If Raul and Vierro
weren't able to destroy the shuttle, Lu wouldn't have any way of
knowing the reason. And at that point his only recourse would be
to sail for the Bahamas with his tail between his legs, which
opened up the possibility of Bracken stopping phase two.

Good trick, but how?

He looked at the tank, then the hose, then the compressor.
Traced the various lines, the exhaust system, and finally the air
intake which led up through the deck head. The fitting was
relatively crude. Some shipwright in Cuba had bored a three-inch

hole through the deck and had fitted a collar. On deck was some kind of air filter with complicated baffles, obviously custom made for the installation. The flexible air intake hose was strapped onto the collar by a hose clamp.

The air intake hose was what interested him. There are many dangers in scuba diving. Most of them dealt with how a diver used his gear, what depths he could go to, and how long he had to wait at various stages during the ascent to the surface to prevent the formation of nitrogen bubbles in the bloodstream.

Another, more dangerous level of potential disaster for a diver resided in the quality and maintenance of the diver's equipment. The rule of thumb is that you bought the best gear and were fanatical about maintaining it.

But a fundamental danger of scuba diving and one that is often overlooked is the potential contamination of air that is used to charge the diving tanks.

Bracken had taken a diving course at Petit St. Vincent resort back in the late sixties. The instructor, a big, affable Australian of immense competency and a godawful accent, had gone through the basic training. Bracken had promised to but had never pursued the finer points. But the instructor had repeatedly stressed the danger that when a diving compressor was run, the air intake must be positioned so that there is no possibility of its picking up any exhaust fumes from a gasoline or diesel engine because exhaust gas containes carbon monoxide. Carbon monoxide is tasteless, has no smell, but even in minute concentrations is deadly to a diver. Bracken couldn't remember what concentration was deadly or even how it affected a diver, but he was willing to use Raul and Vierro as guinea pigs. His idea was to err on the side of massive contamination.

Bracken first cracked the valve on the tank he had just recharged, bleeding off the pressure in the bottles to 2,000 pounds. He then reconnected the compressor high pressure pipe to the tank manifold with a wrench.

Next he examined the generator's exhaust system. It was of all-welded construction—no possibility of breaking into it without destroying the system and, worse, creating a loud racket from the raw exhaust noise.

But there was an answer, although it involved risk. He undogged and eased open the porthole in the engine room. Directly below the porthole was the generator exhaust fitting. The *Pampero* was not heeled very much, and through the porthole he could see the reflection of the sea; small waves curling and licking the side of the ship as she proceeded north in the light wind. How much exhaust fumes would the compressor intake pick up? A lot or a little? He had no way of knowing. But it was the only idea that he had to work with.

He closed the porthole but didn't dog it down, went into the galley, and with the ice pick chopped up all the remaining ice, then poured ice water from the fridge into the bucket. It would do.

On his way back to the engine room he listened at the salon door, then carefully opened it a crack. Lu wasn't up yet, and the aft cabin door was still closed. Bracken again shut the door to the salon, entered the engine room, then wedged a crowbar against the door to keep it from being easily opened.

He removed the clamp from the compressor air intake hose with a screwdriver, wiggled the hose off its fitting, and dangled it out of the porthole so that its free end swung near the generator exhaust fitting. Not quite good enough. The intake of the hose was swinging around, sometimes in the direct downwind flow of the generator and sometimes gyrating out into the clean night air. Bracken ripped off some duct tape from a roll and plastered the hose against the side of the hull. The hose obediently nuzzled against the exhaust outlet, ready to suck up diesel smoke, moisture, carbon monoxide, and death.

Bracken threw the compressor motor switch and listened to it chug up to speed. The pressure gauges on the scuba tanks started to jiggle a little, their pressure slowly rising.

How much carbon monoxide it would take to ice Raul was, as they said, in the laps of the gods.

18.

July 19, 0445 hours

The stars were now obscured by the thickening clouds, a slow swell from the north beginning to overlay the small wavelets from the south, when Lu came up on deck.

He glanced down at the compass, then toward the scattered points of light on the western horizon. Minutes passed. Finally, he glanced again at his watch. "I've received the launch time from the *Victoria,* so we're going to start heading back toward the Cape. Come to port until you're heading two five five degrees. When you're on that heading, the lights of New Smyrna Beach should be dead ahead."

"Call up Walrus. I'll need help."

"Forget your first mate. I want the timing right. Just turn to the heading."

Bracken made an exasperated noise. "You want me to lose the spars? This is a sailing vessel, Lu. The wind is abaft the beam and we're on the starboard tack. I've got to gybe all the sails over, run both the topmast and main backstays, then trim up on that heading. This isn't a power boat, where you just spin the wheel. I need somebody up here who knows what they're doing."

He wasn't exaggerating. Bracken would be turning the *Pampero* away from the wind. And as the wind came directly astern, the leach of the sail would flutter as the flow of wind shifted from one side of the sail to the other, then fill, slamming the boom across the deck in an uncontrolled gybe.

"*Yob tvoyu mat,*" Lu swore. He beat his fist on the aft cabin hatch and yelled down instructions in rapid-fire Spanish. Half-Ton was on deck in thirty seconds, Walrus in fifty.

Bracken turned the helm over to Lu, coaching him to turn the wheel slowly, pause when dead downwind so that the main could be sheeted in, then ease over onto the new tack. As the *Pampero* turned to port, Bracken and Walrus overhauled the mainsheet and foresail sheet until they were taut, shifted the backstays, then readied the headsail sheets for gybing.

Like a duck tacking downwind, back side to the breeze, the *Pampero* came about. The main and foresail booms came over with a *whoomp,* the Dacron sails refilling on the opposite tack and yet restrained by the sheets. Bracken and Walrus eased the sheets on the fore-and-aft sails, then gybed the headsails over. It took more than five minutes and Lu was furious, his neat navigational timing blown away. He ducked below to get another satnav fix, and Bracken, in anticipation, headed farther south along the coast. Doing a rough estimation of time and distance, Bracken figured that the *Pampero* would be abeam Titusville by 0515. Which meant that the launch of the shuttle would be somewhere in the 0645 to 0730 bracket.

The problem was, he was less sure now about the carbon monoxide. By his rough calculation, even assuming that the intake hose was right over the exhaust fitting, he doubted that the concentration of carbon monoxide would be more than five percent—possibly less. Raul and Vierro might eventually die, but would they die soon enough to be prevented from destroying the shuttle? And something else nagged him. Lu had said that a maximum of two attempts would be made within twenty-four hours. Security was certainly part of that decision. How long would the Coast Guard allow a vessel to stooge around in the waters off the Cape before they did some checking? But the idea of the Soviets chucking it in without some kind of backup operation seemed unlikely. Which, in his mind, again confirmed that phase two was an alternative plan to destroy the shuttle in flight, not dependent on Lu destroying it during the launch phase. Something that could be done from as far away as the Bahamas. Which could mean only that a highly directional radio signal would have to be used to trigger the destruction of the shuttle.

He thought back to Les Saintes, trying to remember details of the *Victoria,* and it slowly fitted together. That was why the *Victoria* had a dome aft of the bridge. Not for point-to-point earth communications via a commercial satellite, but for a precision up-link which would track the shuttle's flight path and transmit the destruct signal.

He thought about it, becoming more and more convinced, except for one nagging question. Why would Lu want to first try to destroy the shuttle on the launch pad with all the attendant risks of the security of putting two men on the beach if it could reliably be destroyed by a simple radio signal sent from outside U.S. territory?

The only answer had to be that the project was so important that there had to be both a primary and backup plan that were each damned near perfect, collectively pushing the odds to near unity.

Lu had come back on deck and was munching on an apple, balancing himself with the slow roll of the ship. The lights of New Smyrna Beach twinkled in the unstable night air, growing in brightness as the *Pampero* closed the coast. He turned and glanced down at the compass, apparently satisfied.

"Might be an interesting day, Bracken. I just picked up a radio talk show originating out of Fort Lauderdale. A spokesman for the protesters camped on the causeway says that at dawn four thousand of them are going to storm the National Guard positions. What is even more interesting is a report leaked by a local UPI news stringer. Fourteen of the top Star Wars scientists from Lawrence Livermore Laboratories were secretly flown in to the Cape yesterday by a military aircraft."

"Why's that such a big deal?"

"Eight of them are nuclear physicists who have worked on the nuclear-pumped X-ray laser experiments that have been conducted underground in the Nevada desert. This launch has all the appearances that your country is pursuing a secret nuclear weapons-in-space program."

"What about your own country's Star Wars program? I've read stuff about that phased-array radar site in Krasnoyarsk and the illegal testing of Soviet anti-ICBM missiles. *Jane's Defense Weekly* was quoted as saying that the USSR has spent 150 billion bucks on Star Wars over the last ten years. And you're telling me that the Soviet Union has clean hands?"

"Not absolutely clean, Bracken. Slightly smudged but not dirty. But if the U.S. successfully tests a nuclear-based Star Wars defense system, the more determined elements in the Politburo would argue for a preemptive strike before the U.S. could deploy such a system in depth. If *we*"—emphasizing the word—"stop this madness, we'll buy the world another decade of peace."

Nicely said. Convincing. But Bracken now knew that "stopping the madness" wasn't going to be bloodlessly done by the World Court serving a subpoena or the Soviets submitting electronic evidence to the U.N. Security Council. Nothing that neat. It was going to be done by the assassination of five military astronauts and the destruction of seven billion dollars' worth of hardware, all before the eyes of 260 million Americans glued to the tube. And if he could, he wasn't going to let that happen. Not if he died trying.

"Don't you agree?" Lu prompted.

"Whatever it takes."

Lu nodded, satisfied, and flicked the apple core overboard. "Good. Perhaps after this is over, Bracken, we'll think of each other as friends. And if not friends, then at least as associates who worked together for peace."

"I damn well doubt it," Bracken answered under his breath, but Lu didn't hear him, wasn't listening.

Lu glanced at his watch. He nodded toward the shore, now only a few miles away. "Once we cross the three-fathom line, I want you to turn farther south and parallel the shore. We have to be abeam the red flashing buoy by 0509. If you're running too fast, reduce sail. If we're behind schedule, use the engine to boost the speed."

"And then . . . ?"

"And then I'll tell you what to do. I'm going below to get a final satnav fix."

The stars were completely veiled over, the wind shifting into the northwest, picking up a little, blowing ten knots but gusty. The front was coming in faster than the forecasters had predicted. Bracken figured that even a launch schedule of 0715 would be cutting it close. He considered what would happen if NASA canceled and rescheduled for a day later.

The second time around would be Lu's last chance, he thought. Then considered the inherent danger. The *Pampero* had brought the Soviet/Cuban team to the right place at the right time. Lu and his buddies might not be able to sail the vessel, but they could operate it under power. Vierro had taken the trouble to check out the systems, knew how the engine was started, where the controls were. Plenty of diesel fuel, and Lu seemed to be a competent navigator. Bracken suddenly realized that his usefulness was at an end.

The left side of his brain's cold logic was interrupted by Lu coming back on deck, followed by Raul, Walrus, and Half-Ton bringing up the vanguard with an SMG slung over his neck at the ready.

Lu motioned Bracken. "We're nearly in the proper position. Turn south."

Putting the helm over, Bracken eased down to 180 magnetic and steadied on. As he fed out the mainsheet, Walrus trimmed the headsails.

At 0509 the *Pampero* was abeam the red flashing buoy. Lu checked the depth sounder and commanded, "Come about and anchor. You've got eighteen feet of water under the keel. Now, Bracken!"

Bracken gave a soft whistle and Walrus scuttled forward. Rounding up into the wind, Bracken let the schooner lose way, then whistled two long notes. The anchor let go, the chain running out, the *Pampero* snatching up hard. Walrus rang the ship's bell twice to indicate that the anchor had set. Then Bracken and Walrus dropped the main and headsails, just leaving the foresail up as a steadying sail. "Hook's down," he said to Lu. "What next?"

"Inflate the dinghy and attach the outboard motor. Make sure that the gas tank is full."

"What's the deal on the Walther?" Bracken whispered as they inflated the dinghy.

"Firing pin's still not working right, but it's getting better. Might take another hour of work."

"Damn!"

By the time Bracken and Walrus had pumped up the dinghy, launched it overboard, and attached the eighteen-horse outboard, Lu had his men mustered forward on the port side for some kind of last-minute briefing. Half-Ton stood aside, listening but holding a machine pistol negligently pointed in Bracken's and Walrus's direction. Trusting sod.

Lu flashed a penlight on the deck, and Vierro started to hand down the gear to Raul, who had dropped down into the dinghy. Sweet dreams, Bracken thought. There had been enough time to contaminate only six of the air bottles with the generator exhaust gas, but Bracken had selected the six bottles that were obviously new. The other three were scratched and slightly rusted, probably a backup set.

The loading took very little time, Lu driving them on with oaths. First the watertight container containing the ZSU, about six feet long and heavy by the look of it. Then a plastic bag which contained two underwater flashlights, a bang stick, and shells for it.

Until now Bracken hadn't been able to understand why Vierro was going in with Raul, but now it made sense. Raul was the shooter, and Vierro was in charge of protecting Raul from the occasional shark or barracuda. Due to the nearness of the Gulf Stream with its vast variety of game fish, sharks were a reality that the Florida Tourist Board didn't like to mention except in fine print. Lu had done his homework.

Bracken had owned a bang stick once. Just a simple single-shot gun barrel loaded with a .357 Magnum cartridge. If something with a bigger mouth than brains moseyed up to a diver, the bang stick could be jammed against the fish's snout and the impact fired the shell, blowing out the fish's brains. Messy but very effective.

Both Vierro and Lu were now passing down the scuba bottles; sets of three each, connected by a manifold with a regulator attached.

Even in the dim light of Lu's flashlight, Bracken saw that the second set of scuba bottles were not the new ones that he had contaminated with exhaust gas but the older ones he hadn't touched. He had just assumed that they were a spare set.

"Hey!" he cried. Half-Ton raised the machine pistol to Bracken's chest level as he approached Lu.

"What's the problem?" Lu's voice was flinty.

Pointing down at the bottles, Bracken shook his head. "Those were the spares. I didn't pump them up all the way because I ran out of ice to chill them down."

In the darkness from the dinghy, Raul swore, then took a flashlight and examined the pressure gauges. *"Dos mil ochocientas libras!"*

Wheeling on Bracken, Lu grabbed his Windbreaker, yanking him close with surprising strength. "Stupid bastard! You were supposed to fill all three sets of bottles. These are Raul's own personal bottles."

"Don't sweat it. I'll get the other set. They're pumped up to thirty-four hundred. Won't take a minute."

Raul spat out a stream of rapid-fire Spanish, too rapid for Bracken to understand.

Lu turned to Bracken. "He says he will dive only with his own bottles. They were a personal gift from Fidel, with whom Raul dives on occasion. The pressure is low but adequate, and we can't spare the time it would take to pump them up. The *Victoria* reported that the launch is scheduled for 0720 and there have been no delays in the countdown. Our man on the Cape reported that NASA is calling it a 'letter perfect' countdown. The Coast

Guard will be issuing a notice to mariners within an hour or so to clear the prohibited zone." Lu turned back to Raul. "You can get seven hours out of the bottles?"

"Sí, puedo. At least six and a half if I slow breath. But when I come back, I will want to talk to our captain. Alone." He flashed his teeth. "Just for a little while."

"Then go. And do your work well."

"It will be done, not well, but perfectly," Vierro replied. He flicked Lu a salute.

Half-Ton passed the machine pistol to Lu, then dropped lightly into the dinghy. On the second pull the engine started. Lu cast off the dinghy painter, and the inflatable boat disappeared into the blackness.

Long after the sound of the outboard engine was masked by the rising wind and sea, Lu stared into the darkness. He then turned, fished a cigarette from his pocket and lit it. "Humberto—Half-Ton as you call him—will be back in fifteen minutes. I want you to be ready to up anchor and head south by that time." The machine pistol was slung over his shoulder and he touched it. "I am going to monitor the radio channel from the Victoria. That will be a final confirmation that the launch is going well. You and your first mate will remain on deck. No lights, nothing unusual. I'm switching off the circuit breakers for the anchor windlass, the deck lights, navigational lights, and engine controls."

Bracken took a casual step toward him, but Lu brought up the machine pistol. "Nothing personal, Bracken. It's gone well. I want to be sure it ends that way. I'll pass up two beers. Just stay on deck and wait for me to give you further orders."

"Your show," Bracken said, freezing in place.

"Yes, actually it is." Lu stepped backward until he was at the companionway, then edged down the steps, the muzzle of the weapon covering the opening. Once down below, he closed the hatches, then was in the engine room throwing circuit breakers. The compass light blinked off. Bracken tried the spreader lights. Dead.

"Any doubts left?" asked Walrus.

"None." He glanced down at his watch. About an hour, forty minutes to launch. Not a long time. "Vierro will probably be dead fifteen minutes after he straps that air bottle back on, if not dead, then incapacitated. But Raul has clean air." He explained the contamination process to Walrus. "Any way you look at it, we have to go after Raul or alert the Coast Guard."

"Good luck on the Coast Guard, skip. From what I've seen, they'll still be asking you for your documentation number, whether your fire extinguishers are type-approved, and how many life vests you've got on board before they do bugger all."

Sad but true. In other maritime nations the Coast Guard recruits were drawn from coastal fishermen stock and allowed to exercise initiative. But for some bizarre reason, the U.S. Coast Guard thought that they could take farm boys, put them through twelve weeks of training, and then assign them to the rough coastal waters. The results were a disaster, although, credit to the kids, they tried. They tried so hard it hurt. Walrus was right. Slim chances of getting help from them.

The foresail traveler banged against its stops. In the predawn the wind was beginning to rise.

"How soon's Half-Ton going to be back?" Walrus asked.

Bracken glanced at his watch again. "Twelve minutes, maybe ten."

"So we just wait until he comes back? Then the score is two to two, but Lu has a weapon and we don't."

"Look, Walrus. Maybe Vierro conks out, maybe he doesn't, but Raul is still within thirty yards of the beach. Unless we get to him, he'll destroy the shuttle."

"Any ideas?"

"We've got to nail Lu." Which had a dismal chance of succeeding. A banzai charge down the companionway, facing a 40-round clip of 9mm shells would be suicidal, and they both knew it.

The foresail slammed against its stop again. The wind was picking up, and as the *Pampero* tacked over her anchor and the wind shifted, the foresail thundered from one tack to the other.

"We've got to drop the foresail," said Walrus. "Stitching isn't too good. The sail won't take it for much longer."

"Half-Ton will be back in less than ten minutes. Leave it up."

"Five more minutes and the damn canvas will split a seam."

It took two people on deck, minimum, to get the damn thing down and furled. Three was better. Click. The right side of Bracken's brain came through. "Okay, Walrus. We'll drop it. I'll get Lu up on deck. When I yell 'let go,' cast off the peak and throat halyards and the topping lifts all at once. Let everything run free—no easing it down."

"It'll drop like a rock." And then showed his white teeth in the darkness. "Gotcha!"

"Lu," Bracken yelled. "On deck!"

A muffled voice floated up from below.

"Get back, Bracken." Lu appeared in the companionway, two bottles of beer in his left hand, the machine pistol in his right. "What's the problem?"

"We've got to drop the foresail. The canvas is flogging itself to death. We'll need that sail to get across the Gulf Stream, and I don't have a spare."

"Then drop it, you damned idiot!"

"I need three—Walrus on the halyards, me to muzzle the booms, and one other person to help furl. I can't furl the damn thing myself." Which was pure baloney. To emphasize the point, the *Pampero* surged off on a port tack and the foresail whammed over, the traveler stops snatching up with a smash of metal on metal, the whole deck reverberating. Lu winced.

"All right, Bracken. You get on the outboard end of the booms and I'll try to keep the canvas from flogging. Just one thing—I don't want you to get within ten feet of me. You stay on the other side of the boom, and that goes for your mate." He waved the machine pistol. "I trust you to a certain extent but no further."

"No problem. We all want to get to the Bahamas in one piece. My word that we won't get near you."

Slinging the machine pistol's strap over his shoulder, Lu took up his position amidship, his hands lifted against the sail. Bracken was delaying, waiting for the *Pampero* to tack back over her anchor chain once more. It took another thirty seconds but she snatched up on the chain and tacked. Perfecto. Only another five seconds. He cast off the foresail sheet and yelled to Walrus, "Make ready to let go."

"Set!"

The foresail is a trapezoidal-shaped sail. The foot of the sail is laced to the foresail boom, which is kept horizontal by a topping lift made fast to its outboard end. Normally, the sail is lowered by slacking away on both the peak and throat halyards so that the gaff boom which is laced on to the head of the sail is lowered both evenly and gently. Eventually, if the process is done properly, the gaff boom rests on top of the foresail boom and then the sail can be furled between both booms. That's not exactly what Bracken had in mind.

"Let go!" Bracken yelled.

Six hundred and ten square feet of twelve-ounce Dacron came thundering down, along with the eighteen-foot foresail boom, followed by the even longer gaff boom. From aloft Bracken heard the twang of a line under great stress let go, howling through the topping lift's fiddle block.

Holding his hands up to muzzle the falling sail, realizing too late that not only the gaff boom was falling totally out of control but there was no topping lift line secured to stop its fall, Lu took the full weight of the foresail boom on his head and shoulder. The strap of his machine pistol broke under the force of the impact and went spinning away into the darkness. Bracken jumped on him, pinning his shoulders down under the mass of flogging canvas. Walrus piled on both of them, and together they wrestled Lu clear of the mess.

Lu was semi-conscious, his nose smashed flat. He spat out blood and retched.

Walrus hog-tied him with some sail ties, feet behind his back, legs strapped together and tied to his wrists. He played a flashlight on Lu to check his work, then on the sail. "Dammit! Blood and puke. Be a bastard to get the stains out."

Least of Bracken's worries. Now it would be two to one in Bracken's favor. "Let's get with it. Half-Ton is due back any minute. We can take him easy as he climbs aboard. He won't be armed."

"Guess again," said Walrus. "He carries a backup snub-nose revolver in an ankle holster. Thirty-eight caliber. Cop job."

"Shit!" Bracken made his decision. "You stay on deck. Find Lu's machine pistol and keep a listen out for Half-Ton. I'm going to try getting hold of the Coast Guard. Even if we don't nail Half-Ton, then at least someone will know." Without waiting for a reply, Bracken leapt over the coachroof and dropped down into the companionway, grabbed the banister railing and hung a U-turn into the aft cabin.

The cabin was a pigsty, bunks unmade and filthy, cigarette burns in the carpet, the head unspeakable.

The satnav was still on, spitting out redundant numbers, indicating that the *Pampero* was fixed in one position, speed zero, going nowhere. Radar off. Single-sideband radio off.

The VHF was screwed into the top of the dresser. He flicked the switch on, switched the channel selector to sixteen, and picked up the mike.

Two fishermen were yammering away on sixteen, both with powerful signals. Something about Lucy who worked at Freddie's Raw Bar.

Tits like you couldn't believe, buddy. She starts swinging them things and she'll damn near beat your head into mush. Lots of hard belly laughter.

"*Mayday, Mayday,*" Bracken yelled into the mike.

As Bracken released the mike button, he heard Old Buddy Number One, the stronger signal, still yacking about Lucy. His voice was so loud, it sounded as if he had swallowed the microphone. Bracken tried it again, shouting *Mayday* a couple of more times and no response from anyone, least of all Old Buddy Number Two, who was now giving a monologue on how his bank was fuckin' him over jus' 'cause he had missed a couple payments on his Camero.

Bracken switched to twenty-one, the Coast Guard working frequency.

"*Mayday, Mayday.* Yacht *Pampero,* Whiskey Bravo six five four zero. Anyone copy this transmission?"

Immediately, a soft-spoken Florida cracker voice answered back, the accent smacking of deep-fried magnolia blossoms, hush pone, and corn puppies. Or whatever the hell it was that they ate down here.

"*Vessel calling, please say again your vessel's name and callsign. Here is U.S. Coast Guard Station, Vero Beach, Florida.*"

Bless you, my man, he thought, then keyed the mike. "Yacht *Pampero,* Whiskey Bravo six five four zero. I have an emergency."

"*Capt'n, is your vessel in immediate danger of sinkin' or do you have a critical medical emergency on board?*"

As usual, he had put his mouth in motion before engaging his brain. "No. But we're off the Cape and there's a guy swimming in . . . no . . . actually he's in a dinghy but . . ." He couldn't think of how to phrase it. "He's got a rifle," he blurted out.

Corn Puppie paused to digest this and then came back. "*State your position, Capt'n, and say again the name of your vessel.*"

Walrus rapped hard on the aft cabin hatch, and Bracken cranked it open.

"Trouble, skip. I can hear the dinghy motor."

The speaker on the radio crackled. "*Vessel in distress. I say again. State your position, Cap, and give me the name of your vessel, identifying information, name of the owner, and documentation number.*"

Bracken ignored the radio. "Did you find Lu's machine pistol?"

"Nowhere. It must have gone overboard when he got hit by the boom."

"*Balls!*" No time for the radio now. No time for anything except stopping Half-Ton. Ran to the engine room and threw all the circuit breakers on, then made it up the companionway in three triple-step strides. Couldn't hear the outboard over the sigh of the rising wind, then did. Somewhere behind the *Pampero*, coming up slowly, cautiously, the engine throttled down to an idle.

"You got any ideas, skip?" said Walrus, suddenly beside him, crouched down.

Bracken didn't. "We rush him, I guess."

Walrus passed Bracken a belaying pin. It seemed puny, but it was solid bronze, weighing maybe eight or nine pounds.

Bracken had a lead lump in the stomach, his nerves fluttering like a flag in the wind. Belaying pins versus a .38 Special would be no contest. "Okay, we give it a go. But if he drops the bow painter to the dinghy, the first one of us free dives overboard and goes after it. We'll need the dinghy to get to Raul."

"Hate like hell getting salt water in the mustache," Walrus said under his breath.

They both moved aft, scrunched down, then stretched out flat on the deck either side of the mainsail sheet traveler. Half-Ton could come up either side of the cockpit, a fifty-fifty proposition.

Dinghy motor louder now, twenty feet, ten, then only a few feet away. The engine throttled back and died. Bracken could hear the waves slapping under the bow of the dinghy as it drifted in under the transom. It sounded like Half-Ton was on the port side, Bracken's territory to defend. He gripped the belaying pin tighter, the sweat making the pin slippery in his hand.

A coil of line snaked up into the cockpit; the dinghy painter. Half-Ton was getting ready to come aboard.

There was a guttural call in Spanish. Repeated twice more.

The radio squawked from down below, calling the *Pampero*, followed by an unintelligible list of questions. Bracken could hear Half-Ton's sharp intake of breath. He might not understand English well, but the radio was a dead giveaway that something unplanned had happened.

From the opposite side of the cockpit Walrus stood up, almost casually. "Your boss is down below on the radio. He asked me to give you a hand." Walrus's voice was even and casual, as if all this were what he had been told to do.

Half-Ton suddenly stood up in the dinghy, almost at eye level with Bracken, but with the .38 traversing toward Walrus. There wasn't room for Bracken to swing the belaying pin, so he stiff-armed with the end of it, thrusting into Half-Ton's face.

It wasn't a solid hit, more of a glancing blow. The .38 roared, the explosion deafening, the muzzle blast blinding. One more shot with the simultaneous shock wave concussion of a bullet passing too close. Too damn close. Bracken caught a glimpse of Walrus overhanding his belaying pin and a clatter of metal on wood. Then nothing for thirty seconds.

Walrus's voice close to him. "You okay?"

"Think so."

"I caught a quick glimpse of him. He's hunched down in the dinghy. I think you hurt him but not that badly. I missed."

"You wounded?"

Walrus flattened himself onto the deck. "Nicked my flipper. Stings, but it's all right. Any other fuckin' bright ideas?"

The dinghy painter line was slowly paying out, as though either Half-Ton were retrieving it or the dinghy were just floating astern, dragging the line with it. Bracken grabbed the bitter end of the painter and threw it over a cleat, then took two turns to secure it. The line paid out some more, then came taut. Time for plan two, whatever that was.

"So here's the situation," Bracken whispered, falling into the set solutions of Officer's Leadership Training 101. Lesson one: Let the troops in on your plan even if you don't have one. It was supposed to build confidence. "He can't come over the transom without risking us bashing him. And he can't get a direct shot at us without standing up and exposing himself. But we're pinned down."

"Terrific! So what do we do? Sling beer bottles at him?" Walrus hesitated for a heartbeat, then gripped Bracken's wrist. "Listen up!" There was the faint sound of sawing, a slight vibration on the dinghy painter. "He's cutting the painter, trying to get away."

Which meant that Half-Ton had to be leaning over the bow of the dinghy, probably holding on with one hand, using his knife with the other. And unless he had a third hand to hold the .38 . . .

Uncleating the painter and passing it to Walrus, Bracken

whispered, "Yank on the painter—everything you've got when I say 'Go.'"

He reached across the cockpit, tracing down the row of switches with his fingertips until he found the right one, turned back to Walrus, who now had the dinghy painter in both hands. "And ready . . . set . . ." He flicked on the switch to the mainmast spreader lights, then jumped to his feet, the belaying pin swung back. "*Go!*"

Half-Ton had the .38 in his right hand, a knife in his left, still bent over trying to cut the painter, now looking up. Bracken threw the belaying pin, which careened off Half-Ton's shoulder. With Bracken frozen, silhouetted against the spreader lights, Half-Ton raised the revolver, taking aim just as the dinghy painter jerked taut. The shot went high and wild. The dinghy was jerked forward and Half-Ton, caught off balance, stumbled backward. Another jerk and Half-Ton fell over the dinghy's outboard, getting off another shot as he fell, then landing flat on his back in the water. There was thrashing. Half-Ton had dropped the revolver, his arms churning at the water, frantic, trying to swim back to the dinghy.

"Poor bastard can't swim too well," Bracken said. He picked up a horseshoe life preserver and tossed it, the preserver, caught by the wind, sailing past the Cuban's windmilling arms.

Half-Ton seemed to hesitate, then turned downwind, stroking doggedly toward the white shape of the preserver that bobbed on the waves.

"Why the hell did you do that?" Walrus yelled. "Let the bastard sink!"

"He can't swim back here with a life preserver wrapped around his neck. Minimum of a half-knot current running. He'll be in Palm Beach by tomorrow morning if the sharks aren't hungry."

They watched for another minute. The automatic strobe light on the preserver winked on, but it diminished in intensity as it blew downwind. No one, Bracken realized, could swim for long against a half-knot current. He realized he was shivering and yet not cold.

Walrus lit a Camel and flicked the match away into the darkness. "Seems we won the first inning, skip."

"Yeah, but like the man said," Bracken replied, "it ain't over till it's over."

*　　*　　*

About half an hour to sunup. First pale streaks of dawn already lit in the windy sky. Bracken had some time to play with, but not much.

Between the two of them, they had humped Lu below and strapped him down in one of the aft cabin bunks. He wasn't in good shape, still semi-conscious, dribbling blood from his nose.

"May be internal hemorrhaging, possibly a concussion," Walrus said.

"We can't do anything for him right now." Bracken cinched up the last strap, then laid on a couple of overhand knots. Lu, even in the pink of health and vitality, wasn't going anywhere. "I'll try the VHF," he said over his shoulder.

He called Corn Puppie on Channel 21. No reply at first. Then a slick East Coast voice came up on the frequency.

"Pampero, *this is U.S. Coast Guard, Vero Beach. You read me?*" The voice of authority, obviously an officer or petty officer.

Bracken stiffened, now cautious. "Vero Beach, this is the *Pampero*. I've got an emergency situation. You copy that?"

"Pampero. *This is Lieutenant Commander Gage of the U.S. Coast Guard. Please state your position and the name of the master of the vessel.*"

Involuntarily, Bracken's eyes flicked to the satnav. Twenty-eight, thirty-seven point five north, eighty thirty-three point six west. He was about to reply when he saw Walrus shaking his head.

"What's the matter?"

Walrus was watching him intently, hand wrapped in a bloody rag. "You gave them the *Pampero*'s name and call sign before. Think about it. They undoubtedly checked their computer like good little bean counters. The *Pampero* has a lien on it, and you're still listed as master. You've got a felony rap on record for leaving the country illegally. Add to that what your lady said about you being suspected of drug running. The Coast Guard and the Drug Enforcement Agency probably share their hit lists. Regardless of what you tell them, the Coast Guard is first going to want to lay their grubby hands on both this boat and your body before they do anything else."

And if they didn't believe him right now and act on his information, the shuttle would die. With the mike in his hand, he was caught between the extremes of what *is* and what *if*. There was no choice. He had to make them believe.

"Coast Guard, Vero Beach, this is the *Pampero*. You've got hostile Cubans in the water off Cape Canaveral."

"*Say again, sailing vessel* Pampero. *Your last transmission was broken up.*"

Bracken raised the mike to his lips, about to transmit again, but Walrus snatched it out of his hand. "So maybe they didn't read your last transmission, but think hard, skip. You ever tell them that you were a sailing vessel?"

"No."

"Then how in hell would they know? That sucker screwed up by blurbing information he got off the computer but regardless, you can bet your ass that what he's trying to do is get you to talk long enough so that his people can get a radio bearing on you."

Another case of damned if you do and damned if you don't. Walrus was right. Bracken nodded and turned off the power to the radio.

Bracken checked his watch. Five thirty-eight. Dawn would be in another ten minutes. And with first light there would be patrol choppers and aircraft sweeping the area off the Cape, herding stray vessels out of the impact zone. Followed by patrolling Coast Guard crash boats until just before the launch, but they would be too late to stop Raul.

"We have to go in and find them," Bracken said.

Walrus shrugged. "I figured."

They weren't able to put together much in the way of equipment—only an old scuba bottle which Bracken kept on board in case the prop fouled on a fish-pot float, a regulator and weight belt, a corroded spear gun, assorted flippers, and face masks.

The light was stronger as they pulled away from the *Pampero* in the dinghy. Bracken was steering the outboard, running in on the range that was shown in the photographs—two eight one degrees magnetic, lined up on a railroad water tower north of Titusville.

Bracken shifted forward on the port gunwale of the dinghy, opposite Walrus. The Zodiac inflatable slowly picked up speed as it came up onto the plane.

Spray from the steep chop pelted them, the occasional larger sea throwing solid water in sheets which were wiped by the wind across their bodies.

As the light became stronger, Bracken could begin to pick out launch pad 39 to the south; a mass of angled girders and

multiple cylindrical shapes of the shuttle gleaming under spotlights in the half dawn.

"He's going to hear the outboard coming," Walrus yelled
over the roar of the motor.

Bracken nodded. A diver underwater would first hear the
buzz of the outboard's prop, then the hollow cough of the outboard's engine exhaust long before an outboard could be heard
over the open water. Except that Raul and Vierro had instructions to stay on the bottom until fifteen minutes before the time
of the launch. Raul would hear but he wouldn't react.

"How we doing on the cross bearing?" Bracken shouted.

Walrus took the hand-bearing compass and swung it toward
the north, sighting over it. "Another twelve degrees to go. Say a
quarter of a mile on your present heading. You figure what we're
going to do?"

Bracken throttled back. The Zodiac came off the plane and
mushed down to a crawl. They had covered the distance faster
than he had estimated.

It was easier to talk now with the noise abatement program
in effect. Bracken then shifted to neutral and cut the engine. The
Zodiac slowed, then wallowed sideways in the swell.

He started to strap on the scuba tank harness. "I'll swim
toward the shore on this heading. Raul and Vierro are down on
the bottom somewhere just outside of the surf line. I should be
able to find them."

"Give me the scuba pack, skip. You're getting too old for this
stuff. I'm a better diver, I'm eight years younger, and you don't
know snot about hand-to-hand combat."

Bracken, bent over adjusting the belt strap, looked up at
Walrus. He thought about it. Everything Walrus said was true
except that one additional problem complicated the situation.
Neither one of them had discussed the obvious—that Raul had a
.44 Magnum bang stick for killing sharks. Substitute the word
man for *sharks* in this case. Walrus was right except that he was
wrong. This wasn't his fight. He shook his head.

Walrus shrugged. "What do you want me to do?"

"Head north for a minute or so at low speed, then alter
heading straight toward the shore. If he hears the outboard
motor, he'll be distracted. It'll divert his attention. I'll come up
behind him."

"And if you don't get him?"

"Hide in the dunes. He has to set up the rifle, sight the damn thing in. Nail him with a rock. Stick a scorpion up his ass. Use your imagination, Walrus."

"Honest to God, skip. I keep telling you that you've been reading too many of those Clive Cussler novels." Walrus quickly lit a cigarette. He passed it to Bracken, who took a puff and passed it back. "You sure you want to do it this way?"

"Yep." He stuck out his hand and Walrus held it briefly.

"Good luck," Walrus said softly.

Bracken stuck the regulator in his mouth, grabbed the spear gun, and rolled backward into the sea.

19.

July 19, 0611 hours

The muffled splashing of waves and whistling of wind diminished as he dove deeper, replaced by the hollow sound of his own irregular breathing, the rasp of the regulator as he inhaled, and the burble of expanding air bubbles trailing upward from his exhaust valve.

Visibility was less than twenty feet, limited by a blue-green haze of plankton and debris slowly sinking toward the seabed. A couple of small mackerels swished by him, curious, S-turning as they looked back, then darting away into the dusky depths.

Bracken checked the compass. Not a proper diver's compass, but the hand-held one Walrus had used. It was difficult to read but adequate. He would have to drop it once he spotted the Cubans. Scratch one hundred and eight bucks of gear bought at Loulou's in St. Barts. Right now it was invaluable at any price.

He kicked downward, clearing his ears as he went, trying to keep his breathing regular, conserving precious air.

Bearing. He looked down at the compass again. He was twenty degrees off heading. Damn hard to swim on a straight heading in this murk. He altered course, trying to compensate.

Unexpectedly, he brushed the bottom, not seeing it immediately. Almost featureless sand; just a few blades of sea grass sticking up and the occasional mound which marked the habitat of a shellfish. Checked the compass once more. On heading.

He guessed he was at fifty feet of depth, maybe slightly less. Still kicking his swim fins, he flippered along on his heading, following the bottom contour, trying to keep his visible profile as minimal as possible.

The spear gun was Spanish made, three years old. As usual, he had bought the cheapest model, just something suitable to nail reef fish with for the dinner pot or for charter guests to ward off imaginary sea monsters. The damn thing was a toy, a nickel-and-dime gadget that wouldn't stop a three-foot moray eel, let alone a man.

Enough time had elapsed for the contaminated air to be taking effect on Vierro. Raul's only options would be to share his own uncontaminated air by buddy-breathing or to abandon Vierro. Bracken could guess which course he would choose. Raul was a professional with all the compassion of a block of ice.

Bracken tried to put himself in Raul's head. Lying on the bottom, perhaps shifting around in the undertow, sucking air at a slow-breathing rate, concerned with Vierro. There would be no direct evidence of anything wrong, but Raul would reasonably conclude that Vierro's tanks had been contaminated, had been contaminated during the top-up charging on the *Pampero*.

What would he be doing now? Watching the minutes tick by, perhaps super-sensitive to any sound or dusky shape on the limits of his vision, fingering the bang stick, ready. Unlike his own spear gun, the bang stick could tear away flesh in a great gouge of red-black blood and entrails. Which would bring in the sharks, first milling around, then in slashing attacks and a feeding frenzy until the sea was a pool of bloody offal. Not good thoughts. Not something, Bracken realized, he should be thinking about.

Bracken picked up the faint hum of the outboard. Not distinct but still there: a muffled blur of sound to his right, the noise first getting closer, then slowly fading, its direction indeterminate.

What would Raul be thinking now if he heard it as well? Panic? Not likely. He would probably be wondering what kind of boat was up there on the surface and what it was doing: a local fish boat, Coast Guard, maybe just some kind of NASA patrol sweeping up the coastline in the last few minutes before the launch, checking the area for stragglers?

Still, Raul's instructions covered that contingency. Stay on the bottom until fifteen minutes before the scheduled launch time and then surface. Get a last-minute update by radio, then go ashore in the dunes and set up the long gun with the telescopic sights, sighting in on launch pad 39B, zeroing in on the solid rocket booster between stations 1491 and 1498, just above the field joint, just as the manual instructed. All the press, all the media pundits, all the Monday morning quarterbacks, all the NASA and Department of Defense–bashers would say with suitable sorrow, "We told you so." And their proof would be endlessly replayed videos of flaming wreckage cartwheeling out of a cloud of smoke and fire.

The seabed began to rise beneath him, slowly sloping upward. He stroked past a few outcroppings of fire coral, past slowly waving sea fans, past an immense squadron of tiny silver fish, all of them swimming individually, yet each perfectly spaced apart from its wing mates and maintaining precise position in the formation as the squadron instantaneously changed direction. How in hell did they do it? What signals were given, who led the pack, why such abrupt changes in direction and where were they going? He made a mental note to find out. Probably in some back issue of the *National Geographic* if he lived to read about it.

Checked the compass again. About five degrees to the right, but he estimated that it was a good heading, offsetting the inshore counter-current drift to the south.

Which way would they be lying? Facing to seaward or toward the shore? The bang stick—what was its lethal range? All unknowns. Bracken tried to clear his mind of doubt.

The visibility was clearing slightly and he felt the surge of wave action above him as he swam upward, following the rising seabed. Bracken's ears popped with the decrease in pressure. He looked above him through his fogged swim mask and saw the surface, the roiling interface between water and air, the dawn light dimly backlighting it with shafts of red and orange.

He consulted his compass again. Maybe a little off to the north of the bearing. Raul and Vierro had to be somewhere along this contour, most probably to the south, and if Raul had followed the range in toward the shore, no more than fifty yards away.

Bracken checked the spear gun. Cocked to the second notch. He thumbed off the safety, holding the gun out in front of him, and flippered through a slow turn to the left. He knew that he had the element of surprise going for him, but he would have only one shot.

More fish now, patrolling the backwash of the waves, the biggies feeding on the smaller ones. The torpedo shape of a big barracuda flashed by him, also heading south. Overall size, five feet, maybe six. The 'cuda then circled to the east, lost momentarily in the low visibility, and came roaring by again, its walleye glaring at Bracken as if he were intruding on exclusive territorial domain.

Barracudas were safe, right? That's what everyone said. Bad eyesight but not man-gobblers, right? They swam with their mouths open, displaying great interlocking sets of jagged teeth. He had heard it all before on dry land, not deep in a hostile sea with a hundred pounds of lethal propellant and a warhead of teeth whistling by.

The 'cuda disappeared in the haze ahead of him, undoubtedly pulling a fast U-turn to make a pass. Bracken had heard of the rare 'cuda attacks. Not in clear deep water, but in surf where the visibility was restricted. They went for bright flashy stuff, like wristwatches and ID bracelets. Like *my* diving watch—a Japanese digital thing with a polished stainless steel band. He froze, drifting toward the seabed, tucking the spear gun under his armpit, then frantically pulling at the catch on the wristband. It came loose and he stuffed it in the crotch of his swimsuit. Dumb! You couldn't get any dumber. And in the present circumstances, dumb equalled dead.

He caught the movement out of the left side of his face mask and turned toward it, decreasing his profile. Slowed his kick, getting the spear gun up and aimed. Still too far away, maybe fifteen yards, just on the limit of visibility. Bracken eased down toward the bottom, trying to minimize his profile, a sea fan racking over his chest with a feather brush of soft black lace.

He couldn't make out which one of the Cubans it was because both had been wearing wet suits and dive masks that covered most of their face, but then he saw that the tanks on the man were the newer ones, a dull uniform gray. Vierro! But where the hell was Raul?

Bracken swiveled his neck around trying to see him, holding his exhalation so that no air bubbles would give away his position.

Vierro was lying on the sandy bottom, body movements sluggish, weakly paddling his hands as if he were trying to go somewhere. By now he would be half brain-dead. It was Vierro that had the bang stick. Like they said, God was on the side of the Big Guns.

Using his left hand to claw at the sea grass, he pulled himself forward slowly, closing the distance, the spear gun held at the ready in his right hand. He allowed himself a slow exhalation and gulped in fresh air. Distance now to five yards, closing, closing.

Then he saw Raul, first just the top of his head, then his face. Raul was directly behind Vierro, kneeling in the sand, methodically going over Vierro's hose connections and pressure gauge. He must have heard the eruption of bubbles, because he looked up suddenly.

And saw me, Bracken knew. Couldn't miss me.

Scrambling, Raul was raising a cloud of fine sand and silt, searching for something on the seabed, and came up with it, the muzzle of the bang stick swinging toward Bracken.

It wasn't the type of bang stick that Bracken had used some six years back. In those days, a bang stick was a single-shot defense weapon that you actually had to forcefully prod against whatever it was you were trying to discourage from eating you. But this thing was all the rage with the macho diving set, built in California and aptly called the Big Banger. It was reloadable underwater, and instead of being shoved against a predator, it could be fired with a trigger and still had a lethal range of over three feet underwater. Bracken had seen one advertised in *Sport Diver* a month before and thought the whole idea of bang sticks was silly. Then. Not now. Not as he looked down the bore of the muzzle, which held a .44 Magnum cartridge.

Bracken was still over six feet away. If Raul fired now, the projectile might make a dent in him, but it wouldn't be lethal. But there was no choice. He had to get closer because his own spear gun was a low-powered toy, and any killing shot would have to be to the chest or gut from within a few feet of range.

All his brain cells were screaming at him to turn and run. But he knew that was the ultimate trap because Raul was at least fifteen years younger and not burdened with soggy muscles and residual alcoholic calories. That would be a closed-end contest with the final act being a bang stick shoved up his buns. He extended his spear gun, rushing toward the two bodies in a blur of bubbles and silt, gulping air like a hungry compressor.

Raul had his hands around Vierro's waist, doing something. Then Vierro's weight belt dropped away and, free of the lead weights, he started to drift toward the surface, making little pawing movements.

Distraction. Bracken had lifted his spear gun as Vierro rose from the bottom, then had to bring it back down to Raul, but Raul was also rising behind Vierro, the bang stick retraining on Bracken's chest. As his hand aimed the bang stick, he exposed more of his body and head.

Bracken squeezed the trigger, feeling the spear gun buck in his hand. Then ducked, flailing his feet, porpoising downward toward the bottom, not even knowing where the shaft had gone, knowing only that he had to put distance between himself and Raul, who would be firing any second.

The torpedo flew past Bracken's head, only a foot away. He had the impression of an endless freight train passing him at high speed. Like when he was a kid and the gang that he ran with dared one another to see how close they could stand to the tracks when the southbound from Portland rattled through. But this time the freight train was a barracuda on a strafing run.

There was an explosion in the water in front of him, then a mushrooming cloud of black-brown blood and guts blossoming outward from the core of the concussion.

Backpedaling, unable to slow himself, twisting his body, trying to avoid swimming in the mess, he skirted through the edge, a string of bloody intestine and gore flowing past his face mask, the entrails slithering over his shoulder.

The 'cuda had bought it, its belly blown away but still working its jaw, fins still flopping, not knowing that it was dead.

Bracken discarded the spear gun and pulled out his knife from the plastic sheath on his leg. Caught sight of Raul, all in one piece, shifting sideways, blocking Bracken's escape route. He was frantically reloading the bang stick.

Bracken rang up flank speed to his failing leg muscles and flailed his flippers, closing the distance.

Mistake, bad mistake, because Raul, cool as ice cream, made a calculation of deflection, distance, and closing speed, then rammed home the cartridge and locked the breach. In slow motion he raised the bang stick and homed in on Bracken's chest, waiting for the collision between projectile and body, more than a half second ahead of time.

Reaching out to his full stretch, Bracken deflected the bang stick with his left hand, rolled half inverted, and sliced across Raul's chest with the sawtooth edge of the blade. Felt the impact right up through his stiffened arm, jarring against his shoulder socket. Saw Raul's face close up, just the eyes wide in pain, and the sudden explosion of bubbles from Raul's face mask. The Cuban pushed Bracken off with his feet, desperately trying to bring his bang stick up for the fatal shot.

There was a raw slice of red across Raul's chest, but his rib cage had deflected the point of the knife. He was leaking blood but no open flaps of skin, just seepage.

Curtain time. In the back of Bracken's brain his clever, ever-clamoring neurotransmitters calculated that it was now three to zero and even the Little League would ship Bracken out to the sandlots for this kind of continued dud performance. Except he wasn't listening, just reacting. He twisted upright, clawing for the surface, waiting for the slug to tear a tunnel through his belly.

He felt then heard the explosion, the shock wave of the slug as it tore through the water next to his left ear, realizing that Raul had also missed, then folded his body double and kicked downward.

Raul already had another cartridge out, chambering it. Not quite.

Bracken battered into him with the knife, gouging out a streak of flesh from Raul's shoulder. Overshot, twisted, turned, flippered back, Raul locking the breach of the bang stick, raising it, finger curling around the trigger. In Bracken's mind, each microsecond an individual frame of film, all action nearly stopped, as if there were a near suspension in time.

As with the birth of the universe, his neurotransmitters recorded for posterity the big bang. Molten-hot iron tore through his side, end-all, be-all, world without end, praise God, the Father, the Son, and the Holy Ghost were on his lips except that it was over and finished and just beginning. Clawing up toward the surface, sunlight hard on the interface of sea and sky, then breaking through the waves, seeing raw daylight.

Another express train knocked him aside, heading south and down, whooshing the wind out of him and tearing off skin from his shoulder with a ten-foot sheet of coarse sandpaper.

Bracken flung off his regulator and face mask, gasping for air, choking on a lungful of seawater.

Two more sharks were coming in from the east like a pair of Doberman pinschers competing for a platter of raw meat. He bunched his body up in the fetal position, unconsciously covering his testicles with his hands because there was that thing he had read in a magazine and it had stayed tucked away in the ultimate-fears locker of his mind: the bastards always ate the most tender parts first.

The twin set of sharks streaked past him, fins clipping the surface of the water and then going under in a streak of foam, the famous first pass, maybe even a second, but then the attack.

Bracken tried to turn to face them, pulling his legs up against his body, taking salt water in his mouth and eyes, his neat neurotransmitters no longer detached and logical, all of them howling together in a chorus of primitive fear.

The water around him was laced with tendrils of blood and

offal, all boiling up to the surface like stew in a giant cauldron. More sharks to the south, maybe five boring in. Slashing at one another, twisting, screwing up and down through the water, breaching the surface in a feeding frenzy.

He never heard it coming. His arm was nearly yanked from its socket. He started to lash out with his free fist, then realized what was happening. The dinghy was next to him, still moving fast. Walrus had a wrist lock on him, trying to pull him up over the gunwale. The rubber fabric was slippery, and Bracken was coughing explosively, the salt water that he had swallowed gagging him.

"Get in the goddamned boat! Two of them are headed right for you!"

Flailing his feet, grabbing wildly with his free hand for something to get a hold on, Bracken floundered over the side of the gunwale and collapsed on the floorboards of the dinghy. He braced himself for the impact. There was a violent thump and the dinghy rocked sideways as if it had hit a submerged rock, then slewed around through 180 degrees in a smother of foam. A second fin streaked past, the tip a good two feet clear of the water, the skin mottled white and laced with scars, the eye of the shark as big and black as an eight ball.

Walrus twisted the grip on the motor, increasing the speed of the outboard, then turned and headed out to sea. Bracken hung on grimly, the pounding of the dinghy against the waves an agony, thinking he was going to faint, bile filling his throat. He retched over the side, spewing vomit against the side of the dinghy. Then looked back. The twin set of sharks were matching the dinghy's speed, arrowing in on them. Bracken didn't have to tell him, because Walrus had seen them, too, and increased the power setting to maximum. The dinghy came up on the plane, snapping off the tops of waves, starting to outpace the sharks, who then unaccountably veered off to the south on a divergent course.

Walrus pointed. Twenty yards off to starboard was Vierro, scuba tanks still strapped on, wallowing in the sea, a spear sticking in his shoulder. He waved weakly and took a stroke toward the dinghy.

The sharks hit him in an explosion of white water and foam, turning the sea red. Like two unruly children disputing the ownership of a rag doll, they tore off in separate directions, parts of Vierro clamped in their jaws. It was all over in seconds. A smaller shark came in to clean up the picnic area while the twin set peeled off inshore for bloodier pastures.

Walrus slowly eased off on the throttle, smoothing the ride. He tore off his T-shirt and leaned down to Bracken.

"One hell of a way to lose weight, skip," he said, pressing the cotton into the wound on Bracken's side.

Just after dawn, with the sun a red hot disk on the eastern horizon, the wind building from the north, and the seas kicking up whitecaps, Walrus boosted Bracken out of the dinghy, over the rail, and onto the deck of the *Pampero*.

He braced Bracken up against the coachroof and went below, then came back with the medical kit. "I'm not going to give you a full syringe of morphine—just prick around the wound with a third of a tube to give you a local anesthetic. That okay with you?"

Bracken nodded. He wanted the whole damn thing, but he also knew that Walrus would need him to get the *Pampero* out of Florida waters and on its way to the Bahamas.

After punching around the edge of the wound, Walrus washed out the torn flesh with vodka, dusted it with antibiotics, and sutured it with a sail needle and Dacron thread. "Just a flesh wound," he commented, pulling up the last stitch and tying it off with an overhand hitch. "Clean through the fat on your hip. Maybe nicked a rib. How's that feel?" Bracken groaned convincingly. "Okay, so it hurts. Don't make a big deal over it."

Putting a compress over the wound, Walrus cross-hatched it with silver duct tape. "Take two large bottles of Mount Gay and call me in the morning." He wiped his hands on his jeans. "You think you got Raul?"

"He was leaking blood from a couple of pokes that I gave him. Don't think that it was enough to kill, but the sharks will take care of that. Raul's most likely getting a close-up look at some hammerhead's intestinal tract by now." Giddy with the morphine, Bracken giggled. Figured that by noon Raul would be shark shit—tanks, mask, weight belts, and all.

The sun had turned from red to gold, now above the horizon by the span of a couple of fingers. They had to get going, to get out of there before the Coast Guard patrols started sweeping the area. If they were boarded, then there would be no way to get Jean off the *Victoria*.

Bracken started the engine, then put the gear in forward, motoring up over the chain as the anchor windlass pulled in the links. Walrus heaved on the halyards, raising the main and foresail. With this weight of wind, Bracken thought it would be prudent to tuck in a reef, bend on the smaller jib, but there wasn't time and he couldn't afford to be prudent.

The colonel would be waiting for word on the radio that the shuttle had been destroyed. If it wasn't, what then? If he understood it right, the colonel would wait for the launch and then somehow destroy the shuttle.

The thought occurred to him again. Call the Coast Guard? But that would require them boarding the *Pampero* and the inevitable delays involving coordination with the Bahamian authorities. Bahamian sovereign territory. And there wasn't good blood between the two countries.

He thought about the single-sideband radio. Long range hardware. He might be able to contact NASA directly, but on what frequency? Lu would know how to work the damn thing. But even if he were able to fire up the transmitter and find the frequency, there would be the question of credibility. At best, they'd figure he was some crazy; at worst, they'd believe him, resulting in a squad of Bahamian police storming the *Victoria*. No win either way. He only had one card to play. Lu's knowledge of phase two—the password.

With the mainsail and foresail up, the anchor chain came taut and broke out of the sandy bottom. Walrus catted it, then hoisted the fore staysail and jib. In ten minutes the *Pampero* was hammering across the Gulf Stream on a broad reach, seas breaking heavily across the deck. More than ninety miles to go, but with luck, he'd be there by sundown. What he'd do when he got there, he hadn't a clue.

0812 hours

Bracken was on the helm, his side a dull ache, woolly-headed. Walrus had gone below earlier and now reemerged with two warm beers. "Lu's coherent but he's bitching about the pain. Wants a pill. There's some rat poison under the galley sink."

Bracken turned the helm over to Walrus. "Steer about one forty-five. I'll check the satnav on the hour and give you a course alteration."

A duck of the head from Walrus in acknowledgment.

On deck, the *Pampero* had felt solid, but below he sensed the whole structure of the ship shuddering and working as she slammed into the combers of the Gulf Stream. Already, he heard bilge water sloshing against the cabin sole. It would be an endless day, and already short on sleep and long on pain, he didn't know whether he would see another dawn. He smiled to himself. What the hell, I need the rest if it works out that way.

Lu's face had the texture and color of unbaked bread dough, pasty gray, and was sweating beads of moisture. His eyes were open. He rolled them sideways as Bracken entered the aft cabin.

"Where are Vierro and Raul?" His voice was a raw whisper.

"Fish food."

"Humberto . . . ?"

"Half-Ton, you mean. Don't know exactly. He decided to go swimming. Probably all the way down to West Palm by now. But no sweat. As soon as he wades ashore, the immigration people will give him on-the-spot citizenship, a year's supply of food stamps, and a lifetime membership in the polo club."

Lu turned his head away. "Your sense of humor evades me, Bracken. The shuttle . . . ?"

"It hasn't been launched yet. If it had, we'd have seen it go. Sorry about the loss of your twenty-three-millimeter telemetry gear. I'd love to have turned it over to the World Court or the U.N. Wonder what the result would have been."

"Nothing, Bracken. Both Vierro and Raul were Cuban DGI operatives that were sent to the U.S. during Carter's Mariel boat lift. Each of them has a U.S. residency permit. If they had been caught, it was set up so the authorities would have concluded that they were terrorists from some radical anti-Castro group. Obviously, that's why we used Cubans in this part of the operation. No Soviet fingerprints on the operation." He turned back to Bracken. "I want to be untied, Bracken. And some painkiller."

He wanted to enjoy this moment but couldn't. Tried to dredge up memories of his arm sockets popping out, of the bamboo rods, of Willie, but it seemed so distant, so vague. "Where's it hurt?"

"Shoulder and chest. Nose is broken. My head, mainly. Throbbing."

Bracken bent over him, first examining Lu's eyes. Funny. One contact gone, the other still in—one eye blue and one eye brown like a Siamese cat that Penny had owned. The pupils were dilated, not a good vital sign. Felt Lu's forehead. Cold and clammy, profuse sweating. He had not the foggiest idea of a prognosis, only that Lu might have a concussion.

The nose not just broken, it was mashed flat. There was swollen tissue; the flesh under the eyes was turning purple. He stripped back the shirt. Bruised, rash burns, and contusions but nothing obviously broken. Then the head. A real egg but nothing mushy, only tender as hell.

"*God!*" Lu screamed as Bracken probed.

"Nothing wrong with you. I've seen worse. Problem is, what to do with you."

"Cut me loose." Still trying to control, Bracken thought. Some people never give it up.

"Don't go away. I've got to see whether I've got anything to kill the pain."

Bracken popped up the companionway. Walrus was into the second beer, muttering to himself.

"Any signs of a launch?" yelled Bracken, competing with the wind.

Thumbs down.

Down below again, Bracken turned on the ship's broadcast radio. It took five minutes of sports scores and three minutes of commercials before he learned the fate of the shuttle. Gun shy, the countdown was still holding, but there was some speculation by the experts of rescheduling the launch for the next morning. High wind shear and cold weather precipitated by the cold front which had blown into the state several hours before it was forecast had caused the delay.

Bracken flicked the switch off. With the mission probably canceled for twenty-four hours, the colonel would be expecting the *Pampero* to remain somewhere off the Cape with an attempted second try at dawn the next day and thus wouldn't be expecting the *Pampero* to show up in North West Cay that evening. He glanced at his watch. Eight twenty-one.

From the ship's safe he withdrew one of the prepackaged syringes of morphine. Three left. He wanted one for himself but rejected the idea. Make do with codeine.

He staggered aft, bracing himself against the roll of the ship. Held up the morphine once he was in the aft cabin. Briefly, Lu's eyes glittered in anticipation.

"Brought the dope, but maybe we could chat a little first."

Lu stared up at the overhead for a few seconds, then turned his face to Bracken's. "You get no information. Nothing."

"Okay. So I get nothing. Neither do you. Fair trade." He sank down on the opposite bunk, leaning back against the bulkhead. "We're headed for North West Cay. It'll be a rough trip."

"Damn you, Bracken. I need something to stop the pain."

"So sue. Everybody else does. Don't forget the suffering bit. And add some punitive damages to the bill. Good for at least a million. Shit—I'll even throw in the name of a New York law firm that specializes in marine insurance ripoffs."

Long silence. Lu turned his head away, his jaw muscles clamped down hard, whether in pain or determination it was hard for Bracken to compute.

"I don't know anything that you don't already know. The whole thing was compartmentalized. My job was to get the *Pampero*, Humberto, Raul, and Vierro up to the Cape." His eyes were watering. "Give me the shot, Bracken. I've told you what I know."

"Like Humpty Dumpty, phase one. You told me all about that, huh?"

Lu looked startled. "How did you find out . . . ?"

"Yours is not to question why." He lay his fingers over Lu's broken nose. "Bad twist to your sniffer, Lu. Needs straightening. Had an uncle who was a farmer. Broke his nose with a slipped wrench, trying to tighten up a fitting on a tractor. Just gripped his sniffer and twisted." He pushed against the swollen flesh, and Lu screamed.

"Tender, isn't it? Not as bad as an arm popped out of its socket. Not like a leg festering until it's ready to fall off. Not long and drawn out like starving on rat shit and pumpkin puke, right? Just a little tender." He pressed harder, clamping the nose with both fingers and twisting it gently. Lu screamed in a long, protracted cry, bucking his body against its bonds, then sagging back on the mattress.

"Humpty Dumpty. That was phase one, but your boss didn't entirely trust you to bring it off, so he had a backup plan. Somehow, he can destroy the shuttle once it's in orbit, right? By a radio signal, I'd guess. What's the code word for phase two, Lu?"

"I don't know any of the details. He wouldn't tell me, and it wouldn't do you any good, Bracken, even if I did."

Back to basics. Bracken prodded the most swollen part of

Lu's nose with his index finger. Lu screamed and squeezed his eyes shut, tears streaming down his cheeks. "Morphine!" he screamed.

"Not until I get the password." Ducking out of the cabin, Bracken went to the engine room. Bad sloshing sounds. He started the generator, threw on the bilge pump circuit breaker, and pulled a pair of pliers out of the tool drawer.

Lu was struggling against his bound hands and feet, thrashing under the restraining straps.

Opening and closing the pliers, Bracken approached Lu. "My own version of phase two. Fingers were phase one, pliers are phase two."

"Get away!" There was actual fear in his eyes, and Bracken knew that he had to follow through. He held the pliers over Lu's bent nose and lowered them, just touching the edges to the flesh. Lu was staring up at him, his eyes pleading.

"Bad bend in your beak, Major Lu. But I'll fix it for you right now with my old trusty rusty nose-straightner." He squeezed lightly.

" 'Jabberwocky,' " Lu screamed at him. "That's the name of the poem but that's all I know. Not the actual lines, not how phase two works. Nothing except that it's a plan to transmit a low-powered radio signal to the Japanese GINGA satellite from the Victoria's satellite dish. But what happens when it's received, I don't know."

"You can do better than that. If he told you the name of the poem, why didn't he give you the words?"

"I was his backup based on his superior's insistence."

"Why would he need a backup?"

"He has a bad heart, he's overweight. Already a couple of strokes. If he died, fell into a coma, got dead drunk, whatever. If he was in any way disabled, I was to obtain the phase two code words from the Victoria's ship's safe and send the radio signal based on that information."

"Who wrote the poem?"

Lu flopped his head from one side to the other. "Lewis Carroll. The colonel was stationed in England as an intelligence officer after the Second World War. English literature is one of his passions."

"Why did he even tell you that much?"

"He was drunk. And when he's drunk, he talks too much for

his own good. I prompted him along and he told me the name of the poem. I tried to get him to tell me more about phase two the morning we left Cuba, and he got very angry."

Laying the pliers down, Bracken picked up the morphine. Lu's eyes were on the syringe, watching like a starving man would watch a platter of roast beef and potatoes about to be put on the table.

"Where are the rest of the weapons? Vierro had a .22 pistol and there was another machine pistol."

"Pull out the bottom drawer in the dresser. Down behind it, wrapped in plastic garbage bags."

Bracken retrieved the bags and emptied them on the cabin sole. The .22 would be about as useful as teats on a boar hog, but the machine pistol, a Cuban 9mm SMG-22, had two full clips of forty rounds each.

"Now the morphine, Bracken. I've told you all I know."

There were a lot of unanswered questions. Information that he wanted, but he had to stay with the essentials for now.

He held up the syringe and removed the cap. "Not yet. Not quite yet." He pulled up his T-shirt. The duct tape was holding but the compress was saturated with red slime. "This is the last of the morphine, Lu. See here? A big-caliber hole from a bang stick. Two inches to the left and he would have killed me, but I'll tell you something. It hurts like hell. So I'm stuck with this dilemma. Whether the morphine goes to me or you."

"You promised. Damn you, Bracken, you promised!"

Phony surprise on his face, forehead wrinkled. "I did? I don't think I promised, Lu. But I'm tired. Can't think straight, but it doesn't really matter, does it? Seeing as where you are and I'm where I'm at."

"There's nothing more to give you. That's the absolute truth."

It didn't sound quite right. Too quick. Bracken had a sixth sense nagging at him. He carefully laid the syringe on the dresser. "What else, Lu? What about the stuff?" He was winging it, not knowing if there was anything else, but stuff was a good word— animal, vegetable, or mineral. Or permutations thereof.

Lu hesitated long enough for Bracken to know that there was "stuff." Whatever it was.

"What about the stuff, Lu?" he repeated.

Lu shook his head, but his eyes were lying.

Bracken took the syringe and turned his back, moving toward the cabin door.

"In the bilge under the galley floorboards . . . there are ten kilos of plastic explosive. The detonator's on some kind of a time-delay fuse."

"How's it fired?"

"There's a plastic fishing line from the detonator which runs up to a molding under the refrigerator cabinet. When we got to the Bahamas, the *Victoria* was going to send over the two women. Once they were on board the *Pampero*, my men and I would take the launch back. Just before coming on deck, I was to pull the line. There's a sixty-minute delay. You'd have been in deep water heading south by the time it went off."

"Cute, Lu." He plunged the syringe into Lu's hip and pressed the plunger. Almost immediately, Lu arched his head back on the pillow, his eyes wide and then, slowly, his features relaxing, the muscles in his face going slack. "I didn't think you'd give it to me, Bracken."

"When you're ready for the next one, we'll talk some more."

Lu actually smiled as he slid down the endless chute to euphoria.

0950 hours

"You got a new course laid out?" Walrus shouted over the howl of the wind as Bracken came up the companionway. It was cold, below fifty, and the wind was stiff from the north, blowing thirty-five.

"One thirty-two magnetic. How's it going?"

"Rougher than a cob. You check the bilge?"

"Just turned the pump on. We're leaking a tad."

Walrus wiped a fist across his dripping mustache, squeegee-ing saltwater from the drooping hairs. Walrus didn't trust electric bilge pumps. As he always said, the most reliable pump was a man scared shitless with water sloshing over his kneecaps and a bucket real handy.

"I'll be back up in a minute," Bracken yelled.

"Bring my pea jacket, skip. I'm freezing my balls off."

Bracken ducked below, chewed down a tablet of codeine, grabbed foul weather gear and jackets, and made a quick run through the galley, where he snatched up a bunch of bananas and two beers.

Back on deck, he scrambled back into the cockpit and ducked down just as a sheet of spray swept the decks.

"How's our friend?" The banana went into Walrus's mouth and disappeared in two bites. He flung the peel away to leeward, and it disappeared astern in a smother of foaming wake.

"I shot him up with some dope. He'll live."

"Find anything out?"

" 'Jabberwocky' is the name of a poem. The lines of the poem contain the code words to unlock phase two."

"Shit! I've heard of it." He snapped his fingers. "English author—ah, ah, on the tip of my tusks . . . *Dodgson!* Charles Dodgson. From *Through the Looking Glass*."

"Wrong. Lewis Carroll."

"Pen name. Lewis Carroll was Dodgson's pen name."

"Since when did you read anything other than Melville, Mansfield, and Mickey Mouse?"

Walrus gave Bracken a black look. "So what the hell's wrong with poetry?"

"Nothing. Just surprised. How come you remember it?"

"Carroll wrote 'The Walrus and the Carpenter,' also part of *Through the Looking Glass*."

"Do you have it on board?"

Walrus sank back against the helmsman's seat, thoughtful, then shook his head tentatively. "Probably not the entire poem, unless it's in abridged form. I've got the *Penguin Dictionary of Quotations*. Should be in there. Did Lu drop any other pearls of wisdom?"

"We're sitting on a bomb. They put it aboard in Cuba, maybe even before. Ten kilos of plastique."

Walrus arched his dripping eyebrows. "How's it set up to be detonated?"

"Timer on a detonator. Pull a line, and sixty minutes later it goes off. You know anything about that kind of stuff?"

The *Pampero* bit into a huge sea, burying her bow, spearing through it, then lifting, blue water cascading down the deck. He felt a shudder run through the ship, the masts visibly surging against the rigging. Christ, he wondered, how long could she take this kind of punishment before coming unglued?

Walrus was shouting something back, but it was lost in the wind.

"I said, had the usual training in explosives at Camp Lejeune when I was in the Corps. No big deal in disarming it unless the Cubans booby-trapped it."

"That's the first priority, the book second. You want to take a look?"

"That's what you pay me for, skip. To take dumb chances." Walrus slid out from behind the helm, held it until Bracken replaced him. "You want the inflatable life raft on deck?"

"Why should I want the fuckin' life raft on deck?" Bracken replied.

"In case I get my wires crossed."

"If she blows, Walrus, you're fired and we're both dead."

"Yeah, like they say, ashes to ashes, dust to dust. The bright side is that we're all recyclable." He scuttled forward to the companionway and down the stairs.

"I hope to hell you didn't sleep through that class," Bracken shouted after him. Of course, he would soon find out.

1200 hours

Still blowing a real blue norther, but they were through the worst of the Stream, the seas smoothing out into long aquamarine rollers boiling out of the north. The muslin sky had been bleached white by the cold front, and the horizon, where sky met sea, had a hard, jagged edge of breaking green water.

Walrus had laid out a Penguin paperback on the salon table, the page marked. But it was the explosives that he checked first.

Bracing himself against the salon table, Bracken studied the plastique. Walrus had cushioned it with towels and packed the whole mess in a beer carton, then strapped it down with shock cord to keep it from shifting. The detonator was a small cylinder with a pull ring on it, a fifteen-foot plastic fishing line attached to it. Exactly what Lu had described except one thing. The timer-detonator had characters etched into its barrel which read 10 SEGS. Abbreviation for *segundos*. Meaning seconds. Lu wouldn't have had time to even make it on deck before the ship blew. The *Pampero* carried three hundred gallons of diesel fuel and a couple of tanks of propane cooking gas. She would have gone up like tissue paper in a brushfire. So the colonel didn't want loose ends. Interesting. He wondered how Lu would react to that news.

Next, Bracken checked the satnav. They were making good time. He plopped down at the nav station to work out the fix and his estimated time of arrival at North West Cay. Dividers, parallel rules; spanning off the distance and tapping the results into his calculator. After 1900 hours at the earliest, he figured. Just the last of twilight with darkness imminent. He then turned to the Nautical Almanac. Moonrise 0011—eleven minutes after midnight.

He realized that he was going through the mechanics of moving the *Pampero* from point A to point B but with no idea what would happen when he arrived at point B. Bluff it through with the proposed swap? Unlikely with only Lu left to trade for Jean and Pam. Yet it was the only possibility, because an attempt to storm the *Victoria* would result in eight or nine automatic weapons against his one. To pull it off with even the slimmest possibility of success, he'd need Lu's cooperation, albeit unwilling. But a gun in the back was powerful persuasion.

Unconsciously, he had been doodling, drawing a bird. The jabberwocky? Seems that he remembered the poem from his high school days. A nonsense rhyme that neither he nor his classmates understood. Vaguely, he remembered his English teacher had given some esoteric reason for studying the poem, but in those days Bracken's concentration was centered more on how to entice Mary Sue Zborowsky into the backseat of his 1937 Chevy sedan.

Jabberwocky: the key to phase two. He opened the book to the marker. He scanned for some mention of "Jabberwocky" but found only one:

> *Beware the Jabberwock, my son!*
> *The jaws that bite, the claws that catch!*
> *Beware the Jubjub bird, and shun*
> *The frumious Bandersnatch*

Promising. Very dark overtones to the poem. In the captain's cabin he pulled Jean's portable computer from the storage place beneath the bunk where she had told him she had hidden it. He powered it up according to the instructions on the lid and typed in the lines of the poem.

The computer hiccuped and admonished him with a screen display that read:

PASSWORD(S) INCORRECT

Tried to remember what Jean had said. Something about the best passwords were gibberish. Computers, in trying to crack an encrypted message, sought familiar patterns of spelling and letter frequency.

He tried two other quotations without success, then turned the page.

> Twas brillig, and the slithy toves
>   Did gyre and gimble in the wabe;
> All mimsy were the borogoves,
>   And the mome raths outgrabe.

His hands shaking, he keyboarded in the words. The computer sighed a little, as if it were unhappy to give up this soon and printed out on the screen:

PASSWORD(S) APPROVED PHASE II
SELECT MENU ITEM

20.

July 19, 1235 hours

It was all there, in five different files: the predicted polar orbital track of the shuttle keyed to its liftoff time, timing assumptions of shuttle passes within radio range of the Bahamas, cutaway drawings of the kick stage motor, the clinically phrased details of the events that would happen once the radio signal was transmitted from the *Victoria,* and an outline of the Soviet cleanup operation. Phase two all laid out in a neat, radioactive nutshell.

After all the paranoia that Bracken had gone through, he now realized that the Soviets *weren't* going to directly destroy the shuttle. Not that simple, not that direct. He had made the obvious assumption, but it had been an erroneous one. He scanned through the files, then focused on a table of the REM count buildup and intensity.

Atomic physics he didn't savvy, but he did understand the basic principles and the result. It came down to REM counts, and they were big mother numbers, building to over eight thousand in the first fifteen minutes after the radio signal was transmitted.

Phase two was as subtle as a sledgehammer. If the Soviets could pull it off, the American manned space effort would probably be delayed for a decade or longer. There would undoubtedly be chaos and recrimination in the Administration, massive and multiple lawsuits, a congressional inquiry lasting years, and the nation would undergo self-flagellation for decades. For better or for worse, Star Wars would die on the drawing boards and in the laboratories. But perhaps most important, the Soviets would leap a couple of generations in space defense technology, guaranteeing that a Soviet first strike would go unpunished. The implications were terrifying. It was all so damned simple and yet absolutely brilliant.

"Skip! Up on deck, quick!"

Bracken made the top of the companionway in five seconds and looked up to where Walrus was pointing. A brilliant point of flame on a shaft of white exhaust angled upward through the troposphere, heading south toward a polar orbit. Mesmerized, Bracken watched until it was a pinpoint of fire, then was absorbed into the blackness of deep space. So NASA had held to the maximum allowable time limits and then launched!

A newscast from Miami confirmed it. An unexpected and errant low pressure area from the Gulf of Mexico had obligingly drifted in over the Florida panhandle by mid-morning, diminishing the winds aloft and rapidly raising temperatures to the south. Someone high up in NASA with maybe more guts than brains had argued for a quick launch, and NASA had gone for it with their collective fingers crossed. The final quick countdown and liftoff was described as "flawless" by the newscaster. Checking his watch, he guessed at the launch time, then checked the orbital predictions on the computer. There would be enough time but not by much.

Back on deck, Bracken slumped down next to Walrus. "They can do it."

"Who can do what?"

"The *Victoria*. Kill the shuttle." He laid it out in simplified language.

"Those bastards! Those fucking borscht-eating bastards." Walrus's face was a mask of white anger. "What's the earliest time that they would transmit?"

"I just checked the polar orbital predictions on Jean's computer. The shuttle would be within radio range of the Bahamas by roughly 2120 tonight. We should reach there by 1930."

"A maximum of an hour fifty minutes, which should leave us enough time," said Walrus. He lit a waterlogged Camel, puffing furiously like the Little Engine That Could to get the damn thing drawing.

"Pam and Jean—" Bracken hadn't intended to say it, it just came out.

"Don't, for Christ's sake, even consider them. When the Corps tells you to take the hill, you don't ask questions and you don't think too much about the people next to you. Just salute smartly, lock and load, then charge up the hill for all your worn-out ass is worth. You have to keep going until you're over the top. Then you count the casualties."

Bracken nodded, realizing how slim the odds were.

"You have any idea of what we're going to do?"

"For inventory, we've got one Cuban SMG with two forty-round clips, the .22 semi-auto with one clip, the Walther if you can get it working, and the plastique. I figure if we try to storm the *Victoria* together, we'll get shot out of the saddle before we even make it on deck. Way I see it, we have to independently try to blow up the *Victoria* and to wreck the radome. Either way, the firing signal couldn't be sent and it would double our chances of getting the job done. Walrus, you're more experienced with explosives than I am. Think you can handle the demolition end of things?"

"Already been thinking about it. Yeah, I can handle it."

"I'll take the radome. Are the covers on those things very tough?"

"It's a thin shell; no big deal. Inside is the dish and all the actuators that allow it to keep locked on and tracking a satellite; in this case, the shuttle. Saw the same kind of installation on *Shango II,* the big stinkpot that Gordo used to skipper. All you'd need to do would be to bust up the dome enough to make sure the antenna inside was permanently disabled."

"A forty-round clip would do it?"

"More than enough. The dish is kept aligned by hydraulic drives, driven by a computer-controlled gyro. Cut just one hydraulic line and it'd be fritzed. Better yet, hit the dish itself or the electrical cabling that controls the actuators. If you set up on the beach and fire from a prone position, you could get it."

Bracken nodded. But firing from the beach wouldn't be close enough. It would have to be closer. Very close. From on board the *Victoria* to make sure that the job was done properly. "I'm going to get the dome, but if I can, Walrus, I'm going to get the women off first. That's my problem. You do your job and then get out if you can."

Walrus leaned back against the seat, looking out at the softly heaving sea. Then finally turned back to face Bracken. "I've been thinking. After I plant the explosives, I'll swim back to the beach. I figure that I can buy you some time with a diversion, then cover your flank when you come ashore with the ladies. But just remember, you've got to get everything tidied up before 2120 or you and the ladies will go boom with the rest of them."

"Bullshit, Walrus. You do your job and get back to the *Pampero.* Shorten up on the chain, get the engine going, and if you hear any firing from the beach, get the hell out."

"You don't pay me enough, Bracken, to tell me what I can or can't do. If I want to stay, then I stay. Besides, Pam turns me on.

I may not get the Silver Star, but maybe I'll collect on her undying thanks."

Bracken didn't believe it; knew that Walrus was throwing in his lot for hell or high water, but Bracken gradually accepted it because he knew that he would have done the same.

It just came out, before Bracken could tie his tongue. "She's a hooker, you know."

"Aren't we all?" said Walrus, looking away, smiling a little. "We just charge different rates for our services."

1630 hours

The colonel bent over the shoulder of the *Victoria*'s first officer, watching the radar scope. It was scanning out at its maximum range of thirty-six miles.

"Anything?" he asked.

"Nothing new, Comrade Colonel," the man replied. "Only the small freighter that was heading south. She's still on a straight course, probably headed for Port Everglades."

The colonel touched the man's shoulder. "Call me if you see anything coming in on a bearing from the northwest. It will probably be a weak return."

"The schooner?"

"Yes." The colonel breathed deeply and exhaled. "The schooner." He turned away and went to the bar and poured himself a shot glass of vodka. He would have to control his drinking until it was all over with, but right now he needed something to warm his blood.

It would be roughly another five hours, a long time. Until then the shuttle would be out of radio range, well over the horizon, circling between the poles as the earth turned, cutting tracks across the meridians every ninety-two minutes. But by 2121 hours the shuttle would be streaking over Alabama heading southeast, well within ultra-high frequency radio range of the *Victoria*. The cargo bay doors would be open to allow the cooling panels to function and the shuttle would be flying inverted as it did when in free orbit, thus finally allowing the satellite in the cargo bay to receive a radio signal.

He added more vodka to his glass. The colonel was a functional alcoholic. He accepted the fact, even embraced it, because it was part of the job, of the life-style, and it numbed the grinding tensions that he carried. He handled it well, balancing between his body's needs and his body's performance. He had managed for the last thirty-nine years, except for his heart going sour on him and the occasional flutter in his hands after a long night with the bottle.

The air-conditioning on the bridge hissed softly. He felt just the smallest vibrations of the generators humming through the soles of his shoes. He eased down into the captain's steering chair, looking out over the bow of the vessel, slowly sipping at the vodka, rationing himself.

The *Victoria* was anchored in Union Bay on the leeward side of North West Cay. The island itself was inhabited by only a few local native families, most of them living on the Atlantic side in a village called Hopeville. On the south side of the island were a couple of transient fishermen's shacks, an abandoned fish processing plant, and a ramshackle pier. The island was out of the path of the drug runners and too unattractive to be of interest to developers. But it was perfect for the colonel's needs.

Another small sip of vodka. He held the cold fire in his mouth, his fillings aching, then swallowed it. Felt a flush of confidence flow through him. Then lit a cigarette.

Where was Lu, and what had gone wrong? That was what bothered him. The single-sideband radio report that Lu had sent last night indicated that he was in position with no problems. But less than thirty minutes earlier, the coded report had come in from Moscow indicating that the shuttle had been launched successfully and that phase two was to be implemented.

But what *had* happened? He mentally ticked off the possibilities:

1. Lu had scrubbed the whole operation and fled. The colonel rejected the idea. Lu's life was now centered on getting out of the Soviet Union and living in "retirement" with his son.

2. Bracken and his first mate overpowered Lu and three other well-armed men.

Impossible. Lu would have been very tight with the security in the last critical phases of the operation. He took another sip of the vodka, watching the sun's dazzle on the waters of the bay. Then what?

3. Raul had missed or the weapon had misfired.

Possible. But improbable. Raul had practiced in all kinds of conditions, the projectile never impacting more than half a meter outside of the target area. And the weapon was both simple and reliable.

4. Vierro and Raul had been apprehended by the Kennedy Space Center security forces.

The most likely possibility. It had always been a risk, of course. But the colonel wasn't immediately concerned about the consequences.

Raul was a professional assassin, a man who specialized in long-distance marksmanship with high-caliber weapons. He had been used twice by Qadhafi, once by the Bulgarians, and several times before by the KGB.

If Raul and Vierro were caught, they had been instructed not to resist arrest. Neither would they talk, except to babble in Spanish about how the U.S. had let down the anti-Castro forces at the Bay of Pigs, how John Kennedy had betrayed the whole Cuban freedom-fighter movement, and how their self-styled organization, *Muerte a los Traidores,* would avenge these American betrayals.

Over the last six weeks the Miami police had been carefully fed snippets of information on both Raul and Vierro by anonymous street informers. The FBI would conclude that these two Cubans were a couple of criminally insane men released by Castro during the time of the Mariel boatlift. The files would speak of drug connections that financially supported their passion for radical right-wing Cuban political activism. In Raul's South Miami fleatrap apartment, the police files would be backed up by "evidence": crudely printed leaflets, a tape recording to be telephoned into a local Miami radio station of how the terrorist group *Muerte a los Traidores* had avenged the Cuban freedom fighters' honor by blowing up the shuttle, and a notebook detailing the purchase of a ZSU cannon from a Colombian drug runner who, conveniently, was no longer among the living. His body had been found two weeks earlier by the DEA on the MacArthur Causeway leading over to the Beach, the concrete beneath his crumpled body soaking up blood, his tongue hanging out in a Colombian necktie. A convenient wrap-up from the standpoint of the police.

There would be a few strings still dangling, but the FBI, NASA, and the Administration would not ever want to admit that crazies could get that close to the shuttle, so it would be hushed up. A deal would be cut: psychiatric examination, a little stroking by prison shrinks, some "re-education," reduced sentences, and then deportation to any country that would take them provided that Raul and Vierro kept their mouths shut. Of course, the colonel knew that Raul and Vierro would never live out their sentences.

There was the scuff of shoes behind him and heavy breathing. Mirrored in the glass plate of the wheelhouse, he saw Sanchez's bulging head emerging from the staircase that led up to the bridge from the lower deck. He didn't bother to turn.

"You've carried out my orders?" he asked in a monotone, knowing that Sanchez would bog down the answer with trivial details and Latino puffery.

Huff . . . puff. Sounds of labored breathing. "It is done, Comrade Colonel. I have overseen all the critical elements myself, personally. The second generator is on line." *Huff.* "The crew, except for the man on watch in the engine room, the first officer who is presently monitoring the radar, and myself will all be fed in the crew mess quarters at 1800 hours." Another long *huff* to emphasize the strenuous labors of Señor Sanchez.

"Is the satellite dish functioning properly?" The colonel knew it was, but he wanted to see whether Sanchez had actually checked it out.

"It is my pleasure to report that the dish is operating perfectly. You need only to give me the track, azimuth, and coordinates for the satellite you wish to acquire."

"That, Sanchez, I will do myself when the time comes."

Sanchez slumped down on the leather-cushioned bench behind the colonel. "As you wish. You are pleased thus far?"

"I am reasonably pleased," said the colonel.

"Good. I am pleased that you are reasonably pleased. I would like to order a drink for myself. The day is exceedingly hot and the work demanding."

Waving his hand toward the bar, the colonel nodded, then lifted his own glass, which was now at low tide. "Get it yourself and one for me as well, Sanchez."

"I will call the steward. A plate of toast, pâté, and cheese would also be appreciated." Sanchez sounded a little put off. As he probably saw it, men of his station did not get drinks for themselves, let alone drinks for others.

"No steward. Just the drinks. Far be it for me to inconvenience you, but I need to discuss some very confidential information with you. We need to be alone—absolutely alone. You *comprende?*" He hadn't quite been able to keep the taint of distaste out of his voice. He saw, in the reflection of the glass, Sanchez pull a grimace on the blank, moonlike landscape of his face. Sanchez didn't know what the mission was, was just paid by the KGB to keep the *Victoria* running, but he was obviously itching to know what was going on with the same compulsion as a farm boy on a collective who couldn't resist peeking through a knothole in the horse-breeding stable.

"Of *course*, Comrade Colonel," Sanchez replied, heaving his bulk to a vertical position. "It is a pleasure for me to act as your host under circumstances that require confidentiality." He didn't really say it as if he meant it. But it was part of the face-saving routine—a touch of acquiescence, a touch of rebellion.

Sanchez returned with two glasses, the colonel's slopping over at the rim.

I'll have to watch the booze, the colonel thought, taking the glass. And eventually get some food in me. It will be a long night. But an even longer one for the Americans.

The colonel intentionally waited until Sanchez had settled his bulk on the cushioned bench. "Close the damned door, Sanchez! Or do you want the first officer to hear what I'm going to say?" Stupid *durak*, he swore to himself.

Returning, Sanchez dropped down on the bench. His face was red. "Is that satisfactory?" Sanchez asked with noticeable acidity.

The colonel lit another cigarette from the butt of his previous one. He decided to throw out a bone. "Forgive me for my abruptness. It's the tension of an important mission. How are the women doing?"

Sanchez looked mollified. "Locked in the cabin. I am sending their meals in rather than allowing them the use of the salon."

"You haven't molested either one of them?"

A look of acute piety. "They are both whores. Diseased. Do I look like a fool?"

The colonel shrugged. "Don't tempt me to answer that truthfully, Sanchez." He paused and sipped the mother's milk of Russia. "The engines . . . have they been serviced?"

"Of course."

"Now show me the way that the anchor winch and autopilot are activated."

Sanchez showed him, babbling, eager to please. The colonel had a whole checklist in his briefcase, had gone through the procedures on a mock-up in Russia, but he wanted, as in all things, to be positive. He finally patted Sanchez on the shoulder. "Excellent. You know your work. Please sit down again and listen carefully."

Sanchez repositioned his bulk on the bench, radiating conspiracy. "This mission of yours, Comrade Colonel. It is obviously important."

"And you will play an important part." The colonel leaned back in the cushioned chair and closed his eyes. "When the crew start to eat, you will personally tell them that due to the very sensitive nature of our mission, they will be locked in the crew mess for a few hours."

"Lock them in?"

"That's what I said, Sanchez. You will issue them a few bottles of Cuban rum and a case of beer to go with the meal. The first mate will distribute it equally. Tell them we will be leaving shortly after 2200 hours. You and I will get the *Victoria* under way, then allow them out of the mess so that they can resume their duties. Tell them that we should be back in Cuba by late tomorrow afternoon. At that time I will return the command of the *Victoria* to you along with a written statement praising you for your invaluable services rendered to the international socialist cause. I should imagine that Fidel will be proud of your work."

Sanchez beamed. "You are generous, Colonel, but I don't understand why just you and I will get the vessel under way by ourselves."

"It's unlikely, but the schooner may arrive before we depart. I am unclear on this point, but if it does, it will have to be destroyed. The *Victoria*'s crew might talk. What they don't see they don't know."

"Ah, I now understand. It is a pleasure to work with a man such as yourself, who is so thorough in his planning."

The colonel flicked off the thanks with a lift of his wrist as if a fly had landed there.

"And my duties?"

"First, order the chef to prepare a meal for the two of us. We will eat at 1900 hours. Following the dinner, you will remain at the radar console and keep a watch for the *Pampero*. When and if the schooner arrives, you will take one guard and the two women in the launch, make the transfer, and bring my men back. Once they are on board, we will leave immediately."

"Nothing more than that?"

"If the need arises, I'll tell you."

"What of the tubes? Comrade Lu told me that they contained charts for the Bahamas phase of the operation and that I was to keep them in a secure place until he returned. Will you need them?"

"What charts? I have all the charts I need." The colonel tapped the ash of his cigarette against the frame of his seat, agitated.

Sanchez stood up, lifted the seat of the bench, and withdrew three large-diameter plastic tubes, each about a meter long, the ends sealed with caps and waterproofed with tape. He passed them to the colonel.

Using his penknife, the colonel slit the tape on one of them and removed the cap, then pulled the contents out a few centimeters. It was a painting.

He was thinking rapidly. So this was Lu's retirement fund. The colonel knew little of the value of artwork, but he could guess. Even deeply discounted in the art world's black market, the paintings would bring millions.

"All right, Sanchez, I'm beginning to remember. Comrade Lu made some reference to the charts while we were in Cuba."

"Perhaps we should take them out and inspect them."

The colonel turned and looked at him with the expression of an undertaker measuring a client for a pine box. "Our conference is over, Sanchez. Get me another glass of vodka. Then close the door. I have some work to do."

For a long time the colonel fingered his glass. He placed it against his forehead, letting the coldness soak into his skin, trying to numb his mind.

Lu. The traitor Lu, the foreigner Lu. The Lu that he had nurtured through these last two decades, bringing him along in the Establishment, probably faster than he deserved. Lu, the running dog of capitalism who was deserting the country of his birth; selling out for a few pilfered oil paintings and his sick love for a boy he had never known. The colonel had already made up his mind months before. Lu would be extinguished, a dangling thread snipped neatly away from the fabric of the operation.

He drank down more of the vodka, then, with the door to the bridge shut and locked, the colonel powered up the portable computer and punched in the first two lines from "Jabberwocky," then leafed through the files.

Damn Lu. All that expense. The man was an incompetent. Destruction of the shuttle in the first few seconds of flight would have been ideal. Not only would the shuttle have blown up right in the Americans' faces, but the contamination from the plutonium 239 buried in the propellant of the kick stage motor would have eventually killed the very cream of NASA and the scientists who were conducting the leading edge of Star Wars research. The Cape would have remained contaminated for years, and with the wind from the north as it had been in the morning, most of Miami as well. But then again, there was phase two, equally worthwhile, perhaps, in the colonel's mind, better. "A technically sweet solution" was the phrase of the Soviet scientists who had planned it.

He moved his fingers on the keypad, calling up the cutaway drawing of the kick stage engine. Normal in almost all respects. The motor would gimbal on command, the guidance package worked, all had been tested and proven in the checkout sequences at the Cape. But what the technicians at the Cape couldn't do was fire the engine. The solid rocket propellant was a simple pyrotechnic, no more complicated than the black powder in a skyrocket. To test it would be to destroy it. To probe into the propellant would alter the propellant's burn characteristics. It was just a given that a skyrocket would fire once you touched a match to the fuse.

The cutaway drawing showed the propellant to be a solid, homogeneous mass, except for a box, six small lumps clustered in the upper end of the propellant, and, separating the lumps, small shutters of metal.

Each lump was a kilo sphere of plutonium; in all, six kilos of the purest plutonium that Soviet gaseous diffusion plants could fabricate. The shutters were eight-millimeter-thick strips of cadmium, each a small guillotine, set in slots machined out of the solid explosive, ready to be withdrawn by screw actuators. The box was just a simple radio receiver with a lithium battery strapped to it with wires running off to the actuators.

It wasn't a nuclear weapon but, rather, a crude reactor core. Each sphere of plutonium was placed exactly twenty-two centimeters from its closest mate, more or less in the configuration of six peas stuck uniformly over the surface of a Ping-Pong ball. With the cadmium strips in place, the rate of neutron emission was less than the rate of neutron splitting. The pile was "subcritical."

But once a signal was received by the radio, small electrical currents would flow out to the actuators. Slowly, very slowly, the cadmium strips would be withdrawn from between the plutonium blocks, allowing the pile to go critical. The neutron count would begin to climb, slowly at first, doubling each minute for the first ten minutes, then cascading into a reactor runaway. Intense heat would be generated and, with it, a torrent of high-speed neutrons would flare out in all directions. The count would rise to over 8,000 REM within the first fifteen minutes.

It would be the equivalent of a reactor "meltdown," except, in the absence of gravity, the plutonium would not melt *down* as in the classic "China syndrome." Actually, it wouldn't go any-where; simply mass in a ball of boiling liquid metal, spewing out deadly subatomic particles traveling at the speed of light.

The relatively thin bulkheads of the shuttle would not stop the neutrons. In the first few minutes the astronauts would notice nothing except that their broad-spectrum radiation counters would start to chatter. Solar flare, part of the Van Allen belt, what? As the radiation count climbed, the astronauts would be panicking, trying to identify the source. Mission Control would be helpless, dumbfounded.

The on-board radiation counters would then be tuned to greater selectivity. Not cosmic rays, not alpha, not beta, not gamma but—neutrons. And the only conceivable source of that great a concentration of high-speed neutrons was an atomic weapon that somehow fissioned. And the only possible conclusion would be that the shuttle had a fission weapon on board and it had inadver-tently gone critical.

The astronauts were military men on this launch. Tough, disciplined, but they knew the effects of radiation and how they would die. One of them might blurt out a curse: that the mission they had been briefed on was supposed to be the launch of a chemical laser satellite, not nuclear. And the interchanges be-tween Houston and the shuttle would be recorded, to be played back endlessly by those other than NASA.

In less than ten minutes the astronauts would first become hyperexcitable, irrational, then lose muscle coordination. Finally, near death, they would begin to vomit up blood, lose control over their body functions, and ultimately fall into a stupor. In thirty minutes they would be dead or close to it. In an hour there would be no doubt as the pulsing hills and valleys of heart and breath-ing functions would collapse on the oscilloscopes of Mission Con-trol into flat lines of light.

The colonel leaned back and lit a cigarette, blowing the gray smoke at the overhead. It had been the idea of a nuclear physicist in Kasputin Yar, one originally brought in to calculate what the biological effects of the plutonium would be if the shuttle exploded during the launch—phase one.

Sergei . . . Sergei something. Sergei Chuchkin. A little weasel-faced atomic physicist who had calculated that if the load of plutonium was above the critical mass but was broken down into six segments, separated and dampened by the cadmium control plates which could be slowly withdrawn on command, then the plutonium would go just above criticality, and from that simple idea phase two had evolved.

Sergei had died in an automobile accident because of his brilliance. The colonel ordered it under the justification of "loose strings."

He threw down the remaining vodka. Didn't feel anything. Loose, perhaps. Relaxed. But he would have to clamp down on the rationing. He turned back to the computer and called up the file titled Recovery Operations.

Soyuz 881 was already in a steeply inclined orbit, projected to link up with the MIR space station in twenty-one hours. It was manned by four of the best men in the Soviet Corps of Cosmonauts, each of them trained in the layout of equipment aboard the shuttle. Three of them had extensive experience with EVA— the untethered space walks the Americans loved to do on camera for the slobbering masses.

He checked his watch again—1715. Slightly more than four hours to run. Add another thirty minutes for the plutonium to melt down. Say 2150 hours. By then the world would know that the shuttle was manned by corpses who were killed by a deadly American Star Wars experiment that had gone wrong.

Of course the Soviet Union would offer its help, whether they were asked to or not, but being begged by the Americans would be a nice touch. The colonel smiled at the thought. Either way, the Americans would be helpless because it would take a minimum of nine days to prepare another shuttle launch. No, the Soviets would rendezvous with the shuttle, all in the name of humanity: a new twist on the old tradition that men who go to sea in ships must selflessly offer their assistance to those in distress.

Firing its main engines, then its thrusters, *Soyuz 881* would be realigned to match the orbit of the shuttle, then fire again to overtake it. In all, the linkup would consume more than nineteen hours.

Of course the American astronauts would be dead, but the source of radiation would still be intense. In fact, deadly.

One of the Soviet cosmonauts aboard *Soyuz 881* was Nikolai Sitnikov. A promising young cosmonaut, his dossier read, destined for excellence. Except that he had contracted multiple myeloma, a fatal bone cancer. The prognosis was that he would live for no more than three months.

Once *Soyuz 881* was within a kilometer of the shuttle, Nikolai Sitnikov would don a space suit and jet pack, then span the distance between the two craft. The means by which the Japanese satellite was attached to the floor of the shuttle's cargo bay was known from intelligence provided by the Japanese. There were two mechanical locks to overcome, then an electrical one. Nikolai had the tools to do the work. He would free the satellite of its restraining straps, pry open the locks, then manually trigger the ejection mechanism. It was not much more than a coiled spring, but it provided sufficient thrust to propel the satellite out of the cargo bay at a velocity of .42 meters a second. In forty minutes the satellite would be more than a kilometer away from the shuttle and the neutron emission from the plutonium 239 would be harmless at that distance.

Unfortunately, Nikolai would never live to tell the tale to his grandchildren. He knew that he would die from neutron radiation but that there would be an unusually generous pension for his family, posthumously awarded medals, and a plaque on the Kremlin Wall to commemorate his valor. It would be more than enough.

And then the recovery operation would begin.

Soyuz 881 would fire its thrusters and move in closer to the shuttle, then dock to it with tethers. Two of the Soviet cosmonauts would enter the shuttle by the air lock. They would find five dead men but the shuttle absolutely intact with all systems functioning. They would then reestablish communications with Mission Control, taking care to transmit on a clear channel and not through the scrambler so that the whole world could listen in to the grim details of disaster. It would be the propaganda coup of all time.

First they would tell about how Nikolai had freed the Excalibur satellite in the hope that the American astronauts could be saved, not realizing how intense the radiation source was. Nikolai would be reported to be now comatose with his last conscious words spoken in gasps. "I tried to save them. They are men just like us, trying to reach for the stars." It was a nice touch, the colonel thought, a phrase that would live in history books, even though a bit shopworn.

Of course, the shuttle was a treasure ship. The equipment of vital interest would be stripped and transported to *Soyuz 881*. Not everything but the really leading-edge equipment. The colonel had the Soviet space scientists' wish list:

Inertial flight control black boxes
Laser ring gyro
IFF code packages
Data and voice encryption software and hardware
Star tracker backup navigational system
Infrared deep-spectral band sensors
Main computer CPU and EPROMS
Superconductivity S-2 experimental chip in compartment
   28M-B11, port side of upper flight deck
All operating manuals and blueprints

And finally . . . the Excalibur satellite itself. *Soyuz 881*'s cargo bay had been especially modified to take the satellite. Although weighing tons on earth, in space it would be weightless but still have great mass. It would take two cosmonauts more than an hour to transfer it from the shuttle to *Soyuz*, but it could be done, would be done.

Of course, no mention would be made by the Soviet cosmonauts of the technological transfer. But they had well-rehearsed scripts narrating, in gut-wrenching detail, the tragic deaths of the Americans. There would be a brief memorial service broadcast from the shuttle. By then, with radio communications on a clear channel and with real-time TV coverage, the whole world would be listening and watching—literally the whole world.

As in traditional shipboard burials, the dead men would be commended to their Maker and buried in the deep of space. With a hand-held camera, one of the cosmonauts would record this event—the American bodies suited up, shifted to the open cargo bay, the traditional words of the shipboard burial at sea read by a Russian cosmonaut in stilted English. Then the Americans would be deployed into space with a gentle shove. Their bodies would slowly cartwheel, the sun glinting off their faceplates, the white of their suits brilliant in the glare of the sun but growing smaller in the distance against the blue and white backdrop of the planet. It would be a scene never to be forgotten by anyone who viewed it.

Following the American ceremony, Soviet cosmonaut Nikolai Sitnikov would also be buried in space. The camera would pan to the two other Soviet cosmonauts in the cargo bay. They would first lean down to touch their faceplates to his, then stand back, ramrod straight, and slowly salute. The words in the script memorized by *Soyuz*'s first officer were, "We salute you, Nikolai. Go in peace and sleep well, with the assurance that no crime like this will ever be committed again in the purity of space."

The message would be clear to all who listened, to the entire world. The United States had transgressed the law by putting nuclear weapons into space. The resulting condemnation by the world would be awesome and final. The United States would now be the outlaw, the loathed, and the isolated.

The colonel leaned back in his chair and lit yet another cigarette. He exhaled, blowing blue smoke against the hard light. The sun was going down, and it would be night soon enough. He was hungry, and with the supper meal he would have one of the last remaining bottles of Georgian wine and a few glasses of the Azerbaijanian brandy. It would be a long evening, and he considered it necessary to eat and drink well when he was under pressure because it gave back to him a sense of normalcy, of pacing, of judgment.

He scanned through the rest of the program, tapping the keys and running through the chain of events.

Initially, the Soviet planners had considered trying to recover the shuttle itself by leaving one cosmonaut aboard, then attempting reentry. But the bean-counter statisticians had forecast less than a one in four probability of success, the most likely result being that the shuttle would burn up on reentry. Not that the shuttle was needed for the Soviet space program. They already had their own project, and it was different and more ambitious than the eighteen-year-old American effort. So a neat compromise was made. Just prior to vacating the shuttle, the Soviet cosmonauts would briefly fire the shuttle's thrusters in the retrograde mode for a precise number of seconds. Slowly, the shuttle's orbital path would decay, and within six hours it would start the irrevocable process of reentry, culminating in a fiery breakup of the shuttle as it entered the atmosphere somewhere over Michigan. Soviet orbital physicists predicted an impact area for the remaining shards of twisted metal to be near Houston, Texas.

Again, a nice touch, the colonel thought. Houston Center would have their own space junk impacting in their own backyard.

Silently, he raised his glass and toasted the shuttle, now 224 kilometers out in space and streaking over India for the North Pole at nearly 30,000 kilometers per hour. "You are ours," he pledged.

21.

July 19, 1740 hours

Jean played with her hair, listlessly stroking a brush through the long strands, her mind distracted. She glanced at her watch for the umpteenth time. She stood up and moved to the porthole, looking out over the anchorage. Low hills to the east, really just sand dunes with a few wisps of saw grass and scrub brush. She had not seen anything on the beach move in the last day, and the foreshore remained trackless. It was like the last place that God had made and, displeased with the result, promptly forgot about it.

She turned back to her bed and sat down noiselessly so as not to wake Pam. Pam was on the matching bed, wrapped up in a terry-cloth robe, her head thrown back, without makeup, mouth open, and snoring softly. In the hard afternoon sun that poured through the porthole, Pam's features were cast in half light, half shadow.

Jean had wanted to hate this bitch of a woman because Pam had made it a game of trying to seduce Bracken. But now she found it increasingly difficult to do. So the lady carried her own pharmacy loaded with uppers, downers, and things that made her go sideways, but still, there was something basically *decent* about the woman. Most of the facets of Pam's personality were rough-edged—such as her coarse language—but other facets that Pam took care to conceal were flawless.

She talked openly about hooking for a living. It paid the bills and it was occasionally fun, but she didn't like kinky men. Then on the second night after a second bottle of wine, she talked about three Hispanic and two black kids in Liberty City that she supported through donations to a Catholic foster children's home. Knew their names, had photos of them, agonized when they made poor grades, rejoiced when they did well. One kid, Emanuel, had started to take a real interest in mathematics and was potentially business school material. Another one, a stunning black girl by the name of Faith, was all fired up about the media and was now doing public address announcements over the school's system and writing for the school's newspaper. Pam talked about "her kids" with animation and love, as if they were her own. And in a way they were, because no one else cared as much.

Lessons of life: We shouldn't make moral judgments too soon, Jean thought. What you see is not always what you get.

She realized that Pam hadn't moved, but her eyes were open, a slight smile on her face. "You're gonna wear that brush out, lady. Either that or your hair."

"Just nerves. Nothing to do, nowhere to go. And I'm worried about Bracken and Walrus."

"They can take care of themselves would be my guess." Pam sat up, shaking her hair like a wet dog, then smoothed it by running her hands through it. She lit a cigarette. "God! I'm down to my last pack. We gotta get outta this chicken coop. What's happening?"

"Nothing. They didn't bring any lunch, so I didn't bother to wake you up. Heard some footsteps in the corridor outside just after four. The generators are running, the lights still turn on, the shower works, the water's hot, but nothing else is happening. It's like being in a cozy morgue." Then she realized that was an unfortunate choice of words.

Pam swished over to the porthole and stared at the beach. "What a terrific view. Nothing going on except sea gulls making more sea gulls."

Not exactly a porthole, Jean thought, because it was a pane of half-inch-thick smoked plastic, about eighteen inches wide and twelve inches high, set into an aluminum frame that was designed to pivot upward and inward. The swinging frame was secured to a fixed matching frame screwed into the hull and secured by six aluminum threaded bolts and matching wing nuts. It had been difficult for Jean to unscrew the wing nuts in Cuba in order to pass the cassette tape to the *Pampero,* but now it would be impossible.

Sanchez had come into the cabin ten minutes after the *Pampero* had pulled out of the anchorage and found the porthole still open. Cursing, he dogged the porthole down and left. Within minutes one of the engine room mechanics had come into the cabin and, under the supervision of Sanchez, had hammered the threads of the screws flat with a hammer, making it impossible to loosen the wing nuts again.

"I will say nothing of this to anyone else," Sanchez hissed, his face flushed with anger, "and for that, you should be very grateful. The air-conditioning works well. You have no need to smell the sea air." Then he'd slammed and locked the door.

Pam was still gazing out at the beach. The late afternoon light had a reddish quality to it, deepening her tan. Forties maybe, Jean thought, but still damned attractive. Pam turned back to her.

"You think the *Pampero* is coming back?" She sat down on Jean's bed.

"Honest to God, Pam, I don't know. If they can, they will."

"But if they don't? You know what will happen, don't you? Like Stackhill. I swim like a fish but I *hate* those damn things with big teeth that zip around down deep where it's black." Her eyes welled up with tears. "God—I don't want to die that way."

Pam was getting down to the real nitty-gritty, beginning to pull her fears out of her own personal closet of horrors. The old game of "what if," except that "if" was now not so much in question.

Jean had duplicated the interior dimensions of the porthole by bending coat hangers from the closet into a rectangle frame of eighteen by twelve inches, then tried to slip it over her body. It scraped a little but it fit. Pam was bigger across the shoulders. But there would be no real way to know whether either one of them would fit until they actually tried. Maybe ease through the porthole frame like a greased pig if some of those special and magical night creams Pam carried in her makeup kit were applied liberally.

"We can get out," she said softly. "Or at least we can make a damn good try at it."

"Bull!" Pam snapped back. "Those damn nuts won't turn because Sanchez buggered up the screws. Broke two fingernails trying."

"Maybe we can knock out the plastic."

"Oh, yeah? Just get rid of half an inch of thick plastic. You'd need a sledgehammer to knock that stuff out if that's all it is. But this stuff isn't just plastic, babykins. It's *Lexan*. Bulletproof. I know a guy over on Miami Beach who has a couple of associates who'd like to see him get a bad cold, the local slang for terminal, immediate, and very violent death. He spent over fifty grand bulletproofing the body of his stretch Mercedes limo and then had Lexan windows installed. Looks like glass but it'll stop anything up to a Magnum slug." She nodded toward the porthole. "I'm damn sure that's the same stuff."

Key in the lock, turning, not preceded by a knock.

Sanchez with one of the Latino mess boys in front of him.

"Food," he said tersely. It consisted of a tray with a large bowl—beans and rice mushed together in some kind of black gravy, plus a couple of spoons and some cellophane-covered six-packs of crackers.

"The cuisine in this joint is going downhill fast," Pam said, her voice cold and brittle as glass.

"It is the quality of the guests that determines how one caters to them," Sanchez shot back. "It's simple logic: You give whores food fit for whores."

She spat at him. Accurately, because the little wet blob of saliva splattered his sunglasses. His face flushed red and he gave her a quick jab to the stomach with his right, then backhanded her face with his left. She slammed against the bulkhead and slid down.

He turned to Jean, his voice harsh, sarcastic. "Please excuse me now. Other work requires my attention." He slammed the door behind him. The key turned.

When management got nasty, it was time to pay the bill and leave quietly. But she doubted that Sanchez took MasterCard.

Pam wasn't really out, just doing a fair job of faking it.

Jean bent down but Pam gently pushed her away. "No sweat. I've gotten worse and I've given worse. That *fucker*. I'd like to cut his balls off with sheep shears."

"How about a Swiss Army knife?" Jean asked softly.

1811 hours

Lu woke very slowly, gradually struggling up the spiral to consciousness, beginning to fit together the puzzle of sounds and senses. He didn't rush it, knowing that it would become clear in time. Like all things, it took only time.

His body heaved softly, as if he were lying on a gigantic sleeping animal that was breathing very slowly. Up through another level of awareness, trying to place where he was. He finally realized that it was only the sea's swell, transmitting its motion through the vessel, through the mattress of the bunk to his body.

He forced his mind to focus on his immediate circumstances.

He was on a boat. With his eyes closed he listened and heard the almost inaudible hiss of water flowing past the ship's planking, the creak of the mainmast in its step, the sounds of blocks groaning under strain, the low hum of the trades in the rigging.

He slowly tried to open his eyes and found that he couldn't, not quite. He could see but his sight was restricted due to the swelling around his nose and eyes. His head pounded, his face an agony, but he was whole and he could move, if barely.

The sail ties that had bound his wrists and ankles had been cut away, but nylon lines spanned his body, criss-crossing from head to foot through holes drilled in the opposing edges of the bunk. He was a fly trapped in the spider's web. Bracken had done this sometime after he had given the morphine shot.

As the schooner gently rolled in the swell, bands of hard sunlight sawed across the cabin floor, slashed across his face, then splattered against the bulkhead next to him. The sun had to be down on the horizon, so it was late in the day. No sounds on the deck, but he could hear the steering gear groaning in response to the movement of the helm.

Bracken had said something about an arrival time at North West Cay around 1930 hours. The sun set in these latitudes around 1830. He would have an hour, more or less, to devise and execute a plan if there was to be any plan at all.

One thing was very clear. He had failed. The shuttle was not destroyed. Maybe launched, maybe not, but definitely not destroyed. So he had to strike a deal with the colonel. But to strike a deal meant that he had to somehow communicate with the colonel before Bracken did.

There was a creak on the stairs of the companionway. Lu slitted his eyes, seeing and yet seemingly asleep. And listened.

Through his lashes he could see Bracken. Bracken glanced into the stateroom, then turned and disappeared. Sounds from the engine room: the generator shutting down.

The door to the engine room banged closed. More sounds from the galley; the fridge door opening, then closing. Rattle of a pan on the stove. He didn't hear him coming. Bracken was there in the doorway of the aft cabin.

"You awake?"

"Yes."

"How's the old sniffer?"

"Hurts. Headache. I want some water."

Bracken was gone a minute and returned with a glass and a

soda straw. He bent it into an *L* and inserted the end between Lu's lips. Lu drained half of the glass in one long pull, then the other half, sucking it dry.

Laying his head back on the pillow, he nodded. "Thanks, Bracken."

"Nothing. Got something to show you." He took from his shirt pocket an object that was wrapped in cotton batting, then held it close to Lu's face. "The detonator you told me about. Walrus pulled it out along with the plastic explosives. I thought you might want to know what the colonel had in mind for you." Bracken rotated the small cylinder so that the 10 SEG was visible. "Not a sixty-minute timer, Lu. This would have gone off in ten seconds after you yanked on the fishing line. You wouldn't have made it on deck before the explosive blew. Your boss obviously didn't want you or your buddies to make it back. Why's that?"

It wasn't a surprise. It all fell under the category of "loose ends," and ever since Cuba, Lu had known that he might be one of them. "I don't know, Bracken. Maybe a mistake. The Cubans are sloppy."

"Doesn't bother you?"

Inside his gut Lu was seething, but he kept his face blank, his voice clear of emotion. "Perhaps it does. I don't see that the result for you and your crew will be any different. Either way, the colonel won't allow the *Pampero* to leave North West Cay. Perhaps he intends the same fate for me."

Slumping down on the opposite bunk, Bracken studied the ICOM single-sideband radio. A Japanese marine radiotelephone, compact but very powerful. He nodded at the transceiver. "You have any set radio schedule with the *Victoria*?"

"No. Except for a scheduled brief message that I sent last night telling him in Spanish that 'the fishing was good,' which was to indicate that I was in position off the Cape with no foreseeable problems. We used the names of known fishing boats working out of Key West."

"What if you had problems?"

"I was to use my own discretion. If it was important, I was to call him, using another set of ship's call signs."

Bracken made an exasperated sound. "Okay, Lu. I'm willing to cut a deal. You get on the radio and call the *Victoria*. Tell your boss that Vierro, Raul, and Half-Ton are alive and well, just that they couldn't get up onto the beach because security patrols were all over the place because of the protesters. Without any real warning the shuttle blasted off. Tell him that you left the Cape after the launch and that you should be into North West Cay sometime around two tomorrow morning."

"The shuttle was launched!"

"You bet your socks it was. Beautiful. Walrus and I both saw it go over on the southern horizon this afternoon. The radio stations have confirmed the launch came off without any problems. It's in orbit now."

Lu closed his eyes. Until now he had still retained the vague hope that the shuttle would malfunction and self-destruct. And if it did self-destruct, the colonel would believe that Raul had done his job. But now part one was a failure and the colonel had made it clear what the result would be. Sasha would not be released and Lu would not be allowed to retire except with a bullet in his brain. Unless . . .

"You mentioned a 'deal,' Bracken. What do I get in return for convincing the colonel?"

"Plain and simple—your hide in one piece. We're going to get into North West Cay around 1930. We'll anchor on the eastern side of the island, where their radar won't pick us up, then Walrus and I will walk across the island and try to take out the satellite dish on the *Victoria.* After that, if we can, we'll get the women, head back to the *Pampero,* and bug out. Once we anchor, you'll stay aboard the *Pampero* just where you are until we get back. If we do get back, and that's a reasonably big if, I'll drop you off on the beach in one piece."

"I know better. You'll kill me, Bracken."

"I said in one piece, Lu. Alive."

"Why?"

"Because the necessity of your cooperation overrides my desire to poke a gun in your ear. I've got to stop that signal from being transmitted, and I want my woman back, and I want to get the hell out of here. And it's obvious that the colonel wasn't going to let you get off this vessel alive. Somehow, somewhere, I figure the KGB will take care of you in a way that will be a lot more inventive than I could stomach. That simple."

"I'll give you a counterproposal, Bracken. I'll do it just as you say, except that you have to give me your word that you'll kill the colonel. Make absolutely sure that he's dead."

"How in hell can I promise that! I've got to destroy the satellite dish on the bridge deck so that no signal can be transmitted. If I'm lucky, I'll get the women off. And if I've really got my stuff together, I'll be able to disable the *Victoria* so she can't come after us. But he's got about fifteen men aboard now, right?"

Lu shook his head. "Only thirteen, including the colonel."

"And they're armed?"

"Automatic weapons. AK-47s mainly."

"So forget about me blasting the colonel. I've got just the machine pistol and the .22. One clip for the satellite dish and one clip for whatever happens after that. Maybe he gets blown away, maybe not. I can't guarantee it. You have to accept the deal that I'm offering, Lu, because if you don't, you're shark bait."

"You wouldn't throw me overboard. You know that, I know that. You already had the chance when we were off the coast of Florida."

Bracken bent down, his face very close. He was unshaven, his hair wild, his eyes hot, his breath foul. "You killed Willie, Lu. I don't have a hell of a lot of reason not to off you—but if he was alive, I think he'd go along with what I'm offering you because of the stakes involved. Someday, somewhere, your own fuckin' people will pull the plug on you. If you don't cooperate with me now, I'll do the job for them. Make up your mind!"

He didn't really believe it, for all the bluster. Bracken might be wild and at the end of his rope, but he didn't have the strength or will to inflict death. But for himself, Lu knew he would cling to life, if only to work toward the colonel's death—however that might be possible.

He slowly turned his face back to Bracken. "All right. I'll go along with what you want. Untie the lines, help me up, and let me go to the bathroom. You can warm up the radio in the meanwhile."

Leaning down, Bracken studied Lu's face intently. "Fuck me up and I'll have your guts for garters. Keep the conversation in plain, simple language. Did you have any code phrases which would warn him that you were transmitting under duress?"

"If I was about to be boarded by the Coast Guard, there was a code word I was supposed to transmit imbedded in some normal sentence about fishing gear—'broken outrigger.' Other than that, all the talk was to be kept brief but absolutely normal—what anyone monitoring the frequency would expect commercial fishermen to talk about."

"And that's it? Nothing else?"

Lu shook his head slowly. "The bathroom, Bracken. I don't want to soil myself."

The network of line criss-crossed Lu like a shoelace. The cordage was only a quarter of an inch or so in diameter but it did the job. Lu had already tested it with his hands. It yielded but it didn't break.

Bracken undid one knot from the bottom of the bunk and pulled the light nylon line free from the holes in the opposite sides of the bunk, unlacing it carefully. It took a few moments.

Supporting Lu, Bracken moved him to the stateroom door, then across to the head compartment. Lu intentionally sagged, letting Bracken take his weight.

"Sorry. Legs are wobbly."

Bracken braced him against the sink, then opened the medicine cabinet. He took out a double-edged razor and a packet of blades. "Just so that you don't get any ideas, Lu."

He unzipped his zipper and looked over at Bracken. "I have no intention of killing myself. Do you mind if I have some privacy?" Bracken shrugged and shut the door.

The vessel was heeled slightly, and for a second Lu felt a wave of nausea sweep his body. The head compartment had no porthole or skylight, and he lost his sense of balance. Doggedly, he braced his body against the bulkhead and began to urinate into the toilet bowl. With his free hand he carefully and silently pried open the medicine cabinet door. Bracken had taken the razor and blades, probably more concerned that Lu would kill himself rather than believing that Lu's ultimate objective was escape. The shelves were rusty. Not much left. A couple of bottles of over-the-counter pills, a box of aspirin, a can of Band-Aids, a squashed tube of toothpaste, a dental floss container, and a bottle of aftershave lotion.

It wasn't the best he could have hoped for, or the worst. It would do, but it might take a long time. He shoved the object into his Jockey shorts, eased the medicine cabinet door closed, finished urinating, and zipped his fly shut.

As he began to pump the head out, the door opened.

"Finished?"

"Not finished but better."

"What frequency?"

"Four decimal one three three. Upper side band. *Victoria*'s call sign this time will be Tigre. Ours will be Gato Negro. I can't give him all the information you want to, but he'll get the essence of it. How do you want to phrase it?"

Bracken scratched with a pencil on a piece of paper and

shoved it across the dressing table. "Tell him that you'll be in port a couple of hours after midnight. All the crew are fine but a little disappointed. Just that the fishing didn't go as well as expected. Will he buy it?"

Lu initially held his head stock-still, rereading the message, then slowly nodded. "It's vague enough. About what he would expect if he already knows that the shuttle was launched successfully."

"So do it."

Lu punched in the frequency, turned up the RF Gain, adjusted the Mike Gain, and keyed the handset. The colonel came back after the fifth call in a stilted Spanish accent slurred by alcohol.

1843 hours

The sun was just down in the Bahamas, the clouds of the western sky going bloodred, gold, and soft-drink orange in overlapping layers. The wind had fallen to just a whisper but was still from the north.

The colonel replaced the handset on the single-sideband radio and leaned against the sliding door that led out to the wing bridge.

It had been Lu. No mistaking his voice, his inflection, even through the distortion of the radio. So Lu had failed and now he was coming home to his master like a dog with his tail between his legs. It didn't matter. Lu and all the others on board the *Pampero* would be blown into bits of meat no larger than cocktail sausages.

He had taken his plate to the bridge when the call came through, and he now resumed eating. Rack of lamb, roasted breadfruit, carrots julienne, and a sorbet. The wine was some trash that Sanchez had bought in Panama: French, overpriced, and bitter, but with a lovely gold and green label. Sanchez thought it was *exquisite*.

He finished his plate and pushed it aside. There would be time for a short nap. He set his wristwatch to wake him at 2030 hours, then looked into the salon. Sanchez was into his third helping, pushing forkfuls of food into his face. He looked up.

"News, Colonel?"

"Nothing of importance. I am going to rest. You will remain on the radar. Call me if you detect any returns heading inbound."

"Of course, Colonel." He beamed up a smile and resumed his attack on the lamb.

"And the crew?"

"As you instructed. All except three of the best men are in the mess having the evening meal. I personally distributed two bottles of rum and a case of beer and explained that they would be locked in due to the sensitive nature of your undertakings. Like good sailors, they obey their captain without complaint."

It was unfortunate, the colonel thought. That they would all die, and probably not without complaint.

1924 hours

Ink black, the wind just a breath of cold dry air from the north, the fathometer's digital readout showing that the seabed beneath the *Pampero* was suddenly rising.

Bracken was on the wheel, Walrus forward staring toward the black horizon. Ten minutes before, they had turned on the radar for less than a minute and had picked up the faint trace of North West Cay, took a bearing and range on it, then shut the radar down. Bracken was now steering in on that bearing, watching the log as tenths of miles clicked by, watching the fathometer as eighty feet became seventy, then sixty. Less than a quarter of a mile to go and, as yet, no sight of land.

A sharp whistle from forward. Bracken spun the helm and the *Pampero* slowly wheeled through 180 degrees, dead into the wind, dead in the water. He heard the anchor let go, the rattle of chain, then links slowly running out. The fathometer reading flickered erratically between forty and forty-five feet and began to diminish. They had cut it very, very thin because on the eastern side of the island the seabed rose very quickly from deep water to outlying coral reefs which were awash with the beach only another eighty feet inshore.

He felt the schooner surge up against the chain, hold, and then fall off as Walrus slacked out more chain. Fathometer reading now only twenty-eight feet. More chain running out, then snapping taut. Sixteen feet of water under the keel. Thank God the wind was light, because having to anchor on a lee shore was the boogeyman of sailor's nightmares. If the anchor dragged, the old bucket would be up on the bricks in seconds.

Walrus materialized out of the darkness. He bent down,

cupped his hands, and lit a cigarette. "Thirty fathoms of chain out. I've got the chain snubber on and she's holding good."

Bracken looked at the luminous hands of his watch. Nineteen thirty-seven. Seemed that the only time he was ever on time was when he didn't want to be there in the first place. He looked aft and still couldn't see the island. Not specifically. Just a dark mass, darker than the rest of the night.

"Let's do it," he said.

They already had positioned most of the gear on deck. The machine pistol and .22 semi-automatic encased in a green plastic garbage bag, the P-38 with its box of shells, a roll of duct tape, a reel of fishing line, an air mattress, the coil of garden hose and an air bottle, a regulator, a face mask, two sets of flippers, a snorkel tube, and a couple of what passed in yacht chandleries as waterproof flashlights.

Together they picked up the inflatable dinghy and dumped it overboard.

"No need for the motor, right?" asked Walrus.

The plan was, with the wind blowing onshore, they would string out a light nylon line tied at one end to the stern cleats of the *Pampero* with the other end tied to the bow painter of the dinghy. Then, driven by the wind, they would float in over the reef and once in shoal water carry the dinghy up above the tide line. When they returned, they would launch the dinghy and just haul on the line to get back out to the schooner. The operative words were "when they returned."

"Don't think so."

Walrus shrugged. "Fine by me, skip."

"Be back in a second." He ducked down the companionway and hung a left into the aft cabin.

Lu seemed to be dozing. Bracken had left four tablets of codeine on the dresser top, close enough for Lu to reach them. Three of them were gone.

He poked Lu's chest with his finger. "Hey!"

Eyes fluttered open, tried to focus, then crimped shut.

Poking again with his finger, Bracken bent down. "We're going. The boat's well anchored. You should be all right. I'll leave the bilge pump on automatic."

"And if you don't come back?" The voice was hollow, blurred with sleep and dope.

"You'll be all right. No place to go, nothing to do. Just sleep it off."

"But if you don't come back? What happens to me?" The voice a little clearer, a little more insistent. Lu's eyelids fluttered open.

"Use your imagination, Lu," Bracken said.

Lu listened to the footsteps on deck, the rattle of gear being stowed on the aluminum floorboards of the dinghy, some splashing, then silence.

Raising his knees, he brought pressure against the light nylon line, causing it to tauten. Satisfied, he retrieved the dental floss container from his Jockey shorts and, using the small metal hooked claw that cut off the floss, began to pick at the line, severing the fibers one by one. It took him ten agonizing minutes to cut through the line.

He was shaky, his head throbbing as if a hammer were driving a spike into his brain, but he could function. He hadn't taken the codeine, only pocketed the three tablets for later. But aspirin would help the pain without making him drowsy. He found them in the medicine locker and gulped down four.

He had to get going, but he was methodical about it, the list implanted in his mind more than an hour earlier.

Dark blue pea jacket that the first mate sometimes wore—too large but it was dark and warm. He shrugged it on and buttoned it up.

Food. There was half a pot of cold baked beans in the galley sink. He wolfed down the two cupfuls that remained, then raided the fridge and found a package of breakfast sausages. Lu ate three of them raw, almost gagging on the fat.

Briefcase. It held the passports and the traveler's checks. Bracken had pried open the clasps but had not discovered the secret compartment. Using some of the line that had laced his bunk, he tied the lid closed.

How long had it been since Bracken had left? No more than ten, maybe fifteen minutes.

The deck was pitching gently as the *Pampero* bucked against a light swell from the north. For a minute Lu listened, then groped his way forward. The Sunfish sailing dinghy was lashed down on deck, the sail already bent to the mast lashed beside it. In his leisure time in Cuba, where he had the run of the Mariel naval yard, Lu had learned to sail well enough to handle a similar small craft, and he cut loose the lashings with his knife.

His eyes were adjusting to the dark, and he saw the outboard engine still lashed down under a tarp on the port side of the foremast. Curious that they hadn't used it.

He slipped aft, feeling his way past deck fittings until he was at the transom. His night vision was now very good, always had been except when he had been a heavy cigarette smoker, and he immediately picked out the fluorescent swash of small breakers on both the reef and farther in, on the sandy beach. The beach was shockingly close, no more than the toss of a small stone.

A fluttering of white at his feet caught his eye. He looked down. The white line contrasted with the dark water beneath the transom and he knelt down to feel it. Actually, not one single line but a loop running over a block that had been temporarily rigged. He understood. Instead of just drifting ashore, Bracken and the first mate had used a continuous loop of three-eighths-inch nylon to fall back from the *Pampero* toward the beach, driven by the light wind and probably some hand paddling. To get back to the *Pampero*, they would need only to overhaul the slack portion of the line to quickly drag themselves back. Thus they had not needed the outboard motor.

He tugged on the line. Then strained harder but because of the elasticity of the line he could not take anything in. Of course. They would have carried the inflatable dinghy up above the high tide line.

He took all the slack in the line that he could and threw it over the jib sheet winch, taking five turns around the drum. Then applied the winch handle to the socket on top of the winch and began to crank. Nothing at first, just increasing pressure on the winch handle and the humming tension of the nylon line going taut as a bow string. Then suddenly, movement. He cranked furiously. Bow string taut again—a snag. He slacked off the line ten feet or so and furiously cranked again. The line tightened then suddenly jerked free. Broken! He stood up, taking the line off the winch and pulled on it again, bitter at the results of his impatience. He took in thirty or forty feet of the line but then felt a light tension as if he were pulling in a large fish with the fight gone out of it. In two minutes the inflatable Zodiac dinghy was bobbing alongside.

It took him a few minutes to unlash the outboard motor, find the fuel tank, and lower both into the dinghy. Clambering down into the boat, he slung the outboard onto the transom, connected the fuel line, and opened the choke. The motor was similar to the one he had used in Grenada, made by the same manufacturer. He opened the twist throttle about halfway, pulled out the choke, and yanked on the starter cord. The engine fired on the second pull but quickly died. Lu punched in the choke and pulled again. The engine caught, howling up through the rpms, but Lu quickly throttled it back to a rumbling idle. The wind was blowing on-shore and the sound of the engine would carry. Then he knew that it didn't matter. Bracken wouldn't come back, regardless of what he thought he might have heard, because he didn't have time.

Twenty twenty-two hours.

It was now a race.

22.

2027 hours

With her Swiss Army knife, using the file blade, Jean methodically sawed away at the aluminum porthole stud at the junction of the stud and the wing nut. Three of the six were completely severed, their wing nuts now twisted off, and this one was two thirds of the way through with only two more to go.

The file was really a kid's toy, only about an eighth of an inch thick and a couple of inches long, something more suited to buffing fingernails than cutting through three-eighths-diameter metal. But it was working, although slowly. She estimated that it would take another twenty or thirty minutes before all the studs were severed. Then *adíos, Victoria.*

Her wrist was aching from the constant pressure that she had to exert on the blade. The seesaw scratching wasn't too loud, but loud enough, and they had tried to cover it up with other more acceptable noises. She and Pam had taken turns sawing, ten minutes on and ten minutes off, the other one with her ear to the door listening for any sound in the corridor. And at ten after eight, Pam had hissed to stop filing. They both listened, hearts pounding. Soft footsteps up and down the corridor outside and the occasional metallic click of a weapon against the buttons of the guard's uniform. Pam had tried to cover the noise of the file by running the shower full blast, singing, carrying on an inane conversation with herself, and thumping a spoon around in a glass if she were trying to mix the ultimate dry martini. But she had covered her bets by backing a chair up against the knob of the door.

"My turn," Pam whispered.

Jean nodded. The file had cut almost entirely through the stud, but it was starting to catch the sides if she wasn't careful to keep the file perpendicular to the bottom of the cut.

Pam took over filing and Jean, suddenly inspired, dug out

her hair dryer. Good noisemaker. Why hadn't she thought of it before?

"Sheeee-*it!*" Pam stood there, her expression furious but her body slumped in dejection; the file snapped off three quarters of the way down toward the handle of the knife. The broken-off section of the file lay on the rug.

Pam was shaking. "Damn damn damn!" she whispered, teeth clenched, tears in her eyes.

Putting her arm on Pam's shoulders, Jean hugged her a little. "Not your fault. Anyway, comes with a guarantee. Just send it back to the factory for a full refund. You have any emery boards or nail files?"

Pam nodded. "One of each."

"Okay. We both work now, because it's going to go a lot slower, but we'll have the last two studs sawed off in an hour."

Pam looked at her a little strangely, sniffled, and smiled weakly. "Damned right. Let's get on with it, lady. Just make believe that they're parts of Sanchez's anatomy."

They'd give it a good try, but Jean knew. And she knew that Pam knew. It would take hours.

2038 hours

It had taken them more time to cross the quarter mile of the island than Bracken had thought possible. They had planned for a quick jog, carrying the small items in rucksacks and the tank, weights, hose, and regulator in a makeshift sling between them. But what Bracken hadn't counted on were the sucking mudflats and the mosquitoes.

The interior of North West Cay was one huge caked mudflat, probably bone-dry most of the time but after the rains of Hannah, now a morass. And the torrential rains had also brought out swarming, stinging clouds of insects. Finally, both he and Walrus had stopped and plastered their faces and bodies with mud to give some protection from the bites.

Now they stood in the cleft between two large sand dunes and looked out into the anchorage. Nothing. No lights, no sense of anything there except black emptiness.

"You think they skipped?" asked Walrus. "From what I remember about the satellite dish antenna on the *Shango,* the thing can lock on to a satellite even at sea. They could be heading out for Cuba and still do the job."

Bracken didn't answer immediately. The *Victoria* had to be out there, because if the colonel thought that Lu and the Cubans were en route, he wouldn't want to leave until he had disposed of them and the *Pampero*. And it was obvious that they wouldn't have any lights on except very low power illumination that the bronze-toned glass windows would mask. Still, he had expected the vessel to be visible, because he had estimated that it would be anchored fairly close to shore in order to stay out of the swell that was still rolling down from the north.

He padded down to the water and waded out until he was in over his waist. He thrashed around, sluicing the caked mud away, then ducked his head underwater. He was sloshing mud out of his hair when he heard the hum. He paused, resurfaced for a breath, then carefully lowered his head again until it was completely immersed. Not loud but a hum, similar to the sound of a distant outboard motor heard by a diver who was underwater.

He resurfaced. Walrus was standing beside him, also washing off the mud's residue.

"You heard it?" Bracken asked.

"Yeah. Probably a generator. Higher speed than main propulsion engines. She's out there but a helluva lot farther out than I thought she'd be."

"Let's go!"

Together they sprinted back to the cleft in the sand dunes. Walrus attached the regulator, strapped on the scuba tank, coiled the water hose over his shoulder, and waded down to the water's edge. He then put on a set of flippers and rinsed his mask. "Give me about ten minutes lead, skip." They both checked their watches: 2041 hours. "I should be finished well before nine. Then I'll come back to the beach and play target. Figure on things starting a little after nine. Main thing is that I pull the line at 2120, right?"

It wasn't a lot of time. Less than thirty-nine minutes. "Yes. It's cutting things a little close, but it can't be helped. We're running late. If I'm not back here by 2130, take off for the *Pampero*. I left the single sideband set up so that all you have to do is turn it on and call. It's on the Coast Guard frequency for Portsmouth, Virginia. Give them a mayday and see whether you can get them to send one of their big cutters out here, maybe a chopper as well."

"All of which is bullshit! I'll be here waiting. At least until dawn. If you don't show, then it's up to me how I handle it." He stuck out his hand. "I enjoyed the ride, John. All of it."

There wasn't anything left to say that would be adequate. Bracken nodded. "So did I, Tom. Let's go for it."

2046 hours

Huffing and puffing, Bracken inflated the canvas air mattress. Then gathered up the machine pistol which was wrapped in a plastic garbage bag and sealed with waterproof tape. Next he checked the seal on the freezer bag that protected the .22 semi-automatic from moisture, then strapped it to his calf with electrical tape. He wasn't sure why he was taking it but anything that had firepower was a plus.

Wading into the water, he lay down on the mattress with the machine pistol lodged between his chest and the fabric, then shoved off from the shore, stroking overhand in the rough direction where he thought the *Victoria* was anchored.

Occasionally, he paused and rested, coasting seaward, driven by the light wind. Ducked his head underwater again. Humming getting louder—a little more to his left. Checked the sky. All familiar friends, marching in lockstep circles around the pole, only Polaris hanging motionless at true north.

In another eighty strokes he saw the *Victoria*—didn't actually see it, but sensed the hard, elongated profile of blackness that blotted out the stars on the western horizon. No more than forty yards away. The generators were now loud enough to hear above water, and he hoped that they would drown out his puny splashing.

He altered course to pass astern of her, keeping thirty yards off. He had jeans on and a dark turtleneck, a close approximation of what the *Victoria*'s crew wore at sea and dark enough to blend in with the blackness of the water. But he felt naked. If anyone was aft on her deck, Bracken knew that there was a reasonable chance that he would be seen. And to be seen was to be dead.

In theory, the plan was simple. Walrus would do his thing and swim back to the shore, then open fire with the Walther P-38, although it was limited to one round between reloading. The automatic feed was still jammed, and the corroded hammer spring had been replaced by a large rubber band. Still, the Walrus's prognosis was that it would fire, but only as a one-shot zip gun. "Hell of a way to fight a war, skip," Walrus had commented.

Because the *Victoria* swung to anchor in the north wind, the starboard side of the vessel paralleled the shore and Bracken assumed that the colonel would deploy guards on that side of the vessel. As on most powerboats, there was a teak swimming platform jutting out from the hull just above the waterline, and that was where Bracken was headed. Once he was able to climb up onto the platform, a narrow built-in ladder led up through a gangway into the aft guest cockpit. Once Walrus opened fire from the beach and masked by noise of the return fire from the *Victoria*, the grand theory was that Bracken would slip aboard without being noticed. Which was all it was—a theory. From then on in the theory deteriorated into the realm of winging it.

He was now directly astern of the vessel, still thirty yards off. He rubbed the salt water out of his eyes and rested, studying the deck of the *Victoria*. No movement that he could see, no giveaway glow of a cigarette butt, but then who the hell smoked these days anyway?

Time ticking by. Checked his watch: 2053. Time to make his move.

Slowly, he eased over the side of the mattress, let it go, and, holding the machine pistol above his head, stroked with his free arm toward the stern of the *Victoria*.

The sound of the generators was louder now, and his lungs burned from inhaling the exhaust gas. Twenty more yards to go and then ten. Five.

The boat was almost on top of him, slewing in an arc as it rounded in toward the stern, losing way as the driver chopped the throttle. He hadn't heard it coming until it was on top of him because of the generator exhaust noise. Two yards, then one. His lungs heaving, he pulled himself under the swimming platform, having to immerse the machine pistol underwater in the process to keep it out of sight. With one hand he clung to a barnacle-encrusted tube that supported the swimming platform, keeping his face barely above water.

The boat quickly lost speed and coasted up to the platform, the engine idling, then throttled back to cut off. The bow of the boat nudged the swimming platform no more than a foot from his head, and he recognized the letters painted on the bow: the *Pampero*'s Zodiac dinghy! A figure stood up in the boat and heaved a line onto the deck of the *Victoria*.

"Atención! Hay alguien ahí?"

The accent was terrible and the voice distorted as if the speaker had a banana crammed in his mouth, but it was Lu. How in hell had he gotten free? The guy had to be tough as nails—a lot tougher than Bracken would have ever believed possible.

Lu called again to anyone who might be on deck, but still no one answered. Kill the bastard right now? But he couldn't. Both weapons were sealed up in bags and it would take him more than thirty seconds in perfect conditions to get either one of them out. Of more importance, killing Lu was not the point of being here.

It didn't matter anyway. Lu jumped onto the swimming platform, his bare feet landing just inches away from Bracken's hand. Then, in seconds, he was up the ladder. Bracken heard the aft gangway door bang open, snick closed, then heard the pounding of Lu's bare footsteps on the deck, heading forward toward the bridge.

Well and truly, the cat was out of the bag.

2050 hours

He was blind, stroking through ink, all sense of direction gone. He cautiously eased up to the surface and looked around. The profile of the *Victoria,* instead of being behind him, was just off his left side. Crap! He cleared his face mask of accumulated seawater, paddled around toward the dark shore, and submerged again.

Every instinct in him told him to go back, but this was the plan and he knew he had to stick to it. And his part had come off even more quickly than he had estimated.

The end of sixty feet of water hose, filled with plastic explosive which he had carefully and slowly melted in the oven, then poured into the hose, was now looped around the rudder shaft, secured in place with lashings of fishing line.

Groping his way along the keel of the *Victoria,* Walrus had slowly edged forward, hand over hand, feeling for some projection on the hull to secure the other end of the hose to. And finally found it. He carefully explored it with his fingers. Had to be the housing for some kind of underwater speed sensor. The housing protected a small plastic impeller which was set in its aperture. Pretty common fitting: as the vessel moved through the water, the impeller would turn, sending back to the bridge a measurement of speed and distance traveled.

To be absolutely positive, he chanced using the underwater flashlight. Exactly what he had guessed. He quickly switched off the light. Next he looped the hose through the aperture and doubled the hose back on itself with a length of fishing line.

Securely tamped into the end of the hose was the ten-second detonator. One good pull on the ring of that sucker and it would all be over. The detonator would blow the explosive in the garden hose, and tamped by the water and the shallow bottom, the explosive force would rip out the bottom of the *Victoria* from stem to stern. Watertight compartments wouldn't mean snot when something like this thing blew.

He attached the end of a spool of fishing line to the firing ring, withdrew the safety pin, and, gingerly unwinding the spool, flippered toward the shore, taking extreme care not to put any tension on the line.

Just once he surfaced. Couldn't see the *Victoria*, could see the shore but was on a course a little too far to the north. He released the buckle of his diving harness, shrugged off the tank and regulator, and flippered strongly for the two largest dunes of sand that marked where the Walther lay. Let the battle begin, and the truth was that Walrus had never fired a shot in anger. Until now. He intended to make up for lost time.

2102 hours

Lu was nearly up to the bridge before he saw a guard. The man was lazing in a doorway, smoking a cigarette. Suddenly, the man raised the barrel of his automatic rifle.

Lu knocked it aside. "You idiot! Get over on the starboard side. There's going to be an attack!" he yelled in Spanish, turned, running up the empty deck, banging against fittings, then scrambling up the ladder to the bridge. He tried to slide back the door to the interior but found it latched. With his knuckles he rapped loudly on the glass pane. Inside, he could barely make out the dimly lit gauges on the instrument panel and a shaded light over the chart table, all hazed to a deep apricot by the bronzed tone of the glass.

Sanchez was suddenly behind him. "What are you doing here now? You weren't due to arrive until after midnight." There was the sound of a hammer of a revolver clicking back.

With a weapon prodding into his ribs, Lu carefully set his

briefcase down on the deck, then raised his hands. "There isn't time to play games, Sanchez. I have to see the colonel right now."

Sanchez stepped backward as Lu turned, his handgun leveled on Lu's chest, then switched on a flashlight, blinding Lu. "*Dios mío!* What has happened to your face?"

"The colonel. There's no time. . . ."

The door slid back. "Turn off that light, Sanchez!" The colonel took Lu by the arm and dragged him onto the bridge, then angled the chart light toward Lu. "*Mat trayu!* What happened?"

"Bracken somehow secretly manufactured a Molotov cocktail. As Raul, Vierro, and the other Cuban got into the launch, he lit the wick and threw it. They died screaming."

"And what in hell were you doing, you *durak*? It was your responsibility to guard Bracken and the crew while the Cubans were on the mission." He reached up into a cubicle above the chart table, fumbled around, and withdrew a package of cigarettes. He lit one, then offered the pack to Lu, who shook his head.

"Not now. After what happened he hit me with a lead pipe. I fought him, hurt him badly, but I couldn't see. None of this matters. He's headed here."

"What do you mean, he's headed here? There hasn't been anything on the radar."

"He came in around from the east behind the island, then anchored off the eastern shore. The low sand hills in between would block off your radar. He left me tied up, then set off across the island on foot with his first mate. I got loose and stole their dinghy. Bracken knows about phase two, the timing. He's probably going to try an assault on the *Victoria*."

"How?"

"He has a gun. Something that he had hidden on the *Pampero*."

The colonel's face momentarily went white, then flushed red. "Sanchez!" the colonel shouted. "Release all of the men from the mess. All are to be armed with automatic weapons. Put two of them up on the top deck to protect the satellite dome and two others on the spotlights. The rest should spread around the deck. Anything that moves should be shot. Watch out for swimmers. *Get moving!*"

2105 hours

Bracken painfully pulled his body up over the edge of the swimming platform. The salt water had soaked through the muslin bandage. The wound in his side seared blast-furnace hot from the corrosive effect of the salt water. He panted for a couple of seconds on the platform, trying to get it together. Gradually, the pain receded to the point that it was tolerable.

He ripped off the tape and opened the plastic bag, pulling out the machine pistol. The damn thing was saturated with salt water! Probably some of the barnacles had torn the plastic, but the effect was that the machine pistol had to be dried out and fast because with water in the mechanism and barrel, it might not function and worse still, it could blow up in his hands. He shook it like a wet puppy, hoping for the best.

Less than a minute had elapsed since Lu boarded the *Victoria*. Bracken knew he had fourteen minutes maximum remaining.

Jean would be locked away in one of the cabins. He could allocate a maximum of eight minutes trying to free her, and if he couldn't, he had to go for the satellite dish with no looking back.

Slinging the SMG over his back by its strap, he climbed into the cockpit. The teak deck was still warm, a few deck chairs set out around a canopied table. Stooping down to keep his profile below the level of the salon windows, he brushed by them, feeling with his hand for the door to the salon. Found it. Unlocked. He stood up and rotated the doorknob like he owned the place.

"*Me llamó?*" Easy phrase, naturallike, and the Spanish inflection came out good enough. But no one answered.

He slipped inside and ducked down behind the couch. Dark as a crypt, no lights, although there was a crack of illumination under the door that led to the service pantry and galley forward of the salon. Beneath his feet he could feel the gentle pulsing of the generators.

Seconds ticking away, irreplaceable.

He crawled forward past the couch through the thick nap of the salon carpeting, bumping into furniture as he went. Tried to remember the exact layout of the salon and knew that the stairwell that led down to the guest accommodations was somewhere off to the starboard side, next to the wet bar and liquor locker.

With his head down and on all fours, he stupidly plowed right into the hard paneling of a cabinet, making a racket as his machine pistol came unslung and thunked against the wood.

Damn! He paused, listening carefully. Nothing.

He reached up and felt the object. Wet bar and booze locker. Sink with an ice bucket resting in it, two empty glasses still wet with moisture, a booze bottle, and a faucet. His fingers brushed a coiled cord and traced it to the source, a telephone handset hanging from a fixture on the wall. But not a telephone. Intercom. Just like every other cabin or work area in the vessel was equipped with.

Germ of an idea. Possibly workable. He slowly stood up, reslinging the machine pistol, and pulled the flashlight from his belt, hooded the lens, and flashed the slim sliver of light on the bulkhead next to the phone.

There was a list of numbers and locations protected by a clear plastic panel screwed into the wood.

Bridge was *01.*

Engine Room, 02.

Galley, 03.

He ran down the list. *Cabins* was a subsection running from numbers *twelve* to *seventeen*, each identified with their corresponding cabin number. *Cabin C?* Tried to remember. Was that mine or hers? Or D? Either one or the other.

He punched in a one, then a four for cabin C. Two buzzes.

"Dígame."

Damn! "Ah . . . *perdone . . . ah . . . me equi . . . ah . . . voquéelnúmero,"* and pushed down the hook, cutting off the line.

Sweating buckets. Some Cuban was down in C. Sanchez. No, not Sanchez's voice. Probably a guard.

He knew he had to keep trying. If the Cuban in C got a wrong number, he'd be suspicious. But if the phone then rang in cabin D . . . Maybe the galley calling down to see who was up for a late night snack.

Bracken tried D. Two rings. "Hello." Hesitant, low, throaty, feminine, nervous, but the voice not Jean's. Pam's!

She might not recognize the voice on the phone, and he had to connect with her right away or she might hang up on him or blurt out his name. He kept his voice low. "Good evening, ma'am. We're doing a survey on whether you prefer safe sex or celibacy and if you know who the hell this is, don't talk, just keep listening. I'm upstairs in the salon. Is Jean with you and when you answer, call me Sanchez."

He heard her blow out a long slow breath into the handset. "Oh! *Seen-yor* Sanchez. Nice to hear from you. Jean and I have been wondering when we could come up and see you, but the dirty little man outside in the corridor has us locked in. Such a big gun with all those bullets. Maybe instead you could come down and see us, hum?"

"Don't overdo it, kid. Put Jean on after you brief her. Make it quick."

Thirty thumping heartbeats.

"Hello, Sanchez. How . . . ?"

"No time, Jean. What's the deal on the guard?"

She lowered her voice to a whisper. "He's working out of the cabin across the corridor. Uses the bathroom in there and he's been on the intercom a couple of times bitching in Spanish, about getting some dinner."

"What kind of weapon?"

"Don't know. They generally carry those Russian AK-things with the stubby barrels."

"You think you could get his attention. Like knock on the door and ask him something. Real sweet like?"

"When?"

He looked at the luminous hands of his watch: 2107. "Thirty seconds." He hung up.

Bracken gave it thirty seconds, then slowly descended the stairs to the corridor below. He ducked his head around the corner, the SMG at the ready.

But the guard was standing in front of the door of cabin D, a smile on his face, straightening his uniform and slicking back his hair.

The door opened, casting light into the corridor.

Bracken heard Jean's voice. "Can you help us, Comandante?" she said in Spanish. "We are unable to withdraw the cork from the wine bottle."

The guard, his AK-47 slung over his shoulder, staggered slightly, his eyes bulging out. Then he broke into a huge grin. Bracken counted to five and went after him, light on his feet, his weapon held by the butt and barrel like a club.

"*Ay, qué melónes jugosos!*" the guard whispered, staring into the cabin.

Bracken was behind him now, Pam beyond the guard, naked from the waist up. Her eyes flickered to Bracken's, her mouth opening. The guard started to turn, and Bracken smashed the butt of the machine pistol into his head.

Bracken dragged the still-vibrating body of the Cuban into

the stateroom and pushed the door closed behind him. Pam had turned her head away, Jean was in the bathroom, throwing up.

He threw a bedspread over the body and picked up the AK-47. Full clip, one in the chamber, safety on. Time check: 2108. Almost no time left if the computer program had been right with the prediction of twenty past the hour.

He grabbed Pam's shoulder roughly and wheeled her around. "Both of you get dressed pronto. Follow me up into the salon, out the back doors to the sun deck, and over the transom. Try not to make a splash. Head for shore. When you're there, keep the wind on the left side of your face and start across the island. You'll end up on the Atlantic side. Then head north with the wind in your face and you'll see the *Pampero*. Swim out to her and wait. Walrus and I will be along later."

"How much later, dammit?" Jean was wiping her mouth with a towel, her eyes red, her whole body shaking.

"Do like I say for once! You've got thirty seconds to get into something. I'll cover you until you're both overboard."

Pam was already zipping up a gray silk jump suit that gave new meaning to shrink-wrap packaging. She winked at him.

"Cap'n Hook, you damn well did it again. Allah reserves a special place in paradise for hunks like you. So do I." She was smiling now, no fear on her face.

Jean roughly shoved past her, sat down on the bed, and wiggled into denims and a T-shirt.

"Come on, come on! Hustle." He thought about taking the AK-47 and hefted it. Too big. The machine pistol was handier. He handed the Kalashnikov to Jean. "If you have to fire it, hold on with both hands and pull the trigger. The safety's off."

"You expect me to swim with this thing?"

"No. Just dump it in the sea if we get that far. Now let's go!"

He led the way into the corridor. Still nothing. The women followed behind him as he groped his way up the spiral staircase. "Down on all fours." He retraced his path to the door and cracked it open.

The interior sound insulation had suppressed the noise on deck, but with the door open he could hear pounding footsteps and commands being snapped from someone up forward.

He crept out, motioning the women to hold back. Ducking his head around the superstructure, he took a quick peek along the starboard deck. One man was forward near the gangway, an AK-47 in his hands, his figure silhouetted by a spotlight on the bridge deck which was erratically playing over the waters of the anchorage.

Then a sharp command in Spanish from the bridge and the light reversed its direction, sweeping toward the shore of the island.

Bracken checked the port side. Four or five men with flashlights, two of them fitting the base mount of a 12.7 mm Degtyarev heavy machine gun to a socket on the rail, several other men heaving up canisters of ammunition from a hatch.

The women would have to go now or never. "Pam! You first. Keep low, no noise," he whispered.

She pecked him on the cheek as she slipped by. "Later, Hook." In seconds she was through the boarding gate, down on the swimming platform, and in the water. She took off like a sleek seal headed for a seven-course dinner. In a few seconds the blackness swallowed her.

He tugged at Jean's arm. "You next."

She snatched her arm back. "Not going, Bracken. Not without you. I took weapons training in DEA. I'll back you up."

"Like hell you aren't going!"

"Keep your dumb voice down. I repeat. I'm not going. Not as long as you're on board. Period!"

The splat of a bullet glancing off the side of the ship was followed by the sound of a single muffled shot from shore. Mayhem broke loose on the *Victoria* as several automatic weapons began their heavy stutter, hosing streams of tracers toward the beach.

He checked his watch: 2111. "I didn't think he'd be able to do it but, by God, Walrus's got this boat wired with explosives. We've got to get out of here in two minutes, before it blows."

She looked up at him, his face just a trace of pale white against the blackness. "We'll make it together, Bracken, or not at all. Let's go for it." He felt her tensing.

He shook his head. "Wait until he fires again from the beach. When they're firing back at the shore, we'll make a dive for it." He leaned down and crushed his mouth against hers.

Making a show of it, he laid his SMG on the deck, then took hers and did likewise. "Make sure you jump clear of the railing, make it a clean dive, and go deep. Hold your breath as long as you can, come to the surface and grab a breath, then duck again. If no one's firing at us, we'll stroke downwind for a hundred yards, then turn for shore."

She didn't answer, just squeezed his hand.

Thirty, forty seconds elapsed, then another shot from shore. The sound was deafening as the crew of the *Victoria* hammered the beach with automatic weapons.

"Now!" He slapped her butt and started to sprint forward, Jean at his side. She cleared the rail and knifed into the sea.

Bracken slammed up against the rail, watched for her, but she was gone, then picked up the SMG and entered the salon, creeping toward the crack of light that seeped from under the pantry door.

2112 hours

Walrus, lying just behind the dune, chambered another cartridge, thumbed back the hammer, and elevated his sights to compensate for the distance. The bridge of the *Victoria* was partially illuminated by one of the searchlights.

A short burst of tracers from somewhere aft on the vessel stitched the sand in front of him.

He moved the sights slightly to the left, where he had seen the muzzle flash, and gently squeezed. He was rewarded by the sound of a scream. He jumped up. The spotlight swept across the dune, then picked him up in its glare. He dived behind the dune in time to avoid a torrent of slugs tearing through the air above him. He ripped off his sweatshirt to expose his white T-shirt and sprinted around the back of the dune, chambering another round on the run, then cocking the weapon. He had only another twenty-one cartridges in his pocket.

When they ran out . . .

He emerged on the far side of the dune, well over fifty feet from where he had just fired. The spotlight picked him up in four seconds. He snapped off a shot, then dove into the sandy depression. Almost immediately, tracers raked the sand above him.

He was trying to create the impression of two separate men with two different weapons firing from two different places. It seemed to be working, but he vowed that he would swear off beer for a year if he got out of this one with his hide intact. Carrying a load of blubber around, even for a Walrus, had its disadvantages.

2113 hours

On the shortwave radio, Radio Moscow was playing Prokofiev's Classical Symphony in D Major, Opus 25, the gavotte movement. Lu recognized it immediately, as every educated Soviet citizen did. It had been one of his wife's favorites. He could remember lying in her bed with her warm body spooned against his, listening to it after their first lovemaking time.

On deck, the gunfire had died down to sporadic bursts. Sanchez had reported just minutes before that both Bracken and his first mate were pinned down on the beach.

"Radio Moscow's late! They were supposed to give the go-ahead by now!" The colonel banged his clenched fist on the chart desk. "Knew it, I damn well knew it! Khokhlov has lost his balls and he's backing out on me. Either that or the operation was uncovered by the pacifists in the Politburo."

The colonel checked the computer screen again. The projected trace of the shuttle was arcing down over Kentucky, now almost within line-of-sight of the satellite dish. Overhead, the controller for the dish antenna had been set up on coordinates which would immediately acquire the shuttle once it was within range and line-of-sight, and at that point would begin to track it automatically.

With crushed ice wrapped in a towel, Lu held the coldness to his swollen face. Bracken and his first mate were out of the way, and except for a lucky shot, presented no problem. Whether or not the colonel was able to destroy the shuttle was not his problem. His concern lay elsewhere.

"I saved phase two," he said quietly, matter-of-factly.

The colonel cocked his head aside and looked up at him, agitated, his face streaming with sweat. "You saved nothing, you yellow ape. Instead, you transformed a carefully planned operation into a total balls-up disaster. And four days ago I specifically warned you about the price of failure."

Lu wanted to scream back at him, about the years of discrimination, about having been continually lied to, about the terrifying life he had led for over two decades, and about the timing of the demolition charge planted on the *Pampero* which had been meant to kill him as well, but that wouldn't win him the concessions that he wanted. Flies were better attracted with sugar than with vinegar.

"Perhaps I should have done better, but I repeat—by risking my life to come here and alert you to Bracken's plan, I've saved phase two."

"So you want a medal, Lu? Is that it?"

"No, I want my son and my freedom," he said quietly, very reasonably.

"And you wanted to steal a shitload of paintings in the bargain. Paintings worth millions of rubles, a treasure which belongs to the Soviet people."

"I won't deny that."

The colonel fiddled with the dial on the shortwave, fine-tuning it. The opening strains of the finale, Molto vivace, were just beginning.

"I'm taking them back to the Soviet Union," the colonel said flatly. "The paintings are the property of the State and I seem to be the only one left around here that still represents the interests of the Soviet Union."

"I have a man in Singapore who will sell the paintings. A very discreet man, a man that can be trusted. The proceeds from the sale of each painting will be equally divided and placed in two separate numbered bank accounts when the sale occurs. Fifty-fifty."

"You're crazy! What would I do with the money? You think I could bring it into the Soviet Union without raising questions, regardless of how powerful I was?"

Lu kept his face blank but he could sense victory. "I'm sure with your resources and contacts, Colonel, that would present no problem."

There was a small carafe of clear liquid on the edge of the chart table, and the colonel poured the rest of its contents into a glass, then threw it down in one shot. He blew out his lips and grimaced. "What guarantee do I have that you'll give me my fair share?"

"The proceeds will be deposited in two numbered Hong Kong accounts. If I were to cheat on you, I believe that you have the resources to track me down. But if you accept my proposition, you are bound to me in secrecy because you are a co-conspirator. As you can see"—Lu intentionally framed this in the present tense—"our relationship doesn't end tonight. It goes on forever as long as we both may live—a mutual pledge of silence."

"The value of the paintings after this scab's commission?"

"Discounted, of course, from their real market value because of the dubious nature of their acquisiton. But your share would be approximately four million in American dollars."

Another bullet spanged off the bridge structure, followed by several bursts of automatic fire from the deck of the *Victoria*.

"Persistent bastards, aren't they?" the colonel said. No answer required. He drummed his pencil on the chart table, obviously lost in thought.

"I need your decision, Colonel."

"You had this all thought out, even from the beginning, didn't you?"

"Yes, of course. But that didn't prevent me from doing my best. It was just bad luck."

Radio Moscow's transmission suddenly cut off, the music replaced by the white noise of a dead channel. At the same time, the acquisition controller on the satellite winked on, flickered off, then winked on again. The green "tracking confidence" light illuminated and the soft hum of the satellite dish moving permeated the dome overhead.

The hands on the chronometer attached to the bulkhead read 2116.

The colonel dipped into the recesses of the bookshelf over the chart table and lifted out a miniature tape recorder with his left hand, its recording light still on. And with his right, a 9mm Makarov standard issue semi-automatic. He leveled it on Lu's stomach.

"By the power vested in me as your superior officer and under the criteria defining sedition in section eleven, article three, I accuse you of traitorous actions against both the Union of Soviet Socialist Republics and the *Komitet Gosudarstvennoy Bezopasnosti.* You have freely admitted your crimes against the State. Given such admission and under section twelve, article eleven, I am empowered to administer summary administrative action which I now do." The colonel thumbed back the hammer.

23.

2117 hours

Bracken crept on his hands and knees toward the light that leaked from under the door, keeping his head below the level of the salon windows. Twice he saw blurred silhouettes of men running down the deck and muzzle flashes of fire from their automatic weapons as they fired toward the shoreline.

Before pushing the door back, he paused, listening. No movement, no voices. For a second or so he would be exposed by the light, but that was a risk he had to accept.

He nudged the door open, his machine pistol raised, and pushed through, then quickly pulled the door closed behind him.

He had thought it was the pantry, but actually it was an enclosed alleyway that ran athwartship from port to starboard, terminating in watertight doors that opened onto the side decks. Forward were two other doors, also watertight steel with dogs to bolt them down.

The one to starboard was ajar. It revealed a dimly lit pantry area complete with coolers, a dumbwaiter leading to the main galley on the lower deck, and sinks, now stacked with greasy dishes.

The other door on the port side was marked DECK OFFICER'S DAY CABIN. NO ADMITTANCE. The door was closed.

He gently tested the latch. It yielded a fraction. With his ear to the panel he could hear nothing except an electric hum.

He had to get out of the damned alleyway. The light overhead was dim and would be further diminished by the tinted glass as seen from the deck, but he felt terribly exposed. He checked that the safety was off, slowly rotated the latch and rapidly pushed open the door, ready to fire. The room was empty although a hooded desk lamp was on. To starboard was a rumpled bunk. To port, a radar repeater scope, a satnav, desk, and a bookshelf. Binoculars were slung from a rack attached to the outboard bulkhead along with a bin containing a full set of signal flags housed in pigeonholes. The room was as advertised: a day cabin where the officer of the watch could catch a few winks on a long passage and still monitor what the vessel was doing without going onto the bridge.

A door at the forward end of the day cabin was a similarly reinforced steel structure with watertight dogs, marked by a bronze plaque with BRIDGE spelled out in bold relief. Putting his ear against the metal, he could hear voices. Speaking Russian. How many and how well armed? He listened for another twenty seconds. Just two people as far as he could determine. One voice was Lu's, hesitant yet calm. The other one had to be the colonel's.

He tested the handle very carefully. Again, unlocked.

He roughly memorized the layout of the day cabin, turned down the brilliance control on the radar, and then snapped off the desk lamp to prevent himself from being backlighted. He allowed thirty seconds for his eyes to accommodate to the darkness and tested the handle again. It rotated smoothly in his hand. He edged it open carefully, only fractions of an inch, until he had a restricted wedge of vision onto the bridge deck.

The words were louder, much more distinct now. Over to the right, in the dim illumination of the primary radar scope and dash instruments, he could see Lu's back as he sat on a stool of some sort. Lu was tense, his shoulders hunched, his head rigidly locked on the person in front of him.

The other Russian, blocked by Lu's body, was talking now, his voice rough from too many years of chain-smoking. Had to be the old geezer, the colonel.

Bracken could understand only a small part of the dialogue, but the tone was flat and unaccommodating, as if Lu were being royally reamed out. Shouldn't bloody well wonder, Bracken thought, half smiling.

He edged the door open another fraction. The door swung on well-oiled hinges.

In the slit of the partially opened door, he could now see all of Lu's back and part of the colonel's head. Then the older Russian fractionally shifted his body sideways, exposing a slice of his upper body. There was something in his hand, holding it out for Lu to take. Coffee mug? Lu tensed suddenly as if he hadn't expected the offering. Bracken could see it in the set of his shoulders, the mechanical stiffening of his body movements.

Bracken hadn't thought a lot about this moment, deep down, never really believing that he would get this far. He had been able to abstractly accept the possibility of his own death, but now he was gambling not only on his own life but the future of his country's as well.

The colonel's voice had suddenly pitched up into a staccato tirade, almost shouting, and Bracken realized that both Lu and the colonel would automatically blank out their minds to any other distraction.

Bracken threw his shoulder against the door, slamming it open against the stops, the machine pistol leveled. He tried to keep his voice hard, as if he really meant it, no nonsense. Brain giggling.

"Get your hands up. No noise. *Now!*"

Neither of the two Russians moved for a second. As if they hadn't heard or didn't care. Then Lu slowly raised his. Bracken stared at the colonel for over five seconds, neither of them moving, mental gridlock. "You too, asshole. I said *now*. You speak English?"

"Actually, I speak English very well, Bracken," the colonel said agreeably with just a touch of accent. Smiling as if he were really enjoying it. "And what can I do for you? There's some coffee left in the thermos. It's still warm. Please help yourself and then we can talk."

"Raise your hands, lock them behind your neck, and kneel down. Both of you. No noise."

Lu rose slowly from the stool, his hands still high, folding them behind his hairline, interlocking them, breathing hard. But except for the sound of his lungs processing air and background static from a radio, the bridge was silent. The colonel was actually smiling. "Do I get a blindfold and a last cigarette, Bracken?" Seemed as if he thought this was real fun.

Then, without warning and from the speaker of a sophisticated shortwave receiver set into the bulkhead, a radio announcer's voice was saying, "This is the overseas service of Radio Moscow. We regret that due to technical difficulties this broadcast has been interrupted. We now resume our regularly scheduled program. ..." Soothing strains of classical music fading in, strings and bright brass building.

The colonel, his eyes locked to Bracken's, started to chant in a quiet voice like a little kid's, nodding his head in cadence. "One-two-three-four-five-six . . ."

Bracken's brain came off hold and shouted a warning, but it was too late.

The colonel suddenly shifted to the right, two-stepping, shielding his body with Lu's.

"What the hell . . . !"

Two flat hacking coughs of a small caliber weapon in quick succession. Lu in between them, snapping back with the impact, then folding like a puppet, knees buckling. Quick glimpse of the colonel in the classic firing position, two-handed grip, the muzzle of the barrel coming up. Another cough, muzzle blast, and flame, the bullet missing Bracken but the lead projectile splattering within inches of his face against the steel doorframe. Felt fire lance into his face, sudden wetness, dimming, vision gone. Reflexively pulled the trigger on the machine pistol, falling ass over teakettle, his feet stumbling backward over the doorsill into the day cabin, arms and legs flailing, the machine pistol burping out the full clip in a long, shattering staccato, spraying the bridge deck with tracers rising in a stream toward the overhead in response to the recoil of the weapon as it bucked upward in his right hand.

As he fell backward, in dumb desperation, Bracken grabbed at the locking bars on the door with his left hand, somehow pulling it partially closed behind him. Two more dull reports, the impact of bullets ringing off the steel on the other side of the door, then the door slamming fully closed driven by some desperate force behind it, split seconds later the steel dogs sliding home and locking. Yelling on the other side, someone screaming "*Sanchez*," the sound echoing a millisecond later over the ship's public address system.

He was flat on his back, wind knocked out of him, mindstunned, warm mushy wetness all over his face, knowing that he had blown it. He swiped at the blood on his face. Big gash over his right eye, some other wounds from lead fragments.

There were no portholes in the day cabin that he had remembered seeing, and he turned the desk lamp on. He didn't think Sanchez's men would try a direct assault on the day cabin, but he dogged down the watertight door into the alleyway just in case. Then fumbled in his jacket for the other clip and rammed it home. Forty rounds left.

Why had the colonel been chanting? And he knew without thinking any further because it had been there in the computer's files of phase two. Timing. Counting seconds. There would be a clock on the bridge deck, but he had done it mentally, not wanting to take his eyes off Bracken.

Timing. The firing signal was to be transmitted two minutes

and ten seconds after the interruption of Radio Moscow on 9.288 megahertz. And at least thirty of those seconds had already expired.

He had glimpsed the vague contours of the satellite transmitter terminal next to the navigational desk. But the satellite dome was much farther aft on the upper deck, perhaps twenty feet or more. Which meant that the cabling had to run from the transmitter on the bridge, aft through the ship, and up through the overhead to get there. What kind of cables? Walrus said that these things ran on hydraulic power and there would certainly be a coaxial line for the RF power output as well as other electronic control cabling.

Muffled shouts, then the sound of someone trying to open the aft watertight door, the sound of the impact of a heavy gun butt, then a short burst from an automatic weapon, but it didn't yield, wasn't punctured. Sanchez's next step? They would probably use plastic explosive to blow the door from the alleyway, and damn soon. He figured he had no more than a couple of minutes to live. So go for it, because this is why the hell you came here.

He rotated the desk lamp up toward the ceiling: same veneered plywood paneling as on the bulkhead walls.

He scrambled into the far corner and pulled the desk chair in front of him to give him some protection from the ricochets, then squeezed off a short burst where the overhead met the bulkhead. The paneling splintered, chips of wood and foam insulation showering the bunk underneath, a couple of slugs whining off the metal beyond but not hitting him. Another burst, longer this time, spraying back and forth like a gardener with a water hose, soaking with lead the same junction of the two surfaces. Cabin stinking of smoke and cordite, his hand vibrating from the bucking recoil, barely able to see. Another burst, even longer.

Oh, blessed sweet Jesus! Pink hydraulic fluid under very high pressure spurted in a pulsing jet from a bundle of tubing which was now exposed by the shattered overhead paneling.

How many cartridges left? He thumbed out the clip and felt with his fingertips. Fewer than a third left, but now he knew where to go for the gold. He scrambled along the floor until he was directly under the tubing and, holding the machine pistol tightly with both hands, gently stroked the trigger in two quick bursts until the firing pin fell on an empty chamber.

2123 hours

The hydraulic system that drove the satellite dish was dying but it was a slow death from hemorrhaging and not a rapid one from a mortal wound to its guts. Its life blood, pink type A hydraulic fluid, spurted from three of its ruptured arteries, slowing the movements of the actuators which positioned the antennae as they tracked the shuttle, but there was a four-gallon backup reservoir of its life fluid stored in a pressurized accumulator and the transfusion would last so long as any fluid remained. Slightly more than a gallon of the fluid was still left, and the dumb machine, not programmed to understand the symptoms of its own death, still lived and functioned, not perfectly, but after a fashion.

Lu also still lived and functioned, after a fashion. Lying on the teak deck of the bridge, well below the shaded illumination from the navigational table light, he had curled up in the fetal position, blood soaking through his jacket, his skull howling in agony, his stunned cortex unable to function but still alive. After a fashion.

Nothing fitted together, but his jangled memory kept replaying a scene when he was thirteen and had stupidly tried to separate two boys fighting in a school yard. For his trouble he had been pummeled with their fists for interfering. They had walked away together, wary allies sharing a shallow victory, leaving Lu sprawled in the mud with a broken nose and two loose teeth. He felt as much a fool now as he had then.

The deck was cool against his face and he wanted just to sleep, to give his body time to heal, to rest, but his alarm system kept clanging. And piece by piece the events were beginning to fall in place although jumbled and disordered in sequence.

The colonel had fired first, he remembered that much. Before that? A noise. The clunk of the bulkhead door banging against its stops, then Bracken appearing out of nowhere, demanding something. Then the colonel replying smoothly. But as the colonel talked, he had thrust his Makarov between Lu's left arm and rib cage, using his body both as a shield and a gun port. Then two scalding bursts of pain, flame, and noise.

Lu could now remember the colonel pushing him over backward and relived the long fall, timeless, like cartwheeling end over end down an elevator shaft, and while he was still falling, his head had exploded in pain. Stunned, his whole side afire, eyes unfocused on the brilliance of an unbearable brightness, he heard

in the distance more individual shots fired, then the eardrum-
bursting roar of an automatic weapon.

Heard the watertight door slammed closed and locked. Then
the colonel shouting for Sanchez, orders passed, men running. Lu
had then opened his eyes, looked up to see a blurred double
vision of the colonel bending over him, the Makarov in his hand,
the barrel boresighted on a tingling spot of Lu's forehead.

*"You brought him here, arranged it, were part of it, you mutant
bastard!"* His voice lowered, flattened to a whisper. "If you can
still hear me, think about death, Louis. Think about it because I
will give it to you but in my own time, in my own way and very
slowly." He then kicked Lu in the groin. Lu had sucked in his
breath so hard that he hadn't even the ability to cry with pain.

It all seemed a year, a century, a millennium ago. Groggy, Lu
now took inventory. Testicles ached but the toe of the colonel's
shoe hadn't directly connected. He squinted and scowled, trying
to force double images into one. Felt his left side with his right
hand. There didn't seem to be a lot of blood, only this grinding
pain in his side and shoulder. He then tried moving the fingers
on his left hand and couldn't feel them. Either that, or they didn't
work: maybe weren't there.

More automatic weapons firing, could even feel the shudder
of steel-jacketed bullets jackhammering against steel somewhere
very close, heard the slurred coughing stutter of AKs in reply.
Bracken would be dead by now. Then me, he thought. He looked
up toward the colonel's back. He was bent over, a stopwatch in
his hand, ticking off the seconds with little nods of his head like a
mechanical doll.

Resting on the navigation table was the computer, the track
of the shuttle slowly arching over Alabama. And under the colonel's fingertips, the transmitter terminal keyboard.

Lu knew that he was a living dead man. Once the colonel
transmitted the signal, he would make sure that Bracken was
dead, then carry out the promised execution. But Lu was unwilling to die. Not now, not ever. He doubted that he could take the
colonel by brute force and he desperately needed a weapon; a
club, even a hard-soled shoe, *anything*! He snaked out his right
arm, quietly sweeping the floor with his fingertips, looking for
anything that might help him. His fingers brushed a couple of
spent cartridge cases, a ground-out cigar, and a stray pencil.
Then touched the cool saddle-leather covering of his own brief-

case. Working his fingers carefully, he withdrew the concealed pin from the hinge mechanism.

2125 hours

The colonel wasn't a man who cared how things actually worked or what made them tick. He certainly didn't understand radios or computers; barely understood the mechanisms of women or the personal motivations of subordinates. Only *used* them and expected predictable results. Rule number one of good management. It wasn't *how* something worked, only *how well*.

In the last minute the tracking confidence light of the satellite dish controller had twice winked off and then back on. The blasted thing was certainly malfunctioning, the low hydraulic pressure warning bulb now permanently illuminated. Yet he had positive verification that the dish antennae were still locked onto the kick-stage transponder and there were only thirty-four seconds to run before the firing order could be transmitted.

The technicians at the Frunze Institute had been adamant about the timing of the firing signal. There was only a twelve-second window within which the firing signal could be transmitted. If it was sent too soon, the transponder might reject the signal as a spurious transmission and recycle itself, wasting more than thirty seconds, and by then the shuttle would be too far over the horizon for the antennae to reacquire the lock-on. "No more than twelve seconds after the elapsed time of two minutes and ten seconds, the letters absolutely correct and in sequence." They had been adamant on this and the colonel respected precision.

It would be done from the keyboard of the computer. Six keys, punched in sequence, their respective letters echoing back verification on the computer's screen, then hit the Enter key. The computer then processed the sequence into a firing signal and sent it to the transmitter through the RS-232 serial port. The sequence of letters for the firing signal was not difficult to remember because they were the letters of the first six keys on the top row of the computer's keyboard, moving from left to right. *QWERTY*.

Less than twenty seconds to run. Where the devil was Sanchez? Why hadn't his people broken into the day cabin and eliminated Bracken? Or had they? Then his mind registered that the firing had ceased. Maybe Bracken was neutralized, but it didn't matter either way. The door between the bridge and the day cabin was dogged down securely and Bracken would end up a Swiss cheese if he tried to get to the bridge via the side decks. Sanchez was at least competent enough to prevent that from happening.

Fifteen seconds. He wanted a drink badly, but that was for later. After Louis. One bullet behind the ear. In the fifties he had heard it called the Beria kiss. And yet Beria had gone that way too, hadn't he? A warning that would echo through the KGB for those who tried to write their own agenda.

Nine—eight—seven seconds. His heart was pounding with tension and sweat dripped off his forehead onto the keyboard despite the air-conditioning. He positioned his right index finger over the keys, ready to punch in the sequence of letters.

The sting on his leg was no worse than that of a mosquito biting. Initially, he hardly noticed it, so prevalent were they that Sanchez had nicknamed them the buzz bombers which nightly attacked anyone on deck from their staging areas in the inland swamps. Several times on the previous night, even within the air-conditioned quarters of the *Victoria*, the colonel had been fiercely bitten. His legs and arms were a mass of red welts. But now he ignored the insect because he couldn't take the time to swat the damned thing even though its sting was growing in intensity, now almost intolerable.

Three—two—one—zero. The seconds had run out.

He carefully pressed *Q*, seeing the letter echo back on the screen, then *W*. A streak of pain was running up his leg. Heart gyrating against his rib cage like a cat gone wild in a box.

Something frighteningly wrong, either his vision blurring or the computer screen failing, the *W* stringing out into an overlapping series of *V*s like the teeth of a crosscut saw.

He had risked too much to fail, but he realized it wasn't the computer but rather his heart that was betraying him.

It was picking up its beat to the snare-drum-rolling tempo of fibrillation. Three times before it had happened. An ache under his armpit and tightness in his chest, then intense pain, but this time it was worse, much worse. He hit *E* with a senseless finger. Then stabbed at *R*, the letter echoing back multiples of itself on the plasma computer screen. His vision was contracting and dimming as if he had entered a long tunnel with no light at the other end.

A harder jag of pain, going deeper and deeper, the insect boring up his femoral artery like a ravenous maggot, reaching his groin, his bowels, his lungs.

T. Next letter. His body was racked with uncontrollable shudders. Dimly, dimly realized that he was losing control of his body functions, his bladder letting go, sphincter opening.

T prompted his half-dead mind. He stabbed a finger at the key but somehow missed, instead saw a fading *5* echoed back in multiple images on the screen. *Fool!* his dead brain shouted at him over the roar of his heart exploding, and in a final act of frustration, smashed his fist against the keyboard.

He was dead before he hit the floor.

Dizzy from the exertion, Lu leaned over the colonel. Felt for the artery in his neck. No pulse. He sensed a strange sense of loss and yet of triumph. He had hated the colonel, yet respected him—no, maybe just identified with him—in the same bizarre way that the tortured identified with their torturer. And there had been no choice but to kill him. Perhaps in time he would sort out his feelings, but that process was years and continents away.

He reinserted the hinge pin, taking care to reset the hypodermic needle back into its spring-loaded recess, then painfully pulled himself up to his feet. A wave of nausea swept him, but he forced his gorge down, swallowing the acid bile.

The bloody mess of shredded skin under his armpit was bleeding but not badly. He probed carefully with his fingertips under the glow of the navigational table light. Powder burns and torn skin on both the inside of his arm and over his rib cage. It looked bad but wasn't. Experimentally, he breathed deeply, but there was no real chest pain; certainly no punctured lung or shattered ribs. There would certainly be a mass of scar tissue there for the rest of his lifetime, but he was alive.

He pulled the Makarov from beneath the colonel's belt and released the clip. Only two rounds left, then poked around in the cubbyhole from where the colonel had originally drawn it. The holster had a spare clip of seven rounds, standard issue. He inserted the fresh clip and pocketed the original one. Nine rounds total. It would be enough, he thought.

Stacked in the corner were the three plastic tubes. They were sealed and there was no time to open them to be sure of their contents. He collected them from the corner of the cabin and laid them on the settee.

What else? He had to disable the radio and satellite transmitters. It wouldn't do for Sanchez to warn Cuba about what was happening by calling for help.

Both transmitters were housed in steel cabinets, both built by the same Japanese manufacturer. He turned off the power switches to both units, then lifted the hinged maintenance access panels. Like everything else electronic, their interiors were stuffed with circuit boards, microchips, finely wound wire coils, and electrolytic capacitors. Using the butt of the Makarov, he hammered the interiors of both units and then, just to be sure, divided the remains of a thermos flask of coffee between the radios. To test his workmanship, he flipped on both power switches. The satellite transmitter emitted a shower of sparks, then blew its circuit breaker. The other one came on but began to smoke and splutter, the dial light finally flaring up, then dying.

Only one thing remained: To get off the *Victoria*, and for that he needed help.

The explosive charge that Walrus was to trigger hadn't happened but the result would be the same—die by fire or die by water but die he would. More than two minutes had elapsed since Bracken had expended his last rounds into the overhead. There was no way to know whether he had stopped the transmission, and now there was nothing more that he could do except dumbly await his death. And the most immediate probable cause of his death was forecast by the red glow of the aft door as an oxyacetylene cut into the other side.

By now they would suspect that he was out of ammunition, but he doubted that surrender would be an option they would allow him. Once they cut through a circle in the steel, they would spray the day cabin with automatic fire, and he knew when they did that he would not survive for more than three seconds. What the hell, call it four. Either way, he had all of eternity to contemplate his death, the meaning of life after death, and where the Dow Jones was headed. Sort of looked forward to death now that he knew it would happen.

Either the steel of the door was tough or the torch had a flame tip too small for the job and it was going slowly. But surely.

He estimated that in another two or three minutes they would complete the crude six-inch-diameter circle.

He still had the .22, and he unstrapped it from his leg. The barrel and chamber were dry. He had no idea of how many cartridges it held, probably fourteen or so, but he would be lucky to stop a good-sized rat with this toy. And he doubted that he would ever have a chance to use it.

Everything fragmented. Prayed that Jean had made it, was sure that Pam had. Glanced at his watch. Five minutes or more than when Walrus should have blown out the bottom. Something had gone wrong.

But he was sure that Walrus would have the sense to take care of the women once he realized that the skip wasn't going to make it back. Other than that there was nothing left to contemplate except his own death. Irrationally, he wished for a Big Mac, an order of fries, and a bottle of Banks beer before taking the deep sleep.

The intercom softly buzzed-buzzed twice, then twice again. At first Bracken couldn't relate to the sound, then traced it to the headset just above the bunk. Shit! His subscription to *Time* had probably run out. Or they wanted to know what brand of breakfast cereal he preferred. Or maybe there was a deal to be made with the colonel, but damned if he knew what he had to offer in exchange for his life. He picked it up, heard breathing on the other end.

"Forward command post, Seventh Marine Division, Bracken speaking."

"Cute, Bracken. I don't have a lot of time. I'm offering you a deal, no alternatives, no negotiations, take it or leave it."

Lu! "Okay. Let's say you've got my attention. Is this your deal or the colonel's?"

"The colonel's dead. And Sanchez is aft in the alleyway with all of his men. No return fire from the beach, so they presumably killed your first mate. Everyone wants to be in on the kill, so I'm the only one on the bridge. Once they cut through the door, Sanchez is going to throw in a grenade. Not a nice way to die, Bracken."

"Maybe. Maybe not. I've still got a full clip in the machine pistol."

"You're lying, Bracken. There were only two clips on the *Pampero*. You've gone through both of them. You're a dead man."

"So I'm a dead man. God knows I need the rest."

"You could live, Bracken."

Hope when he didn't believe there was any. A tongue of blue flame lanced through the door, the oxyacetylene torch showering the cabin with sparks of molten metal. They must have changed tips or got the pressure settings on the tanks cranked up.

"So what's the deal?"

"I have a weapon, Bracken. I'll release the dogs on the door to the bridge. You push it open only four inches and pass the machine pistol through. When I say so, only when I say so, you follow with your hands laced behind your neck."

"What guarantee do I have that you won't kill me?"

"None. But why would I when you're going to be dead in three minutes anyway without me taking any personal risk? Make up your mind."

"And if you don't kill me, what happens?" The torch had cut through more than a third of the six-inch circle, the edges of the cut glowing molten, slag spraying out under the pressure of the torch. Three minutes, hell. Much, much less.

"No time to explain. Do you want to live or not? Make up your mind."

"Okay. You got it."

The line clicked dead. In seconds the watertight door bolts unlocked and started to retract.

Amazing what hope did to rekindle the spirit, to make the body function, the mind devious. Bracken knew that Lu would have assumed that Walrus was firing the .22 from the beach and that he was armed only with the machine pistol. Conclusion. Lu would not be expecting that Bracken would be armed. He carefully tucked the .22 under the waistband of his jeans with the barrel nestled in the crevasse of his buttocks, pulled his sweatshirt over the lump, picked up the empty machine pistol, and pushed against the door. It opened a few inches and met a rubbery resistance.

From the far side of the door. "As I said, Bracken, the machine pistol first."

Lu was probably standing on the other side of the door, blocking it with his body. Bracken extended the machine pistol, butt first, and shoved it through. The weapon made a metallic clatter on the deck.

"Now you."

The pressure on the door was suddenly released, and Bracken stumbled over the sill, regained his footing, and stood facing Lu, who had some sort of automatic in his hand. His Windbreaker was soaked with blood, already going black. His left arm seemed slack and lifeless.

"Did the transmission to the shuttle . . . ?"

Lu hunched his shoulders slightly, as if he didn't really care. "No. He died before he could send the complete sequence. Anyway, it doesn't concern me." Lu prodded something on the floor with his foot, never breaking eye contact.

Looking down, Bracken recognized the crumpled form of the colonel pushed back under the nav table.

Lu flicked the barrel of the Makarov toward the plastic tubes. "My left arm doesn't seem to be working, Bracken. I can't carry those and this at the same time. Pick them up."

Three lengths of plastic pipe, varying between two and three feet overall and about six inches in diameter, their ends sealed with plastic plugs and duct tape.

He glanced back at Lu, questioning, but Lu responded by impatiently flicking the automatic sideways. "Go on! Pick them up. And the briefcase next to the terminal as well."

Bracken checked the bulkhead clock: 2130. The hose filled with the plastique should already have blown, and yet he knew Walrus would be precise about the timing. He surveyed the bridge. Sliding door to both port and starboard. If the explosive blew, he still would be ready for it. Throw the tubes at Lu while he was disoriented, kill him with the .22, dive overboard, and swim like hell.

"Pick them up, Bracken. *Now.*"

Bracken gathered the whole lot up into his arms. "What's this stuff?"

"I don't have time for explanations. You do what you're told, exactly as I tell you to, nothing else, no questions. If it works out that we get to the beach, you walk away, the same offer you made me."

Bracken believed that like he believed in the tooth fairy. "They'll come after us!"

"No, they won't. I'm going to order Sanchez to get the *Victoria* out of here immediately and head for Cuba. Tell him that the distress channel was broadcasting something about a Bahamian Coast Guard cutter ordered to investigate firing in the area.

He'll have to get into international waters quickly. Leave that end of it to me."

Lu pushed the door to the day cabin closed, then rotated the dogs into place. He nodded his head toward the bow. "Out on the bridge first, then down three steps. About fifteen feet forward of the steps is a hatch that accesses the crew living quarters and mess. Aft of there you'll find the main galley. Aft of the galley is a wine storage area and a door that opens onto the corridor that services the lower guest accommodations. You know the area; you've been there before. When you get to the bottom of the spiral staircase, wait until you hear me snap my fingers twice. I'll be in the salon at the head of the stairs."

Thirty-two after. "What if I meet up with one of the crew below decks . . . ?"

"That would be your bad luck, Bracken. And mine." He slid back the door to the deck, looked aft to make sure there was no one on the side deck, and motioned with a nod.

Lu was still exerting control, but Bracken had no other options left. He was a leaf, blown in the wind.

"It's clear," Lu said softly, grabbing Bracken by the shoulder and pushing him through the doorway. "Go."

He didn't like trusting Bracken, but it was the only alternative open to him. He saw Bracken's profile make it to the forward hatch and disappear below, then turned back to the bridge and picked up the loud-hailer microphone. Overhead on the bridge, a loudspeaker squealed.

"*Comrade Sanchez. Stop the cutting operation right now. Post two of your men at the door and bring the others with you to the bridge immediately. That is an order.*"

Sanchez showed up in less than thirty seconds, puffing, a crowd of men milling around behind him on the bridge wing deck. Sanchez saluted. "We have him! Just a few more seconds with the cutting torch is all that is necessary!" He looked down at Lu's blood-soaked jacket, starting to ask a question, but Lu cut him off.

"There's no time left. The colonel's weakened heart has failed due to the stress caused by Bracken's attack; your fault, Sanchez, because you were responsible for the security of this vessel. I almost lost my life as well. Two of your men are to guard the door leading to the day room. Don't attempt to open it. He's a mad animal and heavily armed."

"But we have him!"

"And unless you get this vessel out of here and into international waters, the Bahamian Coast Guard will have us. Less than a minute ago there was a message from the Bahamian frigate *Squallus* to a smaller cutter about gunfire reported by the natives at North West Cay. The frigate is only twenty miles south of here and steaming at full speed. Get the engines going and head out into deep water, then south for Cuba. We've done what we came for. Bracken can wait until we're at sea."

Sanchez rapped out orders. Two of his men saluted and tumbled down the steps, heading for the anchor winch.

"You take over the bridge, Sanchez. I've got to bandage this wound and then lie down. Wake me in three hours. In the meanwhile you're in command." He brushed by two of Sanchez's men, onto the bridge wing deck, and then aft through the salon.

Bracken was ready. In half a minute they were both in the dinghy, the painter cast off, drifting downwind. Lu nodded at the engine when they were more than a hundred yards from the *Victoria*. "Start it up and head toward the south end of the island, Bracken. The area called Haul Away Bay."

Walrus lay in a depression that he had scooped out of the sand on the beach, his own private foxhole. Seven minutes before, precisely on time, he had carefully taken up the slack until the fishing line was tight. Then pulled smoothly. The line was monofilament, forty-pound test and brand-new off the shelf. The pin would come out of the detonator with less than a pound of pull being exerted on it but, as he increased tension, the line became strumming taut, unyielding, a bowstring. He pulled harder. Nothing.

He pulled even harder, then released it, jerking it with snaps of pressure. No give to it, nothing.

Bracken would be off the vessel by now. Regardless. That had been agreed. Walrus had to believe that he was. But the damn line was hung up on something, probably a coral outcropping.

The firing had ceased several minutes before. Maybe Bracken hadn't gotten off, but he didn't want to think about that right now, only get the goddamn job done. He stood up and started to wade into the water.

"Where you going?"

Jean was behind him, running down from the cleft in the dunes.

"The damn thing hasn't fired. It's hung up. I've got to trace the line."

"Bracken . . . ?"

"I keep telling you, he's okay. He knew when he had to get out," Walrus said, on the edge of exasperation. "Plan was he would swim upwind of the *Victoria* until he hit the beach, then head straight for the *Pampero*. Just going to take him time. Get Pam back to the schooner. You're both freezing. I'll wait for him here once I get things straightened out."

"I'm not leaving, Walrus."

Walrus shrugged. "Didn't figure you would, lady." He waded into the surf and began to flipper along with the fishing line held in his hand.

There was a current in the cove. And the fishing line had snagged, not on a coral outcropping but in the splintered framework of an old, abandoned lobster trap. The tighter the line had been pulled, the deeper the line had wedged into the fractured wood.

Between the *Victoria* and the lobster pot, the fishing line had over thirty feet of slack.

The anchor chain on the *Victoria* began to be taken up, link by link. Underwater, the guttural roar of her exhausts rumbled, fish darting at the suddenness of sound.

The anchor broke out of the sand and cleared the surface. The pitch of the engines increased and the *Victoria* executed a turn, heading for open water. As it did, the line to the detonator snapped tight.

Walrus was less than thirty feet beyond the surf line when the *Victoria* blew, first with a dull *karump*, then with a massive shattering roar, blowing out a long strake of metal plating above her waterline as if she were a newly opened sardine can. The *Victoria*'s lights snuffed out, replaced by slashing flames and series of pulsing orange secondary explosions that followed each other in successive claps of thunder.

Junk pinwheeling upward, men scrambling, backlit by the flames, diving overboard, screams, cracks of metal fracturing, shrieks of metal bending, windows exploding with the heat, men yelling in the agony of dying.

In less than two minutes she folded in half and sank, steam hissing as hot metal met the sea. Then eight tons of oil from her fuel tanks spread out on the waters of the bay around her, ignited, and burned like the fires of hell. Walrus watched in dumb fascination, then slumped down on the sand.

Jean sat down beside him. In the glow of the burning oil Walrus could see the tears spilling down her cheeks. He took her hand in his. "Don't worry. He'll make it." But he wasn't so sure.

24.

2150 hours

Lu looked back at the inferno that had been the *Victoria,* then turned to Bracken. "Professional. I thought you'd make good use of the plastique explosive. Your work or your first mate's?"

Bracken hunched his shoulders. "Walrus's. Lot of noise for just a little chunk of stuff that looks like modeling clay."

Lu nodded absently in return, not concerned. "Nicely done. Too bad that the *Victoria* wasn't in deep water. There'll be some kind of inquiry. But I doubt that anyone will be there to answer the questions." He settled back on the dinghy's gunwale, relaxed. "You can increase power now. Haul Away Bay is only about three kilometers from here."

Bracken had seen Haul Away Bay on the chart of North West Cay. An old fish-processing plant, a dock, and a few shacks, all abandoned when the English company that built it went belly-up more than ten years earlier.

They rounded the point and headed into the bay less than five minutes later. Bracken paralleled the dock, heading for the shore. Seconds later the inflatable dinghy grated on the beach, the outboard motor kicking up in the shallows, the prop cavitating before Bracken could kill the throttle.

The Zodiac rocked in the swell, keel grating on the graveled foreshore. There was the smell of rotting fish and timber, the stink of decay, neglect, and abandonment.

"Get out, Bracken."

In the starlight Bracken could see the outline of the Makarov automatic leveled on the pit of his stomach. He clambered backward over the dinghy's gunwale into the surf and trudged slowly inshore, a spot in his back burning where he knew Lu's weapon was aimed.

"Stop where you are."

"What happens now?"

Lu was wading ashore behind him, no more than five feet away. "As I said, once we get to the beach, you walk away."

"Just like that?"

"I gave you my word, didn't I?"

Which Bracken figured was worth zip. And he was the only one who knew that Lu hadn't been killed in the explosion and sinking of the *Victoria*. Deep down he realized that he wouldn't get ten feet up the beach before Lu pumped a bullet into his back. He had to stall for time, work out some opening move.

"What's with those plastic tubes?"

"My future." He wagged the barrel of the Makarov. "Turn around and get going."

Delay. Any delay. "How about my dinghy? With the outboard motor, it's worth over two thousand bucks."

"I'm afraid that I'll be needing it, but think of it as a fair trade. You've still got your schooner and your life."

For how long? Bracken shifted his feet, then kicked at the sand. The .22 was nestled under his belt. It would take at least a second and a half to get it out, get the safety off, and fire. Lu would react much faster than that. He desperately needed a diversion to buy him two full seconds.

"Not that I don't trust you, but I'd feel a hell of a lot better if you quit waving that gun around."

"You're bigger than I am, Bracken. My left arm is injured. You might get ideas. And I have other people that I might have to deal with."

He couldn't afford to anger Lu for what that was worth. "Yeah, I see your point. Anyway, thanks for getting me off the *Victoria*."

"I don't need your thanks. If my left arm wasn't disabled, Bracken, you would have died on the *Victoria* fifteen minutes ago. I needed someone to get the tubes and the briefcase past Sanchez. You were just my pack horse."

Lu's voice was suddenly cold, as cold as a sheet of pond ice. If Bracken had had any illusions that Lu would let him walk away, they were gone now. At best he figured that he could take off in a weaving sprint, then dive, roll over, and get the .22 out, but it would still take too much time and Lu had both a flashlight and a much larger caliber weapon. The odds were better than just taking a bullet in the back, but not by much.

There had to be something to delay Lu, to catch him off guard or to distract him. He tried to visualize Lu's frame of mind.

No sleep in twenty-four hours, undoubtedly fatigued, the injuries draining him of energy. He had to be dead on his feet, his reactions dulled. Just like myself, he thought.

Bracken suddenly went down on one knee, holding his head. "God—dizzy."

"Get going, Bracken."

"Sure—just give me a second." He shook his head from side to side as if he were trying to clear it. "You have a cigarette?"

"There's time for that." Lu fumbled out a pack of cigarettes and tossed it and a disposable lighter over to Bracken. "Light one for yourself, then one for me."

Bracken shakily lit two cigarettes and tossed one back to Lu, who grabbed it up from the sand with his left hand. Bracken had hoped Lu would use his good right hand which held the Makarov to recover it, but he didn't. Scratch that plan.

He had to keep Lu talking, looking for an opening. "One thing's been puzzling me, Lu. How come you went through all the hassle of trying to destroy the shuttle and then ended up not transmitting the signal. You had it in the palm of your hand."

Lu remained silent for a short time. Bracken couldn't see his eyes, but he could see the outline of the Makarov, which never wavered. Lu finally answered. "To settle old scores, to right years of injustice. And for my son. Funny thing, Bracken—if I hadn't joined the KGB, I probably would have been a dissident. Work that one out if you can. And here, in the end, I am the ultimate dissident—a defector and traitor to the country of my birth." He ticked the end of the cigarette with his finger, showering sparks.

Beyond the pier, far out in the bay, the sea buoy's light flickered on and off, marking the starboard entrance to the channel that led into Haul Away Bay. It suddenly fit together. He had never intended to return to Cuba on the *Victoria*. Lu was using the sea buoy as a rendezvous point to meet another ship.

"What time does it get here?"

Lu lifted his chin a little, looking at Bracken. "You mean the freighter? Sometime between now and first light." He didn't sound surprised at Bracken's question.

It just came out. "You never intended to let me walk away, did you?"

Long pause, almost, in Bracken's mind, an eternity. "No. You're the only one who knows that I didn't die out there with the rest of them. If you don't exist, then neither do I."

"Balls! Why would I say anything? Your plan failed and if I talked, I'd be in real trouble because of my involvement."

"I couldn't risk trusting you, Bracken. I want to believe you but somehow, someday, it would come out." He slowly stood up. "I'm sorry, Bracken. It won't hurt. I give you my word."

"Christ! Just like that? Wham-bang and it's over. With all the emotional distress and guilt of wringing a chicken's neck. Is that what it means to you?"

"I've already told you my reasons. The game ends here, now."

Bracken put a cigarette between his quivering lips but closed both eyes so as not to destroy his night vision. The cigarette tasted like cat hair, and his stomach was burning with acid, his nerves jangling like a fire bell, but the cigarette had bought him a few more minutes. He had to keep the conversation going. "Don't you think it's bloody idiotic fucking stupid that the two of us are here on some deserted beach, both believing in the same fundamental shit—like freedom and love and commitment—and yet there's no solution for either of us outside of trying to kill the other guy? Isn't that the way wars start?"

"I agree, Bracken. That's how wars start. I'd much rather have a drink with you, shake hands, and walk away, but it can't be that way. I've thought it through and there's no alternative. I'm sorry about Vietnam, about Williams, and about how it has to end. I know that you did your best with what you had. You gave me a hard run." It sounded real.

For another minute Bracken nursed the cigarette, willing it to stay burning forever, but the glow edged down to the filter and expired.

In the silence of the night the sound of the hammer cocking back on the Makarov was unmistakable.

"Bend your head over, Bracken. It's painless."

"Not on my knees, Lu, not like the fuckin' NVA executed POWs in 'Nam. On my feet." Before Lu could object, Bracken angrily flicked the butt of the cigarette away and placing his hands behind him on the sand, started to lever his body up. One hand pushing his body off the sand, the other one groping for the butt of the .22. He fumbled the safety off with his thumb and withdrew the automatic from beneath his waistband, dangling it behind his back until he was in a squat. At close range and in the face it would be more than adequate, except that he knew that by sheer reflex Lu would also fire, and at this distance a

9mm slug plowing into any part of his body would probably be fatal. He needed just a minute edge, something . . .

Then looking past Lu, Bracken saw the lights. Dim, very dim and far away. He picked out the red and green running lights, the white range lights at the mastheads. Still miles off but coming straight for the buoy. "And that's the bloody ship you're waiting for?"

He didn't turn, the barrel unwavering, backing away a step. "What are you talking about?"

"The ship that's headed this way."

"But it wasn't due until . . ." Lu's voice trailed off. He took another step backward, then half turned his body and glanced to the south. It was all that Bracken needed.

He fired three times, saw Lu stumbling over backward, then the roar of the Makarov blowing two flaming holes in the night. The muzzle flash blinded him and he fired three times more at where Lu had been, realized that Lu had to be down on the ground, lowered the barrel of the .22 and fired twice more, then dove into the sand and rolled to the left. Ribs screaming with pain, as if there were skewers spearing through his chest. Two more tongues of flame and the sonic snaps of shock waves as two bullets whined past his ear, then reports echoing off the deserted buildings. But he was unhurt and there were probably six more rounds left in the .22. Big difference, because if he had figured it right, Lu had only two more rounds remaining. Three at most.

Rather than move, he kept absolutely still, listening. Could faintly hear Lu's body movements but not see him. A grunt and the sound of sand rustling under Lu's body as he moved. Wounded? Had to be. Bracken was sure that he had at least one hit.

Was Lu backing away or moving sideways? Left or right? It had to be over soon, one way or the other. It wasn't any longer a matter of running away. He had the edge now and he wasn't about to call it a draw. Winning was living and that was what it was all about.

Remembered from his air force survival training at Stead that a man under stress firing a weapon in the darkness tended to pull his shots high and to the right. He assumed that Lu had had similar weapons training. He was, after all, a professional. But he had only two or three rounds left, and that equated to extreme stress.

The trick was to fire a little to the left and below your opponent's muzzle flash. Bracken transferred the .22 to his left hand, extended his arm straight out, and fired in the general direction of where he guessed Lu was, then simultaneously rolled to the right, away from the area where Lu would return fire.

The Makarov barked three times, the slugs kicking up sand to his left. But Bracken had seen the muzzle flashes and carefully squeezed off another round.

No return fire this time. But sounds. A grunt or wheezing. Then a hard sucking intake of breath.

He had lost count of the .22 rounds remaining. Five, six? Lu was probably hit but he wasn't dead. And Bracken knew he couldn't take chances, not now, because he was too close to winning the game. He carefully rolled to the right again, paused, and listened.

Lu was breathing hard, not trying to hide the sound, possibly not able to. Bracken thought about pumping another round in that direction, but he couldn't exactly define where Lu was lying. He decided to give it time, to wait.

Several minutes.

Finally: "Bracken. Do you hear me?" Not close. Twenty or thirty feet away.

He didn't answer.

"Bracken. You're out there, you're listening. My gun's empty. Cease firing and walk away. We'll both live."

He didn't answer, knowing that it had to be a trick.

"Bracken." A bout of hacking, spitting. "There's no sense in going on with this."

But it somehow made perfect sense to Bracken. Something apart from him was running his reactions, no thought given to why he was going to do this, just that he would.

His genes were a product of ten thousand generations of breeding: the enduring and immutable sequence of battle, victory, submission of the vanquished, revenge, death, rape, pillage, plunder. As old as the code of Caesar's legions or the great khans. Older, much older. As old as the beginning of time, when the first warrior picked up a rock and smashed his enemy's face into pulp.

His skin was tingling, adrenaline pumping, body alive, alive forever, kill the enemy and drink his blood from the vessel of his skull. "If it is," he shouted back, his voice hoarse, "turn on your fucking flashlight. Then hold the Makarov up in the beam so I can see it."

Twelve, thirteen, fourteen rapid heartbeats, Bracken counted. Then Lu switched on the flashlight. Farther to the right than he had guessed. A groove in the sand, like a lizard's trail, traced the path that Lu had made, retreating backward.

The flashlight was held awkwardly in his lame left hand. In the right the beam centered on the Makarov. Its slide was locked back as it would when the clip was empty.

"Press the clip release, Lu old buddy. Let the clip drop out, then throw it as far as you can."

The dull black clip dropped in the sand. Lu fumbled around, held it up in the beam of the flashlight, then threw it toward the shore. There was a faint splash.

"Toss the Makarov out in front of you. About five feet and shine the light on it so I can see it."

There was a faint plop in the sand. The beam erratically traced forward and reflected off the slab-sided automatic.

"Excellent move—truly fucking extraordinarily excellent." He was barely in control of his body and mind, but he felt as if he had the world by the ass and he intended to keep it that way. It was debt-settlement time, and he was going to collect. "Now hold the flashlight with both hands out in front of you and shine the beam directly into your eyes. Make like an owl."

"Bracken—I could have killed you anytime I wanted to. But I didn't—I wouldn't have. You have to believe me!"

"Yeah, and I also believe in Santa Claus and the check's in the mail and I'll love you in the morning. The light, Lu. Shine on, harvest moon."

Lu turned the flashlight on his face, his eyes blinking rapidly. Blood trickled from his ear, which was a mangled mess.

Bracken got up into a crouch and scrambled forward, keeping the .22 zeroed in on Lu's face until he stood just five feet away. He kicked the Makarov to one side.

"You mentioned Williams before. You *really* remember him? Remember his stink and his pain and the shitty way he died?"

Lu nodded weakly.

"I promised myself to do something for him one hell of a long time ago. Nothing real elaborate or fancy. Just to kill you. Someday. And that someday's right now, you fucker. I'm finally going to make good on that promise."

Lu lowered his face to the sand. "I don't have anything left in me, Bracken. All the juices have run out. But I won't beg. I want only two things: that you kill me cleanly, and sometime later you write a letter to my son. No return address, no signature, just say that you were a friend of mine. His address is in my briefcase. Just a simple letter telling him that I loved him with all my heart. I know he knew it, but I don't think I ever really said it properly."

Damn it all, shit, shit, shit! He had the .22 sighted on Lu's forehead, his finger tighten on the trigger and suddenly, completely, the hate drained out of him, the emotional plug yanked, nothing, nothing, nothing left except a vacuum. *Damn it Willie, what do you want? Blood? His or mine? Gimme the answer!*

No answer except the hollow wind and the slow beat of small waves on the shore.

Lu had squeezed his eyes shut, his back hunched, the muscles of his face clenched tight. Tears! Goddamned tears! Somehow his body had shrunken, as if he already knew that his blood would leak away into the sand, and by dawn the crabs would begin scavenging his flesh, and by tomorrow nightfall the tide would claim what was left.

Bracken's finger began to tighten on the trigger, independent of self-control. Kept squeezing relentlessly tighter, Bracken willing it not to. As though there were two independent forces inside of him fighting for control, one sane, the other not, both screaming conflicting commands.

His left hand slashed up, knocking his right hand away, the trigger already depressed, the sear springing forward, the firing pin igniting the primer, the gun kicking in his hand, one shot, two, three, the arc higher and higher, four, five, until he fired the last shot at the stars a million light-years away and the magazine was empty.

He slowly sank down to his knees, expended, everything gone out of him. Lu lay still, not moving but sobbing, lungs racking in great gulps of air.

Bracken flung the .22 toward the beach, watching it tumble, catching little smears of reflected starlight on its polished surfaces until it disappeared in the blackness.

There really was a hell, his father had once told Bracken when he still wore knickers. The old man always walked him to the rectory for Saturday morning catechism classes but never went inside. Catechism was his mother's idea, a devout Catholic, a good warm woman; not his father's—he quietly believed that every man had all the God he really needed already fitted up real neat inside him.

Not the kind of hell that the ministers and priests were always giving you hogwash about, his father had said, kicking fallen twigs from the previous night's windstorm aside with his blunt-toed workshoes. Not even such a thing as eternal damnation. Damned fool nonsense. When you died, you died.

"No, hell is a damned sight worse than any of that bunk. The real hell is walking around for a lifetime with the fact that you done something awful and having to live with that fact every day for the rest of your life."

Bracken stumbled down to the beach, the white-hot shock of adrenaline still in his veins, still screaming for the catharsis of killing and yet denied it.

He found the painter and gathered it up, then pulled the bow around.

"You're not taking the Zodiac, Bracken."

He wheeled around. Lu was there, the Makarov in his hand, four steps away just where the wavelets lapped the shore.

"Up yours, turkey. Your gun's empty."

The Makarov spat flame once, the report deafening. "Proof that it isn't. I had a spare clip, but I couldn't take the chance of you getting in a lucky shot. I also knew that you didn't have it in you to kill me. You already proved that before. Now start the outboard engine. The ship's on heading for the sea buoy and I don't have much time."

Bracken's brain was numb. He bent over and pulled the recoil starter cord. The engine coughed, then started on the second pull.

Lu waded out until he was on the opposite side of the dinghy, the separation between them only three feet. "Now walk ashore, Bracken. Slowly, carefully—no stupid moves."

He braced for the impact of the slug that would shatter his spine, tear out his lungs, explode his heart. He willed his legs to run but they wouldn't respond, as if they had been the first parts of him to die. So goddamned tired, the will to fight finished —only to wait like a steer in the slaughterhouse for the final stunning blow.

"Turn around and face me."

Bracken couldn't, frozen, dumb.

"Face me, Bracken!"

Slowly, he found the strength to turn.

For long seconds, an eternity, Lu stood there, the Makarov leveled. Then slowly lowered it and eased the hammer down. A long sigh went out of him. He shook his head. "No, it's over between us, Bracken. The killing stops here—there's already been enough blood spilled, all of it wasted. And I owe you my life. I give you back yours in return."

Lu glanced toward the ship, now no more than a mile distant. "It's time I left." He paused, obviously considering something, then gave a soft laugh and tossed one of the plastic tubes in the shallows at Bracken's feet. "Just a small gift—something that you might like to hang in the salon of the *Pampero* to remember me by."

He then snicked the gearshift lever in reverse, slowly backing into deeper water and shifted into neutral.

"Under different circumstances, Bracken, we might have been friends." He lifted his hand in a formal salute, dropped it, then shifted the gear lever into forward, increasing rpms to a howl, slewing the dinghy around and heading out toward the freighter, spray roostertailing as the Zodiac gained speed until it was lost in the blackness.

Almost automatically, Bracken returned the salute, then let his hand fall to his side, physically and emotionally exhausted.

Friend? Not bloody likely. But no longer an enemy.